The O'Clock Tales

Other books in the Enid Blyton collection:

The O'Clock Tales

Enid Blyton

EGMONT

EGMONT

We bring stories to life

Five O'Clock Tales first published in Great Britain 1941 by Methuen & Co. Ltd
Dean edition first published 1991
Mammoth edition first published 1993
Egmont edition first published 2008

Six O'Clock Tales first published in Great Britain 1942 by Methuen & Co. Ltd
Dean edition first published 1991
Mammoth edition first published 1993
Egmont edition first published 2008

Seven O'Clock Tales first published in Great Britain 1943 by Methuen & Co. Ltd
Dean edition first published 1991
Mammoth edition first published 1993
Egmont edition first published 2008

Eight O'Clock Tales first published in Great Britain 1944 by Methuen & Co. Ltd
Dean edition first published 1991
Mammoth edition first published 1993
Egmont edition first published 2008

This edition published 2010
by Egmont UK Limited
239 Kensington High Street
London W8 6SA

ISBN 978 1 4052 4847 1

1 3 5 7 9 10 8 6 4 2

A CIP catalogue record for this title is available from the British Library

Printed and bound in Great Britain by the CPI Group

Five O'Clock Tales

CONTENTS

The Red and White Cow

Peter was most excited because his father and mother had moved into the country from the town. How different it was! There were green lanes instead of busy streets, big trees instead of tall chimneys, and *such* a lot of animals and birds to see.

'There are thirty-two sheep in the fields and six little lambs!' said Peter to his mother. 'And there are eleven horses at the farm, and I saw two goats this morning and about twelve ducks. I couldn't count them properly because they wouldn't stay still. The hens won't stay still either.'

'What about the cows?' said his mother. 'Have you counted those?'

'I don't like the cows,' said Peter. 'They have big horns and they roar at me.'

'Oh, no,' said his mother. '*Lions* roar. Cows only moo.'

'Well, it sounds just like roaring to me,' said
Peter. 'I don't like the cows at all. They are my
enemies.'

'They are very good friends!' said Mother.
'They send you a lot of presents.'

'*I've* never seen a present from a cow!' said
Peter.

'Well, here is one,' said Mother, and she took
down a jug of milk. She poured it out into a mug
and gave it to Peter. He drank it.

'So that came from the cow, did it?' he said.
'Well, it was simply lovely!'

At dinner-time Mother put down a dish of
stewed apples for Peter. He looked round for
the custard that Mother usually made for him.
There wasn't any.

'The cow has sent you this present instead!'
said Mother – and she gave him a dear little jug
full of thick cream. How delicious it was! Peter
poured it all over his apples. They tasted much
nicer than usual.

'So that came from the cow, too!' said the
little boy. 'Well, it must be a very kind animal!'

At tea-time Mother put the loaf of bread on
the table. Peter was surprised. Usually there
were slices of bread and butter.

Mother put down a blue dish on which there were little rolls of new-made yellow butter.

'A present from the cow again!' she said, and laughed, 'You can spread your present yourself on slices of bread for a treat!'

'Goodness me!' said Peter. 'What a nice friendly creature the cow is! I won't hate it any more or be frightened of it.'

'I should think not!' said Mother. 'Look, Peter – the cow has sent *me* a present too!'

Mother lifted up the lid of the cheese-dish, and underneath Peter saw a big lump of orange-coloured cheese. Mother cut herself a piece, and said it was delicious.

'I shall go and stand on the gate that leads to the cow field and say thank you to the cows!' said Peter. 'I didn't know they were so kind!'

And now he isn't a bit afraid of them, and he likes them very much. He says they are his friends, not his enemies. What do *you* say?

The Clock in the Wood

Once upon a time three children went out to have a picnic. They were Bob, Mollie, and Eileen. They had a basket full of nice things to eat and a ball to play with. They waved goodbye to their mother and set off to Bluebell Wood.

'Please start back at five o'clock,' she called to them. 'Uncle Jim will be here then and he will want to see you.'

'Yes, Mother,' called back the children. 'We've got our watches!'

They soon came to Bluebell Wood. It was a lovely place. There were still some bluebells shining here and there like pools of blue water. The birds were singing in the trees, and the sunshine slanted through the green branches and made freckles of light on the grass below.

'Let's play hide-and-seek!' said Bob. 'We'll put the basket of tea things under this tree while we play. I'll hide my eyes first.'

When the others called 'Cuckoo', Bob ran to find them. He found Mollie – but as he ran after her he caught his foot in a tree-root and over he went! He didn't hurt himself, but, oh, dear, he broke the glass of his watch!

'Look!' he said. 'My watch is broken! Isn't it a pity! Is yours all right, Mollie? We must know the time to go home.'

'Yes, mine's all right,' said Mollie. 'Never mind, Bob – we'll soon get yours mended!'

'What's the time, Mollie?' asked Eileen. 'Is it time for tea yet?'

'It's four o'clock,' said Mollie. 'Yes – we'd better have tea.' So they fetched their basket and handed out the good things – tomato sandwiches, chocolate cake, and an apple each to eat. What a fine tea! There was nothing left at all except three paper bags and the milk bottle and cup when the children had finished!

'Let's have a game of catch now!' said Bob. So they began. It was great fun and they played for a long time. Then Bob wondered what the time was. He didn't want to miss seeing Uncle Jim! He looked at his watch. Oh, dear – it was broken! He had forgotten that. So he called to Mollie.

'Mollie, what's the time?' Mollie looked at her watch.

'Four o'clock!' she cried.

'But it can't be!' said Bob, surprised. 'You said it was four o'clock just before we had tea! Look again!'

Mollie looked – and then she held her watch up to her ear. 'Oh!' she cried in dismay. 'It's stopped. Now what shall we do? Eileen hasn't a watch! We can't tell the time!'

'I can!' said Eileen, suddenly. She ran to where a big dandelion plant grew and picked a big fluffy dandelion clock. She blew it hard. Puff! She blew again. Puff! Still there was some white fluff left. She blew again. Puff! That was 1 o'clock, 2 o'clock, 3 o'clock – puff, 4 o'clock, puff, 5 o'clock!

'It's five o'clockl!' cried Eileen. 'I've puffed all the fluff off. The dandelion clock says it's five o'clock – time to go home!'

'Come on then!' cried the others, and off they all went. Mother was so pleased to see them in such good time, for Uncle Jim had just come.

'It wasn't our watches that told us the right time!' said Eileen. 'It was the little clock in the wood, Uncle Jim!'

The Peppermint Rock

Mollie and John were very pleased because their Uncle Bob had given them a long stick of pink peppermint rock between them. He had been to the seaside for a day and had brought it back with him. It had 'Southsea' all through the middle of the rock in pink letters. Mollie did wonder how the name was put there.

'We'll break it in half,' she said to John. So she broke it – but one piece was bigger than the other.

'I want the big piece!' said John, and he snatched at it. But Mollie wouldn't let him have it. 'No,' she said, 'I'm the oldest of the family – *I* ought to have it.'

'Selfish thing!' said John and he smacked Mollie, which was stupid, because she at once smacked him back.

'Hello, hello, what's all this?' suddenly said a voice behind them. The two children turned and saw the butcher's boy. They did not like him very much, for he was rough and rude. But John told him what they were quarrelling about.

'It isn't fair, Harry,' he said. 'Look, Mollie has broken the rock into two – and she won't give me the bigger piece. Say *I* ought to have it!'

'I'll settle your quarrel for you,' said Harry. 'Give me the rock and let me measure the pieces.'

Mollie gave him the rock. The butcher boy measured them side by side, saw that one was a whole inch bigger than the other and bit off a large piece of the longer one! But he bit off too much, because when he measured the two pieces again, the piece he had bitten was now smaller than the other.

'Huh! I'll soon put *that* right!' said Harry, and he bit a large piece off the longer stick. Mollie and John stared in dismay.

'Don't do that,' begged Mollie. 'Give us the two pieces back. We won't quarrel any more.'

'Wait!' said Harry. 'I haven't got them right yet. One is still longer than the other. If I give you the pieces back like this you will squabble again! Another bite may set things right.'

He took another large bite, measured the

sticks, and, of course, found one still longer than the other. So he bit again, crunching with enjoyment. And now, alas! there were only two very small pieces of rock left, and the children were almost in tears.

'Give us those little bits,' said Mollie. 'You have no right to eat all our rock like that.'

'Oh, indeed!' said Harry. 'And what about my trouble in trying to settle your stupid quarrel for you? What reward do I get for that? Aren't you going to give me anything for trying to put things right?'

'We've nothing to give you,' said John.

'Well, if you think a big boy like me, who earns his own living, is going to settle your quarrels for nothing, you're mistaken!' said Harry. 'I'll take my own payment – the rest of this peppermint rock. Goodbye!'

And with that he crammed the rest of the rock into his mouth and went off grinning. The two children watched him go, with tears in their eyes.

'It's our own fault, John,' said Mollie. 'If one of us had been unselfish enough to take the smaller piece, we wouldn't have lost the lot!'

Brer Fox's Onions

It happened once that Brer Rabbit passed by an onion field and saw Brer Fox hard at work digging in it.

'Heyo, Brer Fox!' he called. 'Are those your onions?'

'They are,' said Brer Fox, 'but it's mighty hard work digging this hot day.'

'Well, I'll come and help you,' said Brer Rabbit, and he hopped into the field and began digging up the onions too. They were nice little round onions, and Brer Rabbit thought of them in hot soup. Ooh, delicious! He felt sure Brer Fox would give him a good handful for helping him – but no, when Brer Fox stopped, he didn't say a word about Brer Rabbit having any onions at all. He took up a small sack nearby and began to shovel the onions in.

'Aren't you going to give me a few?' said Brer Rabbit, in a rage.

'No, not one,' said Brer Fox, grinning. 'You've tricked me a good many times, Brer Rabbit, and I don't feel very kindly towards you. You don't even get the smallest onion!'

Brer Rabbit stood and watched Brer Fox for a minute. 'That sack's too small for all those onions,' he said. 'I'll lend you a bigger one. I don't bear *you* malice, Brer Fox. I do a kindness when I can.'

Brer Fox laughed loudly at that, but all the same he accepted Brer Rabbit's offer of a large sack. Brer Rabbit fetched it – but when he helped Brer Fox to hoist it, full of onions, on to his back, he took a knife and quickly cut a nice little round hole at the bottom of the sack! Then he grinned, said goodbye to Brer Fox and went off, lippitty-clippitty. But he didn't go far. No, he soon came back, picked up the small sack that hadn't been used, and set off down the road after Brer Fox, who by now had turned the corner. Brer Rabbit didn't need to ask the way he had gone, for there, all down the lane, was a string of little round onions that had dropped one by one from the hole in the sack!

How he grinned to himself! He picked them all up and put them into his sack. Then round the corner he went after Brer Fox and saw another line of onions. Into his sack they went too, and when it was full he turned and ran home to his wife. 'Make some onion soup!' he shouted, and flung down the sack.

And when Brer Fox reached home, and put down *his* sack, what a shock for him! Only a few onions were in the sack – all the rest had gone! He ran out and looked down the road! Not an onion was to be seen! He rushed to Brer Rabbit's house, which was fast bolted – but out of the window stole a most delicious smell of onion soup.

'Have some?' cried Brer Rabbit, leaning out of his window and waving a soup spoon at Brer Fox. But Brer Fox, he didn't answer a word!

There and Back Again!

Bob emptied the pennies out of his money-box, It was Mollie's birthday the next day, and he meant to buy her a book. He had two pounds altogether, so off he went to the bookshop. He saw there a book he wanted very badly himself – *Tales of Brer Rabbit* – and he felt sure Mollie would like it. So he bought it, and left the parcel at Mollie's house with a kind little letter.

Now, Mollie was a very naughty little girl. She was spoilt and disobedient, and on her very birthday morning she did three bad things. She poured all the milk from the milk jug into the teapot; she broke a vase of flowers; and, worse of all, she threw a stone at a cat and hurt its leg. So her mother said that, even though it was her birthday, Mollie must be punished. She took the *Tales of Brer Rabbit* away from the naughty little girl, and said she would give it away.

So the lovely book was given away to the

milkman's boy – but when he got home and looked at it he found that it was just the same book as he had already had for Christmas. He was disappointed – but never mind, he would give it to Alan, the little boy across the road, who had been ill.

So the milkman's boy wrapped up the book and left it at Alan's house with a message. His mother unwrapped the parcel – but when she saw it was a book she wouldn't give it to Alan. The doctor had said that her little son must *not* read at all, because his eyes were very bad – so his mother had carefully kept every book out of his bedroom. He was fond of reading, and she felt sure he would find the new book somehow if she kept it.

She wrapped it up again – and then she thought of Alice, the little girl who lived with her grandmother in the next street. Alice would like the book very much. She put on her hat and ran to the house. She left the book there and ran home again.

The grandmother was surprised when she opened the parcel and found the book – but dear me, Alice had gone far, far away! She had left on a steamer for Canada, where her father and mother were, and was not coming back till she was grown-up. The old grandmother wondered whom she could give the book to.

'There's that kind little chap, Bob,' she suddenly thought, 'When Alice was ill he came to see her every day. He always sent her a card for Christmas and often asked her to tea, because her mother and father were so far away. I'll send it to *him*!'

And *how* surprised Bob was when the book he had bought came back to him! He was *so* pleased – and I think he deserved it, don't you?

Snapdragon Snippets

The Snippet Pixies lived in the mushroom fields, where houses were cheap. As soon as a fine mushroom grew up the Snippets snipped out a door and a window, made a stairway inside the stalk and a room inside the mushroom top, and hey, presto! there was a house big enough for two Snippets at least!

But one day it happened that a boy came along who saw the mushrooms and picked them – and, dear me, what a surprise for him when he saw the doors and windows! The Snippets flew out at once and fled away from the field. The boy followed in glee. He thought they were butterflies or moths, and as he carried a net with him he meant to catch them.

The Snippets flew on and on, panting hard. They flew over a cornfield and the boy rushed after them. They flew down the lane, they flew

through a wood, and at last, quite tired out, they flew into a garden.

'We can't fly any further!' panted one little Snippet, sinking down to the ground like a tiny bubble. 'That boy will have to catch us!'

'What's the matter?' asked a bumble bee near-by.

The Snippets told him. 'There's the boy, look, coming in at the gate now!' they groaned. 'Whatever can we do? There doesn't seem anywhere to hide, bumble bee.'

'Quick! I'll show you a place!' buzzed the velvety bee. 'Follow me!'

He flew to a red snapdragon. He alighted on the lower part and pressed it down so that the snapdragon opened its 'bunny-mouth'. In went the bee – and the mouth of the snapdragon closed behind him so that not even a leg could be seen! He pushed himself out backwards to the surprised Snippets.

'There you are! Get inside any of these snap-dragon flowers and you'll be well-hidden!'

The Snippets gave little high squeals of glee. Each one flew up to a red, pink, or yellow snapdragon, and pressed hard on the lower lip of the flower. The mouth opened – the Snippets slipped in – the mouth closed up! Not a wing was to be seen, not even a tiny bare foot!

The boy banged the garden gate and looked round. 'Where are those strange little butter-flies?' he said, holding his net ready to catch them.'I know they flew into this garden, for I saw them. Where have they hidden them-selves?'

He went to the flower-bed. He set the flowers swinging to and fro, so that he might frighten any butterfly into the air. But the Snippets were safe, though their hiding-places swung about as the boy pushed them with his net. It was like being in a cosy hammock. The flowers smelt lovely, too – they made a wonderful hiding place!

The boy soon left the garden, and it was safe for the Snippets to come out. They peeped from their strange hiding place and nodded to one another. 'We can't go back to our mushroom houses now,' they cried. 'Shall we live here instead?'

Everybody thought it was a good idea. They went to buy soft yellow blankets for beds from the gnome under the hedge, and that was all they needed. Each night they crept into the bunny-mouths of the snapdragons and slept on their hammocks of yellow down, and they probably do still.

You won't find them there in the daytime, for then they are at work snipping up fallen flower petals to make frocks and coats – but you might press open a snapdragon gently and see if you can find the Snippets' downy yellow beds made ready for the night!

Oh, No, Brer Fox!

One day Brer Bear gave Brer Rabbit six fine pots of new honey, golden yellow and sweet. Brer Rabbit was very pleased. He put them in a basket and set off home. It was a hot day, and he sat down beneath a tree to have a rest. Soon his head nodded and he fell asleep.

It wasn't long before Brer Fox came padding by. He was just going to pounce on Brer Rabbit when he saw Brer Hare's ears sticking up behind a bush, watching him. So he thought he would take the honey instead. He picked up the basket and padded off with it, grinning away to himself.

Well, of course, Brer Hare told Brer Rabbit what had happened, and Brer Rabbit was as wild as could be! He sat and puzzled hard how to get back that honey. Then he slapped his knee and grinned.

Off he went, back to Brer Bear's again.

'That robber, Brer Fox, has stolen the honey you gave me, Brer Bear,' he said. 'But I'll get it back! Aha, I will! I've got my cousin, Brer Hare, coming in to talk to me tonight – and we're going to plan how to get that honey back. Brer Hare's clever – and so am I – and between us we'll make a fine plan!'

Well, of course, when Brer Fox met Brer Bear that day, as Brer Rabbit had known he would, Brer Bear told Brer Fox what Brer Rabbit had said. Brer Fox rubbed his sharp nose and grinned, 'I'll be under Brer Rabbit's windowsill tonight listening to his plans!' he said.

Well, that night Brer Rabbit set his radio going, very low. There was a lot of talking on it. When he had set it just so, Brer Rabbit put on his cap and slipped outside under a bush. Presently along came Brer Fox, going as softly as a cat. Brer Fox sidled in at the gate and crept up to Brer Rabbit's windowsill. He crouched down there and listened hard.

'Brer Hare and Brer Rabbit are talking mighty quiet!' he said to himself. 'Maybe soon they'll talk up and I'll hear what they are planning.'

Brer Rabbit watched him and he grinned a

big grin all to himself. He went quietly out of the back gate and then set out for Brer Fox's house as fast as ever he could, lippitty-clippitty through the woods. When he got there he opened the door and went in. He looked round – and the first thing he saw on a shelf was his honey, neatly set out, six pots in a row. Brer Rabbit found his basket under the shelf, too, and he quickly popped all those pots into it.

He ran home – and he walked in at his gate as bold as brass, whistling loudly. Brer Fox heard him and stared in astonishment, for he had thought Brer Rabbit was indoors talking away to Brer Hare! Brer Rabbit switched on his torch and turned it on to Brer Fox under the windowsill.

'Heyo, Brer Fox!' he said. 'Still there! Well, well, well!'

'Where have you been?' asked Brer Fox, an awful thought coming into his mind.

'Been, Brer Fox? Oh, I've just been getting honey for my breakfast tomorrow!' said Brer Rabbit, skipping into his house before Brer Fox could catch him. He put his head out again and bawled, 'So glad you like my radio, Brer Fox! Come in some night and hear it again!'

The Top of the Wall

Old Man Greeneyes lived in a little cottage surrounded on all sides by a high red wall. He liked to be sheltered from the winds – and from prying eyes; for Old Man Greeneyes was half a wizard!

Next door to him lived Dame Fiddlesticks and her children. Dame Fiddlesticks was a most inquisitive person and loved to peep at her neighbours. If she went into her bedroom she could just see nicely over the wall into the old man's garden. That *did* annoy him! And then the children took to climbing on the top of the wall and calling to him. That annoyed him more than ever!

At last he decided that he must do something about it. If he had the wall made higher by a foot, and put some glass spikes on top, Dame Fiddlesticks couldn't see into his garden from her bedroom window and the children wouldn't be able to climb up and sit on top. So off he went to Mr Hod the builder.

'Yes,' said Mr Hod. 'It would be easy to do what you want – but you will offend Dame Fiddlesticks mightily. She might throw her rubbish over your wall in revenge, and her children would certainly call out after you when you go walking, for they are not very well-mannered. Take my advice and think of something else. It is usually just as possible to get your way in a kindly manner as in an ill-natured one.'

Old Man Greeneyes nodded his head and went to see his cousin, Mother Tiptap. She heard what he had to say and smiled. 'I've just the thing for you!' she said. 'See, here are some new seeds I have made. Plant them on the top of your wall and see what happens.'

'But no seeds will grow on a *wall*,' said Old Man Greeneyes. Still, he took them and planted them all along the top of his wall. Then he waited to see what would happen. The rain came. The sun shone. Those tiny seeds thrust out roots into the wall-crannies. They sent up small leaves. They grew and they grew.

And then one day in the springtime they

flowered into bright yellow and red – tall plants, over a foot high, with the most delicious scent in the world! Old Man Greeneyes smelt them from his kitchen window and was glad. Dame Fiddle-sticks feasted her eyes on them, for she loved flowers, and when she smelt their scent she was full of joy.

'Don't you dare to climb up on that wall any more!' she warned her children. 'I won't have those beautiful flowers spoilt that that kind old man has planted there. They've grown so high that I can't peep into his garden any more, but what does that matter? I'd rather see the flowers there!'

She was so delighted that she sent in a new cake she had baked to the old man. He went to thank her and asked what he could do in return for her kindness.

'Oh, if only you'd give me a few seeds of those lovely flowers of yours growing on the wall,' she said. 'What are they called?'

'They've no name at present,' said the old man, smiling. 'What shall we call them? Let's ask the children?'

The children knew what to call them, of course! Do *you* know the name?

A Busy Morning

There was once a little boy called William Robert, and his mother used to call him Billy-Bob for short. He was a useful boy, and did all sorts of things for his mother and father. He used to run errands every day, and he really had a very good memory indeed.

One day his mother said, 'Billy-Bob, please go to the grocer's and get me a packet of tea.'

'A packet of tea,' said Billy-Bob. 'Yes, Mother.'

As he went to the door his father said, 'Billy-Bob, please get me a box of nails.'

'A packet of tea, a box of nails,' said Billy-Bob. 'Yes, Daddy.'

As he went down the path, his aunt, who lived next door, called him. 'Billy-Bob, if you're going out, please get me a bag of buns for tea at our baker's.'

'A packet of tea, a box of nails, and a bag of

buns,' said Billy-Bob to himself. 'Yes, Auntie.'

He was just going out of the gate when his uncle came up on his way home. 'Hello, Billy-Bob,' he said. 'Are you off shopping? Here's fifty p. Buy me a paper, there's a good boy.'

'A packet of tea, a box of nails, a bag of buns, and a paper,' said Billy-Bob. 'Yes, Uncle.'

He went down the road. Old Mrs Brown knocked on the window when she saw him passing. 'Billy-Bob!' she called. 'Please get me a pot of cream and a quarter of peppermints, will you?'

'A packet of tea, a box of nails, a bag of buns, a paper, a pot of cream and a quarter of peppermints,' said Billy-Bob. 'Yes, Mrs Brown!'

On he went, and met Mr Jones. 'Hello, Billy-Bob!' said Mr Jones. 'Are you passing the fish shop? Please buy me a nice kipper, will you? Here's the money.'

'A packet of tea, a box of nails, a bag of buns, a paper, a pot of cream, a quarter of peppermints, and a nice kipper,' said Billy-Bob to himself. 'Yes, Mr Jones.'

He went on. Soon he met Jim and Peter, and they showed him their new marbles. Then he met Susan and she told him how she had fallen down, and showed him her bandaged knee. Then after that he met Tom, who gave him a sweet and told him that his mother had made some ginger buns for tea.

'I must hurry!' said Billy-Bob to himself. He went to the grocer's and bought – well what *did* he buy? He went to the ironmonger and bought – can you tell me? He went to the baker's, and what did he get there? He went to the dairy and came out with – what? He went to the sweet shop and put down the money for – can *you* remember? And last of all he went to the fish shop, and there he asked for a nice – do *you* know what it was?

What a lot of parcels he had! Off he went home, and on the way he repeated the list over to himself – and, dear me, Billy-Bob had forgotten something! Yes, he had! What could it be, oh, what could it be? Yes – you are right – he had forgotten his uncle's paper! He met a newsboy and bought one. Now Billy-Bob was happy. He ran off home, carrying seven things – and who can tell me what they were?

The Witch's Egg

Once upon a time Sneaky the elf peeped into Witch Upadee's kitchen and saw her working a spell. First she took a small chocolate Easter egg and put it on a plate. Sneaky knew the kind. You could buy them for twenty-five p each, and they were filled with sticky cream inside. He sat himself on the windowsill and watched to see what happened next.

Witch Upadee took a peacock's feather and stroked the tiny egg. Then she blew on it hard and chanted, 'Grow, grow. Quick and slow. Make yourself sweet for witches to eat. Grow, grow. Quick and slow!'

And, to Sneaky's enormous astonishment, that tiny chocolate egg began to grow big on the plate! How it grew! How it swelled up! My goodness, Sneaky did feel hungry when he saw that great egg of chocolate, all ready to be eaten, growing bigger and bigger! He nearly fell off the

windowsill in surprse – and then, what a shock
he got! Witch Upadee saw him and gave a shout
of rage. She picked up her broom and swept him
right off her windowsill!

'You nasty little sneaking thing, always peeping and prying! Go away! You *shan't* see my
spells!'

But Sneaky had seen enough. He ran home
grinning and rubbing his hands. *He* would
make a chocolate egg grow like that, too –
and my, what a lot of money he would make
by selling it!

He bought a chocolate egg and took it home.
He set it on a plate and then went to borrow a
peacock's feather from his friend next door. He
stroked the little egg with it, and then blew on it
hard, feeling tremendously excited. Then he
chanted loudly the magic song, 'Grow, grow.
Quick and slow. Make yourself sweet for *fairies*
to eat. Grow, grow. Quick and slow!'

The chocolate egg began to grow. How it
grew! You really should have seen it. It was a
most marvellous sight. First it was as big as a
hen's egg. Then as big as a goose's. Then as big
as a swan's. Then as large as an ostrich's. Then
as big as a coal-scuttle – and it went on growing.

Sneaky was delighted. He danced round in joy, watching the egg grow.

It grew and it grew. Crack! It broke the plate with its weight. But Sneaky didn't mind. He could buy lots of new plates with the money for that lovely egg! That the egg grew bigger than the table – and crack! One of the legs gave way, and down went the table and the egg, too. But still it went on growing!

When it was as big as a large wheel-barrow Sneaky thought it was big enough. After all, he had to get it out of the door and take it to market – it wouldn't do for it to get *too* big! So he shouted to it. 'Stop! Don't grow any more, egg!' But the egg didn't take a bit of notice, no, not a bit. It just went on growing – and however much Sneaky begged it to stop it simply wouldn't. Sneaky didn't know the right words to say, you see! Well, it grew – and it grew – and it grew – and at last it couldn't grow any more, because it was as big as the room itself – and poor Sneaky was squashed flat in one corner. And then in pressing itself against the ceiling, the egg broke! Out came a great stream of sticky cream – all over poor Sneaky! After that the egg stopped growing, for the spell was broken.

But do you know – the only way Sneaky could get out of the room was by eating his way through the egg! It took him two days – and oh, the mess he was in! And now, if you meet a small elf who says he simply can't BEAR Easter eggs, just ask him his name. It's sure to be Sneaky!

Chestnut Prickles

Once, when the pixie dressmaker was going home from the Queen's palace, with a bag full of money in her hand, the robber gnomes lay in wait for her. 'She has been paid for all the dresses she has made for the Queen,' they whispered to one another. 'Let us rob her! She is so small and weak, and we can easily take her money.'

The blackbird heard what they said, and he flew to warn the little dressmaker. He sat up in the big chestnut tree and sang to her as she came along. 'Beware, beware! Hide yourself, little pixie! The robber gnomes are lying in wait for you!'

The pixie was frightened. She rushed to the chestnut tree and climbed up on to its stout branches. There she sat, trembling. She hoped the gnomes would pass by, and then she could slip down and run home. But, no – they spied her up in the tree and shouted in glee.

'There she is! We'll wait till she comes down!'
They sat around the tree trunk, and the poor
little dressmaker was trapped!

She began to cry. The chestnut felt her tears
on its leaves, and it whispered to her to comfort
her. It tumbled a chestnut down on her lap,
dressed in its green, prickly case. She picked it
up – and an idea crept into her mind.

'I'll wait till it's dark – then I'll pick lots of
these prickly cases – and I'll sew them together
with my needle and thread and make myself a
prickly coat! Then if I slip down the tree and
the gnomes try to catch me, *what* a shock they'll
get!'

As soon as it was dark the little dressmaker
picked dozens of the prickly chestnut cases. She
sewed them together with her strongest thread,
and made herself a long coat, right down to her
ankles. With four of them she made a prickly
cap for her head – and then she was ready! With
the prickly coat well wrapped around her, and
the prickly cap on her head, she slipped down
the tree. The gnomes at once leapt up in the
dark and pounced on her.

They caught hold of the pixie – but, dear me,
how prickly she was! 'Ooh! Oh! Ah!' cried the

gnomes, letting her go at once. 'We're pricked! We're scratched! It's a nasty little hedghog! Let it go. Sit down and wait again, for surely the pixie will climb down soon.'

They sat down – and the pixie hurried home safely with her money, chuckling to think of the trick she had played on the robber gnomes. '*What* a useful coat I made!' she thought. 'How cross the gnomes will be in the morning when they see I'm gone!'

And I should just think they *were*!

The Remarkable Doughnut

There was once a small goblin called Greedy, who was just like his name. He was very fond of doughnuts, and every day he went to the baker's to buy a large brown doughnut for his tea. They were always fresh, and new, and fat little Greedy enjoyed them very much.

One day as he came home he was caught by a band of gnomes and taken off to be their servant. He was very angry, and so afraid that his doughnut would be taken from him that he held tightly to the bag.

The gnomes took him to their cave. They gave him a pail and a scrubbing brush and ordered him to clean the floor. But Greedy was not going to.

'What!' he cried, his little green eyes flashing brightly. 'You think I, a clever goblin, will be slave to a pack of stupid gnomes like you!'

The gnomes flew into a rage and shook the

cheeky goblin till his teeth rattled like dice in a box.

'Ask us anything in the world and we'll tell it you!' they cried. 'Only ask us. *Then* you will see how clever we are!'

Greedy the goblin turned pale. What could he ask them? They were sure to know everything, really, for he knew they were friendly with the witches and shared all their strange and wonderful secrets.

'Go on, go on!' shouted the gnomes. 'Ask us something! Quick! If you ask us something and we know the answer we'll turn you into a wasp without a sting, just to teach you not to be so cheeky another time!'

Greedy thought that if he took a bite out of his doughnut it might help him. So he took it out of the bag. His mouth watered when he saw its round, sugary surface, and he longed to taste the jam that lay hidden in one corner of the doughnut's inside.

And then the great question came to him. *He* knew what to ask those goblins! Of course he did. He held out the doughnut to them and bade them look carefully at it, seeing that there was no hole anywhere at all.

Then he bit it and the dob of jam gushed out. 'Now tell me, o gnomes,' said the little goblin, 'how was the jam put inside the doughnut, for, as you saw, the brown skin of it was whole and had no opening anywhere.'

The goblins crowded round in surprise. One of them took the doughnut and looked at it carefully. 'A most remarkable thing,' he said. 'Now, let me see – how *could* that jam be put inside? Let me see.'

And while they were all puzzling their heads about it Greedy slipped out and away! He had lost his doughnut, but found his freedom. Do *you* know the answer to his question? Think hard, like the gnomes!

The Wrong Side of the Bed

Long, long ago, the wizard Ten-toes bought a marvellous bed. There were dragons carved at the head, with long, coiling bodies, and peacocks with spreading tails carved at the foot. The dragons had eyes of rubies and the peacocks had eyes of sapphire blue, so you can guess how strange they looked with their eyes gleaming in the dark at night. The wizard liked the bed very much, he said it made him feel more like a wizard than ever.

He had bought it from a witch, and when she sold it to him she said, 'Ten-toes, whatever you do, always get out on the *right* side of the bed. If you don't you'll be sorry!'

She wouldn't tell him why, but she knew quite well. A bad-tempered little imp had made the bed for himself. One day the witch had placed a spell upon him, got him into her power and taken the bed for herself. But she could not get rid of the little black imp. He made himself invisible and squatted down beside his beautiful bed, which he would not leave night or day. The witch found it out one morning by getting out on the side of the bed where the imp crouched.

What a shock for her! He bit her foot, and his sharp teeth sent poison into her – the poison of his own bad temper. And that day the witch couldn't do anything right! How she scolded, how she raged! How she stamped her foot and frowned! It was terrible to see.

She sold Ten-toes the bed, but she wouldn't say a word about the invisible imp that went with it, for she was afraid that if she did he would not pay her so much money. The wizard was pleased with the bed. He slept well in it and was careful each morning to get out on the right side.

One day he forgot. He was sleepy and got out the wrong side. He trod on the invisible imp, who at once bit him in a rage. 'Dear, dear!' said the wizard, surprised. 'I must have stepped on a pin!'

All that day things went wrong for Ten-toes. He lost his temper, he shouted and raged. He hit the man who came to clean the windows, he shook his fist at the woman who sold him potatoes. Really, he behaved very badly indeed. The bad-temper poison was working very strongly in him!

The next morning Ten-toes got out the *right* side of the bed and things went well. The morning after he got out the *wrong* side, and everything went wrong again because of his bad temper. He simply couldn't understand it!

He met the witch and frowned at her so fiercely that she was frightened and astonished. Then she suddenly thought of something.

'Did you get out of bed the wrong side this morning?' she called after him. The wizard stopped and thought. Yes, he had! Dear, dear, dear! So that explained his bad temper, did it? What a peculiar thing! Well, he would be careful to get out the *right* side after that!

That was hundreds of years ago! But it's a strange thing, isn't it, that we still say to a bad-tempered person, 'You must have got out of bed on the wrong side this morning!' Now you know how that saying began!

The Stupid Little Girl

There was once a small girl called Eileen who had very good brains, which she was too lazy to use. She couldn't even say her two times table when she was eight years old, so you can guess how lazy she was, because they are *very* easy, aren't they!

'Eileen, why are you so stupid?' her teacher asked her one day. 'You have good brains if only you will use them. You should be at the top of the class, not at the bottom.'

'Well, perhaps it's because I haven't any brothers or sisters,' said Eileen. 'I am an only child, and only children can't help being backward.'

'Rubbish!' said her teacher. 'You'd be just the same if you had half a dozen brothers and sisters, Eileen.'

'Oh, no, Miss Brown. I'm sure I shouldn't,' said Eileen. 'If only someone would give me a brother and a sister I know I'd be different!'

Now, although Eileen didn't know it, a little gnome was listening to what she said. And that evening he tapped at Eileen's window and called to her.

'Eileen!' he cried. 'Come out! Your brother and sister are here and are longing to play with you.'

'Oh!' said Eileen in delight. 'So I've got a brother and sister after all, and didn't know it. How lovely!'

Out she ran into the garden, and the first thing she saw was a big grey donkey, who gravely held up his fore-foot to shake hands with her. Eilen looked at the gnome astonished.

'It's your brother,' said the gnome. 'Shake hands, can't you? He's just as stupid and obstinate as you are, so you and he will get on very well together. He will be a very good brother for you.'

'I don't want a donkey for a brother,' said Eileen, going red. 'How horrid of you, gnome! Where is my sister? I will play with her, and not with this donkey.'

'Here's your sister,' said the gnome, and he pointed to a big goose waddling down the

garden. 'She will make you a fine sister. I have
often heard your mother call you a silly goose, so
I have found a goose to be your sister. Won't
you have fine times together, you and the donkey and the goose!'

'I *won't* have a goose and a donkey to play
with,' said Eileen in a rage. The goose and the
donkey looked at the angry little girl out of
solemn eyes.

'Is this the child you said would be our
sister?' asked the donkey. 'Well, we don't want
her. She looks too silly for anything. We are
sure she would be too stupid to play with us.
Goodbye, little girl, we will go and find someone
more interesting.'

Off they went and the gnome looked at
Eileen. 'There you are!' he said, disgusted.
'Even a foolish donkey and a silly goose don't
want to know you. You *must* be stupid, even
though your teacher says you have good brains!'

'I *have* got good brains!' shouted Eileen, and
she ran indoors to do her homework. And you
will be glad to hear that she began to use her
brains so that in a few weeks' time she was top of
her class. It *was* a good thing the gnome tried to
find a brother and sister for her, wasn't it?

The Bread and Milk

Binkle the kitten was very fussy one day. He turned up his nose at the nice dish of bread and milk that his owner put out for his breakfast. He wanted fish.

'You shall have fish this afternoon,' said his owner. 'Now eat your breakfast up properly.' But Binkle went away in a corner and sulked. The dish of bread and milk stood in the porch, full to the brim.

Soon the robin spied it. Down he flew and chose a big piece of soaked bread. Four sparrows saw him, and flew down to join him. The robin didn't like eating with other people, so off he flew – and the sparrows pulled pieces of bread about, eating a very good breakfast indeed! Other sparrows heard them chirruping happily and came to join them too.

Then a small mouse peeped out of his hole in the bank not far off, and sniffed with his little woffly nose. How good that bread and milk smelt, to be sure! He really must have a taste! Off he scampered and came to the dish. The sparrows flew off to have a dust-bath, and left the dish to the little brown mouse. He nibbled daintily here and there, and wondered what made the bread taste so very delicious. What a fine breakfast he was having!

A movement under the lavender bush that grew near the door startled him so much that he ran off in a hurry, thinking it might be Binkle the kitten hiding there. But it was only old Prickles the hedgehog, who lived in the garden and ate beetles, slugs, and grubs whenever he could find them. He, too, had smelt the bread and milk and meant to have some.

He ambled up to the dish, tipped it up so that he could drink the milk, and then began to feast. How he enjoyed it!

Just then he heard the pattering of footsteps, and up came Bobs the dog. The hedgehog, who was not afraid of any animal in the world, walked back to the lavender bush and curled himself up there to go to sleep. Bobs knew him well, and left him alone. He sniffed at the dish and licked it well all around.

Now Binkle the kitten began to feel very hungry, and off he went to find his breakfast, thinking that bread and milk wasn't so bad after all – but when he came to the dish it was empty!

'*We* took some,' said the robin and the sparrows, cheekily. '*I* ate some,' said the little mouse, peeping out. '*I* took some,' said the prickly hedgehog, licking his lips. 'And *I* licked the dish,' said Bobs.

'You greedy things!' cried Binkle, in a rage. 'It was *my* breakfast!'

'And ours, too!' said everyone, and *how* they laughed!

The Sulky Sweets

Everybody knew the Sulky Brownie. He was such a miserable-looking creature. He made other people unhappy, and he himself was the unhappiest of all.

Now it is very unusual for any of the Little Folk to sulk, and everyone felt certain that the brownie had caught the disease from someone in our world – for, as you know, there are plenty of boys and girls who suffer from the sulks when they are not very well. So the pixies, the gnomes and the brownies had a meeting about it to see what could be done for the poor sulky brownie.

He wanted to be cured too. A sulky person is so miserable that if he could find a quick and easy way of curing himself he would do so.

'We could ask the old witch Know-all,' said a gnome. 'I live next door to her, and she really is a marvel at curing things.'

'Well, ask her, then,' said the others. So he

went home and asked his neighbour the witch how to cure a person of the sulks.

'That will cost you ten pieces of gold,' said Witch Know-all, greedily. The gnome paid up the money at once. Then the witch grinned and took a packet out of her cupboard. She undid it and showed the gnome some round, flattish white things that looked like sweets.

'These are sulky sweets,' she said. 'If a sulky person takes one of these and sucks them, smiling all the time that the sweet is in his mouth, his fit of sulks will be cured as soon as the sweet is finished. There you are! And the secret is well worth ten pieces of gold!'

The gnome hurried off to the sulky brownie and told him what the witch had said. The brownie was very grateful, for he really did want to be happy, like ordinary people, and get rid of his silly sulking fits. So the very next time he began to sulk, he took the witch's advice. He popped into his mouth one of the sulky sweets and began to suck it. All the time he was sucking it he made himself smile without stopping. The sweet took a long time to disappear – but will you believe it, as soon as it was gone and the brownie thought about his sulks, *they* had disappeared too! Yes, and he felt quite happy. It was marvellous.

But here is the curious thing. *Those sweets were not magic ones at all!* What do you think they were? Just ordinary white acid drops, the sort you buy at any sweet shop! And the very curious thing is that if anyone in *our* world buys those acid drops, and sucks one when he is sulking, smiling all the time, *his* sulks will go too! You might tell this to anyone who sulks, or try it yourself if *you* feel sulky. But don't forget – you must smile all the time the sweet is in your mouth! *I* shan't charge you ten pieces of gold, as the old witch did, but you might let me know if the strange little spell still works!

The Stupid Goblin

One day Snip and Snap the brownies went fishing in the pond belonging to the Red Goblin. They hadn't caught more than three fish when up came the Red Goblin and pounced on them. 'Aha!' he cried. 'I've got you! I'll lock you up in my deep, dark cave!'

He dragged them off, and in a little while Snip began to cry loudly and say, 'I've left my net behind. My nice new net!'

'Well, go back and get it quickly,' said the goblin, crossly, and Snip ran off. But he didn't come back, as you can guess.

'Perhaps he has lost his way and can't find us,' said Snap. 'Shall I go and fetch him?' The goblin let him go – and of course Snap didn't come back either.

The next week those silly little brownies went to gather bluebells in the goblin's wood. Out he pounced and caught them again.

'Aha!' he shouted. 'I've got you again. I'll lock you up safely *this* time.' He dragged them off, howling and crying. Presently Snap clapped his hand to his head and said. 'I've left my cap in the woods. I shall get sunstroke, I know I shall.'

'This is the sort of trick you played on me last time,' growled the goblin, stopping. 'I let one of you go back, and he lost his way. Then when the other went to find him, *he* didn't come back either!'

'Well, let us *both* go back for the cap together,' said Snap. 'Then we shan't lose our way.'

'Go then, and hurry back,' commanded the goblin. 'I will wait here.' Off went the two brownies, and though the goblin waited until midnight, you may guess that neither of them went back! No, they were safely in their beds at home!

In a few days the foolish brownies went to hunt for the first wild rose on the hedge that ran round the Red Goblin's meadows. He was waiting for them and pounced on them in delight, chuckling gleefully. 'I'll lock you up *this* time!' he shouted.

But before they had gone a great distance

Snip began to cry loudly and feel in his pockets one after the other as if he had lost something. 'What's the matter *now*?' asked the goblin, impatiently.

'I've left my purse full of money under the hedge,' wept Snip. 'Oh dear, oh dear, what shall I do?'

'Ho!' said the Red Goblin, stopping and looking slyly at Snip. 'So you're trying to play me that old trick once more, are you? You want to go back for your purse and slip off home again. No, no, brownies, you can't trick an old goblin like me a third time. I shan't let *you* go again – *I* shall go and get that purse while *you* stay here! Ha, ha, that will teach you that I'm too clever for you!'

And off he ran back to the hedge, where he hunted in vain for the purse of money. When he got back to where he had left those two brownies they were gone! Poor old goblin – he wasn't very clever, was he?

The Boast That Came True

Woffles the rabbit was a boaster. He boasted about everything under the sun, and made himself out to be the most wonderful and most powerful rabbit that ever lived.

But there came a day when he boasted once too often, as you shall hear. It happened when a good many animals were all talking together by the pond that lies at the end of a very long field, the other side of Cuckoo Hill. They were chattering busily, when flying through the sky there came a noisy aeroplane.

'Look at that strange bird,' said Prickles the hedgehog, half frightened. 'I hope it doesn't come down here!'

'I could make it come down if I wanted to!' boasted Woffles at once. 'But if it would frighten you, I won't tell it to come down, Prickles.'

'What stories you tell!' said Mowdie the mole,

scornfully. 'As if you could make a great bird like that come down into our field. You are a silly boaster, Woffles!'

'I tell you I *could* make it come down,' said Woffles at once. 'It's only because it would frighten Prickles that I don't tell it to come here.'

'Stuff and nonsense!' said Mowdie. 'Prickles, go down my hole and hide. Now, Woffles, Prickles has gone. Tell that big bird up there to come down and we'll see if you are telling the truth or just boasting as usual.'

'Yes, go on!' cried all the others, pleased to see Woffles looking rather red.

Well, what could Woffles do but tell the aeroplane to come down? He cleared his throat and then said boldly, 'Strange, noisy bird up there in the sky, come down to our field!'

To everyone's enormous surprise and alarm the aeroplane began to circle round and come lower and lower. The pilot had been told that he must land on this long, flat field, and wait for two other aeroplanes to join him there. So down he came!

R-r-r-r-r-r-r-r-r-r! What a noise the engine made as the aeroplane dropped lower and lower.

Then at last it landed on the grass. All the animals were rooted to the spot, frightened out of their lives, not daring to move or to cry out in case the strange big birds with widespread wings should eat them up. Then to their horror, two more of these queer creatures appeared in the sky, and they too began to circle over the field and come down.

With squeaks, shrieks and squeals every animal fled into ditch, hole, and hedge, scared out of their lives. And the one who ran the fastest of all was Woffles the boaster! He fled into the deepest tunnel he knew of and crouched there, hardly daring to move.

'Woffles, Woffles!' someone called, suddenly. 'Where are you? Come and tell those horrible birds to go away. You made them come and you must make them go.'

But Woffles wasn't going to put his nose into that field again, not he! He crept away down another tunnel and was soon miles away, on the other side of Cuckoo Hill. And from that day he was so afraid that what he said might come true that he never once boasted again!

Sly-One is Caught

There was a reward offered in Oak-Tree Wood to anyone who could catch the thief Sly-One. He was a green goblin, cunning and quick. He liked to lie in wait for pixies and elves going through Oak-Tree Wood and pounce on them. Then he would rob them of their money.

The pixie Nimble longed to catch Sly-One. Nimble hadn't much money, and he lived with his pet hedgehog in a very small cottage. One day he sat on his stool and thought of a plan to catch Sly-One. He told it to Prickles his hedgehog, and Prickles agreed.

The next thing that Nimble did was to send a message to his cousin, Niggle, to say he would be bringing him some money on Friday night. He gave the message to Chatter the magpie, and of course, Chatter told the message to everyone in the wood before he took it to Niggle. Sly-One the goblin heard the message and grinned to himself. He would hide in the hazel bush near Niggle's house and as soon as Nimble came up with the money he would jump on him and get it. It would be dark so Nimble wouldn't spy him.

But Nimble sent for Hush-Hush the owl, and begged him to follow Sly-One on Friday night, find out where he was hiding, and come back to tell him. So when Friday night came Hush-Hush followed Sly-One on his silent wings and saw him hiding himself in the hazel bush. He flew back to Nimble and told him. Then Nimble chuckled and told Prickles the hedgehog.

They set off through the wood together. But when they came near the hazel bush Nimble told Prickles to go in front and make as much noise as he could. So on went the hedgehog, shuffling through the leaves, loudly.

Sly-One thought it was Nimble. He leapt out from the bush and flung himself heavily on top of Prickles. Ooh! What a dreadful shock! Pins and needles! Tacks and nails! Whatever had he fallen on?

Nimble rushed up with a torch, and how he laughed to see the green goblin stuck fast on the hedgehog's hundreds of prickles! 'Hold him,

Prickles!' said Nimble, chuckling. 'We've got him now! You can carry him to Oak-Tree Town just like that.'

Off they went, though Sly-One struggled and begged for mercy. It was no good. The thief was caught. As soon as the folk in Oak-Tree Town knew what had happened they all turned out to see the goblin stuck on the hedgehog. How they laughed!

Nimble got the reward, and now he is so rich that he and Prickles have treacle pudding for dinner every day. Aren't they lucky!

Timothy's Tooth

Once upon a time a long, long while ago, the fairies were making a spell in a big cauldron over a fire of blue flames. It was a good spell and a wonderful one – a spell to make sick people better. All the pixies and elves bent over the steaming cauldron and watched the colour in it change from red to orange, from orange to yellow, yellow to green, from green to blue – and dear me, then it stopped! Now that was quite wrong, because the enchanted liquid should change through all the colours of the rainbow, it shouldn't stop at blue! It should go on to indigo and then to violet, when the spell would be finished and perfect.

'Ooooooooh!' squealed the elves, in their little high voices. 'We've missed out something!'

'Ooooooooh!' cried the pixies. 'What shall we do?

Then there was a rush for the big Magic Book

that belonged to the Queen, and a great rustle as the thick pages were turned over. A small pixie found the place and read out loud.

'To make the spell perfect one small white tooth should be added; a child's tooth is best.'

All the little folk looked at one another sadly. 'We shall never get that,' they cried. 'Never! How could we go round pulling out children's teeth?'

'Wait!' said an elf. 'I know a little boy called Timothy, who is very kind. He might give me one of his teeth if I asked him.' So off he flew to Timothy. He told the little boy all about his difficulty, and Timothy listened.

Timothy was seven years old. One of his first teeth was very loose indeed. He often waggled it to and fro with his finger, but he wouldn't let his mother take it out, though he knew it wouldn't really hurt. He liked to feel it waggling. But if the elf wanted it to finish the wonderful spell; why certainly Timothy would give him the tooth.

'As soon as my mother comes in I'll ask her to take out my loose tooth for you,' promised Timothy. The elf gave him a hug. 'Will you put it under your pillow when you go to bed tonight?' he asked. 'I'll come and get it when you're asleep – and for payment you can have a wish that will come true – and perhaps some money too, if I can get some for you!'

Well, Timothy's mother took out the tooth and it didn't hurt a bit. Timothy slipped it under his pillow – and, will you believe it? the next morning the tooth was gone, and a bright shining coin was there instead. Timothy's wish came true, and he was so excited and happy that he told everyone what had happened. The news soon spread, and to this very day, if you put your little white tooth under your pillow, you will find it gone in the morning, and maybe a coin there instead. Don't forget to wish a wish too, will you!

The Four-leaved Clover

A four-leaved clover is very lucky! If you find one and keep it, it will grant you a wish, so the pixies say – and they ought to know, because they make them grow.

One day a small girl called Nora found a four-leaved clover in a field. She was so pleased. She picked it very carefully and looked at it. Yes, it had four little leaves instead of three!

'Now I can have a wish,' thought Nora. 'I know what I shall wish for – that lovely doll in the toyshop window. I've wanted it for ever so long!'

She skipped off, the four-leaved clover in her hand. On the way home she met Tommy and Joan, hand in hand, crying bitterly.

'Our mother's ill and she's gone to hospital,' wept Joan. 'We want her back.'

'Perhaps she won't be long,' said Nora, putting her arms round the children.

'We can't do without her,' said Tommy. 'She puts us to bed each night and gives us our dinner when we come home from school. What shall we do now she's gone?'

Nora was very sorry for the two unhappy children. She knew how horrid it was when mothers went away.

'Look!' she suddenly said to Joan and Tommy. 'I've found a four-leaved clover, and a wish belongs to it. I was going to wish for that big doll in the toyshop window – but if you like, you can wish for your mother to come home tomorrow,' she said.

'Oh, thank you, Nora – you *are* kind!' cried Joan. 'I'll come and tell you when our mother comes home.'

Nora left them and went home. She hadn't seen a lady standing nearby, waiting for a bus. She hadn't known that the lady had heard every word and had thought Nora was one of the nicest children she had ever seen.

The lady went to Tommy and Joan and asked where Nora lived. Then she went to the toyshop and bought the very big doll that sat in the middle of the window. She wrote a little note and put it inside the box in which the doll was packed. Then she asked the shopwoman to send the doll by post to Nora's house, addressed to Nora.

Early next morning Tommy and Joan came running round to Nora's house, their faces beaming bright. 'Our mother is coming home today! The hospital say there's nothing wrong with her! The clover wish came true! We've brought it back again in case you want to wish with it, too.'

'But a clover leaf only has one wish,' said Nora. 'It's no use now. I *am* glad your mother's coming home. Oh, look, here's the postman with a parcel – and it's for *me*!'

It was a very big doll! There was a note, too, that said, 'The clover leaf you found had *two* wishes, you see!'

'Well!' said Nora, astonished. 'Just think of that! Oh, how lucky I am!'

Ah, but she deserved it, didn't she!

Tuppy and the Goblins

Tuppy was a gnome. He was short and round and fat, and he looked after a sack of gold for the Prince of Here-we-are Land. One night he fell asleep instead of doing his duty and the green goblins came and stole the sack of gold.

What a to-do there was! The Prince stamped up and down, and shouted and raged, and Tuppy shook like a leaf in a storm.

'Go and get back my gold or I'll turn you into a caterpillar and throw you to the birds!' cried the Prince. So off went Tuppy like the wind.

The goblins lived at the top of Twinkle Hill. Tuppy climbed up the hill, and crept into a cave near the top. He spied a big round barrel lying on its side there. 'This will make me a fine hiding place!' thought Tuppy, and he crept inside.

He was tired with his climb and he fell asleep. When he woke up it was night and he heard voices. He peeped through a hole in the barrel and saw the green goblins sitting in a ring, talking. In their midst was the sack of gold they had stolen from the Prince. Oh, how could Tuppy get it?

The goblins were quarrelling loudly. Suddenly one of them ran to the barrel in which Tuppy was hidden and dragged it forward with Tuppy still inside. The goblin wanted to stand on it to make himself heard. He stood the barrel upright and jumped up. Tuppy was inside, very much frightened. He heard the goblin dancing about on top, shouting loudly, and he didn't like it. He thought they knew he was in the barrel, and were going to punish him in some dreadful way.

'I shan't stand it!' thought poor Tuppy, shaking and shivering with fear. 'I shall walk away, barrel and all!'

So he began to walk off, and the barrel, of course, went with him. The goblin on top of it fell off with a bang and cried out in surprise and fear. Tuppy went on, the bottom of the barrel bumping against the ground as he walked. It was heavy and very uncomfortable. The green goblins stared in astonishment and alarm when they saw a barrel walking along. Tuppy couldn't see where he was going and he bumped into first one goblin and then another, knocking them all over.

'Ooh! Ow!' they cried, and took to their heels and fled down the hill! Tuppy bumped along, as frightened as the goblins themselves. The barrel over him looked most strange and peculiar as it went along, looking for all the world as if it were walking on its own!

When Tuppy heard no more noise he guessed that the goblins had gone, and he wriggled out of the barrel. In great delight he saw the sack of gold nearby. He stuffed it into the barrel, turned it on its side again, got in it himself, and rolled down the hill! Over and over he went, and the running goblins cried out in terror as he bumped through bushes and hedges, rolling over their toes and sending them flying. 'What is it, what is it?' they cried.

Tuppy wasn't turned into a caterpillar. The Prince was so pleased with him that he made him Chief Taster of Puddings in the Royal Kitchen, and Tuppy is now so fat that he couldn't get into a barrel if he wanted to! He *does* love to tell about his adventure with the goblins. Can you pretend you are Tuppy and tell it too?

The Five Lost Beans

Once there was a small boy called Thomas, and he was very pleased because he had five, hard, polished beans which his teacher had given him from one of the bean-bags at school. It had burst open, and the children liked the shiny purple beans very much. So each child had been given a few.

Thomas put his beans into his pocket, and let them rattle together there. They were nice to feel and nice to hear. He took them with him wherever he went. One day he went to play in the garden, and he and Micky the dog played at policemen and burglars, which was most exciting. First Micky was the policeman and Thomas the burglar. Thomas had to hide somewhere, and Micky had to find him. Then it was the other way about. Micky was really very good at playing games.

Once when he was the burglar Thomas went

to hide right at the bottom of the garden by the rubbish-heap. And while he was crouching there all the beans fell out of his pocket. Thomas was so excited at watching for Micky that he didn't notice them – and when, later on, he found that all his shining beans were gone, he was very disappointed. He hunted for them, but he couldn't find them anywhere.

'Never mind!' said his mother. 'You'll find them one day, I expect!'

But Thomas didn't find them, and soon he forgot all about them. The winter went by, and the springtime. Summer came – and one day his mother was in a great fix. Thomas's uncle and aunt were coming to dinner, and the green-grocer hadn't sent the peas! It was Wednesday, and the shops would soon be closed. There would be no time to fetch the peas!

'Go and see if there is a marrow growing on the rubbish-heap!' called Thomas's mother to him. 'There may be one big enough to cut.' Off went Thomas down to the rubbish-heap, where the marrow plants always grew – but there was no marrow ready.

And then – dear me – he caught sight of something else. Growing up the fence there were some runner beans, full of red flower at the top – and crowded with fine green beans at the bottom! Thomas stared at them in astonishment. Nobody ever planted beans there. However had they come? He didn't wait long to wonder. He rushed indoors, fetched a basket and ran down to the bottom of the garden again. Soon he had picked a fine basketful of tender green beans, and took them to his mother. How pleased she was!

'Where did you buy them, Thomas?' she asked. 'They will be lovely for dinner.'

'I didn't buy them,' said Thomas. 'They are growing at the bottom of the garden, Mother – five fine runner beans. Who could have planted them?'

'I know!' said his mother, laughing. So do I. Do you?

The Wishing Balloon

Once upon a time Chitter the gnome found a yellow Wishing-Balloon with its string caught in a bush. He was delighted, for he guessed it had blown away from some witch. Oh, wouldn't he have some fun wishing wishes with it!

He took it and went on his way home. Soon he met his friend Twink, and he thought he would show off a bit, for Twink had no idea that the yellow balloon was a magic one.

'Hallo, Twink,' he said. 'You look cold. What's the matter?'

'I wish the sun would come out,' said Twink, shivering. 'I *do* feel cold.'

'I'll bring it out for you!' said Chitter, grandly. 'I wish the sun would come out!' At once his wish was granted, and the sun shone out warmly. Twink gaped at Chitter in surprise.

'Ooh, are your wishes coming true this

morning?' he asked. 'Do wish some more, Chitter!'

'I wish for a bag of chocolates for myself and a bag of sweets for you,' said Chitter at once. In his hand appeared a fat bag of big chocolates, and in Twink's hand came a small bag of sweets. Twink was disappointed. He wanted chocolates too.

'You *are* mean, Chitter,' he said. 'I'd like chocolates, too.'

'You'll just have what I wish for you,' said Chitter, crossly. 'Now I'll wish for something else. I wish for a fine red motor car for myself and a blue bicycle for you!'

At once a little red motor car, shining and new, appeared beside him, and by Twink came a pretty blue bicycle. Chitter climbed into his car and tooted the horn proudly. But Twink threw his bicycle roughly down on the ground.

'You are mean and selfish!' he cried to Chitter. 'You wish all the best things for yourself, and not nearly such nice things for me. Wish me a motor car, too.'

'No!' said Chitter. 'You can have the bicycle.'

'I *won't* have it!' said Twink, and he stamped on a wheel and broke it.

'Oh, you horrid, ungrateful gnome!' cried

Chitter, in a temper. 'I just wish you'd fall into a bed of nettles!'

Poor Twink! The next moment he found himself in a clump of nettles and he howled as the leaves stung him. He jumped out, ran up to Chitter and smacked his cheek. Chitter jumped out of his car in a rage and hit Twink on the nose. Then they fought like two little tigers. It was dreadful to see them. In the middle of the fight a wind blew up and off went the yellow Wishing-Balloon, floating in the air. It blew against a prickly holly bush – Pop! It burst and that was the end of it. Chitter heard the pop and looked round. Oh, his lovely Wishing-Balloon!

He began to cry, and then he told Twink what had happened. The two silly gnomes sat and wept. The car, the bicycle, and the sweets had all vanished when the balloon burst. Now they had nothing at all.

'If only we hadn't quarrelled!' sobbed Chitter. 'Perhaps we'll find another Wishing-Balloon some day. Then we'll be more sensible.'

I'm afraid they'll *never* find one!

The Little Stickleback

There once lived a tiny stickleback in a little round pond. He was very happy, for the water was warm, and there was plenty of company for him. The water-beetles always had something to say, the tadpoles wriggled by, chattering, and the newts were always willing to stay and talk.

One day a sparrow came to the pond to drink. She was very happy, and as she sipped the water she chirruped loudly. 'Why are you so glad?' asked the stickleback, swimming up.

'I am happy because I have built myself a lovely nest in a gutter,' said the sparrow. 'And I have laid five eggs there, and soon they will hatch. Then I shall have little ones to look after, and that will be most exciting.' The sparrow flew away. The fish swam off, thinking. He met a newt and the newt spoke to him. 'What are you thinking about, Stickleback?'

'I am thinking of making a nest and getting

a wife to lay eggs there for me,' said the stickleback.

How the newt laughed! He called the tadpoles, the water-spider and the beetles, and he told them what the fish had said. Then they all laughed loudly.

'Whoever heard of a fish making a nest?' said the newt. 'You're a funny fish, Stickleback!'

All the same, the stickleback meant to do as he said. He swam about and found tiny bits of stick, which he took in his mouth. He put them all together in a cosy corner. He found some bits of grass, too, and put those with the sticks, glueing them together. Soon he had made a queer little nest, like a muff! It had two entrances, just as a muff has!

Then he looked about for a nice motherstickleback. He soon found one and asked her to lay some eggs in his nest. She didn't want to at first, but he chased her into the nest and wouldn't let her go out until she had laid a little batch of eggs. But the stickleback didn't think there were enough, so he waited till he saw another mother-fish, and then he chased her, too, till she went into the muff-like nest and laid a few more eggs.

The stickleback thought he had enough. He was very proud of his nest and eggs. He called the newt and the tadpoles to come and see it. They laughed – but if they came too near the stickleback went red with anger and chased them away, all his little spines sticking up straight!

He loved those eggs. He used to float himself into the nest and stay over them. Sometimes he nosed them gently, turning them over. At other times he waved little currents of water over them by working hard with his fins just nearby.

When the eggs hatched into tiny fish the stickleback was so excited! The nest seemed rather a tight squeeze then, so what do you think he did? He took away the top of it! Then it looked much more a like a bird's nest, for it had no top. If another stickleback came near to look at the fish the little father swam straight at him, red with rage.

The baby fish learnt to swim. They swam away from the nest – but if a big water-beetle came along, back they went in a hurry, their little father keeping guard. He *was* proud of his children.

'Well, you may all laugh at me if you like!' he

said to the tadpoles and the newts. 'But I did what I wanted to, and my baby fish are well and happy!'

I wish you could see them! They are all in my pond, as happy as can be, and the father stickleback is the proudest fish in the garden!

Who? Who? Who?

One night there was a great to-do at the court of the pixie Princess, Sylfai. Her crown had been stolen! She looked on her bed, she looked in her wardrobe, she even looked in her shoe cupboard, but there was no shining crown to be seen. Someone, someone had stolen it!

But who? Sylfai didn't know, and her servants ran here and there, hunting and searching, crying, 'Who is the thief? Who has taken the crown?'

Then it was decided that a messenger should be sent out all over the land crying out that the thief must be found. He must be sent that very night. But who should the messenger be?

'We must have someone with a big voice,' said Sylfai, 'and it must be someone who can see in the dark, and can fly quickly.'

'I know!' cried an elf. 'Let's send the brown owl! He has a very big voice, he always flies at night, and he can see everything.'

So the big brown owl was sent for and he came silently flying on his soft wings.

'Go out over the woods and fields and find out who has stolen my crown,' said Sylfai. So he flew off into the darkness, and nobody heard his wings as he went. But they heard his voice, for it was very loud.

'Who?' he cried. 'Who? Who? Who?'

The gnomes in the hills, the elves in the fields, and the brownies in the wood all ran out trembling with fear to hear this strange question shouted through the night.

'What do you mean?' they cried. 'Why do you shout "Who?" like that?'

'*Who* has stolen Sylfai's crown?' shouted the owl. 'Who? Who? WHO?'

Suddenly he came to an old tree. Once upon a time the owl had nested there, for the hole in it was a deep one, well suited to an owl's dark nest. The owl went to peep in it, wondering whether his old nest was still there.

He looked down with his big staring eyes, and saw a small pixie there, called Tvit. 'Who?' cried the owl, remembering his errand. 'Who? Who? Who? WHO?'

'Oh!' shrieked Tvit the pixie, frightened out of his wits. 'Oh! What do you mean?'

'*Who* has stolen Sylfai's crown?' shouted the owl. 'Who? Who? Who?'

Tvit tried to scramble away from the queer, big-eyed creature looking down at him, and as he moved the owl caught sight of something shining. It was the lost crown! Tvit had stolen it!

The owl was filled with delight. He picked up the frightened pixie in one claw, and the crown in the other. Then he flew straight back to Sylfai, calling, 'Who? Tvit! Who? Who? Tvit, Tvit!'

Sylfai was delighted, and gave the owl a gold ring to wear on his ankle as a reward. He was so pleased with his cleverness in finding the crown that he still goes round each night calling the news to everyone. Have you heard him? 'Who?' he cries. 'Who? Who? Tvit, Tvit! Who? Who? Tvit!'

Listen and you're sure to hear him!

Good Old Jock!

Jock was the school dog. He was a little black Scottie dog, with short legs, a waggy tail, and sharp, cocked ears. His eyes were soft and brown, and all the children loved him and petted him.

And how he loved the children! His tongue worked hard, licking their hands and legs. He stood at the school gate each morning waiting for the children to come running up when Miss Brown rang the school bell. He barked to each child, and they all gave him a pat. Some of them brought him biscuits, so he was a lucky dog.

He really belonged to Miss Brown, the teacher, but she shared him with the children. He lay quietly in the classroom while lessons were going on. He had to be turned out in the singing lesson, though, because he wanted to sing, too! And his voice was not the kind that Miss Brown liked!

Now one Saturday morning a horrid thing happened to poor Miss Brown. She was coming down the stairs when she slipped and fell. And when she tried to get up she couldn't! She had hurt one of her legs very badly.

'Oh, dear!' said Miss Brown. 'Whatever am I to do? I must get help somehow. I can't lie here all day.' But there was no way to get help, because no one else was in the schoolhouse. No children came on Saturday. Miss Brown groaned in dismay. What *could* she do? Then up came Jock and yelped in surprise to see his mistress lying there, he licked her and pulled at her skirt.

'It's no good, Jock, I can't move,' said Miss Brown. 'Can you go and get help? Run out of the school gate and bring someone back with you.' Jock understood quite well. He rushed out of the door into the playground. But the school gate was shut! Jock jumped up – but his short little legs were no good at all for jumping! Now what was he to do? If only he could get his friends, the children! Jock could never understand why there were two days of the week when the children kept away. He was always miserable on Saturdays and Sundays. Jock sat down and thought hard. How could he get the children?

Then into his clever doggy mind came the picture of the school bell! What did Miss Brown do when she wanted the children? Why, she rang the big bell, shaking it by its wooden handle! Jock sprang up, his tail wagging. If only he could get the bell from the table!

He managed to get on the table. He pushed the bell with his nose and it fell to the floor with a clang. Jock picked it up by the wooden handle and ran out into the playground. He ran round with it in his mouth, jumping up and down, ringing the bell with all his might.

The children in the village heard the bell and stared in surprise. 'Miss Brown wants us!' they said, and they tore off to the school. You can guess how surprised they were when they saw Jock jumping about the yard, ringing the bell!

It wasn't very long before Miss Brown was found. One of the children fetched her mother and the doctor, and soon Miss Brown was comfortably in bed.

And what a fuss everyone made of good old Jock! But, really, I do think he was clever to ring that bell, don't you?

The Very Old Kettle

Once there was a fine, shiny kettle that lived on the kitchen fire and sang a song every time it boiled. It had boiled water for thousands of teapots and hundreds of hot-water bottles. And then one day when Mother looked into it she saw that there was a hole in the bottom. 'So that's why you make a sizzly noise on the stove!' she said. 'You are leaking. What a pity! You are no good any more. You have done well, but now you must be thrown away.'

The kettle was sad. It loved the bright kitchen. It knew everything in it so well. It didn't want to be put into the dustbin for the dustman to collect. It didn't feel at all old or tired. But as Mother was going to put it into the dustbin Gillian and Imogen came along. 'Oh, Mummy! Can we have that old kettle to play at houses?' asked Gillian. 'We have a pretend house under the hedge at the bottom of the

garden. It will be lovely to have a kettle for boiling water when we pretend to have our tea.'

So Mother gave them the kettle to play with and the kettle was happy. What a fine time it had with Gillian and Imogen! They filled it with water from the tap in the garden and set it on a pretend fire to boil. They filled their doll's teapot with the water. The kettle tried to sing, and it felt glad to be with the two happy children. Bobs the dog came along, too, and sniffed at the kettle. He even drank out of it when he found the water inside was cold. That pleased the kettle very much.

But after a time Gillian and Imogen got tired of playing houses. They left the kettle under the hedge and forgot all about it. They played Red Indians instead. The kettle was lonely and forgotten.

'This is worse than being in the dustbin!' thought the kettle. 'No one comes near me. I am getting rusty and my hole is much bigger. There are spiders' webs inside me. I shall never never be any use again. And yet I don't feel old or useless!'

One day a cock robin came to the kettle. He put his head on one side and looked inside. He called to his mate: 'Here is a fine place for a nest! Look! This kettle will shelter us and our eggs well. It is a good kettle.'

How pleased the old kettle was! It tried to sing as it used to do, to tell the robin how happy it would be if they would build inside it. It wasn't long before the robins began to tuck grass-roots, dead leaves, bits of moss, and many other things inside the kettle! They made a beautiful nest and lined it with hairs that Bobs had shaken off his coat. Then they laid their four pretty eggs there.

And now the kettle is happy all day long. The hen robin sits in the nest and talks to it. The cock robin brings his wife tit-bits and sings. Soon the eggs will hatch, and how pleased the old kettle will be to feel the tiny creatures inside it, safe and sheltered!

How do I know all this? Well, you see, the old kettle and the robins' nest are in my garden! I see them every day as I walk down the path!

Brer Rabbit Plays
Blind Man's Buff

Now one Christmas-time Brer Wolf gave a party and he asked Brer Rabbit and Brer Turkey Buzzard, Brer Terrapin and Brer Fox, Brer Wildcat, Brer Bear, and Brer Mink, and a whole lot of others. Everybody came, and played party games.

Brer Rabbit was skipping round as merry as you please, looking as plump as a Christmas turkey. He won the game of musical chairs, and he always saw the thimble first. Brer Fox, who thought himself pretty smart, was angry with Brer Rabbit. He looked at him, so plump and merry, and thought he could make a fine meal of that cheeky Brer Rabbit. Brer Rabbit, he hopped around in time to the music, wearing a fine yellow crown that he had got out of a cracker, thinking he was king of the party.

'Now we'll have a game of blind man's buff,' suddenly said Brer Fox, winking at Brer Wolf.

Brer Wolf saw that Brer Fox had a plan of his own and he winked back. 'Right!' he said. 'Will you be blind man first, Brer Fox?'

'Yes, Brer Wolf,' said Brer Fox. Brer Wolf took out a large white handkerchief and went to tie up Brer Fox's eyes – but Brer Rabbit stepped up and took it. 'I'll tie up his eyes!' he cried. 'I'm good at tying, Brer Wolf!'

Brer Fox was wild. He wanted Brer Wolf to tie his eyes up because he knew Brer Wolf would leave him a crack to peep out of – but Brer Rabbit, he tied the handkerchief so tightly that Brer Fox couldn't see a thing! Then the game began. Of course, Brer Fox meant to catch Brer Rabbit, and he listened for the patter of his paws and always went after him. And pretty soon Brer Rabbit guessed what Brer Fox was up to and he ran over to Brer Wildcat.

'Change caps with me, Brer Wildcat,' he said. 'I've been king long enough. It's your turn now. I'll have your bonnet.'

No sooner had they changed than Brer Fox managed to catch Brer Rabbit, but when he felt the bonnet on his head instead of the crown, he let him go! And not long after that he caught old Brer Wildcat. He was about the size of Brer

Rabbit – and he wore the crown, too – so Brer Fox was certain he was Brer Rabbit all right!

He picked him up and ran into the passage outside with him. He bit at a whisker – he nibbled at an ear, which seemed very short for Brer Rabbit! He snapped at the tail – and then, dear me, Brer Fox got the shock of his life! For Brer Wildcat lashed out with his twenty claws and Brer Fox let him go at once!

'Stop it, Brer Rabbit, stop it!' cried Brer Fox. 'I was only having a joke.' Brer Wildcat shot into the garden, every hair on end – and Brer Rabbit slipped out into the hall in his place. So, when Brer Fox tore the handkerchief off his eyes, he didn't see Brer Wildcat at all, but Brer Rabbit, looking as calm as could be.

'My, Brer Rabbit, what made you fierce like that?' said Brer Fox, looking at all his scratches. 'I was only having a bit of fun.'

'My, Brer Fox, and so was I!' said Brer Rabbit, and he skipped off as merry as a blackbird. After that Brer Fox kept out of his way, though he couldn't help wondering how it was that Brer Rabbit was wearing a bonnet now, instead of a crown! Poor old Brer Fox – he can't trick Brer Rabbit, can he?

The Birthday Kitten

It was Peter's birthday – and will you believe it, all he had was one card, and one present! Peter lived with his Aunt Sally, and she wasn't very fond of small boys, and didn't really know what they liked. So Peter's one present was a new pair of socks – and socks aren't at all exciting, are they, for a birthday?

'I did so want that big book of adventure stories in the bookshop,' thought poor Peter, as he pulled on his new socks.

Peter went to school as usual, and because it was his birthday the children clapped their hands eight times for him – he was eight, you see – and he liked that very much. On the way home he saw something under a hedge, and he looked to see what it was. At first he thought it was a big grey mouse.

But it wasn't. It was a tiny tabby kitten! Peter couldn't think how it had come there, for there was no house near. It was mewing, for the weather was cold, and the kitten was hungry. Peter was kind and he bent over the tiny creature.

'You poor little thing!' he said. 'I can't leave you here. I shall take you home under my coat.' So he popped the tiny creature inside his coat – it did feel nice there – and ran home with it. Aunt Sally was not pleased to see it. She said Peter could only keep it if it lived outside in the shed.

So Peter made it a warm bed there, and fed it every day himself. The kitten grew and grew. It became fat and sleek. It purred loudly. It loved Peter very much and always ran to welcome him home from school.

One morning the schoolteacher said that, for a treat, the children should have a pet show. They could each bring their pets, and she would look at them all, and see which was the best cared-for. So, of course, Peter brought his cat along, too. It was still a kitten, but big and fat, and its striped fur was as soft as silk.

It was fun that day at school. Ellen brought her canary in its cage. John brought his dog and so did George. Mary took her white rabbit and

Doris had a tortoise, but it was asleep in its box for the winter, and they didn't wake it. Harry had a cat and so had Nellie. And, of course, Peter had his kitten, which he said was his birthday kitten because he had found it on his birthday.

The teacher looked hard at every animal and bird. She said they all looked well-cared-for and happy. But when she came to Peter's tabby kitten, purring loudly and looking so fat and silky and sleek, she really couldn't help picking it up to stroke it.

'Peter, your kitten wins the prize!' she said. 'She is simply beautiful – quite perfect! I can see you love her and look after her well. Go and fetch the prize from the table.'

And what do you think the prize was? Guess! Yes – it was the big book of adventure stories! Peter was so delighted – he had got what he wanted after all!

'You are a real birthday kitten!' he said to his cat. 'You have brought me the birthday present I so badly wanted!'

The Three Hunters

Leslie, Allan, and Mollie had a holiday because it was Saturday. So they were out in the lane with their little dog Joker.

'Let's pretend to be hunters!' said Leslie. 'I've cut myself this stick from the hedge. It will do for a spear!'

'And I've made myself a wooden sword!' said Allan.

'And I've got my bow and some sticks for arrows,' said Mollie. 'What shall we hunt?'

'Let's hunt the cows in the field, and pretend they are lions,' said Leslie.

'But the farmer wouldn't like us to chase his cows,' said Allan. 'We must only *pretend* to hunt them.'

'All right, we'll just pretend,' said Leslie. 'We'll creep through this hole in the hedge and spring out on the lions!'

'I believe there are some tigers there as well!'

said Mollie, fitting an arrow to her bow.

'And I can see a spotted leopard!' whispered Allan, drawing his sword. 'Come on – we'll hunt the wild animals and not be a bit afraid of them!'

They all squeezed through the hedge, Joker the dog, too. The cows pulled at the grass and didn't even bother to look at the children creeping round them – but, dear me, when Joker the dog began to prance round the cows didn't like it at all. They didn't trust dogs!

'Moooooo!' said one cow, in such a loud voice that the children jumped.

'That was a lion roaring!' whispered Allan. 'Come on – we are three of the bravest hunters in the world!'

They went nearer – and so did Joker. But that was too much for the quiet cows. They all lifted their heads and stared hard at the dog and the children.

'Moooo, moooo!' bellowed a cow and took a step towards Joker.

'MOOOOOOOOO!' roared another cow suddenly and put her head down to run at the dog. It looked exactly as if she was going to run at the children, for Joker was nearby them.

Leslie, Allan, and Mollie stopped and looked

at the cows. 'I don't believe they like being lions and tigers and leopards,' said Mollie. 'They look angry.'

'Moooo-oo-oooo!' said a cow in front, and Mollie jumped in fright. She dropped her bow and arrows and ran for the hedge. Allan dropped his sword and ran, too, and Leslie followed, still keeping his stick in case the cows attacked them! But as soon as the cows saw Joker the dog running off, too, they put their heads down peacefully and went on eating.

The children squeezed through the hedge and almost fell into the lane! And there, standing watching, was Mr Straws, the farmer! How he laughed when he saw them!

'Are you hunting the cows or are the cows hunting *you*?' he said. 'Dear me, I didn't think my harmless old cows would send you scrambling off like this!'

Leslie and Allan and Mollie went red. They didn't feel very brave after all.

'You go and hunt for late blackberries,' said Mr Straws, kindly. 'There are plenty in my field on the hill. You'll be quite safe hunting for blackberries – they won't bellow at you and send you running home.'

'Thank you very much!' said the children, and off they ran on another hunt!

Pitter-Patter's Dance

There was once a mischievous little pixie who loved to peep and pry. His name was Pitter-Patter, and this was because he had such nimble, pitter-pattering feet. If you have heard the raindrops pitter-pattering on the window-pane in a shower, then you will know what the pixie's feet sounded like as he ran here and there.

One day, going through the wood, Pitter-Patter came across two boys lying asleep under the trees, for the sun was hot and the boys had walked a long way. The pixie took a grass and tickled their noses. They sneezed loudly and woke up. Pitter-Patter tried to escape behind a bush – but the bigger boy reached his hand out quickly and caught him!

'Oho, so it's a pixie!' said the boy, in surprise. 'I didn't think there were such things! Look, Bill – a real live pixie! I'm going to tie him up with a bit of string so that he can't get away.'

In a flash he had tied Pitter-Patter's feet and
hands together so that the pixie couldn't move.
The two boys sat and looked at the little fellow.
He glared back at them, and begged to be set
free. But the boys wouldn't untie him.

'No,' said Bill. 'You're a great find. We'll take
you to school tomorrow, and give our class the
biggest surprise in their lives!'

'I shall bite and scratch if you pick me up!'
said Pitter-Patter angrily.

'Well, I saw a cardboard box thrown down by
some untidy person in the woods as we came
along,' said Bill. 'I'll go back and find it, Ted,
and you keep your eye on this pixie till I come
back. Then we'll put him in the box and take
him home in that.'

Bill went off. Pitter-Patter looked at the boy
who was left. Then the pixie began to whistle –
and he could whistle beautifully, just like a
blackbird and a nightingale rolled into one!

'I say!' said Ted. 'I wish I could whistle like
that! My word, you *are* clever!'

'You should see me dance though!' said the
pixie. 'When I whistle, and dance to my whistling, my feet make a pitter-pattering noise like
the rain, and you can hardly see them move, I

dance so nimbly. Ah, it's a sight to see me dance! The little folk pay a great deal of money to see me dance.'

'I'd like to see you, too,' said Ted.

'Well, untie my feet, then, and I'll dance for you till Bill comes back,' said Pitter-Patter. 'You can leave my hands tied.'

So Ted untied the pixie's feet, and Pitter-Patter began to dance. How he danced! He kicked up his feet, he pattered them on the ground like sticks on a little drum, he twisted and he turned, and all the time he whistled till Ted's eyes nearly dropped out of his head!

Pitter-Patter danced to a bush and back again. He danced to the oak-tree nearby – and back again – and then he danced all round the bush – and all round the tree – and danced off down the path – and danced through the wood – and danced right away and away!

So when Bill came back with the box, there was Ted looking very foolish indeed – and no pixie! Ah, you see, it needs sharp wits to outdo the fairy folk. *You* might have let that pixie go, too!

Well, Really, Amelia!

Have you a good memory? I hope you have, because it is a very useful thing. Amelia had no memory at all – and usually she didn't try to remember anything, either!

Now one day her mother had to go to see the doctor, so she left Amelia in charge of the house.

'Now listen, Amelia,' she said. 'You must remember to do *three* things for me. Sweep out the yard. Water the lettuces. And, if it rains, bring in the washing.'

'I don't think I shall remember them, Mother,' said Amelia, looking worried.

'Well, you must,' said her mother. She looked at Amelia and saw that she had three big buttons down the front of her dress. She went to her work-basket and snipped off three pieces of white tape. She tied one piece to the top button. 'This will remind you to sweep out the yard,' she said. She tied a second piece of tape to the

second button. 'And this will remind you to
water the lettuces. And this third piece will
remind you to bring in the washing if it rains!'

Amelia was pleased. She said goodbye to her
mother, and then settled down to read her book.
After a while her eye caught sight of the second
piece of tape, tied in a bow on the second
button. She frowned. 'Now what was that for?'
she said. 'Let me see – something about watering, wasn't it? Oh, yes – water the hens, Mother
said!'

Amelia thought she had better get on with the
jobs while she remembered them. So up she
jumped, filled the water-can and went to the
yard. Soon she was watering all the hens, much
to their astonishment.

'I expect it is to make you grow,' said Amelia,
pleased. She looked down at the first button
with its bow of white tape. 'Now what was that
one for?' she wondered. 'Something to do with
sweeping, wasn't it – oh, yes – sweep out the
washing yard! Good!'

She got the big broom and began to sweep out
the yard where all the clean washing was
blowing in the wind. What a dust she made! All
the dirt flew up and down and soon the clean

washing was smutty and black!

She looked at the last piece of tape and frowned. Whatever was it for? Oh – rain! Yes! She had to bring the lettuces in if it rained. She looked up at the sky, and a few drops of rain began to fall, for the clouds were very low. 'I must bring in the lettuces!' said Amelia. So off she ran to the lettuce-bed and cut the lettuces there.

'Now I can untie all these tape-bows,' said Amelia.

But when her mother came home, how cross she was! There was the washing out in the pouring rain, looking wet and surprisingly dirty! There were the hens in a dirty yard, all of them looking surprisingly wet! And there, on the kitchen table, were two dozen fresh lettuces!

'Well, really, Amelia!' began her mother – but Amelia was nowhere to be seen! She had suddenly remembered three things when she saw her mother's cross face. One was that her mother could get very cross indeed. The second was that it would be better to find a good place to hide. And the third was that if she didn't go quickly it would be too late!

The Brownie and the Witch

Once upon a time Snip the brownie found a yellow toadstool with a blue stalk. He was very pleased, because yellow toadstools with blue stalks have a great deal of magic in them, and Snip thought he could use the magic for making all kinds of spells.

But Deep-one the witch heard of his find, and sent to say she would like to buy it. Snip sent back a note to say that he wasn't going to sell it – and that made Deep-one as angry as could be. So she lay in wait for Snip the brownie, and one day as he was on his way home from marketing in the next town, she jumped out at him from behind a tree.

'Good afternoon, Snip,' she said. 'I want your toadstool.'

'Well, you can't have it,' said Snip, 'because I haven't got it on me! You don't expect me to wear it for a hat or use it for a shoe button, do you? It's at home.'

'Don't be cheeky to *me*,' said Deep-one, in a rage. 'I know you've got it at home. I'm coming home with you – and I'm going in at your door – and I'm going to take that toadstool from its hiding place!'

'Oh, you are, are you?' said Snip, thinking as quickly as a rabbit can run.

Deep-one took hold of the brownie's arm very tightly so that he couldn't run away. Then Snip pretended to be very frightened. He went on through the wood, thinking, thinking, thinking what he could do to save his wonderful yellow toadstool. He came to the end of the wood. He went up the lane and round by the poppy field. He went up the hill – and halfway up he came to a dark little cave running into the hill-side.

A curtain of bracken grew around the opening, and a carpet of moss led to the cave. 'So this is where you live,' said Deep-one. 'Well, I shouldn't choose a dark little cave like this, but I've no doubt *you* like it! Now, whereabouts do you keep that toadstool? You'd better tell me, or you'll be turned into a blackberry on a bush.'

'Please, Deep-one,' said the brownie, 'go right in. You'll find a door at the back. Open it, and take the clock off the mantelpiece. You may find the toadstool behind the clock – if you are lucky!'

The witch went into the cave – but Snip didn't go with her! No – not he! That wasn't where *he* lived! It was the cave of the Ho-Ho Goblin! And the Ho-Ho Goblin didn't like visitors at all – especially those that came in without knocking and took the clock off the mantelpiece!

Snip hid behind a tree to see what would happen – and it wasn't long before he saw quite a lot of things! The witch Deep-one had walked into the cave, opened the door at the back, and had gone straight to the little mantelpiece in the room beyond.

She hadn't seen the Ho-Ho Goblin there – but he had seen Deep-one – and with a roar of rage he jumped at her, shouting, 'Thieves! Robbers! Burglars!'

The bad-tempered little goblin caught up his broom and swept the witch off her feet! He swept her out of the door! He swept her out of the cave! Down the hill she went rolling over and over, in the most terrible fright, for she really didn't know what was happening at all.

As for Snip the brownie he laughed till he

cried, and called out to the witch, 'Didn't you find the toadstool behind the clock after all? Well, well, well!'

And after that Deep-one left Snip alone – he was much too smart for her!

Grunt! Grunt!

Jack and Doris wanted to go blackberrying.
They knew that the best hedges for blackberries
were in the farmer's fields, but they were not
allowed to go there unless they asked politely at
the farm. So they took a basket each and went
off to the farmhouse.

'Please,' said Jack to the farmer's wife, 'may
we go into the fields and pick blackberries?'

'Certainly,' said the farmer's smiling wife.
'But see that you shut the gates as you go, and
don't frighten any of the animals, or chase the
ducks.'

'We'll remember,' promised Jack and Doris.
They went off through the farmyard to the
fields. The farm was a big one. There were cows
in one field, horses in another, and sheep in
another. Pigs grunted not far off, and geese
cackled by a pond. Along the stream-side sat a
row of white ducks, basking in the sunshine,

and hens ran everywhere, clucking and squawking. Jack and Doris loved the farm and all the fields around.

They went past the pigs' field and into the next one. Here was a high hedge, black with ripe juicy berries. What fun! Jack and Doris began to eat them as fast as they could. There would be plenty left to fill their baskets, too.

'Oh, look, Jack! Here are the biggest blackberries I've ever seen!' said Doris. 'Let's stop eating, and fill our baskets with them. Mother will be so pleased to see such lovely ones. She will be able to make a fine pudding with them!'

So they filled their baskets full. How nice they looked, brimming over with the ripe berries! The children set them down on the grass, for they were heavy. They went a little way up the hedge to look for more to eat.

And then they heard a strange sound! Grunt! Snort! Grr-unt! They looked round. Five big pigs had come into the field and had run up to the baskets of blackberries! A pig upset Jack's basket, and began to gobble up the berries!

'Oh! Oh!' cried Jack, in a rage. 'Go away, you naughty pigs! Go away!'

But the pigs took no notice at all. They upset

the other basket too, and before the children could save their lovely blackberries, not one was left! Then the pigs came running to the children for more, and sniffed and snuffed round their legs in a most alarming manner. They did not mean to hurt them, for they were quite harmless, friendly animals, but they did like those blackberries, and wanted Jack and Doris to get them some more!

Jack began to shout loudly. 'Go away! Go away!' Doris began to cry big tears all down her cheeks.

The farmer's wife heard their shouts and cries and came running to see what was the matter. The children told her.

'Dear, dear!' said the farmer's wife, very sorry. 'What a pity! Look – someone has left the field-gate open, so that the pigs wandered in from the next field. I wonder who was silly enough to do that.'

Then Doris and Jack went very red. 'Oh, dear, I'm afraid we forgot to shut the gate,' said Jack, in a small voice. 'It's all our own fault!'

'Well, you will know better next time,' said the farmer's wife. 'Come again tomorrow – and remember to shut the gate!'

Brer Rabbit Plays Ball

Once upon a time Brer Rabbit looked over the wall that ran round Brer Fox's garden, and he saw a plum tree there, full of the finest yellow plums he had ever seen.

'My!' thought Brer Rabbit to himself. 'Maybe Brer Fox would offer me a few of those plums if I go and ask him how he is! I could do with some plums, for it's a thirsty morning!'

So he opened the gate and went to Brer Fox's house, swinging his stick and whistling a little song. But no sooner was he at the door than Brer Fox put his head out of the window and said:

'I guessed you'd be along this morning, Brer Rabbit – and I guessed right. As sure as I've got fish in my larder, honey in my cupboard, and plums on my tree you come along just as saucy as a jay-bird. Well, I'm not opening my door to you – and if you don't get out of my garden pretty quick I'll jump out of this window and get you!'

'Now, now, Brer Fox,' said Brer Rabbit, in a hurt voice. 'Who cares about your plums? I've come to show you my fine new ball. I thought maybe you'd like a game.'

He took a brand new ball out of his pocket. Brer Fox opened the door and had a look at it. It certainly was a fine ball – red, yellow, blue, and green – and it bounced so hard that it caught Brer Fox under the chin and made him bite his tongue almost in half!

'Come out and have a game of catch,' said Brer Rabbit. 'Brer Bear told me no one could beat you at catching a ball, Brer Fox.'

So Brer Fox went out into the garden with Brer Rabbit. But first he said, 'Now, no asking me if you can have plums off my tree, Brer Rabbit.'

And Brer Rabbit said, 'What! Has your tree got plums on? Well, well, well, fancy me not seeing those! No, Brer Fox, I won't ask you for a single plum. Plums always upset me at this time of year. Catch!'

He threw the ball so suddenly that Brer Fox missed it, and it went over the wall. Brer Fox gave a grunt and jumped over to get it – and just as he bent down to pick it up, Brer Rabbit made a grab at the plum tree and picked two ripe plums! He put them into his pocket and then held his paws ready to catch the ball when Brer Fox threw it.

Brer Fox caught the next three balls and Brer Rabbit praised him up to the skies till Brer Fox felt he was as clever as twelve foxes rolled together. But then Brer Rabbit threw another high ball, and over the wall it went! And over the wall went Brer Fox – and into Brer Rabbit's pocket went two more plums! So it went on, till Brer Rabbit's pockets were so full he couldn't put any more plums into them at all!

'Well, Brer Fox, I guess I'll be going now,' said Brer Rabbit at last. 'Thanks for the game of ball. It was fine!'

And when he got halfway down the road he yelled out, 'And thanks for the plums, too, Brer Fox! Mighty nice plums they are, just ready for eating!'

Then Brer Fox took a look at his plum tree – and he jumped over the wall and made after Brer Rabbit as fast as ever he could. But Brer Rabbit was down a burrow, laughing as hard as can be at his wicked game of ball!

The Little Bird

There was once a little bird who told tales about other people all day long. He was a perfect little nuisance!

When he perched on Dame Winkle's windowsill one morning, he saw her putting on her shoes – and dear me, she had a big hole in her stocking. So he flew all round the town that day, whispering in people's ears, 'Dame Winkle has a hole in her stocking!'

Another day he saw Snip-Snap the brownie climb over into the next-door garden and pick up some apples. The little bird flew off, and all that day he told his tale to everyone he met. 'Snip-Snap took some apples that didn't belong to him!'

Nobody was safe from that little tale-teller! He peeked in at windows, he pried into every corner. Many people tried to smack him when they saw his pointed beak poking round the

corner – but he was always just a bit too smart for them!

And then one day he told a tale about Goggins the witch. He had flown down into her garden one afternoon and seen her sitting in a chair having a snooze. He had hopped nearer – and nearer – and nearer. And then he had noticed a shocking thing – Witch Goggins hadn't washed her neck! Dear, dear, dear! He flew off in delight and soon he was telling the tale all over the town. 'Witch Goggins doesn't wash her neck! Fancy that! Witch Goggins doesn't wash her neck!'

Now it was a rule in that town that everyone should wash properly, and as soon as Mr Blueboy, the policeman, heard what the little bird whispered in his ear, he marched off to Goggins and scolded her sternly. The witch said she was very sorry, and asked who had told Blueboy the news.

'That little bird,' said Blueboy, pointing to where the little bird was sitting on the wall, listening. Witch Goggins went indoors to wash her neck, and she vowed to herself that she would catch that little bird and punish him!

But do you suppose she could get near enough

to that cunning little bird to catch him? No, she certainly could not! He flicked his wings and flew off as soon as he saw her. He wasn't going to be caught by Witch Goggins! She would probably turn him into a fly and then send a spider along to eat him!

At last Witch Goggins prepared a little can of water to throw over him, and in it she put a spell to make that horrid little bird invisible. She thought that if no one could see him, nobody would ever listen to his tales. She hid behind a curtain and waited.

And at last she got him! He flew down to peep in at the window to see what he could spy – and the witch flung the enchanged water over him. At once he disappeared! The spell had worked.

But do you know, although he couldn't be seen he still had a voice! And he still went about perching on people's shoulders and whispering tales in their ears! He didn't dare to stay in Fairyland any longer, in case Goggins the witch really caught him the next time. So he came to our world, and he still goes on telling tales.

Sometimes people know something you would rather they *didn't* know, and when you say to them, 'How did you know?' they say,

'Aha! A little bird told me!' Then you know that nasty little tale-teller has been in *your* house – but you'll never see him because he is still invisible!

The Bunch of Carrots

Ronald was pleased and proud. He had grown some lovely young carrots in his garden, and today he had pulled them all up, washed them carefully, and tied them into a bundle. He was going to market to sell them.

'Aha!' said Ronald, trotting down the lane to catch the bus to market. 'I shall get at least two pounds for my bunch of carrots. Imagine that!'

He came to the bus-stop, which was by a gate that led into a field. The bus was not in sight. There was no one to talk to but an old grey donkey who leaned his head over the gate and stared at Ronald. Ronald turned his back on him and went on thinking about his bunch of carrots.

'If I get two pounds for my new young carrots, I shall buy two old wheels from the ironmonger and put them on to that wooden box I have at home,' said Ronald. 'That will make a fine cart. Then I shall go to Mrs Brown and Mrs Jones and Mrs Hughes and Mrs Mack and tell them I will do their shopping for them and bring it home in my cart for two pounds a week each.'

He waved his bunch of carrots in the air and went on planning his plans. The donkey stared at him and wondered who this little boy was, talking away to himself. But Ronald took no notice of him.

'In no time at all I shall have about five pounds,' he said. 'I shall buy a hen at the market for five pounds and it will lay me an egg every day! I shall sell the eggs and soon I shall have ten pounds. Then I shall buy a little pig and fatten it up. I shall sell it for fifty pounds when it is big enough. Fifty pounds! I *shall* be rich then!'

He stood and thought for a moment. 'What shall I do with fifty pounds? I shall buy a donkey! I can get one for fifty pounds. Not a silly old creature like this one that keeps staring at me here – no – a nice fat young donkey that will take children for rides on the sands. I shall charge fifty p a ride – no, a pound, I think! Oooh!'

Ronald stood up straight, looking very proud. 'I shall buy myself a new suit with long trousers.

I shall buy a fine hat and wear it just a bit on one side of my head. I shall buy the biggest and best marbles in the toy shop. I shall get that fine blue top that everyone wants – the top that spins for twenty minutes without stopping. And do you think I shall let Tom and Dick and Leslie and Jack play with my marbles or my top? No – I shall point my finger at them and say, "Go away! I don't want to play with dirty little boys like you!"'

Ronald stuck his chin into the air and threw out his hand as if he were telling people to go away. But in his hand was his bunch of carrots – and it so happened that he stuck them just under the donkey's nose!

The grey donkey was pleased and surprised. He thought Ronald was giving them to him. He opened his mouth and took the carrots. Crunch! They were most delicious!

'Oh! Oh!' shouted Ronald, swinging round in a fury. 'You wicked donkey! You've eaten my carrots! Oh, my lovely wheels – my little pig – my pretty donkey – my new suit and hat – my marbles and top! You've robbed me of them all!'

'Hee-haw!' said the donkey, galloping away still munching. 'You've only yourself to blame!'

Little Miss Dreamy

Do you know anyone who really seems half asleep and dreams the day away? I expect you do, because people are always saying, 'Wake up!' to the dreamy person! There may even be one in your class!

This is the story of a dreamy little girl called Jenny. Whatever she was doing she always seemed to be thinking of something else! Her mother used to get so cross with her at mealtimes, because Jenny *would* sit and dream, instead of eating her dinner.

'Jenny! Wake up!' she would say. 'You will never grow big and strong if you don't eat your dinner properly!'

'What will happen to me then?' asked Jenny.

'Oh, you'll grow small instead of big!' said her mother. 'Your clothes will get too large for you – you will look a funny little thing and everyone will laugh at you! Now, do eat your dinner!'

That afternoon at school the teacher told the children that they were to change their cloak-rooms. The big children were to use the small children's cloakroom to hang up their hats and coats and keep their shoes – and the small children were to use the big cloakroom. The change was made because there were more small children than big, and so they were to have the bigger room.

'I will show each of you your new peg and the hole for your shoes,' said Miss Brown. 'Please remember them or you'll get into a muddle. Jenny, wake up! Do you see your new place in this cloakroom?'

'Yes, Miss Brown,' said Jenny.

But, will you believe it, when afternoon school was over, Jenny ran off to the *old* cloak-room and went to her old peg and hole! She quite forgot that it belonged to a big child now! She took the hat and coat off the peg and changed her shoes, putting on those in the hole. Then off she went home.

But, dear me! The coat belonged to a much bigger child and so did the school hat! So did the shoes – so before long Jenny felt most uncomfortable! The coat nearly reached the ground!

The hat slipped over her nose and she couldn't see! The shoes slopped all over the place – and the gloves she tried to put on were no use at all!

All the children passing by laughed at her. She really did look so funny! Jenny stood still and looked down at herself! Why were her clothes so large – they seemed to be falling off her!

The little girl gave a cry of fright.

'I've gone small! Mother said it would happen if I didn't eat my dinner! It's come true! I'm growing down instead of up! Oh, oh, what shall I do?'

She ran home crying as if her heart would break. Mother wondered whatever was the matter – and when Jenny told her how she had gone small, and her clothes didn't fit her any more, she began to laugh – and laugh – and laugh!

'You silly little dreamer!' she said. 'You have someone else's clothes on! Whatever will you do next? You are just the same size as usual – but you have taken a bigger child's clothes!'

Jenny got into trouble over that, for Miss Brown was very cross. But she *was* glad she hadn't gone small after all, and you can guess that she made up her mind not to dream any more!

Brer Fox's New Suit

Once upon a time Brer Bear sent out invitations to a picnic party. Brer Fox had an invitation and so had Brer Rabbit, and everyone else. They were all as excited as could be.

Now Brer Fox had a fine new suit, and he longed to wear it. Brer Rabbit had a new suit, too; but he didn't think he could very well wear it at a picnic. He thought maybe people would only wear old clothes at a picnic party. He wondered if Brer Fox would wear his grand new coat and trousers. Brer Rabbit hoped he wouldn't, because Brer Fox's new suit was much grander than his.

Now, when the day came, Brer Rabbit decided to put on his old clothes. It was a fine sunny day, and he thought there would be races and rolling on the grass. So he put on his old blue trousers, his rather dirty coat with a patch in one elbow, and his hat that had been sat on by mistake once or twice. Then he set off down the road, lippitty-clippitty.

But Brer Fox put on his fine new suit. It was very grand indeed. It had green trousers with braid down each leg and a yellow coat with silver buttons. Oh, Brer Fox felt mighty fine in his new suit! He set off down the road, swinging his stick.

And then he saw Brer Rabbit – in his oldest clothes – grinning away as if he saw something mighty funny in Brer Fox and his new suit!

'Are you going to *town*?' asked Brer Rabbit. 'I thought you were going to Brer Bear's picnic to play hide-and-seek and run races and all that.'

Brer Fox felt silly in his new suit when he heard all this talk of races and games. He scowled at Brer Rabbit, turned on his heel and went home again. He took off his nice new suit and put on his old brown trousers and his old coat and cap. Then he set out once more.

And what about Brer Rabbit? Ah, no sooner did that artful rabbit see Brer Fox trot home to change his suit – than *he* trotted home, too, to change *his*! He meant to put on his *new* suit now and make old Brer Fox feel simply dreadful!

He slipped into his nice new things. He

waited until Brer Fox had gone down the road again and then he walked out, as smart as a newly minted coin!

Brer Fox was a bit late – and he found, to his horror, that Brer Buzzard, Brer Terrapin, and all the rest were in their best things, and so was Brer Bear! 'Still,' thought Brer Fox, comforting himself, 'Brer Rabbit will be in *his* oldest things – so I shan't be the only one!'

But when Brer Rabbit turned up he was smarter than anyone there, in his beautiful trousers and coat! Brer Fox stared at him in horror and dismay. Brer Rabbit had played *another* trick on him!

Brer Fox didn't enjoy the party one bit. He felt so dreadful in his old clothes. Brer Bear was cool to him, too, and said loudly to Brer Rabbit, 'It's a pity people can't take the trouble to clean themselves up a bit when they come out, isn't it?'

'It is indeed,' said Brer Rabbit, grinning at Brer Fox. 'I wouldn't ask Brer Fox another time, Brer Bear.'

'You wait till I catch you!' Brer Fox hissed to Brer Rabbit.

'I'll have to wait a mighty long time for that,' said Brer Rabbit. 'Oh, a *mighty* long time, Brer Fox!'

The Two Cats

Once upon a time there were two cats. One was a beauty, with long blue-grey fur, a thick, bushy tail, and great yellow eyes. She was called Princess, and thought a great deal of herself.

The other was a little cat, black, with a little white shirt-front, green eyes, and rather a skimpy tail. Her name was Tibs.

Tibs lived in the kitchen. Princess lived in the drawing-room. Tibs had a raggedy old cushion in a wooden box for a bed. Princess had a round basket lined with blue, and a velvet cushion to sleep on. Tibs ate out of a broken kitchen dish. Princess had a lovely blue bowl with her name all round the edge.

One day the master of the house said that he had lost a great deal of money. He would have to sell his horse. He would have to tell his gardener to go. He would have to buy cheaper clothes to wear and cheaper food to eat.

'You, too, wife,' he said, 'will have to go without things for a little while, until I make some more money for you. How many cats do we keep? Could you not do with one?'

'Well, I only keep two,' said his wife. 'But certainly one would do. I will help you all I can.'

Now, Princess, the beautiful cat, heard all this, and she yawned. 'Ha!' she thought. 'This will be a shock for that common little kitchen cat! She will have to go! Then I shall be the only cat in the house! I will tell her this very day.'

So, when Tibs came padding along to say good morning, Princess told the little black cat the bad news.

'Mistress is only going to keep one cat now,' she said. 'You will have to go. Well, no one will miss you, an ordinary little thing like you, always smelling of rats and mice!'

Tibs was sad. She loved her home. She loved the fat old cook who so often let her come on her knee at night. She loved her raggedy cushion in the wooden box by the kitchen fire. She drooped her skimpy tail and ran away, moping.

The mistress went to the kitchen. She told the cook what the master of the house had said.

'We must only keep one cat now,' she said. 'It

will have to be Princess, of course.'

'But why, Madam?' said the old cook, in surprise. 'What good does that cat do? It eats expensive food, it wants care and fussing – and it never does a bit of work for its living. Yes – I know she's beautiful – but that's no excuse for not working! Look at Tibs, now! She only gets a few scraps a day – but that cat works as hard as I do! She catches mice and rats by the dozen. She never lets one come *near* the larder to eat the things I store there! She saves you pounds and pounds!'

'Dear me!' said the mistress. 'You are quite right. Tibs is too valuable to give away. We will keep her and Princess must go. Tibs works hard for us and deserves her home.'

What a shock for Princess! She was packed into a basket one day and sent away for good! But, as for Tibs, the little kitchen cat, she is there still, happy and busy working hard all night long!

'I'd rather be busy than beautiful!' she says to herself. 'People think much more of you!'

Little Suck-a-Thumb

Once upon a time there was a nice little girl called Hilda. She was clean and neat and pretty, and she had such a kind heart that everyone loved her, even the fairies that lived at the bottom of her garden.

But, although she was quite a big girl, she had such a funny habit – she sucked her thumb! When she was thinking hard, or doing nothing, or going to sleep, her thumb popped into her mouth, and she sucked it hard! She had always done this ever since she was a baby, and her mother couldn't cure her of the funny habit.

'Does your thumb taste nice?' she used to say to Hilda. 'Are you making a good meal of it, my dear? I don't expect you will want any dinner, will you?'

Now it didn't really matter when Hilda was very small, except that it made her nice front teeth grow a bit crooked – but it did look rather dreadful to see her busily sucking her thumb when she grew bigger! Her teacher scolded her, her mother scolded her, her friends laughed at her – but still Hilda went on sucking that little pink thumb of hers! And then one day something cured her. Just listen!

Hilda's birthday was coming near and the fairies thought they would give her a present. So they held a meeting about it and thought of many things. Then a small fairy spoke up loudly.

'Hilda loves to suck her thumb – but it can't be very nice to suck. If it were made of toffee or liquorice it would be much nicer for her! Let's change her thumb into something sweet and she will have a fine treat each day, sucking it.'

So they worked a spell, and when Hilda awoke on her birthday and put her thumb into her mouth to suck, she *did* have a surprise! It tasted sweet! It looked a bit funny, too, because it was made of toffee – a little toffee thumb! How very queer!

Hilda sucked it again. Yes – her thumb really *was* made of toffee. How nice! The fairies must have planned this surprise for her. The little girl sucked away and enjoyed her thumb very much.

But, goodness me, when she next took it out of her mouth, she got such a shock! She had sucked half her thumb away! Yes, really! It did look odd. And what use would it be if she sucked it all away? She wouldn't be able to do up her buttons – or her shoes – or write – or do her handwork! Hilda stared at her tiny thumb in dismay. This wouldn't do at all!

She dressed and ran down to the bottom of the garden. The fairies were there waiting to wish her a happy birthday – but Hilda burst into tears.

'You have spoilt my thumb!' she wept. 'I have sucked it nearly all away!'

'Oh, dear, we didn't think of that!' cried the fairies in a fright. 'Never mind – we'll make a new thumb grow each day – a candy one tomorrow – and a liquorice one the next day – and . . .'

'I don't want sweetie-thumbs!' wept Hilda. 'They are all right to suck, but no use for anything else. I want my own thumb back.'

So they gave her back her own little pink thumb. She was so glad. Do you suppose she sucked it after that? No, she didn't! And she

says if you know anyone who sucks his thumb
just tell him what happened to hers. So don't
forget it, will you!

Lazy Kate

'Kate! Time to get up!' called Mother. Kate was fast asleep in bed. She grunted, but didn't open her eyes.

'KATE! You'll be late for school!' cried Mother.

'She always is,' said John, Kate's brother, sitting down to breakfast. 'She just simply *won't* get up!'

It was quite true. Kate was the laziest little girl you ever saw! Sometimes her mother ran upstairs, and pulled all the bed-clothes off Kate to make her get up – but even then she would go on sleeping, though she had no blankets on her!

'I don't know what to do with her!' said her mother, in despair. 'So lazy and slow – it's really dreadful. She will never be any use to anybody!'

One morning a very strange thing happened. Mother went to call Kate as usual. No answer. She called again. Still no answer. She ran into the bedroom and shook Kate by the shoulder. Kate grunted and turned over the other way.

'Do get up, Kate!' said Mother. 'It's prize-giving day at school today and you mustn't be late!'

'All right, Mother,' said Kate, without opening her eyes. Her mother thought she would really get up now, so she went down to give John his breakfast. But Kate fell fast asleep again!

Then the strange thing happened. Her bed began to groan and creak, and to mutter to itself! Kate took no notice. The bed lifted up one of its feet and put it down again. It grunted loudly. Kate didn't hear.

Then the bed lifted up another foot – and this time it took a step towards the door! Goodness! What a funny thing to happen! Kate's bed was very small, and it got through the door with a squeeze. Then, very carefully, it made its way downstairs, carrying Kate with it! She was dreaming peacefully, and didn't even stir!

Right down to the bottom of the stairs walked the bed, and then, as the front door stood wide open, out it went! Nobody heard it, for the dining-room door was shut.

Down the street walked the bed, carrying Kate under the bed-clothes! How everyone stared! The children were going to school, and they ran after the bed in delight.

'Look! Look! There's a bed walking – and there is someone in it! Oh, what fun! Where is it going?'

Well, it was taking Kate to school! What do you think of that? Just as the bell stopped ringing, and all the children were standing in rows – in walked the bed at the door!

The children squealed and shouted in delight. 'Look, it's come to school! Oh, do look! Who is it in bed?'

They made such a noise that Kate woke up in a fright. She sat up and rubbed her eyes – and then, how she stared – and stared – and stared! Then she went very red indeed, for she felt ashamed to have come to school in her night-dress, and in *bed!* She lay down under the bed-clothes and pulled them over her red face. Oh, dear, oh, dear!

The bed wouldn't walk home again – it liked school so much – so a van had to be fetched to take it and lazy Kate back home.

And do you suppose Kate was ever late again?

No – as soon as that bed gives so much as the smallest creak Kate is out on the floor, dressing!

Are any of you sleepyheads? Be careful your bed doesn't behave like Kate's!

Well, Really, Brer Rabbit!

One day Brer Rabbit went by Brer Fox's house and smelt a fine smell of fresh-caught fish. He stood still and sniffed. Brer Fox poked his head out of the window and grinned. 'Ho!' he said. 'Don't think you'll get *my* fish, Brer Rabbit! I'm up to all your tricks now!'

Brer Rabbit didn't say anything. He walked on, and when he came to Brer Bear's house he sniffed a most beautiful smell there of fresh-picked onions. Brer Bear saw him sniffing and looked out of the window. 'Sniff away, Brer Rabbit!' he said. 'That's all you'll get of *my* onions – just the sniff!'

Well, Brer Rabbit scowled and walked on. Pretty soon he did a little dance, and then ran off to his house. He hunted about until he found a nice long piece of string. He coiled it up, took up his ruler, and went off again. He knew quite well that Brer Fox and Brer Bear would be coming along that way soon to do their marketing – and he just hung about and waited till he saw them. Didn't he get busy then! He measured this and measured that, and then unrolled his string, and looked about as if he wanted something.

'Heyo, Brer Rabbit,' said Brer Fox, strolling up. 'What are you doing?'

'I'm thinking of building a house just here,' said Brer Rabbit. 'I'm just wondering how much ground I'll need. See here, Brer Fox, you might just hold the end of this string for me while I measure out the ground.'

Well, Brer Fox didn't see a mite of harm in that and he took the end of the string. Brer Rabbit went some way off, and then walked behind a big bush. He waited for a moment and then spied old Brer Bear ambling along with his basket. 'Heyo, Brer Bear,' said Brer Rabbit, raising his hat politely. 'Would you be good enough to hold the end of this string for me just a moment? I'm doing a bit of measuring, and it's difficult to use my ruler and hold the string too.'

'All right,' said Brer Bear, and he took the end of the string. Brer Rabbit ran round the bush, disappeared under another one – and ran chuckling through a burrow he knew very well indeed.

Brer Fox stood and held the string for ten minutes or more. Then he grew tired and tugged it. Brer Bear, who was at the other end, felt the tug and tugged back, for he, too, was growing mighty tired of waiting so long. Brer Fox, thinking it was Brer Rabbit at the other end, tugged again – and Brer Bear, feeling cross, tugged back hard. Then first one tugged and then the other, and they both got very angry.

'Stop it, I tell you!' roared Brer Fox.

'Stop it yourself!' shouted back Brer Bear. Then they both began to walk in a rage up the string – and when they got to the big bush they met face to face!

'What are *you* doing holding this string?' growled Brer Fox in amazement.

'Well, what are *you* doing?' grunted Brer Bear, astonished. 'It was Brer Rabbit who gave it to *me*.'

'Well, but why did he do such . . .' began Brer Fox – then he stopped and let out a fearful howl.

'My fish!' he cried, and shot back home.

'My onions!' yelled Brer Bear, and trundled off at top speed.

But it was too late. Their larders were empty, and far away in the wood sat old Brer Rabbit, grinning away as he ate the finest meal he had had for weeks. Well, *really*, Brer Rabbit, whatever will you do next?

Little Black Bibs

Long, long ago, Mother Chinky used to hold a New Year's party each year sometime in the month of January. To it she used to ask the cock and hen chaffinches, the cock and hen robins and the cock and hen sparrows.

There was a big tea of crumbs and small sugar biscuits, which everyone enjoyed. Then there were games, and after that a bran-tub, into which each bird dipped his beak and took out a present. There was one present for everybody, so you can guess it was a big bran-tub.

First the cock robins used to line up and peck out a present each. Then the cock chaffinches and then the cock sparrows. After that it was the turn of the hens. But the strange thing was that there never seemed to be enough presents! There were always some little sparrows who had no present at all because the bran-tub was empty when it came to their turn to peck. They would put their beaks excitedly into the bran, and peck it about hopefully, trying to find a present – and there wouldn't be a single one left!

It was very strange! Mother Chinky really couldn't understand it. She counted the birds. There were forty-eight – and she knew quite well she had put forty-eight presents into the tub. What in the world could have happened?

It was one of the little cock robins who told her at last.

'Mother Chinky!' he whispered. 'It's the little cock sparrows who take too many presents. You see, they first of all take one present each, when they line up as cock sparrows – and then the naughty little creatures line up again with the *hen* sparrows and find presents a second time. So you see there are never enough presents for the last sparrows of all.'

Mother Chinky listened and frowned crossly. The naughty little cheats! The cock and hen sparrows were so much alike that of course she would never notice whether the cocks did come twice or not. It was easy to see that the chaffinches didn't, because the cock had a bright pink breast and the hen hadn't. The robins never cheated, so although they looked just alike Mother Chinky was sure they would never play such a trick.

But the sparrows – ah, those cheeky, rude little birds with their loud voices and pushing ways – yes, it would be just like them to cheat.

'Still, I like the noisy little creatures,' said Mother Chinky to herself. 'I want them to come to my party. But I must certainly stop them cheating! Now, what can I do?'

She thought of a splendid idea the next year. What do you think she did? Why, as the sparrows pushed into her little house, she stood at the doorway with a pot of black paint – and she gave each cock sparrow a bib of black as he passed her!

Then, when the time for the bran-tub came, it wasn't a bit of use the cock sparrows lining up again, with the hens, to peck out a second present for themselves. No! They could easily be told by their black bibs – and for the first time there were really enough presents for everybody.

People say that Mother Chinky still gives her New Year's party each January, but whether she really does or not I don't know. The strange thing is that cock sparrows always appear with black bibs under their chins then, so perhaps she does! You might look at your sparrows and see if you can tell cocks from hens now. If you can, you'll be as clever as Mother Chinky!

Six O'Clock Tales

CONTENTS

When the Moon Fell Down!

One evening, when the moon was full and shone out in a cloudy sky, Prickles the Hedgehog went out to look for a beetle or two for his dinner. When he was under a chestnut tree a large chestnut fell down on his back and made him jump in fright. At the same moment the moon disappeared behind a cloud.

'Ooh!' cried Prickles at once. 'The moon fell down on my back! Ooh! I felt it! It's fallen out of the sky! I must tell Frisky the Squirrel.'

He found Frisky and told him. 'The moon has fallen out of the sky!' he said. 'It hit my back. I felt it. What shall we do?'

Frisky was excited. 'We must tell Hoo-Hoo the Brown Owl,' he said. So they went to where Hoo-Hoo was sitting on a branch and told him.

'The moon has fallen out of the sky!' said Frisky the Squirrel. 'It hit Prickles on the back. He felt it. What shall we do?'

Hoo-Hoo was astonished. He looked up into

the cloudy sky, but he could certainly see no moon there.

'We must tell Sly-One the Stoat,' he said. So all three set off to the barn where Sly-One was watching for mice.

'Sly-One, listen!' cried Hoo-Hoo. 'The moon has fallen out of the sky! It hit Prickles on the back, he felt it. What shall we do?'

Sly-One could hardly believe his ears. He jumped up excitedly. 'We must tell Velvety the Mole,' he said. So they all hurried off to where Velvety was making a big tunnel in the field.

'Listen, Velvety!' cried Sly-One. 'The moon has fallen out of the sky! It hit Prickles on the back. He felt it. What shall we do?'

'Why, go and find it, of course!' said Velvety at once. So they all ran to the place where Prickles had felt certain that the moon had fallen on his back, and began to hunt about.

The wind blew a little, and a few more chestnuts fell down. Bump! One hit Frisky the Squirrel on the nose. Bump! Another hit Sly-One the Stoat on his arched back. Bump! A third hit Hoo-Hoo the Owl on his beak.

'Why, the chestnuts are falling!' cried Frisky, picking one up and nibbling it. 'It must have been a chestnut you felt, Prickles. What a silly you are!'

Prickles didn't like being called silly. He stood all his spines up on end at once. 'I tell you, it was the moon!' he said crossly. 'Don't I know the difference between the moon and a chestnut?'

And dear me, at that very moment the moon sailed out from behind a cloud and lit up the wood with its bright silvery light!

'Ho, ho!' laughed all the creatures. 'There's the moon in the sky, after all. So you *didn't* know the difference between the moon and a chestnut! Funny old Prickles!'

But Prickles wasn't there! He had crept away to hide in a ditch, quite ashamed of himself. Poor old hedgehog!

Jean's Little Thrush

Jean had a nice little garden at school. She was very proud of it because she had three rose trees in it, and a border of blue lobelia and white sweet alyssum. The other children had sown seeds of candytuft, poppies, nasturtiums and clarkia, but Jean's was the only garden with rose trees.

She had saved up her money and bought them herself, because she loved roses. There was a tree that would bear red roses, one that would bear pink ones and the third one was yellow. Jean hoped to be able to have a fine bowlful of roses for her schoolroom, and a bunch to take home to her mother.

The head mistress of the school called the little gardeners to her one day and promised a prize for the best-kept garden with the loveliest flowers. Jean did hope hers would be the best, and every day she went to weed it and water her plants, which were growing very well.

One day when she was weeding her garden she heard a loud squeaking noise not far off. It sounded like a gate creaking and Jean wondered what it was. She looked all round but could not see anything at all. The noise still went on so she ran off to find out what it was.

It wasn't long before she discovered what was making the noise. It was a small baby thrush! It sat on the ground beneath a flowering lilac and squeaked with fright. Nearby was the mother thrush making little comforting noises. Jean looked at the frightened baby bird.

'It's too small to fly,' she thought. 'It must have fallen out of its nest. I wonder where the nest is?'

She looked up into the lilac bush. It wasn't there. She looked into the next tree, a chestnut, big and spreading – and there, set neatly in the fork of three small branches she spied a thrush's nest! Over the edge of it peeped a brown head – another baby thrush!

'There!' said Jean. 'I was right! This little thing has tumbled out of its nest. Oh dear, what shall I do? I can't possibly climb up there.'

She stood there, thinking. The baby thrush at her feet kept on squeaking. Jean felt sure a cat would hear it soon if it didn't keep quiet. But it didn't know anything about cats. It just thought that if it went on squeaking someone or something would come to its help.

'I know!' said Jean, at last. 'I'll get the little ladder that Miss Brown keeps in the shed. Then I can climb up and put the bird back quite easily.'

So off she went. She soon got the ladder, and although it was rather heavy it wasn't long before she had set it up against the chestnut tree. She picked the baby thrush up very carefully in her hand and then climbed up the ladder. The mother thrush flew round her as she carried the squeaking bird, and cried out in fear, afraid that Jean was going to harm her little bird.

Carefully Jean put the little thrush into the nest and then climbed down the ladder again.

'Stay in your nest till you are big enough to fly properly!' she called to the baby thrush. 'I might not be near if you fall out again.'

She put the ladder back and went on with her gardening, glad that the little thrush had stopped its frightened squeaking.

Soon after that Jean caught a cold and had to stay at home for a week. When she came back, anxious to look at her garden, what a shock she got! The leaves of her rose trees were all stuck together, and when she pulled them apart she found little green caterpillars all over the trees! They were eating great holes in the leaves, and were even starting to nibble at the nice new rosebuds.

Jean stared at the spoilt rose trees with tears in her eyes. How unlucky that the caterpillars should have come just the week she was away! In a fortnight's time the head mistress, Miss Brown, was going to look at the school gardens and give the prize. Unless Jean could get rid of all the caterpillars in a short time, her rose trees would certainly not be worth looking at!

Then she saw a speckled thrush come hopping over the lawn, followed by three wobbly baby thrushes! The mother thrush was teaching them to look for food. She hopped over to Jean's garden and put her head on one side, looking up into the rose trees. Then, with a quick peck she snapped at a green caterpillar, and, hopping back to her three babies, she popped it quickly into one of their open mouths. Jean was delighted!

'Oh, do take away all the caterpillars that are spoiling my rose trees!' she begged the thrush.

'Trilla-trilla, pretty pretty, trilla!' said the

thrush at once, which Jean was sure meant: 'I will! You once saved one of my babies, and now I will do your garden a good turn!'

The school bell rang and Jean ran in to her class. For the next two or three days the mother thrush came to her little garden a dozen times a day and very soon there was not a caterpillar left!

Jean was so pleased. She carefully picked off all the half-eaten leaves and nipped off the spoilt buds. There was over a week before the head mistress was going to judge the school gardens. Perhaps there would be a chance for Jean after all!

You should have seen Jean's rose trees in a week's time! They had put out nice fresh leaves and every tree had some beautiful roses blooming. The sweet alyssum and the blue lobelia round the little bed were all blossoming gaily, and there wasn't a weed to be seen.

The head mistress looked at all the gardens, but when she came to Jean's she stopped and admired it very much.

'Yours is beautiful,' she said to the proud little girl. 'There isn't a weed to be seen, and your rose trees are lovely. I was afraid they would all be eaten by some caterpillars I saw on them a fortnight ago.'

'Oh, a kind thrush came and ate them all,' said Jean.

'And who was the kind little girl who did a good turn to a baby thrush?' asked Miss Brown. 'I saw all you did from my window, Jean. Well, you were kind to the thrush, the thrush returned your kindness and ate your caterpillars – and now I shall give you the prize for the best and prettiest garden in the school! You deserve it!'

Everyone cheered, and Jean walked proudly up to take the set of fine garden tools that Miss Brown held out to her. And just as she was taking them a thrush up in the trees began to sing a loud, glad song.

'There's your friend the thrush cheering you!' said Miss Brown. And I shouldn't be surprised if it was, would you?

You Can't Please Everybody!

Flip and Flap were two jolly gnomes who tried to please everyone. But once they tried too often, as you shall hear!

It happened one day that they wanted to go to market to fetch some potatoes in their barrow and Flap thought it would be a good idea to take with them a sack of apples to sell. So they fetched the big wheelbarrow and filled a sack full of their best apples. Then they set off.

Now Flip was very tall and thin and Flap was very short and stout, so they looked an odd pair. Flip wheeled the barrow and Flap took the sack of apples on his fat shoulder. It was a hot day and the road to the market was a long one. Many people were going to market that day, and some of them stared laughingly at the two gnomes.

'Look at that little fat one carrying the sack!' cried a big brownie, pointing his long finger at Flap. 'What foolish gnomes they are! Why don't they put the sack in the barrow and wheel it?

Then it need not be carried!'

'Dear me!' said Flip, stopping and looking at Flap. 'We might have thought of that, Flap. Put the sack of apples in the barrow and I can easily wheel it.'

So Flap thankfully put the sack into the barrow and walked on his way, glad to be rid of his load. But tall, thin Flip found the barrow rather heavy to push and every now and again he gave a little groan. Some pixies passing by heard him and they stopped and pointed their fingers at fat Flap, swinging along by himself, whistling.

'Look at that strong, fat gnome selfishly walking by himself, letting his poor thin brother push that heavy barrow!' they cried. 'For shame! He ought to push the barrow himself!'

The gnomes stopped and Flap went very red. He took the handles of the barrow from Flip at once.

'Better let me push the barrow, Flip,' he said. 'I don't want people to think I am selfish, for I am much too fond of you to be unkind. You walk and I will take the barrow.'

So tall, thin Flip walked beside the barrow whistling gaily, while short, fat Flap pushed it. The sun was very hot indeed and soon Flap panted and puffed with the heat. He pushed the barrow along, and felt little drops of water running down his face, because he was so hot.

A large gnome and his wife came jogging up on their donkey and the wife pointed her finger at Flip in disgust.

'Look, husband,' she said, 'do you see that tall gnome there walking by his poor little brother who is working himself to death pushing that heavy barrow? For shame! Why doesn't he help him? Surely he could give him a hand?'

Then it was Flip's turn to go red. The tall gnome stopped and looked at Flap, who was still puffing and panting as he pushed the barrow.

'Look here!' said Flip. 'Hadn't we better push the barrow together, Flap? You can take one handle and I can take the other. Then everyone can see we are helping one another.'

So Flap took the right handle of the barrow and Flip took the left handle, and off they went again down the road.

Very soon a big party of pixies rattled by in a wagon, and when they saw the two gnomes both pushing the one wheelbarrow they screamed with laughter and pointed their small fingers at them in scorn.

'Look! Look! Those gnomes are so weak and

feeble that it needs both of them to push one barrow! Oh, what a funny sight! Poor things! They ought to eat lots of eggs and butter to get up their strength. Then it wouldn't need two of them to push one small barrow!'

The gnomes put down the barrow with a bang and stared angrily after the cheeky pixies.

'*Well!*' said Flap, snorting down his nose in rage. 'We can't seem to please anybody this morning! What are we to do now?'

'Well, it's no use one of us carrying the apples and the other wheeling the barrow,' said Flap, 'because we were laughed at for that.'

'And it's no good you wheeling the barrow alone or me wheeling it either,' said Flap gloomily, 'because people think we're selfish then.'

'And they think we're poor, weak things if we wheel it together,' said Flip. 'But wait – *I* know what we'll do, Flap! You carry the barrow over your shoulder, and *I'll* carry the sack of apples! Then we shall neither of us be called stupid, selfish or feeble. Isn't that a good idea?'

'Fine!' said Flap, and he hoisted the barrow on to his head. The weight of it bent him over and he couldn't see where he was going, so he told Flip to walk in front of him and guide him.

Flip went in front and together they made their way to the market.

The road began to get very crowded, and pigs, hens and ducks were all over the place. Suddenly a little pig ran between Flip's long legs and over he went with the bag of apples. They rolled all over the road and the pigs gobbled them up at once! Then Flap fell over Flip and down came the barrow, crash! Its wheel broke in half and both the handles were cracked.

'My goodness me!' said Flap, sitting up and looking in dismay at the pigs gobbling the apples and at his broken barrow. 'Look at that, Flip! This is what comes of trying to please everybody! *Next* time we will please ourselves!'

And I really think it would be better if they did, don't you?

The King of the Trains

Malcolm had a big red engine for his birthday. You should have seen it! It was the biggest toy engine he had ever seen, so big that Malcolm and his sister Janet could easily get into the back of it and sit there together!

Malcolm had a rope tied round the red funnel and he used to pull Janet round the garden in the engine. Then he would have *his* turn at riding and Janet would pull. It was great fun.

One day a very strange thing happened. The children were in the garden and had squeezed themselves into the engine together. 'I wish the engine would go off by itself and take us along,' said Malcolm.

Just as he said that the children heard a sound in the distance like the loud whistle of an engine. At once their own engine gave a start as though it had heard. Then, to the children's enormous surprise, it began to puff away down the garden path!

Yes! It really puffed! Smoke came out of the funnel, and it went faster and faster down the path! It was a very strange and peculiar thing!

'Goodness!' said Malcolm in astonishment. 'Whatever's happening?'

'Hadn't we better get out?' asked Janet, but the engine was now going much too fast for them to get out. It puffed and puffed, and rattled along out of the gate and down the lane as fast as ever it could.

As it went it seemed to puff a sort of song, and Malcolm listened to see if he could hear what the words were. It seemed to him as if the engine were singing again and again: 'I *might* be King, yes I *might* be King, I *might* be King, yes I *might* be King!'

'How funny,' said Malcolm. 'Whatever does it mean, Janet? I say, isn't this an adventure!'

The engine tore on down the lane and the two children clung tightly to the sides. At the bottom of the lane they came to a small turning to the right and the engine puffed up this. Janet and Malcolm were astonished.

'I never knew there was a turning here before!' said Janet. 'Did you, Malcolm?'

Malcolm didn't either. But there certainly was, for the engine tore on down the little path, rocking from side to side when stones came in its way. It went on and on and at last came to a steep hill that rose up to a point. The children thought the engine was going to puff right up the hill but it didn't. It ran up to a doorway set deep into the hill and whistled loudly three times.

The door opened at once and the engine ran in, taking the two children with it. As it went in Malcolm heard a noise behind them and he turned round. To his surprise he saw three more engines behind him, one nearly as big as his own, and the others smaller.

They all went down a long passage, chuffing and puffing. At last they came to an enormous cave and there, to the children's great astonishment, they saw hundreds of wooden engines, some painted red, some yellow, some blue and some green. Some were small and some were very big. Malcolm thought his engine must be the biggest of all.

A large red engine whistled for silence, and all the engines stopped chuffing and were still. Then, with a good deal of puffing and blowing, the big engine shouted to the others.

'The King of the Wooden Engines is dead,' he puffed. 'He was broken to pieces yesterday. Who is to be our King now?'

At once all the engines puffed and snorted in excitement, and Malcolm's engine and two other very big ones made their way to the front.

'We are the biggest!' they chuffed. 'One of us must be King!'

Then all the smaller engines rushed round them and whistled excitedly. Malcolm and Janet sat still in the cab of their engine and listened. It was all most exciting. They did hope their engine would be chosen for King!

'This one shall be our King!' puffed the small engines, and they surrounded Malcolm's engine. 'It is the biggest and brightest of all! Where is the paint-pot?'

The big red engine whistled loudly, and a small brownie man rushed in with a pot of bright gold paint. In a flash he had painted a little golden crown round the funnel of Malcolm's engine. Then all the engines whistled at the same time and puffed: 'We greet you, King! Long life to you!'

Malcolm's engine whistled back so loudly that the two children were nearly deafened. Then it put itself at the head of all the engines and began to make its way back to the door in the hillside. Out they all went, the big engine leading the way, puffing and panting a happy little song as it went: 'I'm the King of the Wooden Engines! I'm the King of the Wooden Engines!'

You should have seen the sight as all the brightly painted engines wound their way down the path to the lane. They whistled and puffed merrily. None of them had any children in them except Malcolm's engine, and Malcolm couldn't help thinking how lucky it was that he and Janet had happened to be riding in his engine just when it had rushed off to be made King.

At the end of the path Malcolm's engine turned down the lane that led to their house. The other engines whistled goodbye and went the other way. Malcolm's engine rushed back to the garden and put itself in the very place from where it had started.

'Well!' said Malcolm, as he helped Janet out. 'That *was* an adventure! Fancy, Janet, we've got the King of all the Engines! Aren't we grand?'

They still have that engine. You will know it by the little golden crown painted round the funnel.

Pixie Pins

Lightfoot was a small pixie dressmaker. She was very clever indeed, and she had even made a dress for the Pixie Queen herself. She used spider's thread for her cotton, and rose petals for her material, and she trimmed her gowns and coats with twinkling dewdrops or strips of moonshine. So, you see, it was no wonder all the Little Folk came to her whenever they wanted a new party dress.

One day she had just finished a lovely dress for Princess Peronel. It was made of two yellow rose petals and had a trimming of kingfisher down, so it was very pretty. The kingfisher himself had given Lightfoot the little bits of blue and green down, and he had watched her making the dress.

It was so pretty that he flew all over the place telling everyone about it.

'Lightfoot has made the loveliest gown in the world,' he cried. 'It's the prettiest dress ever I saw!'

Now there was a red goblin who heard him saying this, and he pricked up his big pointed ears. His little wife was always asking him for a new dress, and he wondered if he could steal the new one that Lightfoot had just made. So he followed the kingfisher and asked him some questions.

The kingfisher was only too pleased to tell him all about the new dress.

'Lightfoot has just finished it,' he said. 'She is taking it to the Princess Peronel tonight to fit it on for the last time. It is the loveliest thing ever I saw!'

'Which way is she going to the palace?' asked the goblin slyly.

'Oh, down Cuckoo Lane and past the big horse-chestnut tree!' said the kingfisher, and off he flew, calling out his news about the lovely dress.

The goblin had found out all he wanted to know. That night he hid himself under the hedge in Cuckoo Lane and waited for Lightfoot to come by. Presently he heard her coming, humming a little song. She carried her work-bag with her, and in it she had put the new dress, her measuring tape, her box of pins and some hooks and eyes.

The red goblin pounced out at her with a yell.

She gave a frightened shriek and rushed off down the lane thinking that all the witches and goblins in the world were after her. The red goblin followed her, and poor Lightfoot began to puff and pant. Her work-bag was heavy and she did not dare to drop it, for she didn't want it to be stolen.

She came to the horse-chestnut tree. It stood at the end of the lane, a big tree with umbrella-like leaves. It heard Lightfoot puffing along and called to her.

'Lightfoot! What's the matter? Come, hide inside my trunk if you are frightened! There is a little hole at the bottom where a mouse lives.'

Lightfoot looked for the little hole. She saw a tiny woffly nose looking out of the tree and she guessed it belonged to a mouse. So she ran to it and sure enough, there was the hole in the trunk! She squeezed thankfully into it and heard the red goblin go running past. He didn't know she had hidden in the chestnut tree.

Lightfoot stayed there until all the danger was past. She was very grateful to the tree.

'Can I do anything for you in return for your kindness to me?' she asked.

'No, no; nothing!' answered the tree, and all its leaves whispered: 'No, she can't!'

But the little mouse spoke in Lightfoot's ear. 'There *is* something you can do,' she whispered. 'You know the chestnut grows a lot of fine conkers, and wraps them up in green cases. But the goblins come along and pick them each night before the conkers are ripe, and the tree never has any to throw down for the children. Can you think of a good idea to stop the goblins picking them?'

'Yes, I can!' said Lightfoot, and she took out her box of pins. 'Look, mouse! I'll stick these pins into the conker cases, head downwards, then when the goblins come to pick them they will prick their fingers on the sharp pins, and will soon leave the conkers alone!'

So, after Lightfoot had taken the dress to the Princess, and found that it fitted her beautifully, she flew back to the chestnut tree. She spent the whole night sticking pins head downwards into the green conker cases, and she *did* make them prickly! And when the goblins came slinking along to steal the conkers what a shock they got! They pricked their fingers and scratched their hands terribly, and they howled in surprise and pain.

'It serves you right!' whispered the chestnut leaves in delight. 'It serves you right!'

And ever since then all horse-chestnut
conkers have been shut up in very prickly cases
to stop the goblins from stealing them. Have
you seen them? It's a very good idea, isn't it?

The Adventurous Clown

There was once a clown called Tuffy, who lived in a toyshop with hundreds of other toys. Some of them were very grand toys who wouldn't even look at the little clown, with his painted face and pointed hat. Some were not so grand and the clown would often talk with them.

Tuffy the clown longed to be a hero. He longed to do something grand, something noble so that all the toys in the toyshop would cheer him and cry out that he was a hero. He thought his little corner on a toyshelf was dull. Nothing ever happened there. How could he be a hero when nothing ever happened?

'Why do you grumble so?' asked Timothy, the puppy dog with boot-button eyes and a tail that really wagged. 'Be happy and contented with us, Tuffy. We are a nice little family here on this shelf. Why do you want to go off and have adventures? They might not be nice.'

'Oh, yes, they would be,' said Tuffy.

'Adventures are always exciting. I want to do something really fine. Save someone from a fire or something like that. That would make all the grand toys sit up and take notice. It's so dull up here on our shelf. Why, we only get dusted once a week!'

That night Tuffy the clown climbed down from his shelf. He had made up his mind to seek adventures. There must be lots of them down in the shop. He had heard all sorts of exciting noises at night. Surely grand things must happen down in the shop!

Now that night there was to be a grand race between two wooden horses and carts, driven by wooden farmers. The race was just starting as Tuffy climbed down to the floor. One cart came racing by Tuffy, the farmer standing up and yelling for all he was worth.

Tuffy stood and gaped.

'Goodness! An adventure already!' thought Tuffy. 'A runaway horse! Ha, now is my chance to be a hero!'

The horse and cart came round again, and Tuffy sprang at the reins. He held on to them and dragged the horse to one side. The cart fell over with a crash, and the farmer tipped out. Tuffy stood by, helping him up, feeling very

proud that he had stopped the horse.

But the farmer was terribly angry.

'What do you mean by spoiling my race like that!' he yelled. 'Now the other horse and cart will win! And look at my cart, all on its side! And I've spoilt my best hat, too! You silly, interfering little clown. Take that – and that!'

And the farmer cracked his whip at poor, astonished Tuffy.

'Ooh!' cried Tuffy, rushing away. 'You don't understand! I'm a hero!'

He ran out of sight, and sat down in a toy farm, wiping the tears from his eyes. Horrid man! How dare he crack his whip at him like that when Tuffy had tried to be a hero?

As Tuffy sat there he noticed a doll's house in a corner of the shop – and, dear me, what was that coming out of one of the bedroom windows, in great curls? It was smoke!

'Fire, fire!' yelled Tuffy, jumping to his feet at once. 'Another adventure! Fire! I'll put it out at once!'

He rushed to get a ladder leaning against a haystack. He put it up against the wall of the doll's house. Then he found a big bucket which he filled with water from the farm pond. Up the ladder he went, yelling: 'Fire, fire!'

He threw all the water in at the window, and was just going to climb down for another bucketful, when someone caught him by the collar and roared:

'And what do you think *you're* doing, playing a silly trick like that!'

Poor Tuffy was hauled in through the window and shaken like a rat.

'D-d-don't d-d-do that!' he panted. 'I'm a hero! I was p-p-p-putting out the f-f-f-fire!'

'Fire! What fire?' said the angry voice, and Tuffy saw that he was speaking to a sailor doll who was smoking a large pipe. 'Can't I smoke my pipe without you coming and throwing water all over me? I'll teach you to throw water at people!'

The sailor doll dragged poor Tuffy downstairs and held his head under the cold water tap till he was quite soaked. Then he let him go.

Tuffy staggered out into the shop, shaking the water from his head, and squeezing out his pointed hat.

'They w-w-w-won't let me b-b-b-be a hero,' he sobbed. He walked off, angry and hurt, and sat down on a seat to dry. And as he sat there he heard a cry, and looked round. There was a big globe of water nearby, and in it were swimming two fine goldfish – and in the water was a small doll!

'She's fallen in!' shouted Tuffy, jumping up at once. 'I'll rescue her! This is a real adventure at last!'

He caught hold of a little net which was used to catch the goldfish when they were sold. He clambered up on to a chair and dipped the net into the water. Soon he had caught the little doll and hauled her out – but she slipped out of the net and fell bump on to the table.

She banged her head and began to cry. Up came a policeman doll and said, fiercely: 'What are you doing, catching that doll and making her bump her head like that?'

'I was saving her from drowning!' said Tuffy. 'I am a hero. You ought to cheer me!'

'I was having such a lovely swim!' sobbed the little doll. 'I am a swimming-doll, policeman, and I swim with the goldfish every night. But that horrid clown caught me in a nasty net, and I fell out of it and bumped my head. He isn't a hero. He's just a great, big, interfering NUISANCE!'

'You'd better come along with me,' said the policeman, jerking the clown up with a hard hand. 'Now then – any wriggling and I'll give you a good shaking!'

'I tell you, I'm a hero and –' began the clown, struggling hard. The policeman shook him till all his teeth chattered and his hat fell off. Then off he was marched to prison.

The policeman locked him in a room in the police station and left him there. The clown sat down and put his head in his hands.

'Adventures are horrid,' he groaned, 'Being a hero is silly. If only I were back again on my nice, quiet shelf with Timothy Dog and the others.'

Suddenly he heard a little noise outside the window of the room. 'Tuffy! Tuffy!' barked a little voice. 'It is I, Timothy. Here is the key to the door, coming in at the window!'

Tinkle! The key fell to the floor and the clown quickly undid the door. He and Timothy ran off together and climbed up to the shelf. Tuffy hugged the kind little dog and thanked him very much.

'*You're* the hero!' he said. 'All the things I did were silly, not wonderful or noble. I didn't stop to think. But you saw I was in real trouble and saved me.'

'Don't mention it,' said the toy dog, blushing. 'I don't want to be a hero, I'm sure.'

'Oh, how lovely and peaceful it is up on this shelf,' said Tuffy, looking round happily. 'I never want to leave it again.'

And, until he was sold, he never did!

The Money That Flew Away

Malcolm and Jessie were most excited because Mummy was going to take them to the Fair that afternoon. They had all saved up, and Mummy had a ten-pound note in her purse to take them. That would pay for their tickets, their tea, some coconut shies and some roundabouts. What fun they would have!

That morning Mummy opened her purse to take out some money to pay the baker – and, oh dear me, what a dreadful thing, the ten-pound note fell out and was blown away by the wind!

'Quick, quick, go after it, children!' cried Mummy. They ran out into the garden, and chased the flying note, which was being blown away fast by the wind. Suddenly Malcolm and Jessie lost sight of it. They hunted here and they hunted there – but it was gone. Wherever could it have flown to?

The children hunted for more than half an hour, but they couldn't find the ten-pound note.

They were very unhappy. Suppose Mummy said they couldn't go to the Fair now?

That's just what she *did* say! 'I'm very sorry, dears,' she said, 'but I really can't afford to take you if we've lost that ten pounds. Isn't it a shame?'

Mummy looked so miserable that Malcolm and Jessie flung their arms round her and kissed her.

'Never mind, Mummy!' they cried. 'We won't make a fuss! Perhaps it will turn up some other day and we can buy something nice with it.'

It was kind of them to be so good about it, wasn't it? Mummy was very pleased.

'Would you like to take a broom each and go to sweep up the dead leaves in the garden?' she said. 'I know you like doing that. You can make a bonfire of them if you like.'

'Yes, we'd love that!' cried Jessie, and off they went with a broom each. They were pleased to think they could help to tidy up the garden for their mother. They swept up the leaves into a big heap, and then ran indoors for some matches.

Jessie lit the dry leaves and they flared up – and just as the bonfire was burning up merrily,

Malcolm gave a loud shout.

'Jessie! There's the ten-pound note, all among the leaves! Quick, give me that stick and I'll try to rake it out before it's burnt!'

He just managed to poke it out before the flames caught it – and then, shouting in excitement the children rushed indoors to their mother.

'Mummy, Mummy, we've found the ten-pound note! It had blown among the dead leaves, and that was why we couldn't find it. Can we go to the Fair now?'

'Of course!' said Mummy, delighted. 'I *am* glad! Just think, children, if you hadn't been so good and helpful, you would never have found the money. Well, you really do deserve your treat!'

When the Toys Walked Home

Sheila had a lovely dolls' pram and she took her dolls and her teddy-bear out in it every day for a nice long walk. She never missed a day, and all the toys enjoyed their walk very much.

One day the little girl next door asked Sheila if she would lend her pram just for that morning.

'Oh, do, Sheila,' she begged. 'I have never had a pram, and I would so like to wheel one just once. Do lend me yours.'

'But my dolls will miss their walk dreadfully if I let you have my pram this morning,' said Sheila. 'Besides, you might break it, or run into something on the pavement.'

'I wouldn't,' said Ann, the little girl. 'I would be very careful, I wouldn't take your pram out on the road, Sheila. I would just wheel it round and round my garden.'

'My dolls will be so disappointed if I don't take them for their ride,' said Sheila, looking at them as they all sat ready in the dolls' pram.

'Well, can't you take them for a walk instead?' asked Ann. 'You could take their hands, couldn't you, and let them walk with you for once, instead of riding in their pram.'

'Don't be silly!' said Sheila. 'Toys can't really walk. You know that! I only wish they could. I'd love to see them walking down the road just like you and me. It would be lovely. Well, Ann, I *will* lend you my pram just for this morning, if you'll be careful with it. And I will take my toys in the wheelbarrow just for once. It will be a change for them.'

So Ann wheeled the pram into her own garden and put *her* dolls into it. And Sheila fetched her little wheelbarrow and sat her three dolls and her brown teddy-bear in it. It was rather a squash but they didn't seem to mind.

Off she went to the woods. She thought it would be nice and shady there, and there might be blackberries ripening. It would be nice to pick some.

There *were* some blackberries! Sheila began to pick some from a big bush – and then she suddenly saw the funniest little man she had ever seen, picking blackberries from the *other* side of the bush! As she watched him, she heard him say to himself, 'Bother! Oh, bother, bother! Here's my basket gone and got an enormous hole in it just when I wanted to take home enough black-berries to make some pots of blackberry jam!'

Sheila peeped over the bush at his basket. It certainly had a very big hole in it and the blackberries were dropping out as fast as he put them in. He really looked ready to cry!

Then he saw Sheila and he stared at her in surprise. 'Hello, little girl!' he said. 'Just look at my basket! Isn't it too bad! Now I shan't be able to take any blackberries home to make into jam, and my wife will be *so* cross with me.'

'I'm very sorry,' said Sheila, politely. 'I haven't brought a basket with me or I would have lent you one. I'm just taking my toys for a walk in my wheelbarrow.'

'Wheelbarrow!' said the little man excitedly, running round the bush to see it. 'Just the thing! *Just* the thing! Will you lend it to me to carry home my blackberries, little girl? I could put heaps of them into that nice big barrow, and my wife would be so pleased.'

'But what about my dolls?' said Sheila. 'I can't carry them all home, you know!'

'Why can't they walk?' asked the little man, at once.

'Don't be silly!' said Sheila, quite cross at having the same question asked her twice in one morning. 'You know toys can't walk. I only wish they could! If they could, I'd lend you my barrow at once!'

'Will you!' cried the little man, in delight. 'Well, I can easily make your toys walk. Dolls and teddy-bear, get out of the barrow and walk home with the little girl!'

And then, to Sheila's great astonishment, the three dolls and the teddy-bear all climbed quickly out of the barrow and ran up to her, holding up hands and paws for her to take. She stared at them in surprise and delight.

'Well, look at that!' she said at last. 'They have all come alive and will walk home with me. Whatever will people say!'

The little man ran to the empty barrow and wheeled it to his side of the bush. Then he began very quickly to pick blackberries and throw them into the barrow.

'I'll bring your barrow back tomorrow,' he called. 'Thank you so much, little girl. Goodbye!'

The toys dragged at Sheila's hands, and she turned to go home again. She called goodbye to the busy little man and then took the hands of her two smallest dolls, who in their turn took hands with the third doll and the bear. Then all five walked homewards through the wood. You should have seen how delighted Sheila was! The toys walked very nicely indeed, and laughed for joy at having such a treat.

Sheila met two or three people on the way home and you should have seen how they stared! Sheila felt so proud to be taking out a toy family. As she passed Ann's gate, Ann came runnning up – and how *she* stared to see Sheila and the toys all walking home together!

Sheila told her what had happened, and Ann was delighted.

'It's a reward for you because you were so kind and lent me your dolls' pram!' she said. 'But look, Sheila, the littlest doll is looking so tired. Here is your pram – let's put the toys in it, for they are not used to such a long walk.'

So into the pram they were all packed, and Sheila wheeled them into her own garden. She felt so excited and pleased to think that her toys had walked home with her. She was sure that such a thing had never happened to any other little girl.

In the morning she found her wheelbarrow in the garden, left there by the little man. And what do you think was inside it? Why, a little tiny pot of blackberry jam, put there for Sheila, in return for her kindness in lending her wheelbarrow. Isn't she lucky?

Twelve Little Pigs

Once upon a time a dozen little pigs ran into Miss Trippy's garden. She saw them from her bedroom window and she tapped on the pane, crying: 'Little pigs, little pigs, go out at once!'

But they took no notice of her at all.

Then she sent for her dog, Rover, and told him to go and chase the pigs away. He went and barked at them, but they were having such a good time, nibbling the lettuces and gobbling the peas that they took no notice of him either.

'Wuff, wuff!' he barked. 'Go out at once, little pigs!'

But they stayed among the peas and didn't even turn to look at him. Then Miss Trippy sent for her cat, and told her to go and chase the pigs away.

So Cinders the cat ran out, snarling and hissing.

'Little pigs, little pigs, go out at once!' she mewed. 'Miaow! S-ss-ss!'

But the little pigs took no notice of Cinders at all. They had found some carrots and were rooting them up in delight. Poor Miss Trippy! She wondered whatever she could do.

Then she sent for Captain, the big carthorse that belonged to the farmer, and told him to gallop up to the pigs and chase them away.

So he came trotting up to the garden gate, and galloped up the path to the kitchen garden. Cloppity-cloppity-clop, his hoofs went, and he neighed loudly. Ha! *He* would frighten away those wicked little pigs!

'Pooh! It's only a horse,' grunted the pigs, and they took no notice of him at all. They were used to horses. There were five at the farm where they had come from.

The big horse neighed again, and galloped about after the pigs – but soon Miss Trippy knocked loudly at the window, because he was doing a great deal of damage with his big hoofs.

So he cantered out of the gate, and left the little pigs still enjoying themselves among the peas and carrots.

Then a boy came by with a big stick. Miss Trippy called to him and begged him to drive away the little pigs with his stick. So in at the gate he went, shouting and halloing for all he was worth.

'Shoo, shoo, shoo!' he yelled. 'Get away, you wicked little pigs! Shoo, shoo, shoo!'

The pigs scattered here and there, but as fast as he drove one away another ran back, and it wasn't a bit of use. They took no notice of him at all!

Miss Trippy didn't know *what* to do! But just then a small wasp, striped in yellow and black, came buzzing by.

'Zzzzzzzzz!' it said. 'Dogs, cats, horses, boys – none of them can chase out pigs! Zzzzzz! But I can though I am only small. Let me come and steal a few of your sweet apples in the autumn, Miss Trippy, and I will chase away the pigs for you.'

'Very well,' said Miss Trippy. 'But it is hardly likely that a little thing like you will be able to do what even a great horse cannot do! You think too much of yourself, wasp!'

'A little thing is sometimes better than a big thing!' buzzed the wasp, and off it went into the garden. 'Zzzzzz!' it buzzed to the pigs. 'Go away at once! Zzzzzz!'

The pigs took no notice, but went on rooting up carrots. The wasp flew to one and stung it on the nose. It squealed with pain and rushed straight out of the gate!' Zzzzzz!' went the wasp. 'Zzzzzz!' Another little pig was stung on the nose and then a third one on its curly tail. The garden was soon full of grunts and squeals, and one by one the little pigs rushed out of the gate. Miss Trippy ran out into the garden and banged the gate shut. The pigs were out at last!

'What did I tell you?' buzzed the wasp, sailing round her head. 'Will you let me have an apple or two when they are ripe?'

'Willingly!' cried Miss Trippy. 'You were quite right, wasp! A little thing is sometimes better than a big thing! Help yourself to as many apples and pears as you wish!'

It did! Not only that but it brought all its relations, too, and *what* a feast they had!

The Little Pop-gun

The day that Willie bought his pop-gun was a
dreadful one for all the rest of the toys in his
nursery. They had never heard of any sort of
gun before, and none of them knew what a
pop-gun was.

Willie brought his gun proudly into the
nursery. Then he stood up his wooden soldiers
in a row, and put the cork into the end of his
pop-gun. It was tied on to the gun by a string.
When Willie pressed the trigger of the gun the
cork flew out with a loud pop and hit one of the
wooden soldiers. He fell over at once. Then
Willie put back the cork in the gun and shot it
out at the next soldier.

Pop! He went over too!

'What a fine pop-gun I have!' cried Willie.
'Now I will shoot all my skittles over!'

So he stood up his big skittles and one by one
he shot those over too. Then his mother called
him to dinner, and he went, leaving his pop-gun

on the floor. As soon as Willie was out of the room all the soldiers and skittles picked themselves up and scuttled back to the toy-cupboard as fast as ever they could go. They were very much afraid of the pop-gun! The teddy-bear and two dolls hid themselves at the back of the cupboard, too.

'What a dreadful new toy that is, that Willie has brought to our nursery!' said the teddy-bear in a whisper. 'It shouts "POP" at us and then knocks us over. I can't bear it!'

'Hi, where are you all going to?' suddenly shouted the pop-gun from its place in the middle of the floor. 'Come and be friendly. Talk to me and tell me all about this nursery I've come to live in.'

'We don't like you,' said the soldiers, all together. 'You shout "POP" at the top of your voice and then you punch us in the middle and knock us down.'

'Pooh!' said the pop-gun, laughing. 'I won't really hurt you, toys. A pop-gun always says "pop" when the trigger is pulled. As for knocking you down, don't mind that. It is only my little cork that knocks you over – it doesn't really hurt you. It's just a game.'

But none of the toys would make friends with

the pop-gun or go near him. He had to stay by himself all day and all night, for, wherever he was, the toys left him alone, and if he tried to talk to them they wouldn't listen. They thought he was a horrid, rough, unkind toy. But he couldn't help being a pop-gun, and he was sad because the toys wouldn't be friends.

Willie had a pet, beside all his toys. This was Whiskers, his little black cat. She slept in the nursery very often and the toys were quite fond of her. She had a little round basket near the fire.

One day Willie looked into Whiskers' basket and gave a shout of surprise.

'Mummy! Whiskers has got four little black kittens in her basket. Oh, how lovely!'

It was quite true. The toys peeped to see, and sure enough they spied four tiny black creatures cuddled up against Whiskers, who was very pleased.

But, you know, when those kittens grew big enough to climb out of their basket, how they teased the poor toys! They were wild, mischievous little creatures, and they used to climb into the toy-cupboard after the toys, and dig their sharp little claws into them till they squealed! They tore the dolls' pretty dresses with their sharp teeth, and they licked all the sweets in the toy sweet-shop. The toys became frightened of the four kittens.

The teddy-bear went to Whiskers one night and spoke to her.

'Whiskers,' he said, 'the toys have asked me to beg you to take your little kittens away somewhere else. They are unkind to us and we don't want them to live in the nursery.'

Whiskers hissed at the teddy-bear in a rage. 'How dare you say my kittens are unkind!' she cried. 'I shall certainly not take them away. They are the dearest, sweetest kittens in the world, and if they want to tease you, they can. You should stand up for yourselves. They are only kittens.'

The kittens grew bigger and bigger, and, dear me, the poor toys were more and more afraid of them. The pop-gun used to watch the kittens scratching and biting – and then, when he saw the very prettiest doll having her hair pulled off her little head, he made up his mind to rescue the toys. They hadn't been kind to him, but never mind!

He called to the teddy-bear.

'Hi, Teddy! I'll help you to get rid of those mischievous little kittens! Come and pick me up and put my cork in. Press the trigger and make my cork jump out at the kittens. They will soon stop teasing you!'

Teddy ran across the floor and picked up the little pop-gun. He pressed the cork in at the end of the gun and then pointed at the nearest kitten, who was running at him to scratch him.

'Pop!' The cork sprang out of the pop-gun half an inch from the kitten's nose. It darted back in fright. The other kittens came round the teddy-bear, spitting and hissing. Teddy quickly fitted in the cork again.

'Pop!' The cork sprang out to the full length of his string, and if the nearest kitten hadn't sprung backwards, the cork would have hit its front paw.

'S-S-ssssssss!' spat all the kittens. Whiskers heard them hissing and jumped out of her basket. She ran at Teddy in a rage, her paw raised to cuff him.

'Pop!' The cork made her stop in fright.

'Mew! Whatever is it?' she cried. 'Come, kittens, this is dangerous. Follow me, and we will go away from this horrible pop-thing. It might eat us up!'

She ran out of the nursery with all her four kittens following her. She took them to the kitchen, where the dog had a basket, and told them all to sleep there. She wasn't going back to the nursery again!

'There!' said the pop-gun, pleased. 'What did I tell you? They've gone and they won't come back. You'll have a little peace now, Teddy, you and the rest of the toys. Go and tell them.'

Teddy put the pop-gun down on the floor and ran to tell the toys. In a moment they all swarmed out of the toy-cupboard and ran to the pop-gun. They picked him up and put him on their shoulders. Then they carried him round the nursery, shouting: 'For he's a jolly good fellow! For he's a jolly good fellow!' till they were quite out of breath.

'We're sorry we thought you were a rough, unkind creature!' they said. 'You have done us a very good turn. Thank you.'

'Well, now perhaps you'll be friends with me,' said the pop-gun, making his cork jump up and down in the air.

'Of course!' cried everyone, and they took him straight back to the toy-cupboard to sleep with them. And ever since then the pop-gun has had so many friends that he has really never been able to count them!

Quizzy the Goblin

Quizzy was a small green goblin who was always poking his long nose into everything. He really was a perfect nuisance. He wanted to know this and he wanted to know that. He always longed to know every secret there was, and if people wouldn't tell him he flew into a rage and blew green flames out of his mouth.

So nobody liked him very much, and most people were afraid of him. He lived in a hole in the middle of an apple tree that tapped against a nursery window. He often ran up the tree and, if the window was open, hopped into the nursery.

Then the toys would sigh and say: 'Oh bother! Here's Quizzy again. Now we shan't have any peace at all!'

Quizzy wanted to know everything. He wanted to know how to wind up the clockwork engine, and how to set the clockwork mouse going. As soon as he knew he set the engine and mouse going, and they bumped straight into one another. The mouse hurt his nose, and the engine had a bump on its front. They were very cross.

But Quizzy laughed till the tears ran down his cheeks. That was the sort of thing he thought was really funny.

Then another time he wanted to know how the musical box worked, and he wound the handle round so often that it became worn out and broke. The toys were very angry about that, for they loved the tinkling music that came out of the musical box. The clockwork clown scolded the goblin for breaking it, and he flew into a rage at once.

Green flames shot out of his mouth and burnt a hole in the nursery carpet. The toys were frightened and rushed to the toy-cupboard. They climbed in and shut the door – but that wicked little goblin blew a green flame through the key-hole and burnt a hole in the big doll's dress. She screamed, and the goblin laughed loudly.

'That will teach you to interfere with me!' he cried. 'I shall do exactly as I like in your nursery, so there!'

With that he jumped out of the window and disappeared down the apple tree. The toys were so glad to see him go.

'If only we could give him a real fright so that he would never come back again!' sighed the big doll, trying to mend the hole in her pretty blue dress.

'But we can't!' said the clockwork clown. 'Because, for one thing, he would never go near anything he was afraid of – and for another thing I don't believe there *is* anything he is frightened of!'

Now the very next day what should come to the nursery but a large red box in which was hidden a jack-in-the-box with a very long spring to make him jump right out as soon as the lid was opened.

The toys all knew what a jack-in-the-box was, for there had been plenty in the toyshops where they came from – but they wondered if the goblin knew. Perhaps he didn't! If he didn't, what a fright he would get if only they could make him open the box! But how could they make him? If they told him to he would certainly think there was some trick about it, and wouldn't go near it!

'I know!' said the clockwork clown, who was always the one to get good ideas. 'I know! Let's pretend to hide the box away, and beg the goblin not to touch it. Then he is sure to wonder what it is, and he is such a one for poking his nose everywhere that he is certain to lift up the lid sooner or later – then whooooosh! The jack-in-the-box will jump out, and *what* a fright he'll get!'

The big doll wrote out a notice and put it against the box. The notice said: '*Do not touch*!'

'That will make the goblin want to touch it as soon as he sees it!' said the doll, with a laugh.

The next time the goblin came in at the window the toys caught hold of the box and pretended that they were trying to hide it away from Quizzy. He saw them at once and ran up.

'What's that you're trying to hide away?' he cried. 'Is it a secret?'

'Yes, it is, and *you're* not to find out our secret!' cried the teddy-bear.

'What's in the box?' shouted Quizzy, excitedly.

'Never you mind!' said the clockwork clown.

'Is it gold?' asked Quizzy. 'Or something nice to eat? Or fine new clothes?'

'It doesn't matter what it is, you're not to look and see!' said all the toys together.

Well, of course, that made Quizzy more determined than ever that he *would* peep inside that box and see what there was in it. How dare the toys have a secret he didn't know.

He didn't quite like to make the toys show him the inside of the box, when they were all so determined not to, so he made up his mind to come back just before cock-crow, when the toys would have climbed into the toy-cupboard to sleep. Then he would open the box and find out the great secret! And if it was gold he would take it for himself. If it was something nice to eat, he would eat it – and if it was fine clothes he would wear them. Ha ha! That would teach the toys to keep their secrets from Quizzy the goblin!

He jumped out of the window. The toys smiled at one another. They knew quite well he would come back at cock-crow!

They were all in the toy-cupboard, peeping, when Quizzy did come back. He tiptoed across the nursery floor to where the box stood with its notice leaning against it: '*Do not touch!*'

The goblin tore the notice in half. Then he looked at the lid of the box. How was it opened? Ah! There was a little catch. If he slipped that back he could open the lid.

He pressed it back. The lid flew off with a bang, and whooooooosh! Out leapt the jack-in-the-box, squeaking with all his might, his red face shining, his black hair standing up on end! He knocked the goblin flat on his face, and then

hung over him, wobbling about on his long spring, a really fearsome sight!

The goblin got up and gave one look at him. Then he yelled with fright and tore to the window as fast as he could run.

'A witch, a witch!' he cried, and jumped right out of the window. Down the apple tree he slid and landed bump on the ground. Then he began to run. He ran, and ran, and ran – and, so the toys say, he is *still* running! Anyway, he has never come back, and you should see the jack-in-the-box laugh when he tells the tale of how he frightened Quizzy the goblin. You'd love to watch him!

The Kind Hedgehog

When John and Sallie went out in the garden one morning, they ran to watch their father taking down the tennis net. Summer was over and autumn was in, making the mornings crisp and cool.

'Can we help to take down the nets all round the court?' asked Sallie. 'We'd like to.'

'Yes,' said their father. 'Unhook them from the posts and roll them up neatly.'

So the children began. Soon they came to a net that seemed to have a great knot at the bottom of it. They shook it but the knot stayed. It was heavy.

'It can't be a knot!' cried John. 'It's something else. Daddy, what's this?' Daddy came over.

'Why, it's a poor little hedgehog that has walked into the net at the bottom and got tangled up in it,' he said. 'I'll have to cut the net to get him out.'

'The naughty little thing!' cried Sallie, as she watched Daddy cut the net. 'The net was new this summer – now the hedgehog has spoilt it. There will be a big hole there next summer for balls to roll through.'

'It's a nasty, tiresome little hedgehog,' said John. 'It ought to be punished.'

Just then Mother came up to see what all the excitement was about. She looked down at the little rolled-up hedgehog that Daddy had cut out of the net.

'Poor little thing,' she said. 'So you came wandering across the grass looking for beetles and grubs, and got caught in the net. How frightened you must have been! And there was nobody to help you or cut you loose till the children found you this morning. I am sorry for you, little hedgehog. I hope you are not dead with fright.'

Mother picked up the hedgehog carefully. It was very prickly indeed, but she knew just how to hold it so that the spines did not prick her.

'We will give it some cat food,' she said. 'It will like that. Come along and help me, children.'

John and Sallie no longer wanted to punish the little hedgehog. They wanted to help it

instead. Off they all went, and very soon they
had the delight of seeing the funny little brown
creature uncurl itself and run to the saucer of cat
food. It ate it all with its funny little snout-like
mouth, and looked at them with bright, beady
eyes.

'Now we will let it run off,' said Mother. The
hedgehog must have heard what she said, for it
ran to the bushes and soon disappeared.

'Let's leave some cat food out for it tonight,'
said Sallie. 'It might come back.'

'I wish it would do a good deed in return for
our kindness,' said Mother. 'You know, our
kitchen is simply full of horrid black beetles at
night. I can't get rid of them. They come out
from under the stove and walk all over the place.
I wish the hedgehog would eat them for me.'

'Let's leave the cat food by the kitchen door,'
said Sallie. 'We could leave the door open a
little way, and if it's a nice kind hedgehog it will
come in and eat our beetles, Isn't that a good
idea, Mummy?'

So that night the two children put down a
saucer of cat food by the back door, and left the
door just a little bit open – enough for a little
hedgehog to creep through if it wanted to.

Next morning the cat food was still there.

Sallie and John wondered if the hedgehog had seen it, but had made up its mind to eat the beetles instead.

'Let's creep downstairs and see tonight,' said Sallie. So that night, when everyone was asleep in bed, and the clock had struck twelve, the two children crept downstairs to the kitchen. They hated to go to the kitchen late at night, because of the beetles there, but they did so badly want to see if the hedgehog had come back.

He had! Well, you should have seen him! He was scurrying about the floor, gobbling up the nasty black beetles as fast as ever he could! They came out from the nooks and crannies under the warm stove, where they had lived for years, and as soon as the hedgehog saw them he ran over to them. His sharp little teeth snapped them up, and that was the end of the beetles!

'Just look!' whispered Sallie. 'That little hedgehog is getting rid of all those horrid beetles that spoil our kitchen! Beetles that live in kitchens have to be destroyed, Mummy says, but she has never been able to send them off before! Now the hedgehog is doing it for us!'

As soon as the hedgehog heard their voices he ran straight out of the kitchen door in fright. The children stayed quite quiet – and soon they saw his sharp little snout peeping in again. 'Is everything quiet?' he seemed to say. 'Then I will get back to my supper!'

Back he came, and soon the black beetles hurried away to their holes in fear. The children went back to bed longing to tell their mother all they had seen.

'We know why the hedgehog doesn't eat his cat food!' said Sallie to their mother next morning. 'It's because he's doing you a good turn, Mummy, and eating all your black beetles for you!'

'The kind little fellow!' said Mother. 'I did hope he would. We will leave a little cat food out each night for him, and as soon as he begins to eat it we shall know he has cleared out all those beetles for us!'

That little hedgehog came back to the kitchen every single night, and in a week's time, when Sallie was sitting in the kitchen, there was not a single beetle to be seen.

'Well, Mummy,' she said, 'all those creepy-crawly beetles have gone. I hope they don't come back.'

'They won't come back, Sallie!' said Mother. 'The hedgehog has eaten them all! Hasn't he been a good friend to us!'

'Well,' said Sallie. 'The hedgehog we got out of the tennis net must have said to itself: "One good turn deserves another!" and that's why it ate your beetles!'

'I shouldn't be surprised,' said Mother. 'It's always best to be kind to everything, big or little, smooth or prickly. You never know when you might need their help!'

The Cold Snowman

It happened once that some children built a great big snowman. You should have seen him! He was as tall as you, but much fatter, and he wore an old top hat, so he looked very grand. On his hands were woollen gloves, but they were rather holey. Down his front were large round pebbles for buttons and round his neck was an old woollen scarf. He really looked very grand indeed.

The children went indoors at tea-time, and didn't come out again, because it was dark. So the snowman stood all alone in the back yard, and he was very lonely.

He began to sigh, and Foolish-One, the little elf who lived under the old apple tree, heard him and felt sorry. He ran out and spoke to the snowman.

'Are you lonely?' he asked.

'Very,' answered the snowman.

'Are you cold?' asked Foolish-One.

'Who wouldn't be in this frosty weather?' said the snowman.

'I'm sorry for you,' said Foolish-One. 'Shall I sing to you?'

'If you like,' said the snowman. So the elf began to sing a doleful little song about a star that fell from the sky and couldn't get back. It was so sad that the snowman cried a few tears, and they froze at once on his white, snowy cheeks.

'Stop singing that song,' he begged the elf. 'It makes me cry, and it is very painful to do that when your tears freeze on you. Ooooh! Isn't the wind cold?'

'Poor snowman!' said Foolish-One, tying the snowman's scarf so tightly that he nearly choked.

'Don't do that!' gasped the snowman. 'You're strangling me.'

'You have no coat,' said Foolish-One, looking sadly at the snowman. 'You will be frozen stiff before morning.'

'Oooh!' said the snowman, in alarm. 'Frozen stiff! That sounds dreadful! I wish I wasn't so cold.'

'Shall I get you a nice warm coat?' asked the elf. 'I have one that would keep you very cosy.'

'Well, seeing that you only come up to my knees, I'm afraid that your coat would only be big enough for a handkerchief for me,' said the snowman. 'Ooh! There's that cold wind again.'

Just then a smell of burning came over the air, and the elf sniffed it. He jumped to his feet in excitement. Just the thing!

'Snowman!' he cried. 'There's a bonfire. I can smell it. Let us go to it and warm ourselves.'

The snowman tried to move. He was very heavy, and little bits of snow broke off him. But at last he managed to shuffle along somehow, and he followed the dancing elf down the garden path to the corner of the garden where the bonfire was burning.

'Here we are!' said the elf, in delight. 'See what a fine blaze there is. Come, snowman, draw close, and I will tell you a story.'

The snowman came as close to the fire as he could. It was certainly very warm. He couldn't feel the cold wind at all now. It was much better.

'Once upon a time,' began the elf, 'there was a princess called Marigold. Are you nice and warm, snowman?'

'Very,' said the snowman, drowsily. The heat was making him sleepy. 'Go on, Foolish-One.'

'Now this princess lived in a high castle,' went on Foolish-One, leaning against the snowman as he talked. 'And one day – are you sure you're quite warm, snowman?'

'Very, very warm,' murmured the snowman, his hat slipping to one side of his head. Plonk! One of his stone buttons fell off. Plonk! Then another. How odd!

Foolish-One went on with his story. It wasn't a very exciting one, and the snowman hardly listened. He was so warm and sleepy. Foolish-One suddenly felt sleepy, too. He stopped in the middle of his tale and shut his eyes. Then very gently he began to snore.

He woke up with a dreadful jump, for he heard a most peculiar noise.

'Sizzle-sizzle-sizzle, ss-ss-sss-ss!'

Whatever could it be? He jumped up. The fire was almost out. The snowman had gone! Only his hat, scarf and gloves remained, and they were in a pile on the ground.

'Who has put the fire out?' cried Foolish-One in a rage. 'Snowman, where are you? Why have you gone off and left all your clothes? You will catch your death of cold!'

But the snowman didn't answer. He was certainly quite gone. Foolish-One began to cry.

The fire was quite out now, and a pool of water lay all round it. Who had poured the water there? And where, oh where, was that nice snowman?

He called him up the garden and down. He hunted for him everywhere. Then he went home and found his thickest coat and warmest hat. He put them on, took his stick and went out.

'I will find that snowman if it takes me a thousand years to do it!' he cried. And off he went to begin his search. He hasn't found him yet! Poor Foolish-One, I don't somehow think he ever will!

The Big Green Handkerchief

Twinkle the elf had a big green handkerchief that he was very fond of. He always put it into his pocket on Saturday, which was market day, for then he could pull it out and show it to a lot of people.

One Saturday he put it into his pocket as usual and went off to market. When he got there he went round looking at all the cows and sheep, and he bought himself three new-laid eggs and a pound of yellow butter.

Just as he was turning a corner he fell over a duck that was wandering about by itself. Bang! Over went Twinkle and hit his head on the pavement. Everyone ran to pick him up and made a fuss of him.

'He's cut his head,' said kind Mother Dimple. 'We must bandage it up.'

A little bit of the green handkerchief was sticking out of Twinkle's pocket, so Mother Dimple pulled it out and bandaged Twinkle's head with it. He didn't notice what she was doing for he really felt quite bad. But soon he felt better, especially when someone brought him a nice hot sausage roll to eat.

He got up, dusted his trousers and said thank you. Then off he went. He hadn't gone very far before he met Mr Whiskers, who had a very fine red handkerchief in his pocket, which he showed to Twinkle.

'See what I had for my birthday,' he said. Then Twinkle put his hand in his pocket to show Mr Whiskers his fine green handkerchief – and it wasn't there! Dear, dear! He turned out all his pockets one after another, but it wasn't in any of them. Whatever could have happened to it? Someone must have stolen it out of his pocket!

He rushed off to see if he could find it. He saw something green in the distance and he ran after it. It was sticking out from underneath Dame Penny's arm. *She* must have taken his handkerchief! Twinkle tugged at it – and oh, my goodness me, it wasn't a handkerchief after all, but a green sunshade!

Dame Penny was angry! She shook her sunshade at Twinkle and said she would spank him with it. He rushed off in a great hurry.

Then he saw something green going round the corner. That must be his handkerchief. Off he raced and turned the corner. The muffin-man was going down the street and on his head was a tray covered by something green.

'That's my handkerchief!' thought Twinkle, and he rushed up to the muffin-man. He tore the covering from the tray – but, oh dear, dear, dear, it was the green cloth that the muffin-man always used to cover up his muffins! He *was* cross with Twinkle!

'I'll smack you if I catch you!' he cried. But Twinkle was off!

Then he saw something green hanging out on Mother Crotchety's line – it must be his hand-kerchief! He crept into the garden and tore the green thing off the line – but Mother Crotchety was there and she boxed his ears.

'What do you mean by taking my nice green duster!' she shouted. 'You naughty little elf!'

Twinkle ran out of the gate. This was dreadful. Wherever in the world could his handkerchief be?

'It's no good,' he said. 'I must go home. I shall never find it.'

So he went down the street to his cottage, feeling very sad indeed.

'I shall never see my handkerchief again,' he sighed.

When he reached home his little wife cried out in surprise to see him with his head bound up.

'Oh, I just fell down and hurt myself,' said Twinkle.

'Well, let me bathe the place,' said his little wife, and she carefully undid the bandage. She placed it on the table and Twinkle saw it. He stared and stared and stared.

'Ooh, my!' he said, in astonishment. 'There's my handkerchief. Was it on my head all the time, little wife?'

'Of course,' said his wife surprised. 'Why?'

'Because I've been rushing about all over the place taking things I thought were my green handkerchief, and all the time it was round my head,' groaned Twinkle. 'What a silly I am!'

He was a bit of a silly, wasn't he!

The Golden Peacock

Once upon a time, many thousands of years ago when the world was very young, a cobbler going on his rounds found something glittering in the dusty road. He picked it up, and found, to his surprise, that it was a golden peacock.

It was small, and most beautifully made. It had rubies for eyes, and in its outspread tail were set many tiny jewels. It was a lovely thing.

The cobbler was an honest man and he took his find to the King.

'Ah!' said the King, turning it over and over in his hand. 'This is a treasure beyond price. See how beautifully wrought this peacock is! How many weeks, how many months have gone to the setting of these tiny jewels in the fine, outspread tail! I should like to buy this golden peacock and set it on my marble shelf where all may see it. I will send a messenger through the land proclaiming the find, asking the maker of the peacock to come forward.'

The messenger was sent out – and the next week, to the King's surprise, two men came to claim the peacock!

'What?' cried the King. 'You both own the golden peacock? That is impossible. One of you is speaking falsely.'

The two men glared at one another. One was called Moola, and the other Gron. Both were workers in silver and gold, and each vowed that he had made the golden peacock himself, and lost it on a journey.

The King looked at them sternly.

'One of you does not speak the truth,' he said. 'It would be easy for me to send to your towns, and ask your friends which of you has made the peacock, for such a marvellous piece of work is sure to be well-known.'

'Sire,' said Moola, at once, 'it would be of no use sending to my town, for no one knows of this peacock. I did it in secret, for my own pleasure, and no one has seen the lovely bird. I was keeping it to take to the great market in the autumn.'

'So!' said the King, mockingly. 'It was a secret! And you, Gron, what do you say? Was the peacock also a secret with you? Will those in your town know of this golden bird?'

'Sire,' said Gron, his hands trembling as he spoke, 'none but myself knows of the bird. I made it in secret, and these words are the truth.'

The King laughed in scorn. 'I believe you both speak falsely,' he said. 'Tell me, Gron, why should you fashion such a marvellous thing in secret? Have you a reason like Moola's?'

'I have a reason,' said Gron, 'but it is not like Moola's. I made the golden bird for my little daughter's birthday. It was to be a surprise, and none knew of it save myself. I spent all my nights on the bird, Sire, and each of those little jewels took me a whole week to set to my liking.'

'False fellow!' shouted Moola, the other goldsmith. '*I* set those tiny jewels in the tail! Many, many days did I work on those finely-wrought feathers, and the beak I modelled no less than eleven times before it was perfect!'

'Silence,' said the King sternly. 'Now this is a puzzle harder than any I had to solve before. So lovely is this bird that I had resolved to buy it from its rightful owner – but it seems that both of you are the owners, though how that can be is beyond my understanding.'

'It is mine!' said Moola, sulkily.

'Nay, it is mine!' cried Gron, falling on his knees.

'Give it to me, o King, and I will sell it to you for half the price you meant to give!' said Moola. The King turned to Gron.

'And you?' he asked. 'Would you also sell it to me for half the price I had meant to give, if I award the bird to you, Gron?'

Gron was silent.

'Answer me,' commanded the King.

'Sire,' said Gron, stammering in his nervousness, 'as I told you, it was meant for my little daughter. I would rather give it to her for whom it was meant.'

The King looked at both the men for a long moment. Then he spoke.

'Seeing that both of you say you own the bird,' he said, at last, 'and I have no means of finding out which of you speaks the truth, I can do no better than to order the bird to be cut in half. Then one of you shall have the head and the other the tail. For that you must draw lots.'

'Agreed, o King,' said Moola, at once. Gron was silent.

'And you, Gron, do you agree?' asked the King, looking at the pale goldsmith.

Gron threw himself down before the King.

'Do not cut the bird in half, Sire!' he cried. 'It is so beautiful! I spent so much labour on it! It would spoil it to be halved. What is the use of a head or tail? The bird is not just gold and jewels, it is a piece of loveliness. I would rather Moola had it in all its beauty, and sold it to you, than that I should see the work of my hands spoilt. Keep it whole, and give it to Moola. I go, o King!'

With that Gron stumbled towards the door, but the King called him back.

'Return to your place, Gron,' he said in a kindly voice. 'The bird is yours. I would not spoil such loveliness. It was a test to find the rightful owner. I knew that he who made this golden bird would never wish to see it spoilt, even though he might lose it himself. Take it, Gron, and give it to your little daughter. And, in your spare time, make me another like it, and charge your own price. I will buy it from you when you please.'

Gron took the golden peacock, hardly able to believe his ears. Tears poured down his cheeks, and he could say no word. He had spent so much time, so much loving labour on the lovely bird, and it had grieved him to lose it. Now he could give it to his little daughter, as he had planned, and with loving care could fashion yet another peacock for the King himself. He was a proud and happy man.

But Moola shook with fear and turned as yellow as a ripe pear with fright.

'Take him to prison,' ordered the King.

'No, let him go, o King,' begged Gron, merciful in his happiness. 'I bear him no malice. Let him go.'

'You have beauty in your soul as well as in your clever hands!' said the King. 'Come to live at my court, Gron – I have need of such men as you.'

So Gron came to live at the court, and spent the rest of his long life happy in making the palace beautiful for his wise master, the King.

The Brownie and the Gnome

The brownie Beppy and the gnome Noggle were having a fierce quarrel. It was the gnome's fault. He said that the brownie had stolen the yellow brooch that he, Noggle, always wore in the front of his coat, and Beppy the brownie, who was a very honest little fellow, declared a hundred times that he hadn't!

'Well,' said Noggle fiercely, 'you were the only person walking with me when I missed the brooch, weren't you? We were walking through the woods together, and suddenly I felt the pin of my brooch open and the brooch fell – but when I looked on the ground for it, it wasn't there. So somehow or other, you, Beppy, must have picked it up and pocketed it!'

'I didn't, I didn't!' shouted Beppy, dancing about in a rage.

'Well, I warn you, Beppy,' said Noggle, pointing his finger at the brownie in a very nasty manner, 'I warn you – I shall come in the middle of one night and take something of *yours*. Yes, I shall! Something you like very much, just to pay you out for stealing my brooch. I expect I shall take your green necklace.'

'You won't, you shan't!' said Beppy angrily. 'Anyway, I shall hear you and chase you away.'

'I shall come so quietly that you won't hear a sound!' said Noggle. 'I shall get a Silent Spell from my aunt Dame Whispers. Then my feet won't make the tiniest noise at all.'

He did just what he said. He went to Dame Whispers and bought a Silent Spell, and then he planned to go to Beppy's and take his green necklace. He thought he had better wait until the moon was out of the sky, for the nights were just then very bright with moonlight. So he waited for six days and nights, and then decided to creep to the brownie's at midnight.

He looked at the little silver watch on his wrist. It was eleven o'clock. He would go in twenty minutes' time, then he would arrive at Beppy's just about the middle of the night when the brownie would be sound asleep. He wouldn't wake him because the Silent Spell would be in his feet, and they wouldn't make a single sound.

In twenty minutes' time he went to the door

and looked out. The night was very dark indeed. There wasn't even a small moon – in fact, the sky was so dark with clouds that Noggle felt certain it would soon rain. So he thought he would take his umbrella with him. He took it out of the hall-stand, looked at his watch again, and decided that it was time to start.

Out he went into the darkness, glad to think he was going to punish Beppy for stealing his brooch. It wasn't raining yet, so he didn't put up his umbrella. He walked along the lane, his feet making no sound at all. The Silent Spell was a very good one.

It was just midnight when he reached Beppy's cottage. Without a sound he opened a window and crept inside. He made his way up the stairs, without a single creak, to the brownie's bedroom. He opened the door and stood inside the room, listening to see if the brownie was asleep.

Beppy was asleep. He heard no sound of footsteps. He heard no creak. He heard no shuffling – but in his dreams he heard something else. His sharp little brownie ears heard the sound of a watch ticking! The watch that Noggle the gnome wore on his wrist had rather a loud tick, and the Silent Spell wasn't made for watches

– only for feet. So the watch ticked out in the darkness and came to the sleeping brownie's ears.

He woke up. He listened to the little tick-tick-tick that he could hear quite plainly. What could it be? It wasn't loud enough for a clock, and anyway, there wasn't a clock in the bedroom. It must be a watch. But Beppy had taken his watch to be mended that very day, so it couldn't be *his* watch ticking.

Then it must be someone else's – and that someone else must be standing in his bedroom in the dark! Ooh!

Beppy was just going to shout loudly when he thought:'Ah! It must be Noggle, come to steal my necklace! He has a Silent Spell in his feet, but he forgot about his watch! I'll give him a fright.'

Beppy sat up quietly in bed.

'I see you, Noggle,' he said, in an awful hollow voice. 'I see you. You're standing over there in the dark, thinking I can't see or hear you. But I can! And I'm going to put a spell on you! I'm going to turn on a tap behind you and make you wet from head to foot. Look out!'

As he spoke Beppy took up a glass of water by his bedside and threw the water at the corner where he could hear the tick-tick of the watch. It fell on Noggle's head and wetted him. He really thought a tap had been turned on behind him, and, howling in fright, he turned and ran down the stairs, almost falling over in his fear.

When he got outside it was pouring with rain. He put up his umbrella at once – and something fell out of it on to the ground. What could it be? Noggle lit a match and looked. Goodness, gracious, it was his little yellow brooch!

Noggle looked at it in surprise. Then he went very red. He guessed at once what had happened. When it had fallen from his coat in the wood, it had tumbled into his umbrella, and neither he nor Beppy had thought of looking there! So Beppy hadn't taken it after all!

'Beppy! Beppy! I've found my yellow brooch!' cried Noggle, rushing back into the cottage. 'It had fallen into my umbrella. I've just found it. Oh, do forgive me for being so nasty. And do tell me how you knew I was in your bedroom tonight.'

Beppy lit his lamp and the two looked at the yellow brooch. They began to laugh – and how they laughed! Noggle poked Beppy in the ribs and Beppy poked Noggle, and they teased one another and forgot all about their silly quarrel.

'Well, *next* time you want to come and take my green necklace, remember to leave your watch at home!' said Beppy. 'I heard it ticking and that's how I knew you were there!'

'There won't be any next time,' said Noggle. 'We'll be good friends now.'

And so they are!'

The Inside-out Stocking

Once there was a little boy called Rex, who was always having bad luck. People were quite sorry for him because he was so unlucky.

If he ran too fast he fell down and hurt his knee. If he climbed into a swing, he soon fell out. If he had a pound given to him, it was lost through a hole in his pocket. That was the kind of little boy he was.

There was one thing he was very good at, and that was running races. He could run really fast, and could beat anyone if only he didn't catch his foot against something and tumble over! He wasn't good at jumping, and he wasn't good at swimming, but it really was marvellous to see him run.

Now in the field near his home a sports day was going to be held. All the schools of the town were to meet there and see which one was the best at running, jumping, slow bicycle racing, obstacle races and other things. It would be great fun.

'I hope you will win the running race for us,' said the headmaster of his school to Rex. 'You ought to, my boy, for you are a splendid runner for your age.'

'I'll do my best, sir,' answered Rex, 'but I'm a very unlucky person, you know. I never win anything. I'm always losing things, or hurting myself, or getting into trouble. I can't seem to help it!'

'Rex is sure to get measles or mumps on the day of the race!' said one of the bigger boys. 'He caught chicken-pox on Christmas Day. He has no luck at all!'

Now Rex had a small sister called Lucy, who loved him very much indeed. She was quite a lucky little person, and she was always very sad because Rex was so unlucky. Just fancy, he hadn't even been able to go to the seaside in the holidays because he had broken his leg and had to go away to hospital!

Lucy was always afraid of what might happen next to Rex. She hardly dared to plan anything nice for him in case something unlucky happened. She was very pleased when she heard about the sports day, for she felt sure that if only Rex were able to run in the race he would win it, for certain! But suppose it was another of his unlucky days?

'I *do* wish I could make certain sure that Rex would have a lucky day instead of an unlucky day on the sports day!' thought Lucy. 'I think I'll go and see old Mother Brown, who lives in that funny little cottage at the end of our village. People say she is very old and very wise, so perhaps she could tell me how to help Rex.'

The very next day she went. She took with her an egg laid by her own little white hen to give to Mother Brown. The old lady was very pleased and told Lucy to sit down in the big rocking-chair.

'Mother Brown, could you tell me how a person can be lucky?' asked Lucy, rocking herself to and fro in the big chair.

'Well, a black cat brings luck,' said Mother Brown. Lucy thought that was no use to her because there were no black cats near her home.

'What else?' she asked the old woman.

'Well, a piece of white heather is lucky,' said Mother Brown. That was no use to Lucy either, for no heather of any sort grew near her village.

'Then, of course, it's lucky if you get up in the morning and put on your stocking inside-out without noticing,' said Mother Brown. 'That's really very lucky – only most people notice what they're doing and turn their stocking the right way out.'

Lucy's eyes brightened. Ah, here was something she could do! Suppose she crept into her brother's bedroom the night before the sports and turned one of his stockings inside-out! If he didn't notice it, it might make him very lucky that day and he would win the race. She would try it!

So on the night before the sports day Lucy lay wide awake in bed, waiting for Rex to fall asleep. When she thought he really *must* be asleep she crept into his room and quickly turned one of his stockings inside-out. Then back to bed she scampered and soon fell asleep herself.

The next morning Lucy looked anxiously at Rex to see if his stocking was on inside-out. It was! He had put it on without noticing it. Lucy was full of delight. Now what would happen?

Everything went smoothly that day. Rex was happy, and felt certain he was going to win the race. He and Lucy went to the sports field at the right time and stood there waiting to be told what to do. Then suddenly Lucy heard one of the teachers talking.

'Look at that boy over there! He's got his stocking on inside-out! How careless of him. It looks very untidy. Lucy, you're his sister, aren't you? Go and tell him to change his stocking and put it right. Quickly, or there will be no time!'

Poor Lucy! She didn't know what to do. Then she made up her mind that whatever happened, she wouldn't take away Rex's luck. She ran up to him, and instead of telling him about his stocking, she whispered to him to go away to the other side of the field with her. Off they went, and the teacher who had sent her to Rex watched them both in annoyance. Whatever was that naughty little Lucy doing?

But the races were beginning! First one race and then another – the jumping – then the slow bicycle race – then the egg and spoon race – and whatever do you think, Rex won that! He didn't drop his egg once, and he was so surprised and pleased.

He won the running race too! Once he stumbled and almost fell – but not quite! He finished well ahead of all the other children and everyone clapped and cheered loudly. Lucy clapped loudest of all.

'Well, wasn't I lucky today!' cried Rex, very pleased and proud. 'I can't think what happened to me! I really can't. Look at my running prize, Lucy – a fine football. You and I will have plenty of good games with it! I saw your excited

face when I was running that race. I shouldn't
be surprised if you brought me luck!'

Lucy didn't tell him what she had done. His
stocking was still inside-out, and he didn't know
it!

'I'll creep into his room each time I want him
to have a lucky day, and turn one of his
stockings inside-out again,' thought the little
girl. 'I mustn't tell him or he might notice
another time. How lovely that I know a lucky
trick like that!'

I think she was rather a nice little girl, don't
you? Rex often has lucky days now, and he can't
think why. But I can!

The Clockwork Mouse
and the Bird

In the toy-cupboard lived a clockwork mouse and a pecking-bird. The clockwork mouse was a dear little thing, and ran all over the floor when he was wound up. But the pecking-bird was a tiresome nuisance.

He was supposed to peck up crumbs from the floor, but instead of that he pecked the other toys! He thought it was very funny to do that. He used to get the old red duck to wind him up and then off he would go, peck-peck-peck, nipping the teddy-bear, pecking the curly-haired doll and jabbing the railway train.

One day he pecked the clockwork mouse and nipped a big piece of fur from his back. It left a bare patch, and the mouse was cross.

'What do you think you're doing?' he cried angrily. 'Leave me alone! See what a nasty bald place you have given me! You are a great nuisance!'

The pecking-bird laughed, and nipped the

little mouse again. Peck! Another bit of fur flew off, and the mouse squeaked in pain. Peck! This time the pecking-bird nipped at the mouse's key and it flew out of his side. The pecking-bird ran after the key, pecked at it, and swallowed it!

Now whatever do you think of that? Wasn't that a dreadful thing to do? The toys all stared at the pecking-bird in horror, because, as you can guess, it is a terrible thing to lose your key if you happen to be clockwork. It means you don't work any more – you can't move, or walk, or run, or peck, or whatever it is you do when you are wound up.

'Where's my key?' squealed the clockwork mouse in excitement. 'Where is it? Give it back to me, you wicked pecking-bird!'

'I can't,' said the pecking-bird, pleased. 'It's inside me!'

The teddy-bear thumped the pecking-bird on his back, hoping to make him choke and cough up the key. But it only gave him hiccups, and the key stayed inside him.

The little mouse wept so many tears that his feet were wet with standing in the tear-puddle he made. The toys were very, very sorry for him, and very angry with the unkind pecking-bird. But they really didn't know what to do, because they were all half afraid of the pecking-bird.

Then the brown toy dog had a wonderful idea. He called the toys into a corner and whispered to them.

'Have you ever noticed,' he said, 'that the key of the pecking-bird always looked just the same as the key of the clockwork mouse? Suppose, just suppose, that the bird's key fits the mouse? Wouldn't that be grand? Then we could give the mouse the key and the pecking-bird wouldn't have one – except inside him, where it wouldn't be any use!'

'Ooh!' said all the toys, in delight. 'We'll wait till the pecking-bird is asleep and then we'll slip his key out of him and try it in the clockwork mouse!'

So when the pecking-bird stood fast asleep in a corner the teddy-bear crept up to him and carefully pulled out his key. Then he hurried up to the waiting clockwork mouse.

It fitted! Yes, it really did! Quickly the bear wound up the mouse and the little creature ran merrily over the nursery floor. The pecking-bird heard him and woke up.

He stared in astonishment at the mouse. Then he called to his friend, the red duck. 'Duck, come and wind me up quickly! I'm going to peck that noisy mouse! How dare he get another key!'

The duck waddled up. She looked first this side of the pecking-bird and then the other.

'I don't see your key,' she said, puzzled.

'Don't be silly!' said the bird impatiently. 'Are you blind? Look closer and you'll see it sticking out.'

'Indeed, I see nothing but a hole where it went,' said the red duck.

Then the pecking-bird became anxious and looked himself – and to his great dismay he saw that his key was indeed gone.

'Where's my key?' he screamed.

'I've got it, I've got it!' squeaked the mouse in delight and ran right up to the pecking-bird to show him.

'You thief!' cried the pecking-bird, trying to peck. But of course he couldn't move his head at all. He wasn't wound up.

'No more thief than you are!' answered the mouse. 'You took my key, and I've got yours. Fair exchange is no robbery, you know! Ho, ho, what a joke! You've got my key inside you and you can't use it!'

'It serves you right!' said the teddy-bear. 'You

were always unkind, pecking-bird, and now you can't be horrid any more. If you hadn't taken the mouse's key this would never have happened. You can just stand in your corner now and be forgotten.'

So there stands the pecking-bird in his corner, never moving. But they do say that every now and again the kind-hearted little clockwork mouse takes out his key and puts it into the pecking-bird. Then for a little time the bird comes to life again – but he is not alllowed to keep the key for long! No – the toys don't trust him, and I don't blame them, do you?

The Spotted Cow

There was once rather a vain cow. She was plain white with two nice curly horns. She thought she looked rather nice – but she did wish she could have some nice black spots over her back. There were no spotted cows in the field at all, and the white cow thought it would be grand to be the only spotted cow.

Now one day, when she was munching the long, juicy grass that grew in the hedge, she came across a small pixie mixing black paint in a pot.

'What are you doing?' asked the cow.

'I'm mixing my black paint,' said the little fellow. 'I'm the pixie that paints the spots on the ladybirds, you know.'

'Oh!' said the cow. 'Well, will you paint some on me?'

'Yes, if you'll give me a nice drink of milk,' said the pixie.

'I don't mind doing that,' said the cow. 'You

can find a tin mug, and milk some of my creamy milk into it for yourself.'

'I'll just finish these ladybirds first,' said the pixie, and he turned back to his work. In a long line stood about twenty ladybirds with bright red backs and no spots. The pixie neatly painted seven black spots on each red back, and the ladybirds flew off in delight.

When he had finished his work he looked at the waiting cow. 'I'll go and find my mug,' he said. 'I'm very thirsty, and I'd love a drink of your nice milk.'

He ran off and came back with a mug. On it was his name: 'Pixie Pinnie'. He milked the cow, and took a mugful of her creamy milk. Then he began to mix some more black paint.

'Are you sure you'd like *black* spots?' he asked. 'You wouldn't like a few blue ones, or red ones? You would look most uncommon then.'

The cow thought about it. 'No,' she said at last. 'I don't think so. I'd rather have black spots. They will look smarter than coloured ones.'

'Well, you must stand still,' said the pixie, 'or I might smudge the spots, and that would look horrid. Now then – are you ready?'

The pixie began to paint the cow. Goodness,

you should have seen him! A big black spot here, and a little one there! Two by her tail, and three down her back. Four in a ring on her nose, and a whole crowd of spots down her sides. She *did* look grand!

At last the pixie had finished. He put away his paints, took another drink of milk, and said 'goodbye'. The cow left him and went back to the field. How grand she felt!

The other cows stared at her. They didn't know her. Who was this funny spotted cow?

'Don't you know me?' said the cow, proudly. 'I've grown spots.'

'Rubbish!' said the biggest cow. 'Grown spots, indeed. You don't belong to us. Go away, you horrid, spotted creature, we don't want anything to do with you!'

Just then the little boy who looked after the cows came along to see if they were all right. When he saw the spotted one he stared in surprise.

'You're not one of our cows,' he said. 'You must have wandered in here from somewhere else. You had better get out of the field, and go back to your own meadow, wherever it is! What an ugly, spotted creature you are! I'm glad you're not one of *our* cows!'

He opened the gate and pushed the surprised cow out. She trotted down the lane angrily. 'I'll go to the next field,' she thought. 'The cows there will be pleased to have such a fine spotted creature as I am!'

But they weren't pleased! They mooed at her and sent her away. She was very miserable.

'I wish I hadn't got spots now,' she thought to herself. 'It was a mistake. I'll find that pixie, and ask him to take them away.'

But he was gone. She couldn't see him anywhere. Then it began to rain. The cow stood under a tree to shelter herself, but the rain was so heavy that she was soon wet from horn to tail – and, dear me, the black spots all came out in the rain! Soon there were none left at all.

The cow didn't know that the rain had washed the black spots away. She stood there, feeling lonely and miserable, and when the rain had stopped she made up her mind to go back to her own field, and ask the other cows to have her back again. So off she went, whisking her big tail from side to side.

The little boy was still there. He saw her as she came, and now that she had no spots, he knew her for one of his own cows. So he opened the gate, and let her through, saying: 'Dear me,

wherever have you been?'

The other cows crowded round her, for, now that she had no spots, they knew her too.

'We are glad to see you,' they said. 'Do you know, a horrible spotted cow came in your place, and said she was you. She's gone now, thank goodness. Ugly creature that she was! How dared she say she was you, for you are so white and pretty!'

The cow didn't say anything. She listened and hung her head. It was better to be white and pretty than to be handsome and spotted. She didn't look so grand now, but she was herself.

'I hope that pixie doesn't give me away,' she thought. 'The cows *will* laugh at me, if he does!'

But I don't expect he will!

The Cross Caterpillar

Once upon a time there was a little green and yellow caterpillar who lived on a big green cabbage with his brothers and sisters. He hadn't been very long hatched out of an egg but he didn't know that. He was just a bit bigger than the others, and he thought himself very grand indeed.

He ate all day long. He chose the tenderest and juiciest bit of cabbage for himself, and was very angry if another caterpillar dared to share it. He would stand up on his tail end then and look very fierce indeed.

He grew bigger and bigger. He had a few hairs on him here and there, and as he grew bigger they grew longer. He was an artful caterpillar too. He knew quite well that if a shadow came across the cabbage it might be a bird hunting for caterpillars and then he would huddle into a crinkle of the cabbage and keep as still as a stalk. Some of his brothers and sisters were eaten, but not the artful caterpillar. Oh, no, he was far too clever.

One day, when he was quite big, a pretty fluttering creature came to the cabbage. It was a white butterfly with black spots. It sat down on the cabbage and waved its feelers about. The caterpillar peered over the edge of the cabbage leaf and looked at it. When it saw that it was a mild and harmless-looking creature, the caterpillar flew into a temper and cried, 'Get off my cabbage! I was just going to eat this leaf!'

'Gently, gently!' said the butterfly, looking at the cross caterpillar. 'This is as much my cabbage as yours, caterpillar.'

'It certainly isn't!' said the caterpillar, standing up on his hind legs and waving himself about. But the butterfly was not at all frightened. It opened and closed its lovely white wings and laughed.

'You don't know what you are talking about,' said the butterfly. 'I have come to lay my eggs here. I shall lay them on the underneath of the leaf you are sitting on. It is, as you have found out, a tender, juicy leaf, fit for my eggs.'

The caterpillar was as angry as could be. The butterfly took no notice of it at all. She began to lay neat little rows of eggs in exactly the place where the caterpillar had planned to eat his dinner. It was too bad!

'Now don't you dare to touch my eggs!' said the butterfly, warningly, as she flew off. 'If you do, I'll tell the pixie who lives by the wall, and she will come and spank you!'

The caterpillar was so angry that he couldn't say a word. But after a while he found his voice and began to talk to the others about it.

'Brother and sister caterpillars,' he said. 'We cannot stand this. Why should those horrid, ugly, flapping butterflies come and steal our cabbage for their silly eggs? Why should they be allowed to laugh at us and do what they like? Is not this our cabbage? Let us eat all these eggs up.'

'Oh, no!' cried the listening caterpillars. 'If we do that the pixie will come along, as the butterfly said, and she might be very cross indeed.'

Just as the caterpillar was opening his mouth to talk again two more white butterflies came up, and when they saw the nice, juicy cabbage they at once began to lay eggs there. The caterpillar was so angry that he rushed at them and tried to push them off. But they flapped their big wings in his face and scared him. When they had gone he sat down and thought hard.

'*I* will go to the pixie who lives by the wall!' he said. 'Yes, I will. I will complain of these horrid, interfering butterflies, and I will ask the pixie to catch them all and keep them in a cage. Then they can do no more mischief to our cabbage!'

'That is a fine idea!' said all the caterpillars, stopping their eating for a moment. 'Go now.'

So the green caterpillar left his cabbage and crawled down the path to the pixie who lived by the wall. She was most surprised to see him.

'I have come to complain of those hateful butterflies who interfere with our cabbage,' said the caterpillar.

'Which butterflies?' asked the pixie in astonishment.

'The white ones with black spots,' said the caterpillar, fiercely. 'I want you to catch them all and keep them in a cage so that they can do no more harm to our cabbage.'

The pixie laughed and laughed, and the caterpillar felt crosser and crosser as he watched her. At last she dried her eyes and said: 'Well, I will promise to do what you say if you will come to me in four weeks' time and ask me again. I will certainly do what you want then.'

The caterpillar went away, content. In four weeks' time all those horrid butterflies would be caught and put in a cage. Ah, that would teach them to come interfering with his cabbage! He was pleased, and proud of himself. He began to eat his cabbage again and in two days he had grown simply enormous.

Then a strange feeling came over him. He wanted to sleep. He was no longer hungry. He felt strange. Some of his brothers and sisters felt sleepy too, and one day they all fell asleep, having first hung themselves up neatly in silken hammocks. They all turned into chrysalides, and kept as still as if they were dead.

After some time they woke up. Our caterpillar awoke first, for he was strong and big. He wanted to get out of the chrysalis bed he was in, so he bit a hole and crawled out. The sun was warm and he stretched himself. He seemed bigger and lighter. How strange!

He saw a white butterfly in the air and at once all his anger came back to him. He would go to the pixie by the wall, for it must surely now be four weeks since he had seen her, and he would make her keep her promise! He set out to walk as he had done before – but to his great amazement he found himself floating in the air.

He screwed his head round and looked at himself. He was flying! Yes, he had four lovely white wings, spotted with black. He was a butterfly!

'I am lovely!' he thought in delight. 'I am a beautiful creature! Look at my fine wings! Oh, how happy I am!'

He flew about in the air, enjoying the sunshine. Suddenly he heard a small voice calling to him and he saw the pixie who lived by the wall. She knew him even though he was no longer a caterpillar.

'Have you come to ask me to keep my promise?' she asked, with a little tinkling laugh. 'I am quite ready to keep it! And the butterfly I will catch first and keep in a cage shall be *you*!'

The butterfly was frightened. He flew high in the air. How foolish he had been! No wonder the pixie had laughed! But how in the world was he to know that one day he would change from a green caterpillar to a white butterfly?

'I am not so wise as I thought I was,' said the butterfly to himself. 'I know nothing! I will be quiet and gentle in future, and I will never lose my temper again!'

Where is he now? In your garden and mine looking for a little butterfly wife to marry – and you may be sure he will say to her, 'Lay your eggs on a cabbage leaf, my dear! It's the best thing to do – and don't you mind what the rude and stupid caterpillars say to you – they don't know anything at all!'

What a Mistake!

Once upon a time the King of Gnomeland had a lovely garden, kept neat and pretty by twenty-one gardeners. The head gardener was a fat and surly gnome called Gurgle. He was a good gardener, but most unpleasant to the gnomes who worked under him. How he scolded them! And never a word of praise did he give them when they did anything good.

They all disliked him, and feared him. He had a horrid habit of creeping round corners very suddenly and pouncing on them to see if they were doing their work properly. He frightened them so much that they dropped whatever they were carrying, and I couldn't tell you how many pots were broken because of Gurgle's sly ways.

Now Gurgle had a special pair of garden scissors that he was very fond of. They were large and sharp, and most comfortable to hold. They were usually kept hanging in the garden shed, and, dear me, wasn't Gurgle angry if anyone borrowed them!

One day the King himself wandered into the shed and saw them. He thought they would be just the thing for cutting off a piece of rose tree that knocked against his bedroom window. So he borrowed them.

And, of course, it *would* happen that Gurgle came along that same afternoon and wanted them himself. When he found that they were not in the shed he was very angry indeed.

He went round roaring and grumbling, and even when he discovered that it was the King himself who had borrowed them, he didn't stop roaring.

'Those are *my* scissors!' he cried. 'I won't have anyone borrowing them, not even the King, that I won't. I'll keep them safely some-where so that no one can borrow them!'

And where do you think he kept them when he got them back? He had a special hat made, and instead of putting a feather into it he put his scissors!

Now Gurgle had a very bad memory indeed. He quite forgot that he had put his scissors into his hat that afternoon, and he went to the garden shed to get them from their usual place. And, of course, they weren't there! How annoying! How aggravating! How very, very vexing!

He began to roar and rage as usual, and everyone came running to see what was the matter.

'My scissors have gone again!' he shouted. 'Who has taken them?'

'Please sir,' said a small gnome, nervously, 'you took them yourself and they . . .'

'I TOOK THEM MYSELF!' shouted the gnome in anger. 'How ridiculous to say a thing like that when I'm looking for them. If I took them myself I'd have them in my hands, wouldn't I?'

'But sir, you've got . . .' began the little gnome, trembling. Gurgle wouldn't let him finish.

'How dare you argue with me!' he roared. 'Go and dig for six hours in the kitchen garden for a punishment.'

Well, of course, nobody else dared say a word after that. They all stood silently round Gurgle, looking at the scissors stuck in his hat, and wishing that Gurgle would remember they were there.

'Now then, who's borrowed them?' roared Gurgle in a fury. 'Whoever it is had better own up before I punish him very, VERY severely. I've got this punishment all written out here and the head cook has promised to come and read it out if I don't get my scissors back at once.'

Nobody said anything at all. Nobody dared to. They stared at Gurgle, wondering whatever was going to happen.

Gurgle clapped his hands. The head cook came running down the path. He was not a nice fellow and the little gnomes didn't like him very much. He was only too pleased to read out a dreadful punishment, and see it happen to one of the gnome gardeners.

'Cook, someone has got my scissors again,' said Gurgle, angrily. 'Will you please stand in the middle of us and read out the punishment. I will stand here and watch to see who the gardener is, and I shall box his ears when I know!'

The head cook cleared his throat and looked at the paper Gurgle handed him. Then he began to read, slowly and loudly. This is what he read:

'Now hear the dreadful punishment for the one who has my scissors at this very moment. May his ears grow long like donkey's ears! May his hair fall out! May his nails grow as long as a tiger's claws! May his nose shoot out like a snake! May . . .'

Gurgle looked round to see who was the gnome to have such a dreadful punishment – and to his surprise no one seemed to change at all! But what was this? Oh, goodness, gracious, what was happening to his ears? To his hair, that was dropping down all round him; to his nails, and to his nose! Oh, his poor nose! It grew as long as a snake and waved about in the air!

Gurgle gave such a shriek that the head cook stopped reading and looked at him in surprise. When he saw what had happened he dropped his paper, began to shake like a leaf, and then ran back to his kitchen as fast as his legs could carry him, crying, 'He's got the scissors in his hat! He's got the scissors in his hat! Ooooooooooh my!'

The gnome gardeners stared at Gurgle with wide eyes. Then they began to laugh. They couldn't help it. Gurgle looked so funny – and to think he had brought his own punishment on himself, too!

'Ho, ho, ho,' they roared. 'Ho, ho, ho!'

The King heard all the noise and came to see what the matter was. When he saw Gurgle standing there looking such a dreadful sight, with tears pouring down his long nose, he didn't know *what* to say.

At last he asked one of the gnomes to explain everything to him, and the little gnome, stammering and trying not to laugh, told the King all that had happened.

The King listened, frowning.

'You are an unkind gnome, Gurgle,' he said, 'to think of such a fearful punishment for someone whose only fault was that they had borrowed your scissors. Why, I myself might have borrowed them again, and this spell would have worked on *me* then. Well, you are certainly well-punished, Gurgle, and I shall do nothing about it. Keep your long ears, your long nails, your long nose and your bald head! It will help you to remember that bad temper and spitefulness always come back to the owner, and harm him more than they harm anybody else!'

So there is Gurgle, humble and ashamed, hoping and hoping that one day he will become his own self once more. He tries to be sweet-tempered, he tries to be fair, and sooner or later he will grow right again. But it is a long time to wait.

What a mistake!

The Cookie Swan

Once upon a time a little girl called Sallie asked a friend to tea.

'Will there be jam and cakes for tea?' Sallie asked her mother.

'You can have some strawberry jam, and I will make you a cookie swan,' said her mother. Sallie was pleased. Her mother could make lovely cookie swans, white, with a black currant eye each side. They swam upright on a cake-plate and looked very grand indeed.

The cookie swan that day was the nicest and best you ever saw. It was so good that when Mother put it upright on a blue dish, the teapot and the jug both cried out in admiration.

'You are just like a real swan!' said the teapot, in a steamy voice.

'You are beautiful,' said the milk jug, in a creamy voice.

'I am a swan,' said the cookie swan, and he actually spread out his wings.

'You're not a *real* swan,' said the teapot. 'You are only a cookie swan.'

'There's no difference,' said the foolish swan. 'A swan is a swan no matter what it is made of.'

'Ah, but there *is* a difference,' said the milk jug, in its rich voice. 'A real swan swims for years on the river, but a cookie swan only lasts a day.'

'How do you mean, only lasts a day?' asked the cookie swan in surprise.

'Well, you are made to be eaten,' said the teapot and milk jug together. 'When Sallie comes in with her friend they will eat you.'

The cookie swan opened his currant eyes wide with fear when he heard this. He had thought himself very grand indeed, and it was dreadful to be told that he was only made to be eaten.

At that moment Sallie and her little friend came running in. Sallie looked at the tea-table and when she saw the big cookie swan swimming proudly on its blue dish she gave a squeal of delight.

'Look!' she said. 'Mother has made us a beautiful cookie swan. You shall eat the head and tail, Lizzie, and I will eat the middle.'

But this was more than the cookie swan could bear. He suddenly flapped his wings and flew straight off the table. When he got to the floor he found his legs and tore off as fast as he could. Sallie shouted when she saw him go.

'Cookie swan, cookie swan, come back and be eaten!'

But the cookie swan only went all the faster, and although Sallie ran after him at top speed he was soon out of sight. He used his wings as well as his legs, and as he went he muttered: 'I won't be gobbled up, I won't, I won't!'

He ran out into the yard where there were many brown and white hens pecking at the ground. They saw him and gazed in surprise. Then the big cock rushed after him, seeing he was a cookie.

'Cookie swan, cookie swan, come back and be eaten!' he crowed.

But the swan only went all the faster, and no matter how fast the cock ran, he couldn't catch the swan. 'I won't be gobbled up, I won't, I won't!' cried the swan as he went down the yard.

He slipped under a gate and came to the pig-sty. The pig was there, rooting in his straw. When he saw the cookie he raised up his snout and sniffed. It smelt good. The pig trotted up to the cookie, who was standing panting for breath by the gate.

The swan saw the pig just in time, and opening his wings, he flew up to the third bar of the gate just out of the pig's reach.

'Cookie swan, cookie swan, come back and be eaten!' grunted the pig.

But the swan wouldn't. He flew up into the air and flapped his way into a dark stable, crying, 'I won't be gobbled up, I won't, I won't!' Inside was a horse, chewing hay from a manger. The swan settled beside him trembling. The horse stopped his chewing and looked in surprise at the swan. A smell of cookie reached his big brown nose and he put back his upper lip to snatch at the swan. But the swan flew down to the ground and ran between his big shaggy hoofs to the door.

'Cookie swan, cookie swan, come back and be eaten!' neighed the horse, disappointed. He tried to go after the swan, but the lower part of the stable door was shut and he could not go out. He stood looking over the top at the cookie swan who was flapping about outside.

'I won't be gobbled up, I won't, I won't!' screeched the cookie swan, as he flapped his cookie wings.

The swan didn't know where to go. Everywhere he went there seemed to be creatures that wanted to eat him. It was dreadful.

Then, away in the distance he saw the duck pond. There were white ducks on it, swimming and diving. It all looked very peaceful and pretty.

'That's the place for me,' said the cookie swan to himself. 'I'll go to the pond and swim about with the ducks. That is what a real swan does, and I will be a real swan. I will not be a cookie swan, made to be eaten!'

So off he went, half running, half flying to the duck pond. He flopped into the water and tried to swim. But cookie swans are not really meant to swim, and he found himself gradually falling over on one side. Splash! He lay quite on his side, one eye in the water. He could not raise himself upright no matter how he tried.

'Help, help!' he cried, as he struggled. A big duck came swimming up at once.

'What's the matter?' she asked.

'I'm a swan and I've come to swim here,' said the cookie swan. 'But I've fallen on my side, and something horrid is happening to me.'

So there was. He was slowly falling to bits in the water. Poor cookie swan!

'If you like, I'll put my beak into the water and you can climb on to it,' said the duck.

'Oh, thank you,' cried the swan. So the duck put her beak into the water and the poor cookie swan scrambled up on it. Then the duck lifted up her beak and began to swim to shore with the swan balanced carefully across it.

But the other ducks saw that this duck was carrying something and they swam after her, quacking loudly. They tried to snap the cookie swan away, and the duck, opening her mouth to quack angrily, found the cookie swan falling down her throat. Oh, what a delicious mouthful! The duck swallowed joyfully, and the cookie swan disappeared.

But as he went, he cried: 'I won't be gobbled up, I won't, I won't!'

And, you know, he never knew he was, so he was quite happy to the very last moment!

Why Did the Giant Laugh?

There was once a kind-hearted giant called Whopping. He was just like his name, simply enormous, with a great big head, long, strong arms, and legs that could stride miles without getting tired.

He was a good-natured creature, and most people liked him. He was gardener to the Lord High Chamberlain of Brownieland, and a very good one he made too, for he could dig twice as fast and twice as much as ten men at once! He could sweep up leaves in a second with his enormous broom, and could carry great loads of bricks or earth in his big barrow. The other gardeners did the planting and the weeding, for Whopping's hands were too big to handle small things. But he loved doing the big things.

Now one day, as he was going home wheeling his big barrow, whom did he see but Mr Dunce and his wife, walking slowly along the road, each carrying a heavy sack, full of carrots and onions for soup.

They had been a long way and they were tired. Whopping felt sorry for them. They lived next door to him, and by the time they reached home he would have had his meal, read his paper, undressed and gone to bed! But then, his long legs took him twice as fast over the fields as Mr Dunce's thin ones and his wife's little fat ones.

The kind-hearted giant stopped and called to the tired couple.

'Hi!' he called. 'Hi, Mr Dunce and Mrs Dunce! Want a lift?'

'Oh, thank you,' said Mr Dunce, looking round. 'But what in?'

'My big wheelbarrow, of course,' said Whopping, laughing. 'It's quite clean, and I can easily take you both. We'll be home in no time!'

'Well, thank you very much,' said Mr and Mrs Dunce. They climbed into the wheelbarrow and sat down side by side. 'We do hope we shan't be too heavy for you.'

'Not a bit, not a bit!' said Whopping. Mr Dunce whispered something to his wife, and they both solemnly lifted up their sacks of onions and carrots and put them on their shoulders.

'What do you want to do that for?' asked

Whopping in surprise. 'Why don't you put your sacks beside you in the barrow? You don't want to be bowed down under their weight all the way home.'

'Oh,' said Mr Dunce, 'we thought perhaps it would be too much for you, carrying us and our heavy sacks too. So I told my wife to put her sack on her shoulder and carry it herself, and I did the same with mine. Then, you see, you would only have *us* to carry, and not our sacks, too.'

Whopping listened and then he roared with laughter. How he laughed! Really, all the trees shook as if they were in a big wind when his laugh went roaring down the road! As for Mr and Mrs Dunce they looked quite offended.

'What's the joke?' asked Mr Dunce, stiffly. 'I don't see anything to laugh at in what I have just said.'

Whopping tried to explain that the two sillies and their sacks were all in the barrow, whether they carried the sacks on their shoulders or not, but he laughed so much that he couldn't say a word. Tears came into his eyes and two of them dropped down Mrs Dunce's neck.

She put up her umbrella at once and sat in the barrow looking most disgusted.

'Rude fellow!' she said to her husband. 'Isn't he an unmannerly, noisy, vulgar fellow, this giant? What does he want to laugh like that for, when you simply make an ordinary remark?'

'I'm sure I don't know,' said Mr Dunce, in a huff. 'A pretty sight we must look sitting in his barrow, and him roaring with laughter behind us as if we were a couple of clowns at a circus! I've a good mind to get out and walk.'

'No, don't let's do that, because my feet are tired,' said Mrs Dunce. 'It doesn't make any difference to him to have us in his barrow, a great, strong fellow like that! Why, I expect he could take ten of us and not feel it.'

Whopping still went on laughing every time he saw the two sacks so carefully perched up on the narrow shoulders of Mr and Mrs Dunce. At last Mr Dunce became very angry indeed, because every time Whopping laughed a great draught blew down Mr Dunce's neck, and he felt sure he would have a sore throat the next day.

He whispered to his wife.

'Wife, put down your sack in the barrow. I will do the same. If the giant is so horrid as to laugh at us for being kind enough to carry our heavy sacks ourselves, he deserves to be punished. He shall now carry our sacks for us as well as ourselves!'

Whopping heard what Mr Dunce said. He saw the little man put down his heavy sack into the barrow and Mrs Dunce did the same. The giant began to laugh all over again. It was too funny, really!

'What are you laughing at now?' asked Mr Dunce, in a temper.

But Whopping couldn't tell him; he was laughing too much. More tears fell out of his eyes and splashed on to Mr Dunce's head. He wiped them off with his handkerchief and spoke loudly to his wife. 'I wish I had brought my mackintosh with me,' he said.

That made Whopping laugh more than ever, and suddenly the barrow tipped over and the two Dunces fell out, sacks and all.

'Oh, dear, I'm so sorry,' said Whopping. 'But really, you shouldn't say such ridiculous things and make me laugh.'

Mr and Mrs Dunce picked up their sacks and walked away huffily. 'You *see*!' said Mr Dunce to his wife. 'As soon as we put our sacks down in the barrow, he wasn't strong enough to carry us and the sacks too, and tipped us out!'

At that Whopping began to roar again, and

the Dunces hurried away as fast as they could. Whether Whopping managed to get home that night or not I have never heard – but I do know that Mr and Mrs Dunce can't guess to this day why Whopping laughed so much! Can you?

Twinkle Gets into Mischief

Twinkle was a mischievous elf if ever there was one! You wouldn't believe the things he did – all the naughtiest things his quick little mind could think of. But one day he went too far, and tried to play tricks on Snorty the Dragon.

Twinkle wasn't afraid of anyone or anything, so when he heard that Snorty the Dragon was looking for someone brave enough to go and paint his cave walls a nice cheerful pink, he thought he would try to get the job. So off he went, carrying a fine big pot of pink paint, whistling gaily as he skipped along.

'Hello!' he said to Snorty, when he got to the cave. 'I hear you want your walls painted a pleasant pink.'

'Quite right,' said Snorty, blowing out some blue smoke from his nostrils.

'That's a clever trick!' said Twinkle. 'I wish I could blow smoke out of *my* nose!'

'Only dragons can do that!' said Snorty

proudly. 'And look at these!'

He suddenly shot out five enormous claws from each foot – but Twinkle didn't turn a hair.

'Splendid!' he said. 'But what a business it must be for you to cut your nails, Snorty! I should think you would need a pair of shears instead of scissors!'

The dragon didn't like being laughed at. He was used to frightening people, not amusing them. So he glared at Twinkle, and blew a flame out of his mouth.

'Ho, *you* don't need matches to light the gas!' chuckled Twinkle.

'That's not funny,' said Snorty sulkily. 'Get on with my painting, please, and make the walls a bright pink. And no more of your cheek, mind!'

'No more of my *tongue*, you mean!' said Twinkle, who did love having the last word. He began to mix his paint and to daub the wall with the bright pink colour. The dragon walked out in a huff and left him to it.

The cave was large and it took Twinkle all the day to do even half of it. When night came there was still half left to do. So he made up his mind to do it the next day. Snorty came back, and ate a sackful of corn for his supper. He liked the pink wall very much.

'Have you heard me roar?' he asked the elf suddenly, longing to give the cheeky little creature a real fright.

'No,' said Twinkle. 'Do roar a bit.'

So the dragon roared his loudest. Well, if you can imagine ten good thunderstorms, mixed up with a thousand dustbin-lids all crashing to the ground at once, and about five hundred dinner-plates breaking at the same time, you can guess a little bit what the dragon's roaring was like. It was really immense.

'What do you think of that?' asked Snorty, when he had finished.

'Well,' said Twinkle, 'how do you expect me to hear you roar when you just whisper like that? I could hardly hear you!'

The dragon was so angry at this cheeky speech that he lifted Twinkle up and opened his mouth and blew smoke all over him. That made the elf angry, and he ran into a corner, very red in the face, making up his mind to play a trick on the dragon the very first chance he had!

The dragon went to bed, and soon the awful sound of his snoring filled the cave. Twinkle couldn't possibly go to sleep, so he looked round for something naughty to do – and he saw the dragon's two pet geese at the end of the cave, their heads tucked under their wings. They were fine birds, as white as snow.

'Ha!' said Twinkle at once. 'I'll paint them pink. That will give old Snorty a fine shock in the morning!'

So he woke up the geese and painted the two surprised birds a brilliant pink. They looked very strange when they were finished. Then Twinkle looked round for something else to paint. He saw the dragon's cat, a great black creature, snoozing by the fire. What fun it would be to give it a pink tail and pink whiskers!

No sooner said than done! Twinkle dipped the cat's whiskers into his paint-pot and then dipped in the tail. What a dreadful sight the poor cat looked!

But that wasn't enough for Twinkle – no, he must do something even more daring than that! He would paint the dragon's beautiful brown tail! So he stole up to the snoring dragon and painted his tail a vivid pink from beginning to end. It didn't suit the dragon a bit!

Then Twinkle hid in a corner to see what the dragon would say. All the pink would easily wash off, so, after the first shock, perhaps the dragon would laugh and think Twinkle was a daring elf.

But, dear me, goodness gracious, buttons and buttercups, stars and moon! The dragon didn't think it was funny, or daring, or clever, or anything else! As soon as he woke up and saw his pink geese, his pink-tailed and pink-whiskered cat, and his own terrible pink tail, he flew into the most dreadful rage that was ever seen!

He roared so loudly that the mountain not far away had its top broken off with the shock. He blew out so much smoke that everyone for miles around wondered where the thick fog came from. He shot flames from his mouth and very nearly burned up his cave, his geese, his cat, himself and poor, frightened Twinkle!

That silly little elf was really almost scared out of his skin. Who would have thought that Snorty would make such a fuss! Goodness gracious! Snorty roared again, and blew out more smoke. Then he began to look for that naughty little Twinkle. Twinkle saw two great red eyes like engine-lamps coming towards him, and he picked up his pot of paint and fled!

How he ran! How he flew! How he jumped and bounded and skipped! And after him galloped Snorty the Dragon, smoke and flames flying behind him and terrible roars filling the air. Right through Fairyland they went, the two of them, for Twinkle didn't dare to stop for a minute.

At last the elf came to the gate of Fairyland itself, and he flew over it. The dragon came up to the gate and roared to the gate-keeper to open it for him – but the pixie shook his head.

'No dragons allowed out of Fairyland,' he said.

'Very well, then, I shall sit here and wait for Twinkle to come back,' roared the dragon, and down he sat, just inside the gate. And there he is still, waiting for the elf to come creeping back again.

But Twinkle is afraid to go back. So he lives in our world now, and he is really quite happy, using his paint and paintbrush all the year round. And what do you think he does? You have often seen his work, though you may not have known it. He paints the tips of the little white daisies on our lawns and in our fields! Go and look for them – you are sure to find a pretty, pink-tipped one. Then you will know that that mischievous elf, Twinkle, is *some*where near. Call him and see if he comes!

How Untidy!

There were once some small brownies who lived in tiny houses at the end of Cherry Wood. They were cheerful, merry little creatures, but how untidy!

Really, you could hardly get into their houses for the mess and muddle they were in! The mats were crooked and needed beating, the curtains were in rags, the chimneys smoked, and every brownie looked as if he could do with a good wash and brush up.

'How untidy!' said the fairies, going by with their noses in the air.

'How untidy!' said the rabbits in disgust.

'How untidy!' said the Fairy Queen herself, as she drove through Cherry Wood and saw the houses of the small brownies. She stopped her carriage and got out.

'Come here,' she said to the scared brownies. 'How dare you keep your houses in such a mess! Now listen to me – if you don't keep them more tidy I shall send old Witch Stamparound to look after you, and you won't like *her*, I can tell you!'

'Oh, please, please, no,' said the brownies, who knew that Witch Stamparound was a terribly strict person.

But they didn't become any more tidy, and one day old Witch Stamparound did arrive! Goodness, you should have seen her! She wore six pairs of spectacles, the better to see any speck of dirt, and her nose was all wrinkled through being turned up in disgust at dirtiness and untidiness!

She set to work to make those brownies tidy. She scolded them, she made them wash, brush, clean, and scrub all day long and sometimes half the night too. They couldn't bear it, and were very unhappy.

'Let's run away!' whispered one.

'She would catch us!' said another.

'Well, let's *fly* away!' said a third.

'That's a good idea,' said the first one. 'The old witch only has her broomstick to fly on. We'll hide that, then she won't be able to chase us.'

'We haven't any wings, so we had better change ourselves into little brown birds,' said the biggest brownie. 'I've got a bird spell somewhere.'

He hunted for it and found it in a dusty drawer. It was a box of tiny yellow pills.

'Where are the spells that will change us back to our own shape?' asked the smallest brownie.

'I've got them safely in my pocket,' said the biggest brownie. 'Now come along, everyone – here's a yellow pill for each of you. As soon as you've swallowed it you'll turn into birds. Spread your wings and fly away. I've hidden the old witch's broomstick!'

They swallowed the pills, and hey presto! each brownie became a small bird, dressed in brown feathers the same colour as their suits had been. They spread their wings and flew away, and although the old witch shouted after them she could not stop them, for she could not find her broomstick anywhere!

But what a dreadful thing – when they arrived at a wood far away, where they would be safe, the biggest brownie, who was now the biggest sparrow, couldn't find the spells to change them back into brownies again. You see, he now had no pockets for he was dressed in feathers, and no matter how he hunted, the pills to change them back again were quite gone!

So little brown birds they had to remain – and they are with us still. You know the sparrows, don't you? How they chatter and chirp, and how they love to come round our houses to be with us!

But, you know, they are still terribly untidy! Have you seen their nests? Go and look for one this year, tucked away somewhere under the eaves, in a gutter pipe. Then you will see how untidy those small brownies are still! Pieces of straw hang down here and there, and the nests really look as if they will fall to bits! And you will say, as the Fairy Queen said about their houses long ago, 'HOW UNTIDY!'

Three Cheers for John!

At John's school they did a great many exciting things in nature lessons. They grew seeds, they kept caterpillars, and there was a big aquarium tank, too, where two little sticklebacks were making a nest. John loved the nature lesson, and he was always going out for walks to find flowers or to watch the birds building their nests and fetching grubs for their little ones.

One child each week took the caterpillars home at the weekend to look after them, for they could not be left on the classroom windowsill from Friday to Monday. John had had his turn, and dear me, the teacher thought they had grown twice as large in John's care! He was very good with everything alive, big or little.

This week it was Billy's turn. He was a careless little boy, and the teacher spoke to him sharply.

'Now, Billy, it's your turn to take the

caterpillars home this weekend and feed them and clean out their box. See you do it well, for they are growing big now and will soon turn into chrysalides.'

'Yes, Miss Brown,' said Billy.

But do you know, he forgot all about taking them home that Friday afternoon! A circus was coming to their village, and all the children were so eager to see it coming through the streets that everyone rushed off and nobody thought of the caterpillars at all. Even the teacher forgot, for it was prize-giving day on Monday, and she was busy arranging all the prizes and putting out the little silver mugs and cups that had been won at the sports by the children. There was a lot to do. She arranged all the things on a table, ready for the parents to see, and went home.

Billy didn't think about the caterpillars that night, nor all the next day, which was Saturday – but John did. He wondered if Billy was treating the little things properly, for he quite thought that Billy had taken them home. So he went round to Billy's house to ask him if the caterpillars were all right.

'Ooh, my!' said Billy, at once. 'I forgot to bring them home!'

'Forgot to bring them home!' said John, in

dismay. 'Oh, poor things! Their leaves will be dead, and they won't have anything to eat. I do think you are unkind, Billy.'

'Well, I can't help it, I'm not going to bother about them now,' said Billy sulkily.

'You ought to go and get the key from the caretaker, next door to the school, and fetch them home,' said John. 'They will die.'

'Well, let them!' said Billy unkindly. 'They are only caterpillars.'

'I don't like you, Billy,' said John in disgust, and he turned away to go home. But those caterpillars worried him. He couldn't bear to think of them dying because their leaves were dead and dry. He wondered what to do. He was going to the circus that night – perhaps he could leave early, get the key from old Mrs White and fetch the caterpillars home himself. He could feed and clean them that night and they would be all right. If they were left till the next day they would certainly die.

So he went to the circus with the others, and slipped away before it was finished, though he badly wanted to see the end of it; but he was afraid that old Mrs White would have gone to bed if he got to her house too late.

But dear me, when he did get there, there was

no answer! The old lady had gone away for the weekend and her house was empty. Now what was John to do? There didn't seem anything to be done at all!

'I'll just go and peep in at the schoolroom window,' thought John. 'I've got my torch with me and I can shine it down on the caterpillar box and see if they are all right or not.' So he went round to the school and walked over to the window.

Then he stopped in the greatest surprise – for there was someone in the classroom – someone with a torch that shone on to the prizes all so neatly arranged on the table. And that someone had come to steal the silver cups!

John crept away from the window and ran to the police station. 'There's a burglar in my classroom at the school!' he cried. 'Quick, sir, he's stealing all our prizes!'

The policeman put on his coat and came at once – and he was just in time to catch the thief as he climbed out of the window with his bag full of the silver cups and other prizes! He was taken to the police station and locked up.

John didn't forget the caterpillars in his excitement. No, he went back to the school, took the box of caterpillars from the open window, shut the window down and went home. He cleaned out the box before he went to bed and gave the poor caterpillars some fresh leaves, for they looked ill and feeble. The next day they were perfectly all right again.

John took them back to school on Monday, and the teacher didn't notice that it was John who brought them back and not Billy. Billy looked ashamed of himself, and thanked John in a whisper – but John wouldn't smile at him. He thought Billy was mean and unkind.

What a surprise at prize-giving time! In the middle of it, when all the parents were sitting watching the boys and girls go up for their prizes, the policeman walked in and spoke to the headmaster. Then he handed a little parcel to him and went out.

The headmaster turned to the waiting people. 'You have all heard,' he began, 'how the prizes were nearly stolen from us on Saturday night and how John Watson helped the police to catch the thief and give us back our prizes. I should like to say that the reason John was here that night so late was because, being a kind-hearted lad, he had remembered that the caterpillars in his classroom had not been taken home that weekend by the boy who should have looked after them – and John had come to see if they were all right. That was how he saw the thief. The police are delighted to have caught the man, as they have been after him for some time – and as a reward to John they have sent him this silver watch – which I now present to you, John, with my best wishes and thanks to you for saving our prizes!'

John came up, blushing bright red.

'I am also pleased to say that John wins the nature prize,' said the headmaster, and gave John – what do you think? – a little camera! John was so delighted that he could hardly say thank you.

'Now what about three cheers for the boy who came to find the caterpillars and caught a burglar instead?' smiled the headmaster. 'If it had not been for John we should none of us have been here at a prize-giving today – for there would have been no prizes. Now then, all together – hip, hip, hurrah! Three cheers for John!'

'Hip, hip, hurrah!' shouted everyone. John *was* proud and happy – and there was only one person there who was even prouder and happier. His mother!

Cuckoo!

Winnie and Tony were playing in the woods together. They had kept houses, played school and had hunted for primroses. Now Winnie was tired and wanted to go home.

'*I'm* not tired!' said Tony. 'I'd like a game of hide-and-seek.'

'I don't want to play,' said Winnie. 'You stay here if you like. I'm going home. I'll tell Mummy you'll come soon.'

Off she went, and Tony was left alone in the wood, halfway up a tree he was climbing.

'Winnie's silly!' he grumbled to himself. 'She might have stayed and had a game. I love hide-and-seek!'

As he was climbing down the tree someone called, 'Cuckoo! Cuckoo!'

'Good old Winnie!' said Tony, pleased. 'She is playing after all! I suppose she found a good hiding place as she ran off, and hid there. All right, Winnie! I'll find you!'

He ran towards the voice and hunted through the bushes. 'Where are you?' he cried.

'Cuckoo! Cuckoo!' came the voice, this time behind him. Tony ran off again, looking behind the trees and under the bushes. Wherever could Winnie be?

'Call again!' he shouted. No answer. Then, after a while, he heard once more: 'Cuckoo!'

'Well, where *are* you?' cried Tony, crossly. 'You're not to dodge about like that, Winnie. Keep in one place. It isn't fair.'

'Cuckoo, cuckoo, cuckoo!' This time it was to the left of him, quite near. Tony felt really cross. Winnie wasn't playing fair. She wasn't hiding in the same place all the time. She was creeping round about him.

'I give up!' he cried. 'Where are you, Winnie? Come out and show me!'

'Cuckoo! Cuckoo!'

'Don't be silly, I'm not playing any more!' shouted Tony. 'Come out, Winnie, and we'll go home together.'

But Winnie didn't come out. Nobody came at all – but still someone called: 'Cuckoo! Cuckoo!'

'All right, then, silly, I'm going home by myself!' said Tony in a huff, and he ran home.

But Winnie was there before him! She opened the door to him!

'How did you get here so soon?' said Tony in surprise. 'You might have told me where you were hiding, Winnie. I looked and looked and looked.'

'But I didn't play hide-and-seek,' said Winnie in astonishment. 'I came straight home. I've been helping Mummy get the tea for ever so long.'

'You couldn't have been,' said Tony. 'Because I kept hearing you call "Cuckoo", Winnie.'

'I didn't,' said Winnie.

'You did!'

'I didn't!'

'You did!'

'Children, children, don't quarrel!' called their mother. 'Tony, you're a silly boy. Listen at the front door for a minute.'

Tony went there and listened – and from the woods came a call: 'Cuckoo! Cuckoo!'

'Oh!' said Tony, going red. 'It's the cuckoo come back to us again after being away all the winter. Oh, what a silly I am! I played hide-and-seek with him!'

And how Mummy and Winnie laughed!

Seven O'Clock Tales

CONTENTS

The Enchanted Shoelace

There was once a little pixie called Skippy who went shopping in his village. As he trotted along his shoelace broke and his shoe came undone.

'Bother!' said Skippy, stopping. 'Now I must buy another shoelace.'

But he didn't need to buy one – for as he went merrily along he saw one lying in the road. His shoes were red, and the lace was green, but that didn't matter. It would lace up his shoe, whatever colour it was!

He slipped the lace into his shoe and tied it. That was fine. Now he was quite all right. Off he went again, skipping along, as happy as a bumble-bee.

Soon he came to a sweet shop and he looked in very longingly. He hadn't any money for sweets – but how delicious those big peppermints did look, to be sure!

'I just wish I had a pocketful of those!' sighed Skippy, and on he went. In a short while he felt something heavy in his pocket, and he put in his hand to feel what it was.

Peppermints! Peppermints by the dozen! Ooh, what a surprise! But however did they come there?

'My wish came true!' marvelled little Skippy. 'Oh, what a wonderful thing!'

He didn't know that he had a magic shoelace in his shoe – a lace that had once belonged to a witch and was enchanted! It came undone and nearly tripped him up.

'Bother!' said Skippy, doing it up. But he couldn't be cross for long with a pocketful of peppermints. He saw a little white kitten playing with its tail in the sunshine. Skippy was very fond of animals and he stood and watched it.

'I do wish I had a little white kitten just like that!' he said.

'Miaow!' Something rubbed against his legs, and Skippy looked down. He saw another little white kitten, looking up at him and mewing.

'Bless me!' said Skippy, in astonishment. 'If that isn't another wish come true! Well, well, well!'

He picked up the kitten and cuddled it. It nestled happily under his coat, glad to belong to a nice little pixie like Skippy. He bent down and did up his shoelace which had again come undone.

'This is really very strange,' thought the

pixie, tickling the kitten under the chin. 'This must be my lucky day, or something. I wonder if another wish will come true.'

He blinked his eyes and thought hard. 'I wish my suit was made of gold!' he said.

In a flash Skippy's red suit changed to a gleaming yellow. He was dressed in gold!

'Ooh!' said Skippy, amazed. 'Look at me all dressed up in gold! I'm a prince! I'm as grand as can be!'

His shoelace came undone again, and trailed on the ground. 'Bother!' said Skippy. 'It will trip me up as sure as eggs are eggs!'

He did it up, feeling most excited. He must tell somebody about his great good fortune. He would go to his friend Tickler the gnome and tell him. How surprised Tickler would be! Aha, he would wish all kinds of things for Tickler the gnome!

Off he went, skipping down the road as gaily as could be. What a day! What an adventure!

He banged at Tickler's door and the gnome opened it in surprise, staring at Skippy and the kitten.

'Why do you knock so hard?' he asked. 'Oh, Skippy – how beautiful you look! Where did you get that fine suit made of gold?'

'Would *you* like one?' asked Skippy, beaming.

'All right! I wish you had a suit like mine, Tickler!'

Hey presto! At once the gnome shone brightly in a suit as fine as Skippy's. He stared down at himself in amazement.

'Oh, Skippy!' he said. 'Skippy! What's happened? Do your wishes all come true?'

'Yes,' said Skippy, happily, and he stepped forward to go into Tickler's house. But his shoelace was undone again and nearly tripped him up. 'Bother, bother, bother!' he said, and did it up. Then he went into Tickler's neat little house.

'I can't tell you why my wishes come true,' he said to Tickler. 'They just suddenly did.'

'But there must be some reason why,' said Tickler, puzzled. 'Have you anything new on you, Skippy?'

'No, nothing,' said Skippy, quite forgetting about the shoelace. 'The magic just suddenly came.'

'Wish something else,' said Tickler. 'Wish for a jolly good dinner!'

'I wish we could have a fine dinner to eat this very minute!' said Skippy at once – and lo and behold, in front of them, on Tickler's round table, appeared a most delicious dinner! A roast chicken sent its tasty smell into the air, and a meat pie stood ready to be served. A large treacle pudding appeared and a plate of big jam tarts.

'Ooh my !' said Tickler, half frightened.

'Let's eat,' said Skippy. So they began to eat, and didn't they enjoy their dinner!

'I'm just going to get some water to drink,' said Skippy, and he hopped off his seat to go to the tap. His shoelace had come undone again, and he fell down on the floor!

'Bother!' he said. 'That shoelace is always tripping me up!'

He did it up and got his water, which he immediately wished into lemonade. Really, it was marvellous!

'Now I shall wish myself a little white pony to ride,' said Skippy. 'And I'll wish you one too, Tickler.'

'I'd rather have a pink pony,' said Tickler. 'That would be most unusual.'

'A pink one wouldn't be nice,' said Skippy, frowning. 'It would look silly. I'll get you a nice white one.'

'I'd rather have a pink one,' said Tickler.

'But *I* shouldn't like a pink pony,' said Skippy.

'Well, it's not you who is to have it, it's me,' said Tickler. 'Wish me a pink one, Skippy.'

'I wish for two nice white ponies,' said Skippy firmly.

At once two little ponies appeared outside in the garden, as white as snow. Skippy got up to run out and nearly tripped over again. His lace was undone.

'Oh, there's that stupid lace undone again!' he cried. He did it up and went outside. 'Come on, Tickler,' he called, 'here's your pony waiting for you. Come and have a ride.'

'I wanted a pink pony,' said Tickler sulkily. 'I don't want a white one.'

'You horrid, ungrateful thing!' cried Skippy. 'Here I've got you a golden suit and a fine meal, and a lovely pony too, and all you can do is to frown at me and look sulky.'

'Well, I wanted a pink pony,' said Tickler. 'A pink pony is uncommon. You were too selfish to let me have what I wanted.'

'I'm *not* selfish!' cried Skippy, in a rage. 'Aren't I sharing all my wishes with you, now? What more do you want?'

'I just want a pink pony,' said Tickler, in an obstinate voice.

'Oh well, have a hundred pink ponies then!' shouted Skippy in a temper – and hey presto, the little garden was at once full to overflowing with small, bright pink ponies!

'Oh, they're treading on my flowers and on my lovely new peas!' shrieked Tickler in dismay. 'Oh, take your horrid ponies away, Skippy!'

'They're not mine, they're yours!' said Skippy dancing about in glee. 'You wanted pink and you've got pink!'

He suddenly tripped headlong over his shoe-lace, which had come undone once more. Down he went, with his nose in the dust.

'Ha, ha, ha! ho, ho!' laughed Tickler. 'That's what comes of being too proud, Skippy. Pride goes before a fall! That shoelace of yours punished you nicely!'

Skippy sat up and looked angrily at his shoe. Yes, that horrid, stupid shoelace was undone again!

'I wish to goodness I'd never put you into my shoe!' said Skippy, crossly, putting out his hand to take the lace to tie again. But it wriggled out of his fingers like a green snake and vanished down the garden path!

And at the same moment all the ponies vanished too! The little white kitten, which had been wandering happily about, suddenly shot up into the air and disappeared like a white cloud.

'Where have all the ponies gone?' said Tickler

in wonder. 'And oh, Skippy, where has your gold suit gone? You've got your old one on again.'

'So have you!' cried Skippy. 'Did you see my shoelace slide off like a snake, Tickler? Wasn't that strange?'

'Where did you get it from?' asked Tickler, suddenly.

'I picked it up in the road,' said Skippy. 'Ooh, Tickler! That's what brought the magic! Of course! When I wished a wish the shoelace always came undone. I remember now – and oh, oh, what a terrible pity, I've wished it away! I've wished my wonderful good luck away!'

'If we hadn't quarrelled it wouldn't have happened,' said Tickler, tears coming into his eyes. 'Oh, Skippy, how foolish we've been. To think we had riches, happiness, everything just for the wishing – and we quarrelled about a pink pony!'

'It shows we weren't big enough to have such a wonderful power,' said Skippy. 'Oh my, oh my, if ever I get a magic shoelace again, won't I just be careful with it!'

But the pity of it was that he never *did* find one again. Do be careful if *you* find one, won't you!

That Little Red Imp

Once upon a time, many years ago, there lived a brownie called Mingy. That wasn't his real name, but he was such a mingy, miserly, mean old fellow that everyone forgot his real name and called him Mingy.

One day he picked up an old kettle from a ditch and looked at it. Yes – if he took it home he could mend that little hole in the bottom and use it. That would save him buying a new kettle!

So he took it home – but, you know, he hadn't looked inside that kettle. If he had, he would have seen that a little red, spidery imp had made it his home, and was very much annoyed at having his kettle taken up from the ditch.

The imp lifted up the lid and took a look at the brownie. He grinned. 'It's old Mingy!' he said to himself. 'I might have guessed. Ho ho! He'll find this kettle a pretty expensive one, before he's done, I think!'

Mingy took the kettle home, mended the hole

and put it up on a shelf to dry. As he turned to sit down there came a knock at the door, and a small elf popped her head in.

'Could you lend me yesterday's newspaper?' she asked. 'I just wanted to see the answer to a puzzle.'

'No, I can't lend it to you,' snapped the brownie, who hated lending even a pin to anyone.

'Mingy, Mingy! Stingy old Mingy!' yelled the little red imp loudly from the kettle.

The brownie looked round, astonished. The imp popped up the kettle lid and grinned at him. 'Mingy, stingy Mingy!' he yelled, in his little high voice.

'Oh, so it's you, is it!' said Mingy, fiercely. 'I'll soon settle *you*!'

The red imp popped out of the kettle and danced up to a higher shelf where some pots of plum jam stood. 'Mingy old stingy! Stingy old Mingy!' he called.

Mingy picked up a duster and flapped hard at the imp. Crash! Smash! Down to the floor came two pots of plum jam and splashed the brownie from head to feet in dark red.

'What a waste, what a waste, Mingy dear!' shouted the red imp. The brownie wiped himself down, in a furious temper. Then he picked up a broom and hit out at the red imp, who had hopped on to the dresser.

The imp took a flying leap on to a shelf full of saucepans and the broom hit a big dish and two glasses. Blim-blam, crash! Down they all came in smithereens, and the red imp jigged about for joy among the saucepans, jumping into first one and then another.

'Mingy, Mingy, isn't he stingy!' he shouted, in his naughty little high voice. The brownie threw the broom at him in a rage, and half the saucepans bounced off the shelf and fell clanging and clanking to the floor, denting themselves terribly.

The red imp hopped back into the kettle, shaking with laughter. Ho ho, old Mingy had got to spend some money now. He must buy new saucepans, a new dish, new glasses!

Mingy suddenly took hold of the kettle and opened the lid. The red imp slipped up the spout and out in a flash. He jumped on to the brownie's shoulder and nipped his ear.

'Mingy, here I am!' he yelled. Mingy put up his hand and tried to slap him, but the imp jumped to the table, where Mingy's tea was set out. The brownie grabbed at him and upset the teapot. The tea went soaking into the tablecloth and into the plate of bread-and-butter.

The red imp jumped into the warm teapot and out again. He *was* enjoying himself. Then he jumped on to the milk jug. Mingy hit out at him – and over went the milk!

Mingy burst into tears. It was too bad! Nasty little imp! Why couldn't he leave him alone?

'Will you go away if I throw the kettle back into the ditch again?' he begged the imp at last. But the red imp shook his head firmly.

'No, certainly not. It's fun living with a stingy old miser like you,' said the imp. 'It's fun to make you break things and spill them, to make you spend your money! Ho ho, I like living with a mingy miser!'

Mingy glared at the imp in rage. Then he put on his hat and went to visit the wise woman next door. He told her his trouble and asked her how he could get rid of the mischievous imp.

'If it's a red imp,' said the wise woman, 'he will love to live with you, Mingy, because red imps love to tease mean, selfish people like you. There's only *one* way of getting rid of him!'

'What's that?' asked Mingy, eagerly.

'Stop being mean and miserly,' said the wise woman, looking over her spectacles at Mingy. 'Then he won't be able to call you names or tease you. It serves you right to be plagued with a nasty little imp like that, Mingy, you know –

you really are rather a nasty little creature yourself!'

Mingy blushed as red as a tomato. How dreadful to have such a thing said to him by a wise woman! He went home hanging his head, and on the way he gave two elves a penny each – a thing he had never in his life done before!

He crept quietly into his cottage – but the red imp was waiting for him.

'Ho ho, here's dear old mingy, old stingy mingy!' he cried, peeping out of the kettle. 'Welcome home, Mingy.'

Mingy said nothing. He hunted about for yesterday's paper and then went out to give it to the little elf who had asked for it. The imp watched him in surprise. When Mingy came back the imp was fast shut in his kettle and didn't even peep out. Mingy was glad.

Tiptap the goblin came knocking at the door that evening and asked Mingy to lend him a little tea. Without a word the brownie opened his tea-caddy and gave Tiptap what he wanted. Tiptap was so astonished that he couldn't say a word. He had never in his life known Mingy to give or lend anything before.

The word soon went round that Mingy was changing. How strange! People said he had a little red imp there too, that sometimes called him names. Stranger still! More and more people called at Mingy's in the next few days to borrow something or to ask for something. Mingy gave them all what they wanted, with a pleasant smile.

A peculiar thing began to happen to him. He felt nice and warm inside whenever he did something kind. He liked the grateful look in people's eyes. He liked their warm smiles at him. It was good to be kind! It was nice to be friendly!

The little red imp had a bad time. It was no good his peeping out of the kettle – no good even to call something rude for Mingy didn't seem to mind.

One day he climbed right out of the kettle and had a good look into Mingy's face.

'Why, I thought you were mean and selfish!' said the red imp. 'I've made a mistake! You are kind! You are good! You're no use to me! I want someone to plague and tease. I want someone to be rude to. Bah! It's no good staying here!'

'Not a bit of good, imp,' said Mingy. 'I'll put your kettle back in the ditch, if you like.'

The imp climbed into his kettle and the brownie threw it into the ditch where he had found it.

'That's the end of *you*!' he thought with glee.

'Now, if I want to, I can go back to my old ways!'

But the strange thing was that he *didn't* want to! There was no fun in being mean! He didn't feel warm and happy when he was being selfish! No, he wanted to smile, and to see others smile. He wanted to be generous and get that nice warm feeling inside. It was much more fun to be kind!

So the little red imp was some good after all! He is still living in his old kettle down in the ditch. You may find him there one day, if you look – but first be sure you're not a mingy fellow yourself, or I shall be very sorry for you!

The Little Fat Dormouse

There was once a fat dormouse who lived in a cosy home in the hedge with his mother and father and four brothers and sisters. His name was Pitterpat because his feet went pitter-pattering like rain along the bank by his home.

Pitterpat didn't like being a dormouse. He was small, too small, he thought. Why couldn't he be big, like a rabbit, or have sharp claws, like a cat? Then he would be Somebody!

He thought he was much cleverer than his family. He was always laughing at them and telling them they were stupid. At last his brothers and sisters turned him out of the nest, and said:

'If you are so clever, go and find another home! Let us know when you have made your fortune and we will come and admire you – but until you have done something great, leave us to ourselves!'

Pitterpat was very angry. He picked up his little bag and set off, vowing to himself that he would soon show his brothers and sisters what a clever fellow he was. Ha, he would be a cow, or a horse, or even a sharp weasel if he could find one who would teach him all the tricks.

Soon he came to a field. In it there were some sheep grazing, and Pitterpat went up to one of them.

'Madam,' he said, politely. 'I am a clever dormouse, but I would like to be a sheep. Will you tell me how?'

'Certainly,' said the surprised sheep, looking at the tiny dormouse. 'Can you baa?'

Pitterpat tried. He could squeak, but he could not seem to baa.

'Well, never mind,' said the sheep. 'You must grow wool on your back.'

'But that would be so hot,' said the dormouse. 'It is summertime.'

'You *must* grow wool if you want to be like us,' said the sheep.

'I don't think I will be a sheep,' said the dormouse and he scurried away, thinking that sheep must be stupid to wear wool in the summer. Soon he came to where a rabbit nibbled grass outside its hole.

'Sir,' he said, 'I am a clever dormouse, but I would like to be a rabbit. Will you tell me how?'

'Well, you must learn to make a great home of

burrows under the ground,' said the rabbit. 'You must use your paws like this to scrape up the earth.' The rabbit scraped a shower of earth up and it fell all over the dormouse.

'That's a stupid thing to do,' said the dormouse, angrily. 'Look how dirty you have made me.'

The rabbit took no notice. 'Then,' he went on, 'you must grow a short, fluffy white bobtail like mine. It acts as a danger-signal to everyone when I run to my hole. My friends see my bobbing tail and run too.'

'My tail is much better than yours,' said the dormouse scornfully. 'I don't think I will be a rabbit.' He ran away, thinking what a stupid creature the rabbit was, covering him with earth like that and talking about bobtails.

He came to a pond after a while and saw a fine white duck squatting beside the water, basking in the sun. He went up and bowed.

'Madam!' he said. 'I am a clever dormouse, but I would like to be a duck. Will you tell me how?'

'First you must quack like this,' said the duck, and she opened her beak and quacked so loudly that the dormouse was half frightened. He opened his mouth and tried to quack too, but all the sound he made was a small squeal.

'And then,' said the duck, 'you must swim, like this!' She flopped into the water, and it splashed all over the watching dormouse, soaking him to the skin.

'You silly, stupid duck, look what you've done!' he cried in anger. 'You've nearly drowned me.'

'Oh, you'll have to get used to a wetting if you're going to be a duck,' quacked the duck, merrily.

'I don't think I will be a duck!' called the dormouse and hurried away. 'Silly creature,' he thought. 'Splashing me like that!'

A grunting noise made him stop. He looked under a gate and saw a large, fat pig in a sty. Ah, how big and fine he looked! The dormouse crept under the gate and spoke to the pig.

'Sir,' he said, 'I am a clever dormouse, but I would like to be a pig. Will you tell me how?'

'Can you grunt, like this?' said the surprised pig and grunted in such a vulgar manner that the dormouse was quite disgusted.

'I shouldn't wish to make such a rude noise as that,' he said, his nose in the air. The pig grunted again and began to root about in the mud of his sty so roughly that poor Pitterpat was sent head-over-heels into a dirty puddle.

'You must learn to root about like this,' said

the pig, twinkling his little eyes cheekily at the dormouse. 'Oh, did I upset you?'

The dormouse picked himself up out of the mud and looked angrily at the pig.

'I don't think I will be a pig,' he said, huffily. 'Nasty, dirty, ill-mannered creatures!'

The pig laughed gruntily, and the dormouse pattered off. Ugh! He wouldn't be a dirty old pig for anything!

Outside the farmyard he met a sharp-nosed rat. This rat was eating potato parings which he had pulled from the rubbish-heap. The dormouse watched the rat, and noticed his clever, sharp eyes and the way in which he held the food in his front paws. Ah, here was a clever fellow, to be sure! Not stupid like the rabbit and sheep, not wicked like the duck, not dirty like the pig. He would be a rat!

'Sir,' said the dormouse, going nearer. 'I am a clever dormouse, but I would like to be a rat. Will you tell me how?'

'Certainly,' said the rat. 'Can you squeal like this?' He squealed shrilly. The dormouse opened his mouth and squealed too.

'Not so bad,' said the rat. 'Now can you hold food in your paws as I do?' The dormouse tried, and found he could do it easily. He was delighted. Ah yes, he would certainly be a rat!

'What else must I do?' he asked.

'You must learn to pounce on your victims like this,' said the rat, and he leapt to one side. 'See, this is how I catch a young bird! And see, this is how I pounce on a frog! And SEE! This is how I pounce on silly little dormice!'

He leapt at the astonished dormouse – but Pitterpat gave a frightened squeal and fled for his life. Down a molehole he went and into a maze of small tunnels. The rat followed him, hungry for a dinner.

The dormouse slipped aside into a tiny hole he knew of, hoping that the rat would pass before he guessed he was there. The rat did pass – and at once Pitterpat turned and fled back the way he had come, never stopping once until he had got back to his own cosy home again, high up in the hedgerow.

As he scrambled into the big, round nest all his sisters and brothers cried out in surprise. 'Oh, here's the clever one back again! Have you made your fortune?'

'No,' said the dormouse, hanging his head. 'I haven't made a fortune but I've made a lot of mistakes. I'm not clever, I'm very stupid. Forgive me and let me live here again with you.'

So his family forgave him, and the little dormouse lived happily in the hedgerow. 'It's

best to be what you are!' he thought. 'I'm *glad*
I'm a stupid little dormouse!'

The Greedy Toy Clown

Once there was a toy clown. He lived in the nursery cupboard with all the other toys, but nobody liked him very much. For one thing he was very thin, and for another he was greedy.

If ever the toys had a tea party he was sure to eat most of the cakes, and once he even put some sandwiches in his pocket when he thought no one was looking. He meant to eat them all by himself in the night.

He was very proud of his blue trousers and red coat, and proudest of all of a lovely glittering brooch that Ann had given him out of a Christmas cracker. Ann was the little girl the toys belonged to. They liked her very much because she played every day with them, and was gentle and kind.

One day Ann had a lovely present given to her. It was a proper little stove! It had an oven inside and saucepans and kettles on top. You could really light it and cook with it. Ann loved it and cooked little puddings for herself of biscuits and sugar.

Now when everything was dark and still one night, the clown awoke and stretched himself. He was hungry. He remembered the little stove. What fun if he could creep out and cook himself a meal on it! None of the other toys were about. Ann had been playing with them such a lot that day that they were all feeling too tired to stir out of the cupboard.

So the clown tiptoed out alone. He went to the little gas stove and looked at it. How lovely it was! He was sure he could cook with it. But what could he cook?

He looked around. He couldn't really see anything to cook for his supper – and then he suddenly saw the little toy sweet shop that Ann had. There were little bottles of sweets in it, and packets of chocolate and lozenges. He would take some of those and cook them.

So he went to the shop, opened the door and went behind the counter. Wasn't it naughty of him? He took some sweets out of a bottle, a packet of chocolate and shook some lozenges into his hand. What a fine meal he would cook with all those mixed in a saucepan together!

He tiptoed back to the stove and emptied the sweets into a saucepan. He took it to the doll's house, turned on the bathroom tap there and half-filled the saucepan with water. That was to cook the sweets in. He thought it would make a lovely sweet-pudding!

Then he found some matches in a box by the fireplace and lit the stove. The flame shot up, and he put the saucepan over it. Now his dinner would cook!

The clown was pleased with himself. Ha, he would have a fine meal while all the other toys were asleep. The saucepan was nearly boiling, his supper would soon be ready. How good it smelt!

He did a little dance round the stove – and then a dreadful thing happened His sleeve caught the handle of the saucepan and over it went!

Splish-splash! The boiling water shot out and some of it fell on the clown's legs. Goodness, how he squealed!

His shrieks woke up all the other toys, of course. They came pouring out of the cupboard wondering whatever the matter was. When they saw the clown holding his leg, and discovered the spilt saucepan, with all the sticky mess on the carpet, they guessed what he had been doing!

'It serves you right!' said the teddy bear. 'You're far too sly and greedy. How dare you take sweets from the shop and use Ann's stove?

Stop making that noise. Go and get some vaseline out of the box on the shelf and tie up your leg with your handkerchief. If you've scalded it, it is a good punishment for you!'

The clown hopped off, crying. The wooden doll tried to scrape up the hot, sticky mess from the nursery carpet – and, oh dear me, it came away with a bit of the carpet and left a hole there!

The toys stared at it in dismay. Whatever could be done about that? Ann would see it, and perhaps Ann would be scolded for something she hadn't done! It must be mended *some*how.

'What shall we do?' asked the teddy bear, quite upset.

'We'd better ask the elf who lives in the lavender bed outside if she'll come and mend the hole,' said the clockwork duck. 'I sometimes see her when Ann takes me down the path, and she's always sewing, so I expect she could easily mend that hole.'

'Good idea!' said the bear. So he went to the window and called the elf softly. She soon came – and when she heard what they wanted her to do, she went back to get her needle and threads. She sat down on the carpet and began to sew. All the toys watched her. You wouldn't believe how beautifully she did it! Her threads were fine but strong, and she matched up the carpet perfectly.

'There!' she said, when it was done. 'Is that all right?'

'It's beautiful!' cried all the toys. 'What would you like for a reward?'

'I should love a little brooch,' said the elf, shyly. 'I haven't one, you know.'

'Clown! Give the elf your glittering brooch!' said the teddy bear, at once, beckoning the clown forward.

'But I don't want to,' he said. 'I like it.'

'That doesn't matter,' said the wooden doll. 'You caused damage by your greediness, and so you must suffer for it. The elf has put things right and you must reward her. Give her your brooch, quickly!'

The clown undid it, with tears in his eyes. The elf took it gladly and pinned it at her neck. It looked fine! She was most delighted.

'Goodbye!' she said. 'I hope nobody will ever notice the mend.' Nobody did – but Ann soon saw that the clown had lost his brooch. She hunted for it everywhere, but of course she never found it. As for the clown, he isn't vain or greedy any more. Fancy that!

Timothy Toad

One morning when Janet was riding down the lane on her bicycle she saw something crawling in the road. She got off her bicycle and went to see what it was – and she saw that it was a big toad, whose hind foot had been squashed by a passing car.

Janet looked at the hurt toad and the toad looked back. He had the loveliest coppery eyes, like jewels, and as Janet looked at him he put up his front hand and rubbed his nose.

'You seem quite tame!' said Janet, who wasn't altogether sure that she liked toads. She looked at him again, and really, it did seem as if he were just about to speak to her. But he didn't, of course. He gave a deep croak and tried to crawl away again, dragging his leg behind him.

'You'll get run over by a car,' said Janet. 'You shouldn't walk in the road. Your poor leg is already squashed by something.'

The little girl didn't like to leave the toad there. She felt sure he would be run over. So she took her handkerchief out of her pocket, wrapped the toad up in it and carefully put it on the side of the road.

The toad stretched out its leg as if to show her that it was hurt. Janet, who was a very kind-hearted child, wondered if she ought to do something for its leg. So she picked it up in her handkerchief and carried it home. Her daddy was working in the garden and called out to find out what she had.

'A hurt toad!' said Janet.

'Let's see,' said Daddy. So the little girl showed him.

'Dear, dear!' said Daddy. 'He *has* hurt his foot, hasn't he! Let's put some ointment on it. That will help it to get better.'

So they doctored the toad's foot. He was very good. He sat on Daddy's hand, looking up with his fine, copper eyes, and then, when they had finished with him he crawled away into the flower bed.

'Will he eat the flowers, Daddy?' asked Janet. 'The tortoise ate our violas, you know.'

'No, he won't touch the plants,' said Daddy. 'He likes an insect dinner!'

Janet looked for the toad the next day, but she couldn't find him. He seemed to be gone. She wondered if his foot was better, and was glad that she had brought him home so that Daddy could see to him.

Daddy was always gardening. He grew such a lot of flowers and vegetables. The broad beans were full of fine pods. The early peas were flowering. The gooseberries were ripe enough to pick. Daddy was very pleased with his garden – except for just one thing.

And that was his lettuces! He had planted out a long row of small plants – and then two days later nearly all of them had gone! Daddy *was* upset.

'The slugs have had them,' he told Janet. 'They really are a pest this year. You might help me this evening, Janet. We'll hunt for them and catch as many as we can. Then I'll plant out another row of lettuces.'

So Janet and Daddy hunted for slugs, and they found a great many. The next day Daddy planted out another row of lettuces – nice little plants with two or three leaves each.

'In a few weeks' time they will be fine big lettuces,' said Daddy. 'Then we can take them in for tea. They will be lovely with new bread-and-butter!'

For a few days the lettuces grew well – and then came a wet day and night. In the night the slugs crept out again from the hiding places under the stone edgings and beneath the pebbles on the bed – and how they feasted on those lettuces!

Really, when Daddy and Janet came to look at them the next day they could hardly believe their eyes! Only about nine miserable little half-eaten plants remained. It was too bad.

'Well, I shall only try once again,' said Daddy. 'I've enough plants for one more time. If the slugs get at those I shall have to give up.'

So once more he and Janet planted them out in neat rows. They sprinkled soot round them to keep off the slugs, but when the rain came it washed the soot all away!

'I don't expect these will escape the slugs,' said Daddy.

But, you know, they did! Day after day Daddy and Janet went to look at the lettuces, expecting to see them eaten up. But not a single lettuce died. All of them shot up strong and green and began to make fine plants.

'It's strange,' said Daddy, in surprise, looking in vain for slugs. 'I wonder where all those slugs have gone to.'

'Oh, Daddy, look!' cried Janet, suddenly. She pointed to a big lettuce – and what do you think was behind it? A great fat toad! As Daddy and Janet looked at him he shot out his tongue and caught a big blue-bottle fly that was sitting on a nearby leaf.

'Why, Janet, there's the fellow who's got rid of all those slugs for us!' said Daddy. 'A toad is a good friend in the garden – he eats all kinds of insects, and loves a meal of slugs. He has certainly saved our lettuces for us.'

Janet bent down to look at him. He stared up at her, his bright eyes gleaming.

'Do you know, Daddy,' said Janet, excited. 'It's the toad whose foot was hurt! Look, it's better now, but you can see where it was hurt. Oh, Daddy! Just think! We were friends to him and now he's a friend to us! He's saved our lettuces. Do you suppose he knew?'

'I can't tell,' said Daddy, 'but I shouldn't be surprised. You never know what a minute's kindness will bring you in return! Good old toad, we'll call you Timothy, and you shall live in our garden all your life!'

He's still there, because I've seen him!

Brer Rabbit Gets in a Fix

Once it happened that Brer Fox found Brer Rabbit fishing in his favourite fishing-place, and he was so angry that he pounced on Brer Rabbit and nearly caught him. But Brer Rabbit was just a little bit too quick, and he got away, leaving a tuft of his fur in Brer Fox's claws.

Brer Fox was so excited to think how nearly he had caught Brer Rabbit that he raced after him at top speed. Brer Fox could go as fast as a race-horse when he liked, and he meant to catch Brer Rabbit this time.

There were no rabbit-holes near the fishing-place, and Brer Rabbit was in a bad way, for there was nowhere he could hide. He just ran on and on, lippitty-clippitty, hoping to find a thick bush or hole.

But there was nothing at all, and Brer Fox was getting nearer and nearer. At last Brer Rabbit spied Brer Wolf's house in the distance, and he ran up to it. He leapt up the gutter-pipe by the side of the house and sat on the roof. Brer

Fox stopped and looked up. The gutter-pipe wouldn't bear his weight – he could see that – but all the same he had got Brer Rabbit very nicely caught! A ladder would get him down all right, and then he would pop him into a pan and stew him for dinner. Oho!

Brer Wolf came out to see what all the noise was about, and he was mighty astonished to see Brer Rabbit sitting up on his roof, panting and puffing, and Brer Fox down below, snarling in delight.

'I've got old Brer Rabbit at last!' said Brer Fox. 'Have you a pan big enough to stew him in, Brer Wolf?'

'No, I haven't,' said Brer Wolf. 'He looks pretty fat to me. He'll need a bigger pan than *I* have.'

'Well, will you just keep watch on him to see he doesn't escape,' said Brer Fox, 'and I'll go and get my biggest pan.'

Off went Brer Fox at a run and Brer Wolf sat down in his garden, his gleaming eyes fixed on Brer Rabbit. But Brer Rabbit didn't seem at all worried. He just sat up on the roof and washed his ears for a little while, and then he began to sniff about round the chimney nearby. Presently Brer Wolf heard him scraping at a tile, and pretty soon it came loose.

'Hey, Brer Rabbit, what are you doing?' shouted Brer Wolf. 'You leave my roof alone.'

'All right, all right, Brer Wolf,' said Brer Rabbit. 'I just thought there was something under this tile, that's all.'

'What do you mean, something under the tile?' asked Brer Wolf.

'Oh, just something,' answered Brer Rabbit, scraping the tile back into place. Just then something fell down the roof and bounced near Brer Wolf. It was a piece of money! Brer Wolf pounced on it and looked at it in surprise.

'What was that?' asked Brer Rabbit, peering over the edge of the roof.

'It's a piece of money!' cried Brer Wolf. 'My, Brer Rabbit, it must have come from under that tile!'

'Or it might have dropped out of my pocket,' said Brer Rabbit. 'You throw it back to me, Brer Wolf.'

'Ho, ho, you think you'll rob me of secret money hidden under my roof, do you?' said Brer Wolf. 'No, I'm not so stupid as that, Brer Rabbit. I'm going to get a ladder and come up there to see what's hidden under that loose tile by the chimney. Whatever's there is mine, because the roof is mine!'

Brer Wolf took up his ladder, which was

nearby and leaned it against the roof. He climbed up and was soon sitting beside Brer Rabbit.

'Now, where's that tile?' he asked him.

'It's just here, by the chimney,' said Brer Rabbit, and he showed Brer Wolf the tile he had moved. 'Hold on to the chimney, Brer Wolf, and you can scrape away the tile with your other hand.'

Brer Wolf held on tightly to the chimney, and began to scratch away at the tile. It was hard to move and he pushed away, quite forgetting all about Brer Rabbit. Brer Rabbit slid down to the edge of the roof, got on to the ladder, and was down it in a twink! He made his way to a bramble-bush, where he knew there was a hole, and there he sat, his whiskers shaking with delight.

Brer Wolf went on scratching and scraping at the tile, and didn't hear Brer Fox coming back. Brer Fox came along dragging a great pan by the handle, and he was most astonished to see Brer Wolf up on the roof and no Brer Rabbit anywhere.

'Heyo, Brer Wolf!' he shouted. 'Where's Brer Rabbit?'

Brer Wolf almost fell off the roof in horror when he saw Brer Rabbit was gone, and Brer

Fox down below looking mighty angry.

'Has Brer Rabbit gone?' he said at last.

Brer Fox nearly had a fit. When he could speak he almost choked with rage. 'Do you mean to tell me that you let Brer Rabbit go when you knew I'd gone to fetch a pan to stew him in?' he shouted. 'And anyway what are *you* doing up on the roof, Brer Wolf, scratching away like mad?'

'Oh, I think there's a fortune hidden somewhere about this chimney,' said Brer Wolf. 'Brer Rabbit got this tile loose and a piece of money fell down to the ground. Come on up, Brer Fox, and don't look so angry down there. If we can find a fortune what does it matter about losing a skinny creature like Brer Rabbit.'

'He wasn't skinny,' said Brer Fox, climbing up the ladder. 'Well, Brer Wolf, if you'll share your good fortune with me, I'll say no more about you letting Brer Rabbit go.'

Soon the tile came loose and fell to the ground and smashed. The two on the roof put their paws down to find the hidden gold they expected – but there was none there! No, not a single piece of money was to be found!

'Brer Rabbit's been telling you stories!' cried Brer Fox, in a rage. 'There's nothing there!'

'I've been telling *no* stories!' said Brer

Rabbit's voice from the garden. 'Didn't I say, Brer Wolf, that that piece of money must have fallen out of my pocket? Well, it did!'

Brer Wolf and Brer Fox glared at Brer Rabbit in a fury – and as they sat up there, glaring, Brer Rabbit kicked the ladder so that it fell flat on the ground.

'You'd better stay up on the roof a bit longer,' he grinned. 'I'm not going to be chased home by two great bullies like you! I'm going home slowly. Goodbye, Brer Fox! Goodbye, Brer Wolf!'

And with that off went Brer Rabbit, sauntering along as if he had all the day before him to get home. As for Brer Fox and Brer Wolf, there they had to stay, up on the roof, and it was a mighty long time before they managed to get down!

The Skippetty Shoes

Mr Winkle was a shoemaker. He lived in a tiny, tumbledown cottage, and all day long he sat outside on a bench and made or mended shoes. He was a merry, mischievous fellow, always ready for a joke. Sometimes he played naughty tricks and made his friends cross.

One time he ran a glue brush inside a pair of shoes that he sold to Father Grumps – and dear me, how Grumps tugged and pulled to get those shoes from his feet! In the end both his socks came too, and Father Grumps was very angry indeed.

Another time Winkle put a squeak into the heels of some boots he sold to Dame Twisty, and when she heard the squeak-squeak-squeak as she walked, she really thought it was a goblin coming after her, and she fled down the street in fright, her shoes squeaking loudly all the time! Yes, really, Mr Winkle was a mischievous fellow.

He got worse as he grew older, instead of

better, People shook their heads and said: 'One day he will go too far, and then who knows what will happen to him?'

Now, one morning, as Mr Winkle sat mending shoes, and humming a little song that went 'Tol-de-ray, shoes for a fay, tol-de-rome, shoes for a gnome,' a fat gnome came by. He stood and watched Winkle at work, and Winkle looked up and grinned.

'You've a lot of time to waste!' he said, cheekily.

The gnome frowned. He felt in his bag and brought out a pair of old slippers, each of which had a hole in the sole. They had once been grand slippers, for there was a gold buckle on each, and the heels were made of silver.

'How long will you take to mend these?' asked the gnome.

'One hour,' answered Winkle, looking at them. 'My, how grand they were once – but they are very old now, and hardly worth mending.'

'They are most comfortable slippers,' said the gnome, 'and that is why they are to be mended, Mr Winkle. Now, set to work, and keep your tongue still. It wags all day long.'

'Better than growling all day long, like yours!' answered Winkle, cheekily. The gnome frowned again, and sat himself down on a stool.

Winkle tried to make him talk, but he wouldn't say a word. He just sat there and thought.

Mr Winkle felt annoyed. What an old solemn-face the gnome was! Cross old stick, thought Winkle, as he began to mend the slippers. His needle flew in and out, and his busy little brain thought about the old fat gnome.

Presently an idea came into his naughty mind. He would play a trick on the gnome. But what trick could he play? He thought and thought – and then he got up and went indoors. Somewhere he had got a little Skippetty Spell – but where was it? If only he could find it, what a fine trick he would play on the old fat gnome!

He hunted here and he hunted there – and at last he found it, tucked inside a milk jug. Good! Winkle hurried back to his bench, and found the gnome looking crossly at him.

'Where have you been?' he said. 'Get on with your work. I want those shoes finished at once.'

Winkle made a face and sewed quickly at the shoes. Into each he sewed half of the Skippetty Spell, grinning to himself as he thought of how the gnome would kick, jump, leap and prance, as soon as he put those slippers on his feet. Ho, ho! That would be a funny sight to watch! That would teach the solemn old fellow to frown at him and talk crossly!

'The slippers are finished,' said Winkle at last. He handed them to the gnome, and took his payment. But still the old fellow sat there on his stool, as if he were waiting for someone.

'What are you waiting for?' asked Winkle.

'The king is coming to call for me here,' said the gnome. 'He said he would fetch me in his carriage. It is his shoes you have mended. They are his oldest ones, but so comfortable that he cannot bear to get new ones.'

Winkle stared in horror. Gracious goodness, were they really the king's own slippers? He was just going to take them from the gnome when there came the sound of galloping hooves, and up came the king's carriage. The gnome stood up and went to the gate. The carriage stopped and the king leaned out.

'Did you get my shoes mended?' he asked.

'Yes, Your Majesty,' said the gnome and gave them to the king. His Majesty kicked off his grand gold boots and slipped his feet contentedly into his old slippers.

'Oh, how nice to have these again!' he began – and then he stopped in dismay. Oh, those slippers! As soon as they were on the king's feet the Skippetty Spell began to work, and what a shock they gave His Majesty!

They jumped him out of the carriage. They

made him kick his legs up into the air. His crown fell off into a lavender bush, and his cloak was shaken all crooked. He pranced round the garden, he kicked high, he kicked low, he jumped over the wall, and he spun round and round till he was quite giddy. Certainly that Skippetty Spell was very powerful indeed!

The gnome stared at the king in horror. Mr Winkle turned pale and trembled. When the gnome saw Winkle's face he knew that he must have played a trick. He was full of rage and he caught the trembling cobbler by the collar.

'What have you done to the king's slippers, you wicked creature?' he shouted.

'There's a Sk-Skippetty Sp-Spell in them,' stammered Winkle. 'Do you know how to get it out? I don't!'

Luckily the old gnome was a clever fellow, and he knew how to deal with a Skippetty Spell. He clapped his hands seven times, called out a strange magic word, and hey presto the spell flew out of the slippers, they stopped dancing, and the king sat down to get his breath.

Mr Winkle knelt down and begged the king's pardon – but he was far too angry to listen.

'Take your tools and go away from Fairy-land!' roared the king. 'I've a good mind to turn you into an earwig, you mischievous little creature! Go away before I think of the right word!'

Winkle was in a terrible fright. He was so afraid of turning into an earwig that he caught up his bag of tools then and there and fled right away. He ran until he came to the borders of Fairyland, and not till then did he feel safe. He kept looking at himself, to see if he were Winkle, or an earwig.

Now he lives in our world. He still makes shoes for the pixies – very tiny ones, gold and black. He has no shop now, so he has to store them somewhere else – and do you know where he puts them? I'll tell you.

Find a white dead-nettle blossom and lift up the flower so that you can peep inside the top lip. What do you see there? Yes – two pairs of tiny pixie slippers, hung up safely by Mr Winkle the cobbler! Aren't they sweet? Don't forget to go and look for them, will you?

Jerry's Lost Temper

Once upon a time there lived a little boy who was always losing his temper. He lost it about six times a day, and that made him most unpleasant to live with.

He lost his temper at breakfast time when his mother made him eat his porridge, and threw his spoon at her. He lost it in the middle of the morning when his spade broke. He lost it at dinner time when he wanted a third helping of jelly and there wasn't any. He lost it twice at tea time because his mother wanted him to finish up his bread-and-butter, and he lost it when he was in the bath, because his duck wouldn't float properly.

So you can see what a bad-tempered child he was! It was really dreadful to see him and hear him.

'One of these days, Jerry,' said his mother, 'you'll lose your temper and not be able to find it again! That will be a great shock to you, because little boys and girls who lose their tempers for always, can never smile or laugh, but can only sulk, frown and cry, and talk in a cross-patch voice! You really should be careful!'

Now, one day, Jerry went to spend the day with his Aunt Marigold, who lived at the very end of Foxglove Village. His mother told him to be sure and behave nicely and to keep his temper, not to lose it.

But he hadn't been at his aunt's for five minutes before he flew into a terrible rage, quite lost his temper, and threw a saucepan lid at the big black cat sitting peacefully by the fire! That was the worst of Jerry. He always threw things when he lost his temper.

The saucepan lid hit the cat on the head. She hissed and jumped aside. Then she turned on the little boy and scratched him hard.

'Oh, dear!' said his aunt. 'Cinders is a queer cat, and whenever he scratches anybody something unpleasant happens. Now, Jerry, don't look so cross. Go out into the garden and don't come in again until you've found that temper you've lost!'

She pushed the angry little boy out of doors, and shut the kitchen door firmly. Jerry wandered round the garden, scowling. Suddenly he heard a call and, looking up, he saw the little girl next door holding out an apple to him.

'Hello, Jerry!' she said. 'Have an apple!'

Jerry tried to smile his thanks – but, to his horror, a smile wouldn't come! Instead a terrible frown puckered up his forehead and his lips pouted into a sulk.

'Oh, all right!' said the little girl, offended at Jerry's black looks. 'If you don't want a nice apple, *I'll* eat it!'

She dug her teeth into it, slid off the wall and disappeared. Jerry was dreadfully disappointed. He wondered what was wrong with his face. No matter how hard he tried to smile, he couldn't make his lips go up – they always went down. And his forehead kept wrinkling into a frown – but, worst of all, when he tried to speak he found that his voice had changed into a fierce growl, like a dog's!

'Oh, goodness gracious!' thought poor Jerry to himself. 'What Mother said would happen has come true! I've really and truly lost my temper this time and it hasn't come back!'

Jerry ran into a corner and cried bitterly. He tried again and again to speak, but he could only growl. He tried to stop frowning but he couldn't. Then he heard his aunt calling him.

'Jerry! Jerry! Here is a piece of chocolate cake for you!'

Jerry loved chocolate cake! He forgot his tears

and ran eagerly to the kitchen door, where his Aunt Marigold stood holding an enormous piece of iced chocolate cake. But, when she saw the scowling, frowning face of the little boy, and heard his growling, angry voice, she stared in surprise.

'What a dreadful, cross face!' she said. 'No, Jerry – you can't have the cake if you look like that!'

She went indoors, and shut the door, taking the cake with her. Jerry banged on the door, trying to say that he didn't mean to look cross and to growl – but his aunt was annoyed with him and wouldn't open the door. So the little boy ran off to the bottom of the garden, more miserable and more frightened than he had ever been in his life before.

What would happen if he never found his temper again, if it was always lost? How people would hate him! He would never get any treats, but would always be left out of everything. Jerry was very, very sad.

'What's the matter?' suddenly asked a high voice just beside him. Jerry looked down and saw a sharp-faced little man looking up at him. He was not a fairy, but looked more like a funny little dwarf.

'I've lost my temper, and I can't find it again,'

said Jerry, in a strange, snarling voice, frowning at the little dwarf.

'Ho, ho!' said the little creature, laughing. 'So that's what's the matter! Well, *I've* got your temper, little boy! I collect bad tempers, when I find them, and sell them to a cross old witch, who lives on the edge of the world. She pays me well for them. I found yours flying round the garden this morning, and I've got it safely in my pocket!'

'Please give it back to me!' begged Jerry, in the same growly voice. 'I can't bear to be like this, all frowns, sulks and snarls! It's horrid!'

'But you're like it a dozen times a day!' said the dwarf, grinning. 'I know you are! I've been close to you for a long time, though you didn't know it – and I knew I should be able to find that bad temper of yours, one day, when you lost it. And now I've got it!'

'Please,' said Jerry, still in his snarly voice. 'Please do give it back to me. I promise you that if I lose it again you may have it for good. I do promise you! But let me have it back again, just this once.'

'Well,' said the little dwarf, putting his hand into his pocket, 'I'm pretty sure you'll lose it again in the next ten minutes, so I don't mind letting you have it. Here you are. Swallow it –

but mind, I shall get it again before very long!'

Jerry took from the dwarf's hand a small, soft, yellow thing, rather the shape of an egg, with bright red ends that gleamed. He popped it into his mouth and swallowed it down – his lost temper!

At once he began to smile, and his own proper voice came back. His terrible frown went, and he looked friendly and pleasant.

'Goodness! That's made a difference to you!' said the dwarf, in surprise. 'Well, well – you'll get your frowns back in a minute or two, I expect, when you lose your temper again. And I shall catch that temper of yours and keep it to sell to the old witch! Ho, ho!'

Jerry said no more to the little dwarf. He ran straight to the kitchen door and opened it.

'Aunt Marigold, Aunt Marigold!' he cried. 'I've come to say I'm sorry I lost my temper this morning, and you may be sure I shall never do such a thing again. Please forgive me!'

And do you know, from that day to this Jerry never *has* lost his temper. He's so afraid the little dwarf will find it and keep it to sell to the witch. I do hope you won't ever lose yours when he's about – wouldn't it be dreadful if he found it and didn't give it back!

Mr Tickles' Green Pen

Once upon a time a brownie called Mr Tickles had a fine green pen. He was very proud of it, for it was a beautiful green, and it wrote very well indeed. It was a fountain pen, and he always kept it full of ink, so that he might write letters at any time.

But he was always losing it! Sometimes it was found on the dresser, sometimes on the mantelpiece, and once in the middle of the best bed, which made Mrs Tickles very angry indeed, for it had left a spot of ink behind.

'Tickles, why can't you keep your green pen in your pocket?' she said, a dozen times a week. 'You are always losing it. You must waste hours and hours trying to find it.'

'I know,' said Tickles. 'It is a great nuisance. I do try to remember to put it into my pocket, but it so often falls out, you know. And besides, I already have two pencils and a notebook in my pocket. There really isn't room for a pen too.'

'Well, why not do as the butcher boy does?' said Mrs Tickles.

'What does he do?' asked Mr Tickles.

'He puts his pen behind his right ear,' said Mrs Tickles. 'He comes every morning to take my order, and he has never to hunt for his pen for there it always is, tucked safely behind his ear!'

'What a splendid idea!' said Mr Tickles. 'I wonder if *my* ear will hold my green pen.'

He hunted about for his pen and found it stuck in a jug on the dresser. He put it behind his right ear and it held it beautifully. He was very pleased.

'Now I shall always know where it is!' he said, rubbing his hands. 'Aha! I shall waste no more time in looking for it again!'

'That's good,' said his wife. 'Now listen, Tickles, I'm going out to do my shopping. Will you please write a note to the sweep while I am gone, and ask him to come and sweep the chimney next Saturday? Now don't forget because it is most important and I shan't have time to do any letter writing today.'

Tickles promised to do the letter, and his wife took her basket and went out. Tickles cleaned his new boots, and then he scraped out his pipe, for it was very dirty. Then he frowned.

'Now, what was it that Mrs Tickles said she wanted me to do?' he wondered. 'Ah, yes – I promised to write a note to the sweep. Well, I'll do it now before I forget!'

He took out his notepaper and sat down. He felt in his pocket for his green pen. But it wasn't there. Bother! Where was it?

'That pen is always disappearing!' grumbled Mr Tickles, crossly. 'Now where did I put it?'

He hunted here and he hunted there. He looked on the dresser, he looked under the table. He went into the bedroom and looked on the bed. He looked simply everywhere! But he couldn't find that green pen.

'Let me see,' said Mr Tickles. 'I cleaned out my pipe this morning and put the scrapings in the dustbin. I believe, yes, I really do believe that my green pen must have dropped into the dustbin. Oh, dear!'

Just then, who should come into the garden but the dustman to take away the rubbish from the dustbin. He picked up the bin and strode out to his cart. Mr Tickles tapped loudly on the window.

'Wait, wait!' he cried. 'There is something valuable in the dustbin!'

But alas! The dustman had already tipped the dustbin into his cart. Mr Tickles ran out and scolded him.

'Why didn't you wait when you heard me

tapping at my window? My green fountain pen, the only one I have, has disappeared, and I'm sure it must have dropped into the dustbin. Now it's gone into the cart.'

'Well, sir,' said the dustman, 'I could go through the rubbish for you, if you like, and find your pen.'

'You'd better do that,' said Mr Tickles. 'I really *must* have my green pen back.'

The dustman began to search through the rubbish. He hunted through the cabbage leaves and the tea leaves, he looked in all the old tins, and he shook out the papers. But he couldn't find that pen anywhere. At last he went back to Mr Tickles.

'I'm very sorry, sir,' he said, 'but I can't find that pen of yours.'

'Dear, dear, how foolish of you!' said Mr Tickles. 'I tell you it *must* be there!'

The dustman took a piece of paper from his pocket and gave it to Mr Tickles. 'If you'll just sign that paper, sir,' he said, 'I'll see that your pen is hunted for once again, when I get back to the works. But I can't stop and look any longer myself, because I'm late as it is.'

'Very well, I'll sign the paper,' said Mr Tickles, impatiently. 'Dear me, I wish I'd looked in the cart myself for my pen – I'm sure I should have found it. It's too bad to lose a fine green pen like that!'

He put the piece of paper on the flat top of his gatepost to sign it. He took his green pen from behind his ear, where he had so carefully put it, and signed his name. The dustman stared at him in amazement.

'Now, what are you staring at me like that for?' asked Mr Tickles, putting back his pen behind his ear. 'Really, really, it is very rude of you!'

'It may be rude,' said the dustman. 'But pray tell me this, Mr Tickles – why do you make me waste my time in looking for your green pen when you have it behind your ear all the time? You have just signed your name with it!'

Mr Tickles put up his hand – and, of course, there was his green pen, behind his ear, just as the dustman had said! He did feel dreadful! He went first pink, then red, then purple.

'How foolish I am!' he wailed, suddenly. 'Oh, Dustman, don't tell Mrs Tickles, will you? See, here are two pounds for all your trouble. Oh dear, dear, dear, what a stupid fellow I am!'

The dustman took the two pounds, grinned all over his face and went back to his cart, whistling. Mr Tickles went into the house, muttering to himself.

'I'll never forget where I put my green pen again, I never will, never, never, never!'

But I shouldn't be surprised if he forgets again tomorrow, would you?

Good Old Tinker-Dog!

There was once a dog called Tinker. He belonged to Billy Brown, and the two were great friends. Billy had no brothers or sisters to play with, so he played with Tinker-dog instead. He gave him his breakfast and his dinner, and sometimes he even spent his Saturday money on a nice juicy bone for Tinker. So you can see how fond he was of his dog.

Now Tinker was a funny-looking dog. He looked a bit like a collie, a bit like a terrier, and his face was very much like a pug. Billy's mother said he was the ugliest dog she had ever seen, and that made Billy sad.

'Don't take any notice of what people say,' he whispered to Tinker. '*I* think you are the nicest dog in the whole world, Tinker, and you play better than any boy or girl I've ever seen!'

Tinker loved Billy. He loved the little boy so much that he even put up with being bathed, though he did so hate that. It was horrid to stand in hot water and be afraid of soap going in your eyes all the time. But he liked being well brushed every day. He liked to feel his coat silky and smooth, right down to the end of his tail!

One day Billy saw a notice on the wall. It said that there was to be a dog show at a garden fair to be held in the rector's garden. There were to be all sorts of prizes for different kinds of dogs.

'Ooh!' said Billy,. in delight. 'Look, Tinker-dog! A dog show! I'll take you, and you're sure to get first prize, a good dog like you!'

So when the day came, Billy asked his mother if she would give him fifty pence, which was what had to be paid to go into the garden fair. 'I'm going to take Tinker-dog to the dog show there,' he said, proudly. 'I'm sure he will win a prize, Mother!'

His mother laughed. 'What, that ugly old Tinker-dog win a prize!' she said. 'No, no, Billy – he never will. He's a nice enough dog for a pet, but he'll never win any prize for you, never!'

Billy said nothing more. He gave Tinker a good brushing, and put on his old collar. He would have liked to buy him a new one but there was no money in his money-box. Then off the two went to the fair in the rectory garden.

Billy paid his fifty pence to the man at the gate, and he and Tinker went inside the lovely garden. There was a big tent in the distance, labelled 'Dog Show', and Billy went over to it.

A lady was at the door, entering the names of all the dog owners who wanted to show their dogs. There were fox terriers, pekes, collies and all kinds of dogs, looking very smart. When Billy's turn came, the lady looked at Tinker.

'But you can't enter *him* for the show,' she said. 'He's a mongrel! He isn't a fox terrier, a peke or a collie, or anything. He's just a funny mixture of all of them! I'm sorry – but I'm afraid it's no use trying to enter such a funny-looking animal.'

'But he's a very, very good dog,' said Billy, almost crying with disappointment. 'Couldn't you give him a chance?'

'I'm afraid not,' said the lady. 'Now move away, please – I must take the name of the boy behind you.'

Billy moved away. He knew he was too big to cry, but he simply couldn't help the tears coming into his eyes. He knew quite well that Tinker was the finest dog in the world, and it was dreadful to hear people saying unkind things about him. He took Tinker to a shady corner, put his arms round the dog's neck and wiped away his tears on his silky coat.

Presently an old man came by and saw the two sitting there. He guessed that Billy had been crying, and he was sorry. He sat down by the little boy and soon Billy had told him about his big disappointment.

'Dear, dear me!' said the old man, shaking his head. 'That's very sad. But, unless I am mistaken, there *is* a competition you can enter your dog for, Billy. I'll just make certain. Stay here for a minute.'

Soon he was back. 'Yes,' he said. 'There is a prize offered for the best-kept dog in the show. Why not put Tinker-dog in for that? He looks very clean indeed to me, and not too fat or too thin – in fact, he's just right!'

Billy cheered up and went with the old man back to the tent. Soon Tinker and a good many other dogs were being walked about in front of two judges – and whatever do you think? Tinker won the first prize for being the best-kept dog!

'He is so clean and so silky,' said one of the judges. 'His teeth are so white, and he is just the right figure, neither too fat nor too thin. He looks such a happy, cheerful dog, too! We are pleased to give him the first prize.'

And what do you think the prize was? Guess! It was ten pounds! Think of that! Billy could hardly believe his eyes when the old man, who happened to be one of the judges, counted ten bright pounds out into his hand.

'Oh, thank you, thank you!' said Billy, his face red with joy. 'I do feel so pleased!'

Tinker-dog wagged his tail hard and licked the old man's hand. He loved anyone who made Billy happy.

'He's a fine dog, a good dog!' said the old man, patting Tinker.

Billy took Tinker home, longing to tell his mother what happened – and on the way he stopped at a shop. He went inside and bought Tinker-dog a fine red collar. You should have seen it!

'Mother, Mother! Tinker's got a prize!' said Billy, rushing indoors. 'Ten whole pounds. See, I've bought him that new red collar. Doesn't he look fine?'

His mother stared at Tinker-dog in surprise. He certainly *did* look fine.

'Well, he's always been a good and loving dog,' she said, 'and he deserves his prize. I'll never say he's ugly again, Billy!'

But Billy doesn't mind a bit now if people call Tinker-dog ugly or funny-looking. He just says: 'Well, he won a prize of ten pounds at a dog show, so he is a very clever dog and I am proud of him.'

And you should see Tinker-dog's tail wagging then! It's a wonder he doesn't wag it off!

Janet and her Friends

Janet always put out the crumbs every morning for the birds – but especially for the little red-breasted robin who stood on the windowsill each day. He looked in at the window with his bright black eyes and trilled a cheery little song as if to say: 'Well, I'm here, I'm here! What about a nice tasty crumb, my dear, my dear!'

One day a dreadful thing happened. The cat jumped up at the robin and caught him! Janet screamed and ran to save him. The cat dropped the bird – but when Janet picked him up, she saw that one of his little legs was hurt.

So, for four days she nursed the robin, and kept him cosily in a small box till he was quite better again. He was very happy, and often trilled to Janet when she came to feed him. He flew off merrily when she let him go, and she was so pleased to see that he could perch just as well as ever, on his two legs.

Now in the early spring-time Janet fell ill. She had to go to bed – and, oh dear me, what a long time she stayed there! Nobody was allowed to see her, and as she couldn't read, the time seemed very dull. She was tired of her dolls, tired of everything. She longed to get up and go and play. She wanted to see people and talk to her friends. But the doctor said no, she must be kept perfectly quiet.

So the little girl grew more and more dull and often cried when she was alone. She sometimes thought of the robin and wondered if he missed her – and one day he came to see her! He *had* missed his little friend, and at last he made up his mind to go and find her. So he hopped on every windowsill and looked in every room – and there, in the small bedroom was Janet, lying flat in bed, crying big tears down her cheeks!

'Trilla, trilla!' sang the robin, outside. He saw that the window was open a little way at the top and he flew up. He sat on the edge of the window and sang again. Janet heard him and was delighted.

'Oh, Robin!' she said. 'I'm so glad to see you. I'm so bored. No one ever comes to see me, and I'm not allowed to get up. Do come and see me every day.'

So after that the robin came to her bedroom every morning. Soon he would fly right inside and sit on the bed, chirping and singing gaily.

Janet loved him very much and looked for him eagerly. She wasn't allowed visitors, she knew, but she meant to have this little robin, all the same! He made her feel so cheerful and happy.

The robin didn't like to see his little friend looking so sad and ill. What could he do to cheer her up? He had just found a dear little wife and he talked to her about it – and she had a wonderful idea!

'My dear,' she said, 'shall we build our nest in Janet's bedroom? You know, if we build it here in the bank, we shall be too busy to go and see her each day and she would miss you dreadfully. But if we could find a good place in her bedroom, we should be in and out all day long, and keep her amused and happy!'

The robin thought that was a splendid idea. So he flew to Janet's bedroom and had a good look round and he thought that the top of the wardrobe would be a splendid place in which to build his nest. It was high up and not likely to be seen.

So, to Janet's great surprise and delight he brought his little wife to her the next day and sang to Janet all about the good idea they had had for their nest. And they began to build it that very same day! Janet soon guessed what they were doing and her cheeks grew red with happiness and her eyes shone. To think that those dear little robins had really chosen her bedroom for a nesting-place! Oh, she did hope that no one would find out. It would be too dreadful if the nest were taken away!

But no one found out for the robins were very careful indeed. They never came into the room when people were there – only when Janet was alone. They built their nest on the wardrobe, so high up that no one but Janet guessed anything about it! They always picked up anything they dropped, leaves or moss, and were careful to leave their new home tidy and neat.

Janet was so happy watching them. She loved to see first one robin and then another flying in at the window with a leaf, or a piece of soft moss for the nest. Then at last the nest was finished. Janet could just see one side of it if she stood up in bed.

'I do wonder if there will be any baby robins!' thought the little girl, excitedly. 'I'm sure the hen robin is laying eggs.'

So she was. She laid four pretty red-brown eggs and then sat on them to keep them warm. Janet watched the little cock robin flying in and out of the window dozens of times a day with a titbit for his small mate. The little girl was very happy and contented now, for there was something to think about and to watch. She had more colour in her cheeks and quite forgot to cry.

Her mother was pleased. 'I can't think what has happened to make Janet so much better,' she said to the doctor. 'She doesn't seem so bored, and she is always smiling. I really think she is much better.'

'She certainly is,' said the doctor. 'There must be some reason why she seems so much brighter lately, but I don't know what it is. Anyway, it is a very good thing!'

And then one day something dreadful happened: Janet's mother thought she would dust the top of the wardrobe, so up she stepped on a chair – and of course she saw the robins' nest on the top of the wardrobe!

'There's a bird sitting on a nest on the top of the wardrobe!' she said. 'What a mess it will make! I shall clear the nest away.'

But then Janet sat up and began to cry bitterly, and said: 'No, no, no! They are *my* robins! I have watched them for a long time, and they have made me so happy. Don't touch the nest, please, please!'

In the middle of all the excitement, in came the doctor. He heard about the nest, and then he turned to Janet. 'So it was the two little robins who made you so happy all this time, was it?' he said. 'They helped you to forget how bored you were, and visited you every day?'

'Yes,' said Janet. 'They made me feel ever so much better. They came and sang to me, and they built their nest there, and I was hoping there were some eggs so that I could see the little ones when they hatched. In the winter I nursed the little cock robin, when he had a bad leg – and now you see, he has been a good friend to me in return!'

'So he has!' said the doctor. 'Well, we'll let the nest stay there, I think. By the time the eggs hatch, Janet, you will be ready to go downstairs again! What do you think of that?'

Janet was delighted. She could keep the robins' nest and see the young ones – and soon she would go downstairs, and then, perhaps, go out. How lovely!

When everyone had gone and she was alone, she called to the robins. 'Robins! Don't be afraid! The doctor knows what good friends you've been to me. Bring up your young ones and then take them into my garden and teach them to sing and fly. I do love you so!'

'Trilla, trilla, and we love you!' said the cock-robin, peeping over the wardrobe. 'There's nothing like helping one another, is there?'

Inside the Doll's House

There was once a small pixie who had a large family of children. They lived in a foxglove, and each child had a flower for itself. But when the flowers fell off the foxglove there was nowhere for the children to sleep!

So the pixie moved to a rose bush. This was prickly, but there were plenty of roses there, opening in the sunshine. Each small pixie took a flower for himself, and for a few days the little family was happy.

Then someone came along with sharp scissors, snipped off the roses and put them into a basket. The pixie children tumbled out quickly, and ran to their mother. She was in despair.

'It's dreadful to have so many children!' she said. 'There doesn't seem anywhere that we can live in comfort. I wish I could get a proper little house, but that's quite impossible.'

'There's a dear little house in that big house over there!' said a passing rabbit. 'I once saw the little girl who lives there carrying this tiny house out into the garden to play with. It's called a doll's house. It would be quite big enough for you and your family, I should think. Why don't you go there?'

The pixie mother was delighted. She went with her children to the big house one night and climbed in at the nursery window. There was a fire in the room and she could quite well see everything. She looked round – and there, in the corner, stood the doll's house! The pixie gave a squeal of delight and ran to it. She opened the front door and went inside.

It was a lovely house. There were six rooms, and a little stair ran up to the bedrooms. The kitchen had a proper stove, and a dresser with plates, cups and saucers. The dining room and drawing room were full of proper furniture, just the right size for the pixies, and the bedrooms had plenty of small white beds.

'Children! Come and see!' cried the mother pixie. The little pixies ran into the house and shouted with joy to see everything.

'Now just get undressed and pop into bed,' said the mother pixie, happily. 'For once we will have a really good night!'

Just as the small pixies were undressing there came a loud knock at the front door. The pixie went to see who was there – and to her surprise, there stood outside a sailor doll, a teddy bear and a golden-haired doll.

'Good evening,' they said, quite politely. 'We have come to see what you are doing in this house. It belongs to Mary Ann, the little girl whose nursery this is. She would be very upset if her nice house was spoilt. We think you had better come out and go away.'

The mother pixie sat down on the front doorstep and cried into her clean white apron. It was too bad to have to turn out just when she had found a house that suited them all so well.

The toys didn't like to see her crying. They felt most uncomfortable. She really seemed a dear little pixie.

'Please don't cry,' said the sailor doll.

'I can't help it,' sobbed the pixie. 'All my tired little pixie children are getting undressed and jumping into those nice little white beds, and I was just making them a chocolate pudding to eat for their suppers. Can't you smell it cooking on the stove?'

The toys could. It *did* smell delicious!

'You shall taste a little,' said the pixie, and she ran to the kitchen. She ladled some of the chocolate pudding into a dish and took it to the toys. They each tasted some and really, it was the nicest pudding they had ever had!

'If you'll let us stay in this house I'll often cook you things,' said the pixie, looking at them with her bright eyes. 'I'll make you cakes when you have birthdays. I'll sew on any buttons, whiskers or eyes that come loose. I'll keep this house spotless and tidy so that Mary Ann will never guess there's a pixie family living here. In the daytime I'll take all my children into the garden, so that no one will see them.'

'Well – ' said the toys, liking the little pixie very much indeed. 'Well – perhaps it would be all right. Stay a week and we'll see!'

So the pixies stayed a week – and you should have seen that doll's house at the end of it. It was spotlessly clean, for all the children scrubbed the floors, swept and dusted very well. All the saucepans and kettles shone like new. The beds were always neatly made after the children had slept in them, and the pixie had even mended a tiny hole in one of the tablecloths – a hole that had been there ever since Christmas!

Each night she cooked something for the toys – and she was a very good cook indeed. Sometimes it was a pudding. Sometimes it was a few buns. Once it was a birthday cake for the brown teddy bear. She knew how to manage the toy stove very well, and it cooked beautifully for her.

'Pixie, we'd like you to stay here,' said the sailor doll, at the end of the week. 'We are very fond of you and your children, and you certainly keep the doll's house even better than Mary Ann does. Stay with us, and let your children come and play in the nursery at night-time, when we toys come alive and have games too.'

So, very gladly, the pixies stayed on in the doll's house – and they are still there! At night the pixie children go for rides in the clockwork train, and ride on the big elephant. They run races with the clockwork mouse and squeal like mice for happiness!

As for the doll's house it is just as spotless as ever, and Mary Ann's mother often says to her: 'Well, really, Mary Ann dear, you *do* keep that house of yours beautifully! I really am proud of you!'

Mary Ann is quite puzzled – for she knows she doesn't do very much to her house. Nobody has told her that a family of pixies live there, for the toys are afraid that if she knew she might be angry. But she wouldn't. She would be just as pleased as you would be, I'm sure!

So if you should happen to know a little girl called Mary Ann, who has a beautiful doll's house, just tell her who lives in it, will you? Won't she get a surprise!

The Cross Little Girl

Belinda was a cross little girl. If things didn't go right she shouted and stamped her foot. If her toys didn't do exactly as she wanted them to she threw them across the room. If she played snakes and ladders and went down the snakes instead of going up the ladders she quite lost her temper and threw the counters into the fire.

So you can guess that her toys, dolls and games didn't like her one bit!

One day Belinda couldn't find a sailor doll she wanted to play with. She hunted all through her toy cupboard, but it wasn't a bit of good, she could *not* find it! Then in a rage she swept every single thing out of the cupboard on to the floor! Crash! Bang! Smash!

The china doll was broken. The little tea-set had its teapot and a cup smashed to bits. The teddy bear hurt its soft nose. The humming-top was dented at one side. Really, it was too bad of Belinda!

Belinda looked at the empty toy cupboard. 'I

think I'll play at houses,' she said. 'I will make
the toy cupboard into a little house for myself.
That will be fun!'

She opened the door wide and then squeezed
herself into the cupboard on the bottom shelf. It
just fitted her nicely!

Then a very peculiar thing happened! The
teddy bear suddenly jumped up from the floor
and shouted loudly. He did make Belinda jump!

'Toys! Quick, let us shut and lock the door on
Belinda, and run away from this nursery! We
are so badly treated! Let us go to the next-door-
neighbour's cottage. He has two kind little
children, and they will treat us better than this
cross little girl.'

At once all the toys jumped up. The bricks
grew legs, the humming-top grew a face, the
tea-set grew legs and arms, and all the dolls
walked and talked. Belinda could hardly believe
her eyes!

She tried to get out of the cupboard, but she
was too late. The teddy bear slammed the door,
and then click! She heard the key being turned
in the lock. She was a prisoner in the toy
cupboard!

Belinda banged on the door and shouted, but
the toys took no notice. She heard their little
pattering feet running to the door and then

down the passage outside. Soon there was not a sound to be heard. They had all gone!

Belinda was frightened and angry. It was all very well to play at houses, but it was horrid to be shut up like this so that she couldn't get out. She began to feel very squashed and uncomfortable.

She shook the door and called loudly. 'Help! Mummy! Nanny! Help!'

But nobody came. Mummy was out, and Nanny had gone down the garden to hang up the clothes.

The little girl began to cry. She didn't like being locked in. She didn't like her toys running away. She felt really ashamed. Suppose the next-door-neighbour's children took them in and loved them? They would never want to come back to her.

Belinda shook the cupboard again, but it wasn't a bit of use. The door would *not* open! Then, suddenly, the little girl heard a sound of pattering feet again, and all the toys came back into the nursery! Belinda could hear their little high voices!

She listened – and she found out that the toys had run down the garden path to the next-door-neighbour's cottage – and had met a big dog who chased them away! They had been very much frightened and had run back to the nursery as fast as ever they could!

'Toys! Toys! Let me out, please do!' begged Belinda, shaking the door. 'I know I've been a cross little girl. But I'll be better in future, really I will! Do, do let me out, I'm terribly squashed in here! Don't run away from me again – give me another chance!'

'No!' shouted the toys, all together. 'We shall not give you another chance, Belinda. You have been a cross little girl for so long that we don't think you can ever be anything else! You shall stay there!'

Just at that moment Nanny came running up the stairs, calling, 'Belinda, Belinda!'

'I'm here, Nanny!' cried Belinda. 'Oh, do let me out. I'm in the toy cupboard.'

Nanny unlocked the cupboard and stared at Belinda in surprise.

'How did you get locked in?' she asked.

'The toys locked me in,' said Belinda. 'They said I was a cross little girl. And they tried to run away from me, but Bonzo, the next-door dog, met them and chased them back.'

'The *toys* locked you in,' said Nanny, laughing. 'Whatever will you say next? Don't be so silly, Belinda! You must somehow have slipped the lock yourself from the inside of the cupboard!'

Belinda didn't say any more. But you may be sure of two things – she never got into her toy cupboard again to play houses – and she stopped being a cross little girl, and became good-tempered instead.

And now the toys wouldn't *dream* of running away! They are much too happy!

The Stupid Donkey

There was once a very stupid donkey. His name was Neddy, and he had long grey ears, a pretty grey coat, and a tail that could swish all the flies off his back.

He belonged to Mr Turnabout, and was very fond of his master indeed. But Mr Turnabout was not so fond of Neddy. Neddy really could be so very stupid. Sometimes he would go ambling along the road with Mr Turnabout on his back, and then he would suddenly stop.

'Get on, get on!' Mr Turnabout would say. But no, Neddy wanted to stop, and he might stop there all day long. It was very stupid of him, especially when he chose to stop in the middle of a bridge so that no carts or barrows could get past him.

Then sometimes he wouldn't allow himself to be caught. No – he would gallop round and round the field with Mr Turnabout chasing him for all he was worth, panting and shouting. But he never caught Neddy if the donkey didn't want him to.

There was no doubt about it, Neddy could be a very stupid donkey.

One day Mr Turnabout heard that Old Man Twiddleabout, his cousin, was badly in need of a grey donkey.

'Ha!' said Mr Turnabout at once. 'Ho! I'll take *you* to him, Neddy. You're too stupid for me. Perhaps Old Man Twiddleabout can do something with you – but I doubt it, for a stupider donkey than you I never did see!'

So the next day Mr Turnabout took Neddy and saddled him. Then he jumped up on to his broad back and cantered off. Neddy was sad. He didn't want to leave his good master. He wished that he wasn't so stupid, but it was hard for a little donkey to be clever.

Now the way to Old Man Twiddleabout's lay through the Witch Country. Mr Turnabout wasn't quite sure of his way, and he wasn't quite sure how the witches and wizards would treat him, either. So he went at a smart rate, and hoped that nobody would stop him.

Soon he lost his way. He stopped and looked round. There was no one in sight except an old witch sitting knitting on the edge of the well at the bottom of her garden. She looked at Mr Turnabout with bright green eyes and he didn't like them much. But there was no one else from whom he could ask the way, so he cantered up to her on Neddy.

'Good morning,' he said politely. 'Please could you tell me the way to Old Man Twiddle-about's?'

The witch looked at Mr Turnabout and saw the fat leather bag he carried at his waist. She had heard the chink of money and her eyes gleamed.

'I'll tell you the way but first you must pay me,' she said, knitting hard.

'How much?' asked Mr Turnabout.

'Oh, all the money you have in that bag,' said the witch greedily. Mr Turnabout grew pale.

'I can't give you all that,' he said. The witch dropped her knitting and took up her stick. She was just going to turn poor Mr Turnabout into a jumping frog when the donkey grew tired of waiting. He was thirsty and he wanted to trot down to a pond he could see and have a drink. So he asked for one.

'Hee-haw!' he brayed, suddenly, opening his great mouth. 'Hee-haw!'

The witch gave a jump, and was so startled at the enormous noise that she lost her balance and fell over the edge of the well. Splash! She went into the cold water and began to scream.

'Help! Help! Save me!'

Her servant heard her and came running down the garden path. The donkey hee-hawed again and trotted off to the pond. Mr Turnabout, very thankful that the witch had fallen into the well, and very much afraid that her servant would get her out before he was well away, tugged at the reins and tried to make the donkey gallop off.

But no – Neddy wanted his drink and meant to have it. Only after he had drunk about four gallons did he trot off down the road again – just as the witch's servant pulled her up to the top of the well in the bucket!

'Just like you, Neddy, to want a drink when we might have been turned into frogs and snails any minute,' said Mr Turnabout crossly. 'Get on now, get on!'

Neddy galloped on. Mr Turnabout wondered very much if they were going the right way, but thought they were. Soon he saw a curious figure coming along towards them. It was a dwarf wizard, a small creature with wicked eyes and a crooked nose.

Mr Turnabout wanted to gallop on but the wizard stopped him.

'Not so fast, not so fast,' he said. 'Give me the money out of your wallet.'

'Indeed I won't!' said Mr Turnabout, not

feeling very much afraid of this small wizard. He bent forward and tried to box the wizard's long, sticking-out ears – but at once the little creature changed himself into a tree and Mr Turnabout banged his knuckles hard on the bark, making them bleed. Mr Turnabout was very angry.

The wizard changed himself back to his own shape. 'Give me that money!' he cried, and tried to grab the bag of coins. But Mr Turnabout kicked out with his right foot, meaning to send the dwarf flying head over heels.

But the wizard changed himself into a hard rock and poor Turnabout nearly broke his toes!

'Oh!' he cried, rubbing his foot. 'Ow!'

The dwarf changed back to his own shape and grinned. 'I said, give me your money!' he shouted.

Mr Turnabout leapt off the donkey and rushed at the wizard, trying to clutch him with his hands. But at once the dwarf changed himself into a tall and prickly thistle, and the poor man pricked and scratched his hands terribly.

Neddy the donkey was standing patiently waiting. But when he saw the big thistle he looked at it in surprise and joy. Ha, a thistle was a fine titbit for *him*! Before his master could say a word he began to munch that thistle!

'You're eating the wizard!' said Mr Turn-about, half pleased, half frightened. Then, not knowing what might happen next, he leapt on the donkey's back and tore off down the lane. Neddy was still munching the prickly thistle which certainly tasted rather odd.

On they went again and very soon Mr Turn-about came in sight of his cousin's house, set on a hilltop in the distance. But before he reached it, he came across a greedy old woman, half a witch, powerful and strong.

'Stop!' she cried. 'I want your donkey! Give it to me at once, for I have a long way to go.'

Now Mr Turnabout saw that this old woman was very powerful, and he jumped off the donkey at once and bowed politely.

'Madam,' he said, 'the donkey is for sale. You may have him for seven golden pounds.'

'Fiddlesticks!' said the old woman. 'I'm having him for nothing!' She went to one side of Neddy to climb on his back, but he at once turned round so that he was facing her. He didn't like her. She went round to his side again and once more he turned to face her.

She grew cross and struck him with her big stick. Neddy pricked up his big ears and brayed angrily. As quick as lightning he turned himself about so that his back was towards the witch.

Then he kicked out with his hind feet as hard as he could.

'Whoosh!' The old witch sailed through the air and came down bump about a hundred yards away, so frightened that she at once got up and ran for her life! Neddy gave a contented bray and looked round for his master.

Mr Turnabout was looking at the donkey very strangely. Then he scratched his head, rubbed his nose and pursed up his lips.

'Neddy,' he said, 'are you really stupid, or are you clever? You've got rid of a witch today by tumbling her into a well, you've eaten a wizard, and now you've frightened that powerful old witch.'

'Hee-haw!' said Neddy, pleased, and he whisked his tail so hard that he knocked Mr Turnabout's hat off. But his master didn't seem to mind, he just went on staring at the donkey.

'I can't make you out,' said Mr Turnabout. 'You do seem so stupid at times and yet you do the cleverest things without thinking about them. I think you really *are* clever but are too stupid to know it. Well, well, Neddy, I shan't sell you to my cousin, Mr Twiddleabout. You're too good a friend. Come on, turn round now and we'll gallop home to tea!'

So round they turned, the two of them, and

galloped home at top speed – and not a witch or a wizard dared to stop them!

Which do *you* think Neddy was? Stupid – or clever? I'm sure *I* don't know!

Clever Old Jumbo

There was once a sailor doll who loved frightening people. He used to hide in dark corners, and when the golden-haired doll came by he would jump out at her and shout, 'Boo!' The doll was dreadfully frightened, of course, and ran away as fast as she could.

The sailor doll frightened the teddy bear too, and the pink cat and the blue rabbit. They would be walking along at night, enjoying a talk, when suddenly that sailor would dart out at them, his face shining and his big eyes gleaming. 'Boo!' he would cry, and off they would all run, screaming.

The toys were most annoyed with him. How could they stop him? They made up their minds to beg him to be kinder, but he only laughed at them.

'No!' he said. 'I love playing jokes on you. It's fun to see your scared faces!'

One day, when Jill had taken the sailor doll out for a ride in her pram, the toys had a

meeting about him. Jill was the little girl whose
nursery they lived in and she would soon be
back with the sailor, so they had to hurry up and
decide what to do.

'Oh, if only we could think of some way to
make him heard wherever he goes!' said the
teddy bear. 'Then we should know where he
was and not be frightened. But he isn't clockwork so we can't hear his works going round,
and he doesn't squeak or do anything like
that.'

'It's a pity he doesn't wear a bell, like the blue
rabbit does!' said the golden-haired doll. 'We
always know when Bunny is coming because his
bell rings!'

'Well, can't we make him wear a bell?' said
the pink cat.

'Of course not!' said the bear. 'Do you
suppose he would let us put a bell on him?
Don't be silly!'

'Look here, I've got an idea!' said clever old
Jumbo, suddenly. 'Let's have some races or
sports, and let him win something. The prize
shall be a bell and I'll tie it round his neck and
pretend it is a great honour for him. He won't
like to refuse – and then we shall always know
when he is coming and he won't be able to
frighten us any more!'

'But he'll be able to take it off, won't he?' said the doll.

'Ha, I'll tie it too tightly for that!' said Jumbo. 'It will be on a thick string and there will be lots of knots, I can tell you! We'll hide the nursery scissors and he won't be able to cut the string or undo the knots. Ho ho!'

'Sh!' said the pink cat. 'Here comes Jill with the sailor doll.'

The next night the toys held their races. The sailor doll was pleased when he heard about them, for he had long legs and could jump very high indeed. He thought he would be sure to win the high jump.

First there was a long race, three times round the nursery, for clockwork toys. The train, the car and the clockwork mouse went in for that and the train won very easily. The prize was a bit of cottonwool for smoke, and the train tucked it into its funnel and was delighted.

Then there was a running race for ordinary toys. The sailor went in for that but he didn't expect to win it because he knew the pink cat could go very fast. She bounded along and easily won the prize – a piece of blue ribbon.

Then came the jumping. Ah, the sailor was going to win that! He had quite made up his mind. He didn't guess that the other toys had made up their minds he should win it too!

They all jumped – but everyone was careful to jump very low indeed. Only the sailor jumped high – and he certainly jumped twice as high as anyone else! He was very pleased with himself.

'Pooh, what poor jumpers you all are!' he said, proudly looking round. 'No one can beat *me* at jumping. I've won the prize! What is it, please?'

'It's a *beautiful* prize,' said clever Jumbo, coming forward. He held in his trunk a brightly shining little bell. He had taken it off a pair of old reins in the toy cupboard and had polished it up till it shone. The sailor doll looked at it.

'Well – I'm not sure I want that for a prize,' he began.

'Very well,' said Jumbo, at once. 'I'll give it to the blue rabbit. He jumped nearly as high as you did, and I'm sure he tried harder.'

The sailor doll didn't like that. He frowned and sulked. 'That's not true,' he said. 'I jumped twice as high as anyone, and I tried the hardest too. I must have the prize. You are not to give it to the blue rabbit.'

'Very well,' said Jumbo. 'I have much pleasure in giving *you* the prize. Let me tie it round your neck so that everyone can see what an honour you have won!'

The sailor doll came forward, pleased. The old elephant tied the bell tightly round his neck, knotting the stout string a dozen times. The sailor thanked him and walked off. Jingle-jingle-jingle, went the bell! It made a very loud sound indeed!

Well, of course, the sailor doll was never able to frighten anyone after that! Wherever he went the bell shook and jingled, and everyone always knew where he was. It wasn't a bit of good for him to hide any more – his bell rang and warned anyone nearby where he was. Then they called out: 'Oho, we can hear you hiding there! You can't frighten *us*!'

Sailor doll was angry. He tried to undo the knots but he couldn't. He tried to find the nursery scissors but they were well hidden under the doll's house and he didn't know where they were. He asked all the toys, one by one, please to undo the string that tied the bell round his neck – but nobody would.

'I believe you put it there on purpose!' he cried angrily to Jumbo one day.

'Of course I did!' said Jumbo, grinning. 'And it will stay there until you promise never to frighten anyone any more. So now you know!'

Sailor promised yesterday – so the bell is coming off today. But *wasn't* it a good idea of clever old Jumbo's?

A Basket of Brownies

John had a bicycle that his uncle had given him two birthdays ago. When it was new it was very beautiful – as bright as silver, with a fine, tinkling bell, a lamp in front, and a brake under the handle that John used when he was going downhill.

But when two years had gone by it didn't look quite so beautiful. It had been out in the rain and the mud, the bell had got broken, and the lamp wouldn't light. John looked at his bicycle sadly one day and made up his mind to clean it well.

So he asked his mother for some polish, an old cloth and a duster, and set to work. He rubbed the polish on with the cloth, and then made the bicycle shine brightly with the duster. His mother was pleased.

'John, you're a good boy,' she said. 'When you've cleaned up your bicycle nicely I'll give you something new for it!'

John was delighted. He did so badly want a

new bell. Then people would know he was
coming when he rang it. So he worked away
hard, and by dinner-time the bicycle shone as
bright as silver, and looked as good as new. His
mother came in from her shopping and looked
at it.

'Well done, John,' she said. 'I've brought you
back something new to put on your bicycle, as I
promised. Here it is!'

She handed John a parcel, quite a big one. He
undid it – and what do you think was inside it?
Not a bell, but a new basket to go on the front of
the bicycle! John was disappointed, but he
didn't like to say so.

'Isn't it a nice basket, John?' said his mother.
'I thought it would be so useful when you go
shopping for me. You can put all the parcels
into the basket and carry them home easily.'

'Thank you very much, Mother,' said John.
He fixed the basket on the front of the handle,
but he did wish it was a new bell! How nice a
fine new, shining bell with a loud ting-a-ling
would have been! The basket was all right, but
it was a very dull sort of thing.

'Do you want any shopping this afternoon,
Mother?' he asked after dinner.

'No, thank you,' said his mother. 'I've done
it all this morning. Why don't you go for a ride

to the woods, John? There may be some blackberries there.'

So John set off, his bicycle shining brightly.
He soon came to the woods, for he could pedal
very quickly. He chose a fairly wide path
through the woods so that his bicycle could go
along easily. When he came to a thick clump of
brambles he jumped off. Blackberries! Fine big
ones, black and juicy! John was soon picking
them as fast as he could, and his mouth quickly
became as black as the fruit!

Now as he was busy picking, he suddenly saw
a very strange sight. It was so strange that he
could hardly believe his eyes. He saw, coming
round the blackberry bushes, a line of very
small brownies, each wearing a red tunic and
green stockings. There were about seven of
them, and they seemed in a great hurry. Just as
they came round the bush, they stopped.

'We shall be very late,' said one. 'I am sure we
shall never get there in time.'

'Oh, I don't want to miss the party!' said
another, and took out a small green handkerchief as if he were going to cry.

'It's a pity we got lost this morning,' said the
first one. 'I know the way now, but we are most
certainly very late indeed.'

Suddenly one of the small brownies saw

John's bicycle standing nearby. He pointed to it in excitement.

'Look!' he cried. 'A bicycle! Just what we want! Let's make it small and then perhaps it will carry all of us to the party in good time! I know how to work it.'

The brownies all rushed to the bicycle, and to John's astonishment one of them took up a stick and began to wave it over his bicycle.

'Hi, hi!' shouted John, suddenly, coming out from behind the bush. 'Don't do that! That's *my* bicycle! If you make it small I shan't be able to ride it. You mustn't do that. It isn't yours!'

The brownies looked round in a fright. When they saw that John looked a kindly little boy they didn't run away, but just looked sorrowfully at the bicycle. What a pity they couldn't use it after all!

'How disappointing!' said one with a sigh 'I did think we had found a way to get to the party in time. Won't you really let us make the bicycle small, little boy? We'd make it big again later on.'

'I'd really rather you didn't,' said John. 'You see, I've only just cleaned it today, and I'm rather proud of it. I should be very upset if you made it small and forgot to make it big again. It wouldn't be any use to me at all.'

'Well, we *might* forget, in the excitement of the party,' said one of the brownies. 'We haven't very good memories. We'd better go on our way, I think.'

The little folk were just turning to go when a great idea came to John. 'Wait! Wait!' he cried. '*I* could take you to your party! I could put you all comfortably into my new basket in front there; it's quite big enough, for you are so tiny! Then, if you could tell me the way, we'd soon be there!'

The brownies began to twitter like birds in their excitement. 'Yes, yes!' they cried. 'Take us, little boy! We can easily squeeze ourselves into your basket!'

So John picked up each brownie very carefully, in his hands and put them all into his fine new basket. How pleased he was to have a basket then! When each tiny fellow was in the basket, he got on the saddle and put his feet on the pedals.

'Now you must tell me the way,' he said.

One of the brownies stood up in the basket and pointed the way to go. Off went John. The path grew rather narrow but on he went. The brownies knew the way quite well, and John pedalled fast. Down this path – and down that – round this tree – and round that one. And suddenly they were there! There was no doubt about it, for, in a grassy clearing, there ran and chattered scores of fairy folk – brownies, pixies, gnomes and many others. How John stared!

'Thank you very much, little boy,' said the brownies, scrambling out of the basket, and sliding down the front part of the bicycle. 'You shall have your reward! Now do you mind going home, because the other little folk might be frightened to see you here!'

'Well – I'm afraid I don't know the way,' said John. 'You see, there were so many twists and turns!'

'Oh, your bicycle knows the way,' said a brownie, and he gave the wheels a push. 'Home, bicycle, home!'

To John's surprise the bicycle turned itself round, and, with him on the saddle, pedalled itself merrily, shot up this path and that, and in a very short while came out into the place where John had been picking blackberries. There it stopped.

'Well, that was a most extraordinary adventure really!' thought John, as he got off to pick some more blackberries. 'I've never seen fairies before, and never thought I should, though I've looked for them often enough! I'm afraid no one will believe me if I tell them! I don't think I'll say anything to anyone about it.'

But he had to – because the very next morning, when he went to get out his bicycle, what do you think was fixed to the handle? Why, the finest, biggest silver bell John had ever seen, and when he rang it, goodness, what a noise! You could hear it a mile away!

There was a small label on it and John read it. It said: 'From seven grateful brownies' – so there was no need to wonder where it came from!

Of course everyone wanted to know where John had got his beautiful bell, and he had to tell them. He told *me*, so that's how I know. I *wish* I'd seen that basketful of brownies, don't you?

The Very Fine Tail

There was once a small lizard who had a remarkably fine tail. It was long and graceful, and Flick the lizard was very proud of it. The other lizards had tails too, but none were quite so fine as his.

The lizards used to play together on a sunny bank, and Flick always showed off his tail as much as he could. The others became tired of hearing about the wonderful tail and laughed at Flick.

'Pride goes before a fall!' they said. 'You be careful that nothing happens to that tail of yours! If it's so grand it may be stolen!'

'Don't be foolish!' said Flick, quite offended. 'Who would steal a lizard's tail?'

'Ah! You never know!' said the others.

When the autumn came, and the nights were chilly, the little lizards began to think of finding a nice cosy hole in which they could sleep the winter away. They peered under stones, they looked into all the holes on the bankside to see which would be best. Flick was too lazy to help.

He lay on the bank in the autumn sunshine, spreading out his long, graceful tail for all the birds and the mice to see.

He fell asleep as he lay there. He didn't hear the excited squeals of the other lizards. He didn't hear the squeaks of the mice as they scurried over the bank, frightened. He didn't even hear the deep, warning croak of the big old toad who sat all day under his damp stone, peering out at the sunny world outside.

'Rat!' squealed the lizards, and rushed for their hole.

'Rat, rat!' squealed the mice, and scurried away.

'Here comes the wicked rat!' croaked the old toad, who knew that the lean brown rat would gobble up any small creature he came across. 'Beware of the rat!'

The rat appeared on the bank, his whiskers twitching. He could smell lizard. Ah, he would dearly love a dinner of nice fat lizard. Then, to his great delight he spied the sleeping lizard just nearby, lying in the short grass, his long tail proudly spread out beside him.

He was just about to pounce on the sleeping creature when all the other lizards, peeping from their hole, squealed to Flick in fright.

'Flick! Flick! Run quickly! The RAT is here!'

Flick woke with a jump. Did he hear someone say RAT? He swung round – and saw the lean grey-brown rat just about to pounce on him.

He tried to run – but he was too late. The rat jumped and caught Flick by his beautiful tail. Flick wriggled in pain but he could not get away.

'Leave your tail behind and run to your hole,' said the old, wise toad. 'Go on! Break it off and leave it. Then you will escape!'

Poor Flick! There was nothing else to be done! He snapped off his tail, and then rushed to his hole, a funny little short-bodied lizard with no tail at all!

The rat was astonished. He was about to rush after Flick when he felt the tail jumping about between his paws. He gobbled it up and then went on his way, sorry that he hadn't eaten the rest of the little lizard.

Then how sad and upset Flick was! He had no beautiful tail. He didn't look like a lizard. He moped in his hole and the others were sorry for him.

'We always told you something would happen to that tail you were so proud of,' they said. 'But cheer up, Flick – it's no use moping. You were foolish about your tail when you had it – don't be foolish about it now it's gone!'

So Flick cheered up and went to help the others to find a nice winter hole. When the little lizards found one they all crowded into it, and, curling themselves up together, fell fast asleep. They did not wake until the warm days came again – and then what a surprise Flick got!

His tail had grown again while he had slept! Would you believe it! It was not so fine nor so long as his first tail. It was short and stumpy, and it didn't seem to fit him very well – but at any rate it was a *tail*! Flick was very happy. He ran about with the others squealing. He helped them when he could, and was more friendly than he had ever been before.

'It's a good thing you lost that old tail of yours, Flick!' said the wise old toad. 'You don't *look* so fine with your new one – but you're a much *nicer* little lizard!'

Mr Stupid and Too-Smart

One day Too-Smart and his friend Tiny the gnome were walking down the road together. Over Tiny's shoulder was an empty sack which should have been full of potatoes – but Too-Smart and Tiny had earned no money that day, so they had not been able to buy the potatoes they wanted.

Now just as they came up to a field-gate who should they see coming out of the field but Mr Stupid, the brownie farmer, carrying over his shoulder a big sack full of something heavy. Too-Smart took a look into the field. It was a potato field. Mr Stupid must have been digging up a sack of potatoes to take home.

'Look!' said Too-Smart, nudging Tiny. 'See that sack of potatoes on old Stupid's back? I've got a plan to get them all from him! Ho ho! All you've got to do is walk behind a little way and pick up what falls out of the sack. See? *I'll* manage the rest!'

Up he went to Mr Stupid and bade him

good-day. Stupid was going very slowly indeed
for the sack was too heavy, and bent him
double.

'That's a heavy load you've got!' said Too-
Smart, brightly. 'If you promise to give me a
basket of carrots, Mr Stupid, I'll wish a wish for
you so that your load becomes lighter every step
you take!'

Mr Stupid mopped his forehead with his big
red handkerchief. The sack was terribly heavy.
He looked sideways at Too-Smart and grinned.
'All right,' he said. 'You lighten my load for me
and maybe I'll give you a basket of carrots.'

'I'll just tap your sack then as I wish,' said
Too-Smart. He waited until Mr Stupid came to
a grassy path that led up the hillside to his
house, for he did not want the old farmer to hear
the potatoes dropping out on the road. Then he
pretended to tap the sack smartly, but what he
really did was to cut a hole at the bottom of it
with his knife.

'I wish your load may become lighter and
lighter!' he said. 'There you are, Mr Stupid.
Now you'll soon find that my wish will work for
you.'

The two went on up the hill together, and
Too-Smart talked hard all the time to hide the
soft plop-plop as something fell out of the sack

at every step. Behind them stepped Tiny, with *his* sack – but to his great astonishment he found that it was not potatoes that fell from Mr Stupid's sack – it was stones! He couldn't think what to do – he couldn't possibly tell Too-Smart, for then Stupid would hear.

'Well, I'd better pick up the stones and put them in my sack, I suppose,' thought Tiny. 'Then I can show them to Too-Smart if he doesn't believe me when I say that no potatoes fell from Stupid's sack.'

So the small gnome picked up every stone that fell from Mr Stupid's sack, and put them into his own. Goodness, how heavy they were!

'Well, Mr Stupid, is your load feeling any lighter?' asked Too-Smart, as he walked up the hill beside Mr Stupid.

'Oh, *much* lighter!' said Mr Stupid. 'Dear me, it's wonderful, Too-Smart. I am very glad I met you, really.'

'So am I,' said Too-Smart. 'I do like doing anyone a good turn. I told you your load would get lighter, and I've kept my word. I'm a smart chap, Mr Stupid.'

'There's no doubt about it,' said the old farmer, grinning to himself as he heard the soft plop of one stone after another tumbling out of his sack. He knew quite well that there must be

someone behind picking them all up. Well, well, if Too-Smart thought his sack had potatoes in it, that was his own look-out! Ho ho!

Poor little Tiny panted behind them, picking up more and more stones. His sack became very heavy indeed and he could hardly carry it, for he was not very big. As for Mr Stupid's sack, it was soon as light as a feather!

When at last he and Too-Smart arrived at his house, Mr Stupid put down his sack without looking at it. He turned to Too-Smart with a smile.

'Well, you certainly kept your word,' he said. 'My load is much lighter now. I hardly felt it, coming up the hill. Wait here a moment and I'll get you your reward – a basket of carrots.'

He went indoors, and no sooner had he gone than Too-Smart ran eagerly to Tiny, who was standing gloomily by the gate with his enormous sack of stones.

'What did I tell you?' he whispered. 'Am I not a smart chap, Tiny?'

'Not so very,' said the little gnome sulkily. 'I suppose you know that that was a sack of *stones*, not potatoes, that old Stupid was carrying? If you don't believe me, look inside my sack. I've picked them all up and carried them. My goodness, my back is nearly broken!'

Too-Smart stared at the stones in horror. Stones! Not potatoes! Whoever would have thought of that?

Just then Mr Stupid came out with a basket of very old, very hard carrots. He walked up to Too-Smart and Tiny.

'Well?' he said to Tiny. 'Did you pick up all my stones and carry them home for me? It really was very kind of you, and *such* a good idea of Too-Smart's! I can't imagine how you thought of it, but I am most grateful. My wife asked me to bring home a sack of flints to edge her new flower garden, and I can tell you it was a terrible load to carry. I was *so* pleased when kind Too-Smart offered to lighten the load for me! Thank you very much indeed!'

'B-b-b-b-b-ut . . .' began Tiny, in anger and surprise, furious to think he had carried the stones all the way home instead of the farmer. 'B-b-but I thought . . .'

'I don't care what you thought,' said Mr Stupid, kindly. 'It was really very nice of you both. Here is your reward, Too-Smart – a basket of carrots.'

He held out the basket, and Too-Smart saw what nasty old ones they were.

'You ought to be ashamed to give us those horrid carrots!' said Too-Smart angrily.

'Oh, donkeys don't mind if carrots are old or new,' said Mr Stupid, cheerfully. 'I don't expect either of *you* will notice the difference, Too-Smart!'

Mr Stupid picked up Tiny's sack of stones, emptied them out by the side of his wife's flower garden, and gave him back the sack with a grin.

'Goodbye,' he said to the angry gnomes. 'Stupid may be my name – but it isn't my nature, you know! *Good*bye!'

He went indoors, chuckling, and soon Too-Smart and Tiny heard him and his wife roaring with laughter – and they knew why. They went home down the hill in silence, and for a long time after that Too-Smart didn't try any tricks at all.

But I've no doubt he will soon again – don't you think so?

The Little Boy Who Cried

Doreen and Harry were very happy. They had two pounds between them, and they were going to buy a new paint-box. They both loved painting, but their paint-box was very old and not very good – and at last they had saved up two pounds to buy one they had seen in the toy-shop. It was not a very big one, but the colours in it were good and there were two paint-brushes as well.

Harry had the money in his pocket, and he carried a parcel in his hand. Mummy had asked him to take her shoes to be mended. The cobbler lived next door to the toy-shop, so Harry said of course he would take the shoes.

They went on down the road, and passed the park on their way. Running in through the gates was a little boy. Just as the children passed the gates the small boy tripped over something and fell flat on his face. A parcel he carried burst open and out fell sandwiches, an orange, and a sticky piece of chocolate cake.

The children heard a tinkle too, as if a coin has fallen and rollen away – and at the same moment the small boy began to howl. Goodness, how he yelled! You would have thought there were six little boys crying instead of only one!

Doreen couldn't bear to hear anyone cry. She ran up to the little boy and picked him up. He had hurt his knee, and grazed his hands.

'Don't cry,' said Doreen, dusting his jacket down. 'You're not much hurt.'

'B-b-b-b-but my d-d-dinner's all spoilt,' wept the little boy, 'and my m-m-m-money's gone!'

Harry picked up the sandwiches, the orange and the chocolate cake – but they were no good for eating. The orange had burst, the sandwiches had fallen into a puddle and the piece of cake was covered with mud. The little boy's dinner certainly *was* spoilt!

'I had fifty pence in my hand and that fell and rolled down the drain there!' wept the little boy. 'Oh dear! How am I to get home? It's the first time my mother has let me go out alone, and she gave me my dinner to bring to the park and let me have fifty pence to pay for some lemonade and my bus-fare home.'

Doreen and Harry didn't know what to do. The small boy would *not* stop crying. It really was dreadful to hear him.

'Listen!' said Doreen, suddenly. 'If you'll stop crying, little boy, we'll buy you some new dinner, and give you the money to get home. We've two pounds between us. We were going to buy a new paint-box, but we'll give you some of the money if you'll cheer up.'

The little boy wiped his eyes and looked at Doreen with a smile. He slipped his hand into hers and squeezed hard.

'I like you,' he said. 'You are kind. Tell me your name and I'll ask my Mummy to send you back the money.'

'Oh no,' said Doreen. 'You needn't bother about that. We can spare you the money because it is our very own.'

Harry took the small boy to the water fountain and bathed his knee and hands. Then they went with him to a baker's shop, and bought him two buns, a cherry-cake and a bottle of lemonade. Then they bought an apple at another shop. Harry unwrapped his mother's shoes and carefully wrapped up all the food they had bought, in the brown paper. He was very much afraid the little boy would fall down again and spoil everything!

'There you are!' he said. 'There's a fine lunch for you! I should go and sit down on that seat by the duck-pond, if I were you, when you eat it.

Then you can watch the ducks.'

'How much is your bus-fare home?' asked Doreen.

'Twenty pence,' said the small boy.

'Well, here you are,' said Harry, giving the little fellow the money. 'Put that in your pocket and keep it safely till your bus comes. I'm sorry we can't stop any longer with you, but our mother will worry if we are too long. Goodbye!'

Doreen and Harry left the little boy sitting happily on a seat with his lunch in the brown paper. They took their mother's shoes to be mended, and then they looked into the shop next door. There was that lovely paint-box!

'We can't have it after all,' said Doreen. 'It's a pity, Harry – but we had to help the little boy who cried, didn't we?'

'Of course,' said Harry. He felt in his pocket and found three twenty pence pieces, which was all that was left of the money he had had. 'Look, Doreen – we've still got sixty pence left. Shall we put it back in our money-box or shall we spend it on something now?'

'Oh, let's spend it now,' said Doreen. 'It will take too long to save up two pounds again! Let's buy an ice-cream each and take some sweets home to Mummy!'

So they had an ice-cream each and bought some peppermints to take home to their mother because she was so fond of them. They told her all about the little boy who cried, and she was pleased when she heard how kind they had been.

'But we couldn't get that paint-box we wanted!' said Harry, with a sigh.

'Never mind,' said their mother. 'Your kindness is worth far more than a paint-box!'

Two days later, when Doreen and Harry were playing in the garden, a little car pulled up outside their door, and out jumped a pretty lady. She had a big parcel in her hand and she ran up to the front door with it. She knocked and the children's mother opened the door.

'Oh, good morning!' said the lady. 'Does Mrs White live here?'

'Yes – I'm Mrs White,' said the children's mother.

'Well, your two children were *very* kind to my little boy the other day in the park,' said the lady. 'He fell down and spoilt his lunch and lost his money – and they bought him another lunch and gave him the money to catch his bus home. He told me all about it – and he told me too that they really meant to buy a paint-box with the money they so kindly gave him, so, in return for their kindness, I've brought them a little present!'

'Oh, how nice of you!' cried Mrs White. 'Doreen! Harry! Come here a minute!'

The children came running. Their mother told them who the lady was, and what she had come to bring. The lady smiled at them and gave them the parcel – and whatever do you think was inside when they opened it?

There were two big, beautiful paint-boxes, one for each of them, and two fine painting-books! The paint-boxes were *very* much nicer than the one that the children had been going to buy and they were full of excitement when they saw them.

'Oh, thank you, thank you!' cried Harry. 'But how *did* you know our name and where we lived? We didn't tell your little boy.'

'No – but you wrapped up his lunch in a nice piece of brown paper for him – and on the paper was your mother's name and address!' said the lady. 'So that's how I knew, you see – and I *was* glad because I did so badly want to give you some reward for your kindness! Will you come to tea with Eric tomorrow? He very much wants to see you again. I will come and fetch you in my car if your mother will let you come.'

So tomorrow Doreen and Harry are going to

tea with Eric – but today they are going to do some painting with their beautiful new paint-boxes. They *are* pleased.

'Aren't we lucky!' cried Doreen.

'Yes – but you deserve your good luck!' said her mother. And so they did!

The Pink Teddy Bear

Once there was a pink teddy bear called Edward. He was quite big, his whiskers were very fine and he had two odd eyes, for one was a brown boot-button and the other was a black one. But he could see very well indeed.

He belonged to Elsie, and she often played with him. Each morning he went for a ride in her doll's pram, and each evening he was put to bed in a doll's cot, so you can see he was a very lucky bear.

One afternoon Elsie took him out into the garden, and had a tea-party. There was herself, the little boy next door, the black kitten and Edward the teddy bear. They each had a cup and saucer and a plate, and real biscuits to eat and real milk to pour out of the teapot. So it was a most exciting party.

'You must clear away everything tidily!' called Elsie's mother, when they had finished. 'It is nearly bedtime, but you've just time to tidy up the garden, and to wash up the tea things.'

Elsie carried the tea things indoors and the black kitten came with her. The little boy next door helped Elsie to wash the plates and cups, and then it was time for him to go home. He called goodbye and ran off.

'Good girl, Elsie,' said her mother, when she saw how nicely Elsie had washed up. She hadn't broken anything at all. 'Now run into the bathroom and turn on the hot tap for your bath.'

Elsie loved doing that, so off she went – and do you know she quite forgot that there was one thing she hadn't brought in from the garden – and that was poor Edward, the bear!

There he sat at the bottom of the garden on the damp grass, all alone. He was very cross with Elsie for forgetting him. Tears came into his boot-button eyes when he saw the light go on in the bathroom and heard the splash of the bath-water.

'Elsie's going to have her bath,' he thought. 'She's forgotten all about me! How horrid of her!'

Elsie had her bath, and then said her prayers and jumped into bed. She was very sleepy. It wasn't long before her eyes closed and she fell fast asleep.

But Edward didn't fall asleep. No, he was far too frightened! A great big thing had just flown over him and shouted, 'Too-whit, too-whoo!' right in his ear! Then a big prickly creature ran into him and scratched him. Edward cried out in pain, but the hedgehog didn't even say it was sorry.

'You shouldn't sit there, right in my way,' it said, rudely, and went on down the garden.

After that a spider ran over Edward's head and began to spin a web between his ears. Edward was very angry. His arms were much too short to brush away the web, and the spider wouldn't stop when he told it he was a teddy bear.

'I don't care what you are!' said the spider. 'I'm going to make my web here!'

Now, in the middle of the night, Elsie suddenly woke up – and she remembered Edward, her bear. She hadn't put him to bed in his nice warm cot! Goodness gracious, where was he? 'Oh, I must have left him out in the garden!' she thought, and she sat up in bed in horror. 'Poor Edward! He will be so sad and lonely! I must go and fetch him.'

So Elsie put on her dressing-gown, and her little red slippers, and down the stairs she crept. She opened the garden door and went into the garden.

It looked so different at night! It was so very

dark, and the grass was so wet. She tried to find the path and at last found herself walking on it. Twigs brushed against her face and frightened her. Soon she had lost the path and was on the wet grass again. She didn't know where she was at all!

'Well, I'm in the garden, I know!' said Elsie. 'But what part of it? Oh, I do hope I don't fall into the pond! It's so dark I can't see where I'm going!'

She tripped over a stone and hurt her foot. Then she walked straight into a tree and bumped her head. She was just rubbing it when a big bird flew near her, crying: 'Too-whit, too-whoo!' at the top of its voice.

'Oh, owl, don't frighten me so!' said poor Elsie. She sank down on the wet grass and began to cry. It was dreadful – she didn't dare to go any further, for fear of falling over or of bumping her head!

Now Edward the bear was not far off. He was frightened out of his life because a big beetle, two earwigs, a mouse and a rat had all run over him, and he hardly dared to move. But when he heard the sound of Elsie crying he forgot all about his fears.

'Why, that's Elsie!' he thought. 'She's crying! She must have remembered me and come out to

look for me in the dark – and she's lost herself!
Poor little girl, how frightened and lonely she
will be, with all these night-time creatures
about. I wouldn't like a spider to make a web
between *her* ears, or a rat to nibble at her nose. I
must go and find her.'

Up got the brave little bear, and, listening to
the sound of Elsie's sobs, he began to make his
way to where she was sitting. How he bumped
his nose when he walked into trees! How wet his
feet were! How he scratched himself when he
fell into a rose bush! But never mind, he was
getting nearer to Elsie.

Suddenly the frightened little girl felt a small
furry paw pushed into her hand, and the growly
voice of the teddy bear spoke to her.

'Don't cry, Elsie. I heard you, and I've come
to find you.'

'Oh, Edward! Is it really you?' said Elsie,
astonished and glad. 'I came out to find *you* and
you've found me instead! Oh, you *are* a dear! Do
you know the way indoors?'

'We'll find it together,' said Edward. So hand
in hand the two stumbled up the garden, not at
all frightened now they had one another. They
soon found the garden door and crept indoors.
They went upstairs and Elsie hopped into bed.

'You shall sleep with *me* tonight, Edward,'

she said. 'Your poor feet are so cold and wet. I'll warm them for you.'

So the two fell asleep together, and Edward's feet soon got dry and warm. He was so happy and excited.

'What an adventure to tell the toys to-morrow!' he thought. 'None of them has ever slept in Elsie's bed before. How glad I am she forgot me and left me out in the garden! Now I know how much she loves me!'

In the morning when Elsie woke up, the bear was still in her bed. She looked at him and remembered what had happened in the night.

'Did it really happen, or did I dream it?' she wondered. 'Oh, Edward, you were alive last night and came to find me in the garden. You are a most *wonderful* teddy bear!'

And now Edward almost hopes he will be left out again – but I don't expect Elsie will ever forget him another time, do you?

When the Stars Fell Down

On Guy Fawkes night little Tweeky the pixie was sitting by a puddle in the lane, eating a late supper of honey and cobweb-bread. He didn't know it was Guy Fawkes night. He didn't know anything about fireworks at all.

So when he heard a rocket go up he nearly jumped out of his skin, and he dropped a large piece of cobweb-bread into the puddle. He was most upset.

He looked up into the sky. To his enormous suprise he saw a crowd of coloured stars dropping out of the black sky towards him. They were the stars out of the rocket, but he didn't know it. He thought they were real stars falling out of the sky, and he was frightened.

He dived under a bush and stayed there for two minutes, shivering. Then he crawled out. Where had those stars fallen? They must be somewhere about.

He began to look. He hunted over the grass at the lane-side. He searched among the stones in

the road. He climbed up the bare hedge and looked along the top. No stars anywhere. Wherever could they be?

Then he thought of looking in the puddle. So he ran to it and looked into the water. Reflected there were the real stars that were shining high up in the sky. But Tweeky at once thought that they were the coloured stars he had seen falling down.

'They've dropped into this puddle!' he shouted in excitement. 'They've fallen splash into this water! Now I will get them out, thread them on a string and give them to the fairy queen for a birthday present. Oh, what a marvellous thing! They have all dropped into the puddle!'

He ran off and presently came back with a net. He put it into the puddle and tried to catch the stars. He seemed to get them easily in his net, but as soon as he took the net out, alas! there were no stars there at all. It was most annoying.

Soon Grass-Green the goblin came by, and looked astonished to see Tweeky fishing in the pool.

'What do you fish for?' he asked.

'Stars!' said Tweeky, proudly. 'They fell from the sky into this puddle as I was eating my supper. Red, green and blue they were – the most beautiful stars I have ever seen.'

'What a surprising thing!' said Grass-Green, peering into the puddle. It was all stirred up with Tweeky's fishing, and he couldn't see anything at all. But he wanted those stars very badly indeed. So he knelt down by the puddle and began to feel in the water with his hands.

'You're not to take my stars!' shouted Tweeky in a rage. 'You're a robber, Grass-Green! Leave my stars alone!'

Pinkity the elf heard Tweeky shouting and came to see what the matter was.

'Tell Grass-Green to go away!' cried Tweeky. 'He is trying to steal my stars. A whole lot fell into this puddle while I was eating my supper. They are mine! I want to thread them on a string and give them to the queen for her birthday.'

'Nonsense!' said Pinkity, at once. 'The puddle isn't yours, Tweeky. If Grass-Green wants to fish in it, of course he can do so! *I* shall fish too, and if I find the stars, they shall be mine! Make room, Grass-Green!'

Grass-Green wouldn't make room, and soon there was such a shouting and a squabbling that it woke up Old Man Pinny-Penny, who was asleep under the hedge not far off. He was half a gnome and half a goblin, and he had a fearful temper. He sat up and scowled.

'Who's making all that noise?' he grunted. 'I'll teach them to scream and squabble at night! I'll knock their heads together! I'll spank them! I'll – I'll – I'll . . .'

Dear me, the things Old Man Pinny-Penny was going to do would fill a book and a half! He got up, and went to the puddle round which Tweeky, Grass-Green and Pinkity were all pushing and squabbling.

'WHAT'S all this?' shouted Pinny-Penny, in his very biggest voice. 'How DARE you wake me up?'

'Ooh!' cried Tweeky in fright. 'We didn't mean to disturb you, Pinny-Penny. We will be quiet. But oh, it is so annoying of Grass-Green and Pinkity, because they are trying to steal my stars.'

'Steal your stars?' cried Old Man Pinny-Penny. 'Now what in the wide world do you mean, Tweeky?'

'Well, a whole lot of beautiful coloured stars fell out of the sky while I was eating my supper by the puddle,' said Tweeky, 'and when I looked I saw they had fallen into the puddle. So I went to get a net to fish them out. Then I shall thread them and make them into a necklace for the queen.'

Grass-Green scooped through the puddle with his big hands, and Tweeky smacked him on the head. He hit back at the pixie, and struck Pinkity instead, splashing him from head to foot. Pinkity danced with rage and hit out with both his fists – but oh, my goodness me, he hit Old Man Pinny-Penny by mistake, and didn't that make him angry!

With a shout of rage he picked up Pinkity and sat him down in the very middle of the pool! He pushed Grass-Green who fell on his face in the puddle, and as for Tweeky, he found himself rolling over and over in the water, his mouth full of mud!

How they howled! How they roared! They picked themselves up out of the puddle and shook the water from them like dogs. Then, still howling, and shivering from head to foot, they ran off to get dry, leaving Old Man Pinny-Penny alone by the big puddle. He looked into it as soon as it had become smooth and quiet, and sure enough, he saw the stars reflected there.

'Goodness!' said Old Man Pinny-Penny, in astonishment. 'So Tweeky spoke the truth. There *are* stars there after all! I'll go and get my net.'

Off he went – but before he came back a grey donkey wandered down that way and saw the puddle shining. He was thirsty so he went to it and drank. He drank and drank and drank – and by the time he had finished there was no puddle at all! It had all gone down his throat, stars and all!

When Old Man Pinny-Penny came back he couldn't find the puddle, though he looked up and down the lane from end to end.

'The stars have flown back to the sky and taken the puddle with them,' he thought mournfully. 'What a pity!'

The grey donkey watched him looking for the puddle, and he thought it was very funny to see Pinny-Penny looking for a puddle that was down his throat. So he threw back his head and laughed loudly.

'Hee-haw! Hee-hee-haw!'

But Old Man Pinny-Penny didn't know what the joke was!

Poor Mr Greedy!

There was once a sharp little pixie called Nab. He lived just on the edge of Giantland, and if there was one thing he liked more than another it was going to the nearest giant's pea-patch and taking a few peas when they were ripe. They were as big as cricket-balls to the pixie, and two of them made a fine dinner for him, cooked with a sprig of mint, and well-buttered when hot.

The pea-patch belonged to Big-Eyes the giant. He could well have spared Nab a few peas now and again, but he was a mean giant, and if he could have counted his peas every day to see that none were missing, he would have done so! As it was he kept a sharp look-out for little Nab, and meant to catch him if he possibly could.

Nab used to slip through the hedge early in the morning before the giant was up. He would slit a big pod with his knife and take out two or three peas. Then back through the hedge he would go, chuckling to think of the giant fast asleep in bed. It was naughty of Nab, and all his friends used to tell him that one day he would surely be caught.

Well, that day came! As he slipped through the hedge early one morning, a big hand came down on him – and goodness me, it was Big-Eyes the giant! He had come out early that day, and had spied Nab running through the fields a long way off. Now he had him at last.

'Oho!' said the giant, in his big voice. 'So I've caught you, Nab! Well, you've often cooked my peas for your dinner – and now perhaps I'll cook *you* for mine.'

Dear me, that did make Nab shiver and shake! The giant had a sack beside him, that he was going to use for his potatoes. He threw Nab into it, tied the neck up tightly, and flung the sack back on the ground.

'You can stay there for a while,' he said. 'I'm going back to my breakfast, and I don't want to let my wife know I've caught you, for she's tender-hearted and might set you free!'

Off he went down the garden, leaving poor Nab wriggling in the sack. Big-Eyes had taken his knife from him, so he could not make a hole with it. He wriggled about until he found a little hole, and then he put his eye to that and peeped through it. At first he could see nothing but the pea-patch.

Then he saw something else. It was a gnome marching along the path, whistling gaily. The gnome was big and fat, and he had mean little eyes set close together. Nab knew him quite well. He was shoemaker to Big-Eyes the giant, who was very fond of him and vowed that Mr Greedy the gnome could make better shoes than anyone else in the kingdom. The two were great friends, though all the rest of the pixies and gnomes hated Mr Greedy, for he was so mean and so very selfish and greedy.

Mr Greedy saw the sack and stirred it with his foot, wondering if there was anything to eat in it. Nab gave a squeal, and Mr Greedy looked astonished.

'Who's there?' he asked.

'Nab, the pixie,' answered Nab.

'What are you doing in that dirty old sack?' asked Greedy, in surprise.

Nab wasn't going to tell him. 'Never you mind!' he said. That made Greedy most curious.

'I believe Big-Eyes the giant has set you to watch his pea-patch for him,' he said. 'Yes, that's what you're doing – and I guess he is paying you a lot of money for it, isn't he?'

'Never you mind, Mr Greedy!' said Nab again.

'Well, I should like to know why Big-Eyes

didn't give *me* the job!' said Greedy, half-sulkily. 'We're great friends, he and I. I would have liked to earn a bit of money watching his peas for him.'

'Well, would you like to change places with me?' suddenly said Nab, watching Mister Greedy through the little hole. 'I'm tired of being in this dark sack. You can have the job of watching Big-Eyes' peas if you want to. I'm sure I don't want to have anything more to do with them!'

'Oh, you always were a lazy little creature!' said Greedy. 'Of course I'll change places with you. I'd enjoy the job very much, and I shan't give you any of the money I get, so there!'

'I don't want any!' said Nab. 'Come on, undo the sack, Greedy.'

Greedy undid the sack, grumbling at the knots. At last the sack was open and Nab joyfully crawled out. He took a quick look round and then fled for the hole in the hedge. He hid there until Greedy had crawled into the sack, and then he ran to him and quickly knotted the string round the neck. Then, chuckling hard, he rushed through the hedge and ran home, vowing to himself that never, never, never would he steal peas again.

Greedy found the sack very dark and stuffy.

No one came to steal the peas. It was very dull. He thought it was a horrid sort of job and he didn't wonder that Nab had given it up so easily.

'I wonder how much Big-Eyes was going to give him,' he thought. 'I'll make him give me double!'

After a while, along came the giant. He picked up the sack and swung it over his shoulder. He carried it up the path, not listening at all to the cries of pain that Mister Greedy kept making as he was bumped here and there.

Big-Eyes reached the kitchen and flung the sack down on the floor.

'Hey, cook!' he called to his servant. 'Here's something for you to cook for my dinner!'

Greedy cried out in fright. The giant went out of the kitchen and the cook undid the sack. She hauled the frightened gnome out by the scruff of the neck and put him on the table.

Greedy at once leapt off and ran to the dining-room, where the giant was just taking off his big boots.

'Big-Eyes!' shouted Greedy, in fright. 'You can't mean to have me for your dinner! Why, I'm Greedy, your shoemaker friend! I've been watching your pea-patch for you all the morning in your sack!'

Well, you should have seen Big-Eyes stare! His eyes nearly dropped out of his head with surprise when he saw Greedy there instead of Nab. He knew quite well that it was the pixie he had caught – but here was Greedy come out of the sack!

'Of course I won't cook you,' he said at last. 'But I don't understand – I put Nab in the sack for stealing my peas and I meant to punish him by having him for my dinner. How did *you* get there?'

Then Greedy blushed red with shame to think how his stupidity and greed had made him so foolish and put him in such danger. He hardly liked to tell Big-Eyes – but at last he did, and how that giant roared with laughter!

'Ho, ho, ho!' he cried. 'What a joke! So you thought you'd take Nab's job and get the money for yourself – and there wasn't a job and there wasn't any money either! Oh, Greedy, you're like your name, aren't you!'

Greedy stole home ashamed, vowing never to be greedy again. He kept his word – and Nab kept his. So it was a good thing, wasn't it, that Nab was caught that morning, for it certainly changed two people for the better, and gave Big-Eyes the giant something to laugh about for weeks and weeks afterwards!

The Great Big Dog

Willie and Joan were coming home from school one day when they saw, coming round the corner of the lane, a great big dog. It was growling as it came, and the two children looked at it in fright. It was really so very big, and looked more like a wolf than a dog.

'Supposing it's a wolf escaped from somewhere!' said Joan trembling. 'Oh, Willie, have we got time to run away?'

'Let's get into the hedge and perhaps it will pass us by without seeing us,' said Willie. So the two scared children squeezed themselves into the big hedge at the side of the road and crouched there as still as mice.

The big dog came on up the lane. It was limping, the children saw. It held up one of its front paws, and every now and again it licked it as if it was in pain. It didn't seem to see the children, for it came right up to where they were and passed them without a look.

When it had gone a few steps past the big dog

stopped and growled. It lay down in the lane and began to lick its bad foot once more, giving a little whine every now and again as it did so.

'Joan!' whispered Willie. 'It must have hurt its foot.'

'Poor thing!' said Joan. 'Oh, I do hope it goes right on down the lane without seeing us, Willie.'

'But, Joan, do you think we ought to see if we can help it,' whispered Willie. 'We would go up to it if it was a little dog, you know. It's only because it's so big that we don't like it.'

'Oh, no, don't let's go,' said Joan, frightened – but the next minute she changed her mind, for the dog gave another whimper that made the little girl very sorry for it. 'All right – let's go carefully up and speak kindly to it,' she said. 'But please take hold of my hand, Willie.'

Willie took his sister's hand and they came out of the hedge. They walked up to the dog, who looked round at them with a growl.

'Poor fellow, poor fellow!' said Willie. 'Have you hurt yourself? Good dog! Poor old fellow!'

The dog pricked up his ears at the little boy's kind voice and whined. He held up his paw to him. Willie put out his hand but did not touch the dog, for his mother had told him always to let a dog sniff him before he touched it. Then, as soon as he saw the dog wag his tail, he would know the dog was friendly to him, and could touch it.

The big dog sniffed at the small brown hand and then wagged its big brown tail. 'We are friends!' it seemed to say. Willie patted the dog gently and the tail wagged harder. Then Joan patted him, after he had sniffed her hand too, though she was really very much afraid of the big fellow.

'Let me see your poor old paw, then,' said Willie. He took the dog's paw in his hand and held it up. The dog whined again.

Willie turned the paw up to see the underneath of it – and then he saw what the matter was. Run into the pad below the paw were two great thorns, like needles. No wonder the poor creature was in such pain and could not walk on his paw.

'Look, Joan,' said Willie. 'He's got great thorns in his paw. Could you hold the paw while I try to pull them out?'

Joan was sorry to see the dreadful thorns. She held the big paw gently and Willie took hold of one of the thorns. He pulled – and it came out between his finger and thumb. The dog yelped and took away his paw. But Joan took it again and spoke gently to him.

'Don't be afraid, big dog. We're only giving you a little pain to save you from a much bigger one. Keep still while Willie takes out the other thorn.'

The dog cocked his ears, and looked at her with his large brown eyes. He kept his paw still and Willie pulled out the other thorn. There was another yelp, and the dog pulled his paw away. He put it to the ground and found that it no longer hurt him. With a joyful yelp he bounded away down the lane on all four feet, barking as we went.

'Well, he might at least have given us a lick for being kind to him,' said Joan.

'Oh, I expect he wanted to get home,' said Willie. 'I'm glad we were able to do that, Joan. Aren't you?'

But Joan was disappointed in the dog. She thought he ought to have stayed a little with them and showed them he was grateful.

'Oh, don't worry about that, Joan,' said Willie, as they went on their way home. 'He won't forget, you'll see! We can't really expect him to stop and say thank you!'

Now the very next day the two children went into the nearest town to buy a present for their mother's birthday. It was the first time they had gone there alone, and their mother warned

Willie to be careful about crossing the roads, and to look out for motorcars.

'I'll be very careful indeed and look after Joan,' said Willie. So off they went. They bought a fine silver brooch for their mother and then, as they had fifty pence left, they thought they would go to a sweet-shop and buy some chocolate.

'Look! There's a nice sweet-shop over there!' said Joan, and she pointed across the road. 'Let's cross over.'

Willie took her hand and looked up and down the road. 'Wait a moment,' he said, 'there's a motor-car coming.'

'Oh, there's plenty of time to get across!' said Joan impatiently, and she jerked her hand away from Willie's. She ran into the road, and then, oh dear me, she fell over on her nose in the very middle! The car was coming very fast and it could not possibly stop in time. Willie rushed out, but before he could reach Joan, something else had shot past him and had caught hold of the little girl by her frock. It was a great big dog!

He galloped up to Joan, and, without stopping except to grip her dress in his teeth, he shot right across the road in front of the car, carrying Joan with him. The car grazed the dog's tail, but went safely by without touching the frightened little girl. It stopped a little way down the road, and the man at the wheel jumped out. Another man hurried up too – the man who owned the dog.

Joan was frightened but not hurt. She looked at the dog who had saved her, and flung her arms around his neck. 'Oh, you're the same dog we saw yesterday!' she cried. 'We took the thorns out of your foot, and I was cross because you didn't seem grateful. But you didn't forget! And now you've helped *me*!'

The dog's owner was astonished to hear all this, and very proud of his dog. 'He's not much more than a full-grown puppy yet,' he said. 'I'm proud of you, old fellow! You don't forget your friends, I see!'

The dog licked Joan's face and then gambolled over to Willie, who had been very frightened. The little boy went up to Joan and took her hand. 'Come along home,' he said. So Joan went with him, after they had said goodbye to the dog.

'Joan, you mustn't ever do that again,' said Willie, as they went along. 'The dog might not be there another time!'

'I won't do it again,' promised Joan. 'But oh, Willie! Wasn't it a good thing we were kind to the dog yesterday. He saved my life today!'

Get On, Little Donkey!

There was once a small fat donkey who lived in Farmer Brown's field at the bottom of the hill. He had a little shed to live in when it was cold, but he liked being in the field best. Every day Bill, the farmer's boy, used to fetch Neddy the donkey and take him up the hill to work on the farm, for Neddy was strong.

Margery lived on the hillside in a little cottage beside the road up which Neddy and Bill went every day. She liked the donkey and each morning and evening she watched for Neddy and Bill and called to them. Neddy was fond of her for sometimes she held out a carrot to him.

One cold winter's day, when frost was everywhere, and the road up the hillside was coated with ice, Bill went down to fetch Neddy as usual. Twice the boy fell down, for the road was very slippery. Margery watched him from the gate and hoped he wasn't hurt. No – he was not at all hurt, but he was in a very bad temper!

'Bother the ice!' Margery heard him say, angrily. 'It's a perfect nuisance!'

Presently she saw him coming out of the field at the bottom of the hill with Neddy. Neddy needed no guiding, for he knew the way so well. He would always go up the hill by himself, without even a hand on his halter. But this morning he was puzzled and afraid.

His feet seemed slippery. He couldn't walk properly on the road! He didn't know it was because the road was covered with ice. He went slowly up the hill until he was just outside Margery's cottage. Then he stopped, frightened. He felt sure he was going to fall down. He didn't mean to walk another step!

'Get on, little donkey, get on!' shouted Bill. But the donkey wouldn't move an inch.

'Hurry up!' cried Bill. 'We shall be late. What's the matter with you? You know the way!'

The donkey stood perfectly still, his head hanging down, his tail twitching. He couldn't explain to Bill that he was afraid of falling.

Bill became angry. He had no stick with him, for Neddy never needed a stick, but this morning Bill wished he *had* got a stick. He went up to Neddy and slapped him hard on the back.

'Get on, little donkey,' he shouted again. But no – Neddy wouldn't move. He stood as firm as a rock on his four stout little legs.

Bill slapped him again. Then he went to the

donkey's head, took hold of the rope-halter and tugged at it to pull the donkey up the hill. But the donkey was far stronger than he was, and not an inch could the boy move him, one way or another.

Bill was in a fine rage. 'Oh, so you think you'll play a trick on me and make me late for my work, do you!' he cried, angrily. 'Well, we'll see about that! I haven't a stick to beat you with, but perhaps a few stones will make you move!'

Then, to Margery's horror – for the little girl was watching from her gate – Bill went to the side of the road where there were many small stones, and, picking up a big handful, he flung them at the startled donkey. The stones hurt him and he brayed – but he wouldn't move. Bill took up some more stones and threw them with all his might. Neddy brayed again, sadly and angrily. Margery couldn't bear it. It was cruel to throw stones at anything.

'Stop, Bill, stop!' she cried, running out of the gate. 'You're not to hurt him!'

'Well, stones are the only thing to make him go up this hill,' said Bill, sulkily.

'You're right!' said Margery. 'But not used *that* way, Bill.'

'What do you mean?' said Bill. 'How can I use them any other way?'

'I'll soon show you,' said Margery. 'Can't you see the little donkey is afraid to walk on this icy road? I saw *you* fall down on it twice, Bill. This is the way to use the stones, look!'

The little girl ran to the side of the road and picked up two handfuls of the pebbles. She ran to the donkey and spread them under his feet. Then back she went again for more stones, and soon she had made a little pathway of stones for the donkey to walk on. Then she took hold of his halter and spoke kindly to him.

'Get on, little donkey! You're all right now!' The donkey felt the stones under his feet, which no longer slipped on the ice. He took a little step forward. The stones stopped him from slipping. He took another step – and soon he was away from the icy piece, and was walking quickly on the sunny side of the road, where the ice had melted away!

'*That's* the right way to use stones!' said Margery – and Neddy the donkey thought so too!

The Magic Wash-tub

Binny and Tucker were doing their spring cleaning. They had moved all the furniture and scrubbed behind it. They had washed all the chair-covers and banged every book to get the dust out of them. The two pixies had worked very hard indeed, and they were tired.

'Oh dear, we've got to wash all our curtains this afternoon,' groaned Binny, tying her apron strings more tightly round her.

Tucker sighed. He really didn't want to begin washing. If only washing would do itself!

That gave Tucker an idea. 'Binny,' he said, 'do you suppose Dame Sooky would lend us her magic wash-tub for a little while? It would do all our washing for us in about ten minutes!'

'Let's go and ask her!' said Binny. So off the two pixies went. They soon came to Dame Sooky's cottage and rang her bell. Jing-jang, jing-jang!

Nobody came.

'Bother!' said Binny. 'She must be out!'

They went round the back to see if she was in the garden. No, Dame Sooky was not there – but, dear me, something else was! The magic wash-tub was there, on its wooden stand! The magic soap was inside and the scrubbing-brush too.

'Ooh!' said Tucker. 'Look at that! It seems just ready for us to take!'

'Well, let's borrow it, then,' said Binny. 'I'm sure Dame Sooky wouldn't mind! She's a great friend of ours.'

So together they carried the wash-tub home, and stood it in the garden. Then they filled it with hot water and put into it all their dirty curtains.

They stood and watched to see what would happen. In a moment or two the soap jumped up from the bottom of the tub and began to soap the curtains thoroughly. The scrubbing-brush scrubbed the dirt out of them, and then the water soused them up and down just as well as if Binny were doing it herself.

'Isn't it marvellous!' said Binny. 'What a lot of trouble it is saving us! Do you think the curtains are washed enough now, Tucker? Shall we empty out the water and put some fresh in for rinsing?'

'Yes,' said Tucker, and he ran to get the water. Binny emptied out the soapy water, and

then Tucker poured in clean water for the tub to
rinse the curtains thoroughly.

The tub soused the curtains well. Binny took
them out, squeezed them dry and went to hang
them up. But just as she had reached the line she
heard a cry from Tucker.

'Binny! Look at our mats!'

Binny turned to look – and she saw a strange
sight! All her mats and rugs were flapping along
in a row to the wash-tub, which was rocking on
its stand, and making a most curious noise. The
mats flopped in the water and the soap and
brush at once began to wash them thoroughly.

Then Binny and Tucker saw something else!
They saw all their dresses and suits come
marching out of the house in a line, all by
themselves! They went to the wash-tub and put
themselves in.

'My best dress!' shrieked Binny.

'My best suit!' shouted Tucker, and they ran
to the wash-tub to pull out their precious
clothes, which were already being well-mixed
up with the dirty, dusty rugs and mats!

And then, how they never quite knew, both
Binny and Tucker suddenly found themselves
pulled into the big wash-tub too! There they
were in the hot, soapy water, all mixed up with
mats, rugs, suits and dresses!

The soap soaped them well. The scrubbing-brush went up and down poor Binny's arms and nearly scraped the soft skin off them. Tucker was soused under the water and got soap into both his eyes. He opened his mouth to yell and the soapy water ran in.

'Ooh! Ouch!' he spluttered, trying his best to get out of the wash-tub.

Binny's feet were then scrubbed so hard that her shoes came off. She sat down suddenly in the water and the tub nearly went over.

'Oh, oh!' she shrieked. 'Tucker, save me! Oh, I'm drowning! Oh, whatever shall I do?'

The tub soused her up and down well. Then Tucker was soused and rinsed, and he gurgled and gasped, trying to catch hold of the sides of the tub to throw himself out.

Just at that moment an astonished voice cried loudly: 'Binny, Tucker! Whatever are you doing?'

It was old Dame Sooky's voice. She had come in to call on Binny and Tucker on her way home – and she was most amazed to see them jumping up and down in their wash-tub, soaked and soapy. She had no idea at all that it was *her* wash-tub they had borrowed.

'Dame Sooky! D-d-d-dame S-s-s-sooky!' yelled Tucker. 'Help, help!'

Dame Sooky ran across the grass – and at once she saw that it was her wash-tub, and she guessed what had happened.

And then – oh dear – Dame Sooky couldn't help beginning to laugh. She just simply couldn't! It was really too funny to see poor Tucker and Binny being washed and scrubbed in the wash-tub with so many other clothes. She tried her hardest to say the words to stop the tub – but she kept beginning to laugh again.

'Wash-tub, st-st-st –!' she began, and then she laughed again till the tears came into her eyes. 'Wash-tub, st-st-stop your w-w-w-w-washing!' chuckled Dame Sooky – and oh, what a relief, to be sure! It stopped washing poor Binny and Tucker and they were able to climb out of the tub. How queer they looked!

'Oh my, oh my, you'll be the death of me!' laughed Dame Sooky, holding her sides.

'Well, your wash-tub was nearly the death of *us*!' said Tucker, wringing the water out of his coat. 'We'd never have borrowed it if we'd known it would behave like that.'

'You should have waited till I got home, and then I could have told you the words to say to stop it,' said Dame Sooky. 'I never mind lending my wash-tub to my friends, as you know, but not many are so foolish as to take it without knowing the right words to stop it when they want to!'

She took the wash-tub, emptied it, set it on her shoulder and went home with it, laughing so much that a crowd of little elves followed her in astonishment.

As for poor Binny and Tucker they were so tired with their buffeting, soaping and sousing that they took off all their wet things, dried themselves quickly and got straight into bed.

'It would have been easier and quicker to do all the washing ourselves in our own little wash-tub,' said Binny.

'Much easier!' said Tucker. 'We won't be so foolish another time!'

And then, in two twinks, they were fast asleep – and I'm not surprised, are you?

The Lonely Rabbit

Benny was a toy rabbit. He was nearly as large as a real rabbit, and he was dressed in pink striped trousers, a blue spotted coat, a bright orange scarf, and tight blue shoes. So he looked very smart indeed.

But Benny was a lonely rabbit. He belonged to Lucy, and she *would* keep leaving him about everywhere. She left him in the greenhouse one night, all by himself. The next night she left him in the summer-house and spiders walked all over his whiskers and made a web on his pretty blue shoes.

'This is horrid,' said Benny to himself. 'Lucy will keep leaving me alone in these nasty dark places. Why doesn't she remember to take me indoors to the nursery at night, when she goes to bed? She might know that I would like to talk to the other toys. It's a lonely life to be left by myself all day and all night.'

Once or twice Lucy did remember to take Benny indoors and then he was happy. But usually she left him on a garden seat or on the swing, when she went indoors to bed, and then poor Benny was lonely and frightened.

One night Lucy took Benny out into the field just outside her garden. She sat him down beside her and then began to read a book. In a little while some big drops of rain began to fall and Lucy looked up at the sky.

'Goodness!' she said, getting up in a hurry. 'There's a storm coming! Just look at those big black clouds!'

She ran to the garden-gate, opened it and rushed up the garden path. Poor Benny was left sitting in the field!

The rain fell faster and faster. The sky darkened and night came quickly. Benny's coat was soaked through and his pink striped trousers began to run, so that a pink patch showed on the grass around him. His tight blue shoes shrank and burst right off his feet.

'This is dreadful!' said Benny. 'I shall catch a dreadful cold. A-tish-oo! A-tish-oo!'

The rain pelted down and Benny sneezed again. 'A-TISH-OO!'

There was a rabbit-hole just behind Benny. A sandy rabbit suddenly poked the tip of his nose out and said: 'Who's that sneezing? Do come inside out of the rain.'

Benny turned and saw the rabbit. He got to his feet and went to the hole. 'Thank you very much,' he said. 'Do you live here?'

'Of course,' said the rabbit, backing down the hole to make room for Benny. 'This is my home. I say! How wet you are! You *will* catch cold!'

Benny walked down the hole. He was wet and shivering, and he certainly didn't feel very well. The rabbit took him to a cosy room lined with moss and dry leaves.

Another rabbit was there, and she looked at Benny in surprise.

'What are you?' she asked.

'A toy rabbit,' said Benny, and sneezed again. 'A-tish-oo!'

'Goodness, what a cold you've got!' said the second rabbit. 'I think I'd better get Pixie Lightfoot here. She can look after you till your cold is better.'

The first rabbit went to fetch the pixie. She came running in, a merry-eyed creature, with dancing skippitty feet.

'A-tish-oo!' said Benny.

'Goodness, what a dreadful cold!' said Lightfoot. 'Bed's the only place for you. Come with me!'

He followed her down a dark passage and at last came to a cosy room in which were chairs, a table and two small beds.

'Now, undress quickly, and get into bed,' said Lightfoot. 'I'm going to put the kettle on the fire and make you a hot drink.'

Benny took off his dripping pink trousers, his blue coat, and his orange scarf. Then he got into the cosy bed and waited for his hot drink. Oh, it *was* good! It warmed him all over.

'Now lie down and go to sleep,' said Lightfoot. 'Good night!'

'Good – a-tish-oo – night!' said Benny – and in two minutes he was fast asleep.

He was much better in the morning but Lightfoot wouldn't let him get up. No, he must stay in bed until his cold and sore throat were better. She had dried his scarf for him and she tied it round his throat. 'That will keep your throat warm,' she said. 'Now here is some warm milk for you.'

It was lovely to be looked after like that. Benny did enjoy it. It was quite different from being left about by Lucy, who didn't care about him at all. He had plenty of visitors. Both the rabbits came that he had seen the night before, and all their pretty little children. A mole came too and told him a great many stories. Everything was lovely.

Three days later Lightfoot said he could get

up. 'It's a fine sunny day,' she said. 'You can go out of the burrow and sit in the sunshine for half an hour.'

'But suppose Lucy comes to look for me,' said Benny, in alarm. He didn't at all want to go back to her.

'Well, you silly, just pop down the hole again like the other rabbits do,' said Lightfoot. 'You needn't put on your coat and trousers – they have shrunk and are far too small for you – but you must keep on your orange scarf because of your throat.'

So out into the sunshine Benny went, and it was so lovely and warm there that he fell fast asleep. And while he was asleep Lucy came and found him. She lifted him up and looked at him.

'Well!' she said. 'I wonder if this can be Benny. I left him here – but where are his shoes – and his pretty trousers and lovely blue coat? It can't be Benny – but this is his scarf round his neck, that's certain! Except for that he looks very like a real rabbit!'

Just then Benny woke up. He opened his eyes and looked at Lucy. What a shock he got! He struggled and leapt down to the ground. Lucy pounced after him – but he was down the hole in a twinkling, and Lucy couldn't catch him.

'It can't have been Benny!' she thought. 'It

must have been a rabbit that had stolen Benny's scarf – and to think I nearly took him home. Oh, I do wish I could find Benny. I'd never leave him about again if only I could find him.'

But she never did find him – for Lightfoot told Benny he could live with the other rabbits if he liked, and do just as they did. 'It only needs a little magic rubbed into your fur to make you just like them,' she said. 'I'll do it, if you like.'

So she did – and Benny became a real live rabbit like all the rest, as happy as the day was long, with plenty of company and lots to do all the year round.

But Lightfoot made him wear his scarf always, because his soaking had given him a very weak throat, and as soon as he left off his scarf he caught a cold. He always remembers to put it on when he goes out of the burrow, and as it is a very bright orange, it is easy to see.

So if ever you see a rabbit playing on the hill-side, with an orange scarf tied round his throat, you'll know who he is – Benny! But don't tell Lucy, will you?

The Little Bag of Salt

Once upon a time the lion, the tiger, the hyena, the zebra, the ostrich and the snake were all met together. They talked of this and that and then they went to drink at the big water-hole.

Now on the way the lion saw something. It was a small bag and it lay on the ground.

'See!' he said. 'A bag!'

The tiger sniffed at it. 'It smells of salt!' he said.

The hyena tried to untie the string that bound the neck of the bag, but he could not.

'Let the ostrich peck a hole in it,' said the zebra, wisely. So the ostrich pecked a big hole and the salt trickled out. All the animals stood and looked at it.

'I will taste it,' said the snake, and he put out his forked tongue. 'It is salt!' he cried in excitement. 'Salt!'

Then the six animals were most excited for they so seldom tasted salt. It was not to be found anywhere, and was a rare treat. Some man must

have dropped this bag of salt and lost it. What a
find! Now they would be able to lick salt each
day!

'It is mine,' said the lion. 'I saw it first. I shall
take it to my cave.'

The tiger growled angrily. 'No,' he said, 'it
must be mine. I was the first to sniff it and to tell
you all that it was salt!'

'Why should it not be *mine*?' asked the hyena
with a sneering laugh. 'Did I not try my best to
untie the string?'

'But you failed!' said the quiet zebra. 'It was I
who thought of telling the ostrich to peck a hole
in the bag. It should be mine!'

'Now come, come!' said the ostrich, stamping
her big foot. 'Was it not I who pecked the hole
and let out the salt for us all to lick? Surely the
bag should belong to *me*!'

'No, no,' said the snake, hissing in rage. 'I
tasted it to make sure it was salt. Why, it might
have been poison! The salt belongs to *me*! I shall
bite anyone who will not let me take it away!'

Then they all began to growl, roar, stamp,
hiss and howl, and made such a terrible noise
that a little jackal who was running along not far
off, stopped in surprise.

'What can be the matter?' he thought. He ran
to see, and was most astonished to find the lion,

the tiger, the hyena, the zebra, the ostrich and the snake all quarrelling noisily round a bag of salt.

'What are you quarrelling about?' he asked. The lion told him, and the jackal listened in silence. Then he scratched his head and thought.

'I can tell you how to decide who shall have the bag of salt,' he said, at last. 'Let me hide it for you, while you all shut your eyes and count one hundred. Whoever finds it first shall have it.'

The animals all agreed to do this, for each one felt certain that he would be clever enough to find it first. So they all shut their eyes, and began to count one hundred, as quickly as they could. They opened their eyes, and began at once to sniff round eagerly, under the bushes, in the trees, beneath the rocks.

The lion pawed here and there, the tiger scraped at the stones. The hyena sniffed, the zebra snuffed, the ostrich pecked about and the snake glided under everything. But nobody could find that bag of salt! It didn't seem to be anywhere at all!

At last the animals looked at one another, tired and angry. 'Where's the jackal?' said the lion. 'We will ask him where he has hidden the salt, and share it between us! Jackal, come forth! Where is the salt? You shall share it with us.'

But no jackal came forth at all. There was silence everywhere except for the wind that blew. The tiger growled impatiently. 'Jackal jackal, come forth!' he roared.

Still no jackal came – and then the six animals turned and looked at one another. They knew where that bag of salt was now – yes, it was with the cunning jackal, wherever *he* was! But nobody knew his hiding-place!

'Wait till I see that jackal again!' roared the lion – but you may be sure that the jackal kept out of his way for many weeks to come!

Poor Sally Simple!

Once upon a time there lived a dame called Sally Simple. She was very rich indeed, and had fine dresses and wonderful bonnets. She was vain and proud, and always loved to show off her fine clothes and to boast of them.

She lived in Twinkle Village and the folk there disliked her very much.

'If she spent a little of her money on other people, instead of on herself, she would be a nicer person!' they said. But nobody liked to tell Sally Simple this.

Now one day Sally was most excited because she had a new red shawl, new red shoes to match, a wonderful bonnet with red roses on, as light as a feather, and a magnificent sunshade with red roses all round the brim.

'How all the folk in the village will stare when I go out dressed up in my new clothes!' she thought to herself in glee. 'How they will envy me! No one has a sunshade like mine – and no one has such shoes, shawls and bonnets!'

On the next hot, sunny day, Sally Simple dressed herself up in all her new clothes. How grand she looked! Her bonnet was exactly right. Her shoes twinkled in and out as she walked, and very smart they looked. Her shawl was of the finest silk, and as for her sunshade, well it was the prettiest ever seen in Twinkle Village!

All the folk there saw Sally Simple going out in her new finery – and nobody smiled at her, or told her how nice she looked. No – they all turned their heads and looked the other way.

'Look at that mean, vain creature,' said one to another. 'She wouldn't give even a penny yesterday to help poor old Tom Pepper who fell down and broke his leg last week. And now here she is all dressed up in expensive clothes! Well – we just won't look at her or say a single word of praise!'

Sally Simple was annoyed and hurt when no one seemed to see her. She was a foolish woman and didn't know that people thought her mean or vain. So up and down the village she went, holding her head high in its new bonnet, and her new shoes making a clip-clip noise as she walked along.

Now to the village that day came Dame Sly-One, on the look-out for somebody to trick. That was how the rascally old woman got her living. She lived on her wits, and was always picking up money or goods by tricking others not so clever as she was. And as soon as she saw Sally Simple she knew that here was someone she might rob!

'Good morning to you,' she said politely to Sally Simple. 'Could you tell me the way to the tea-shop?'

'Certainly,' said Sally. 'I'm going that way. You can come with me.'

So off they went, the old woman throwing glances of great admiration at Sally's shawl and bonnet.

'I hope you won't mind my mentioning it,' said Dame Sly-One, at last, 'but really, I cannot help remarking what a beautiful bonnet that is you have on – and what a fine shawl!'

Sally Simple was delighted. Here at last was someone who was praising her. She was so pleased that she asked Dame Sly-One to go into the tea-shop and have a cup of coffee with her. So in they went.

They had cups of coffee and buns, and all the time Dame Sly-One was busy praising this and that.

'That bonnet looks rather heavy to me,' she said at last. 'It is very lovely – but surely just a bit heavy to wear, with all those red roses on?'

'Not a bit, not a bit!' said Sally Simple, at once. 'Just try it, Dame. You'll find it is as light as a feather.'

She took off her bonnet and the old dame slipped it on. She looked at herself in the glass and exclaimed in delight. 'Truly beautiful and as you say, as light as a feather! Really marvellous!'

Sally Simple was pleased. 'Doesn't the shawl match the bonnet nicely?' she asked.

'Very well indeed,' said Dame Sly-One, admiringly. 'But it looks to me as if it might be a little too hot.'

'Indeed it isn't!' cried Sally. 'Do you suppose I would choose a hot shawl for this weather! No – it is the coolest shawl I've ever had. Try it and see!'

So Dame Sly-One wrapped the lovely shawl round her shoulders and admired herself in the glass once more.

'It is lovely,' she said, 'and you are again right, my dear Miss Simple. It is not at all hot – in fact, it is a very cool shawl. I might have known that you were clever enough to choose just the right shawl for weather like this!'

'Have you seen the colour of my shoes?' asked Sally, putting out her feet. 'Do you not think they match the shawl beautifully? I had such a task to get them just right.'

'They certainly do match,' said the old dame, 'but it seems to me they look rather uncomfortable to walk in. I don't believe you will be very happy in those, Miss Simple! Pardon my finding fault with such lovely shoes, won't you?'

Sally was not at all pleased. She kicked off her shoes at once. 'Try them on and see for yourself,' she said, quite crossly.

Dame Sly-One put off her own shoes and slipped her feet into the beautiful red pair. 'Do you mind if I just walk up the street a little and try them?' she asked. 'Really, I can hardly believe that such small shoes can be comfortable.'

'Yes, do walk up the street and see,' said Sally eager to make the old dame say she was right. So out of the door went Dame Sly-One, up the street as far as the corner. Then she came back. All the folk of Twinkle Village were most astonished to see her wearing Sally Simple's clothes, and they gaped at her in surprise.

'Once again you are right, dear Miss Simple!' said the old dame, sitting down at the table. 'Really, you have a most beautiful new set of clothes, even to your fine sunshade – though I fear it would not be of much use in the sun! It is very pretty, but would not keep the hot sun off your head very well.'

'You don't know what you are talking about!' said Sally, in quite a temper. 'Why, I chose that sunshade because it is both pretty *and* useful! It keeps the sun's rays from my face in a most excellent way. I beg you to take it and put it up. Go out into the sun and walk a little way. I am sure you will once again come back and tell me I am right!'

Dame Sly-One picked up the sunshade, went to the door and opened it. Then she stepped out into the hot, sunny street, and walked up it, carrying the fine sunshade, and wearing the lovely bonnet, the beautiful shawl and the magnificent shoes. She went right up to the corner, and turned round it.

Sally Simple waited in the tea-shop for the nice old dame to come back. She waited and she waited. When she had waited for ten minutes she became impatient and went in her stockinged feet to the door. She looked out. There was no sign of the old dame at all.

Sally Simple was vexed. She stamped her foot and got red in the face as she always did when she was angry. But still the old dame did not come back.

'Have you seen an old lady anywhere, wearing

my new bonnet, my new shoes, my new shawl, and carrying my new sunshade?' Sally called at last, to some passing shoppers.

'Yes!' they said, grinning. 'We saw her get into her old donkey-cart round the corner there and drive off in a great hurry, looking as grand as a queen! She must have gone off with all your things, Sally Simple!'

Well, of course, that is just what *had* happened. How Sally raged! How she screamed! How she wept! But no one said anything to comfort her at all.

'Sally, you deserve it,' said Mother Trippy. 'Who is going to be sorry that you have lost the fine things that caused you to be so vain, so mean and so proud? Dame Sly-One paid you for them – with flattering words and false praise! You have nothing to grumble at. Go home now, and think about all that has happened and get some good out of it.'

Poor Sally Simple! Home she went in her stockinged feet, with her bare head, no shawl and no sunshade, a sadder and a much wiser woman. And, so people say, she *did* get some good out of Dame Sly-One's trick – for she turned over a new leaf and was much kinder and more generous than she had ever been before. But she is still rather foolish, poor Sally!

Eight O'Clock Tales

CONTENTS

The Good Turn

Old Mr Turnabout was always doing good turns to people. He was a nice old fellow, very poor, but always willing to help anyone. You would be surprised at the number of good turns he did in a day.

He would help a child across the busy road. He would take a bundle from a tired washerwoman, and carry it for her. He would take anybody's dog for a walk. Really, he seemed to spend his time doing things for other people.

He was a very happy man, for he had dozens of friends. One of his friends was little Billy Smith, the small boy next door. Billy often used to see Mr Turnabout doing his good turns, and he always knew what the old man was going to say when people thanked him for his help. He always said the same thing: 'Don't thank me for the good turn I've done you! Just pass it on!'

That was a strange thing to say, wasn't it? 'Pass it on!' Billy asked him about it one day.

'Why do you ask people to pass your good turns on?' he asked.

'Because the world would soon be full of good turns if we all passed them on!' said old Mr Turnabout. 'Then we should all be happy and friendly, shouldn't we? And that would be very nice.'

'Well, when *I* do a good turn to anyone I shall say the same as you do,' said Billy. 'I shall tell them to pass it on!'

'Yes, do!' said Mr Turnabout. 'And you'll notice a very strange thing, Billy. Sooner or later your good turn will come back to you! Yes, it will! It will be a different good turn, but it will be the one that you began!'

Billy thought that was very odd – but old Mr Turnabout knew what he was saying. And this is the tale of Billy's good turn and how it came back to him. Just listen!

The very next day Billy went to play with Wilfred, a great friend of his. They played marbles, and had a grand time. Then they thought they would go and call on Timothy, who lived in the next street, and show him their marbles. So off they went – but dear me, on the way there Wilfred's very best marble, a great big one of blue glass with pink stripes inside it, rolled down a grating into the cellar of a shop.

Wilfred stopped at once and looked through the grating in dismay. Now what was he to do? The shop was empty and locked up, for nobody lived there.

'That marble has gone for ever!' said poor Wilfred, almost ready to cry, because it really was a splendid marble. 'The shop is locked up and empty, and there is no way of getting the marble.'

But Billy had an idea.

'My daddy knows the man who has the keys to the shop,' he said. 'If I ask him perhaps he'll ask for the keys so that I can get your marble for you. I could unlock the shop, go down to the cellar and find it.'

'Oh, Billy, but it would be dark down there and lonely,' said Wilfred, looking at his friend. 'Wouldn't you be frightened?'

'Only a bit,' said Billy. 'Anyway, I'll try, Wilfred. As soon as my daddy comes home tonight I'll ask him.'

Billy kept his word. He told his father about Wilfred's beautiful marble and how it had dropped down the grating, and he asked him if he might go and get the keys from Mr White, the caretaker down the road, and find the marble for Wilfred.

'If you like,' said his father. He wrote a note to Mr White and gave it to Billy. The little boy ran off to Mr White's house, and in a minute or two he had the key of the shop in his hand. Good! Now he could go and hunt for Wilfred's marble!

It was getting dark so he took his torch with him. He unlocked the door of the empty shop and went inside. It was dusty and smelt stale and nasty. Billy found the steps that led down to the cellar and climbed down them. The cellar was full of spiders' webs and he didn't like it at all. But he really must find Wilfred's marble. He flashed his torch here and there, and at last found the blue marble in a corner. He picked it up, put it into his pocket and went up the steps again. In a minute or two he was out of the shop and was giving back the key to Mr White. Then he ran to Wilfred's house with the marble.

'You *are* a brick!' said Wilfred, delighted. 'See, Billy, do take one of my little green marbles for getting back my big blue one. You *did* do me a good turn!'

'No, thank you,' said Billy. 'I don't want a reward for doing a little thing like that, Wilfred. But you might pass on my good turn to somebody else. See? Just give somebody a helping hand when you can. It's a nice feeling – and tell them to pass on the good turn, too, won't you?'

'Yes, I will,' said Wilfred. 'It's a good idea.'

The next day Wilfred was running to buy some sweets from the sweet-shop when a lady in front of him slipped and fell. The bag she was carrying burst open and everything fell out. Papers went flying in the wind, books tumbled out, pencils and pens clattered on to the pavement.

'Oh, dear!' said the lady, and tried to clutch at her papers.

'I'll help you,' said Wilfred, remembering that he had a good turn to pass on. So he rushed after the flying papers, picked up all the other things, put them into the bag and handed it to the grateful lady.

She opened her purse to give him a coin, but Wilfred wouldn't take it.

'No, don't give me anything, please,' he said. 'I'm only passing on a good turn. Will you pass it on to somebody else?'

'What a splendid idea!' said the lady, very pleased. 'Yes, I'll certainly pass it on!'

It wasn't long before she was able to keep her word. As she hurried home that evening she saw an old woman standing at the edge of the pavement waiting to cross the road. There was a great deal of traffic rushing up and down the street and the old lady didn't quite like to cross, even when there was a clear space.

The young lady went up to her and took her by the elbow.

'Let me help you over,' she said. 'You'll be quite safe with me!'

She took the old woman safely across, and smiled at her kindly.

'That was a good turn you did to me, my dear,' said the old woman gratefully. 'Thank you.'

'Then pass it on to somebody else!' said the young lady. 'Don't forget! Pass it on!'

The old woman didn't forget. She kept wondering and wondering how she could do a good turn to someone, and at last her chance came.

Mrs Jones, her next-door neighbour, hung out her washing on the line, and then went off to do her shopping. The old woman happened to look out of her window and was just in time to see the washing-line snap in two! Down went all the clothes in a heap!

'Oh my! Oh my!' said the old woman in

dismay. 'Look at Mrs Jones's fine washing! It will all get dirty if something isn't done at once. I'll hurry round and pick it all up myself. I've got a good turn to pass on, and that shall be it!'

She went round to the next-door garden and unpegged all the clothes from the broken line. She was just gathering them all up when Mrs Jones came back from her shopping and saw what she had done.

'Oh, you kind soul!' she said. 'Thank you very much indeed. That's a great help to me. You *have* done me a good turn today! I should have been miserable if I'd come back and found I had all my washing to do again. Thank you for your very good turn!'

'That's quite all right,' said the old woman, pleased. 'Just pass on the good turn, will you?'

'I certainly will!' said Mrs Jones.

She didn't forget. She looked out for a chance to do a good turn and it soon came. Old Mr Lacy across the road was in bed with a bad cold, and Mrs Jones thought she would make him some good hot soup and take it to him last thing at night, so that he could have it before he went to sleep. So she carried him a basinful that night and he was delighted!

'This is really very kind of you,' said Mr

Lacy, gratefully. 'I shall enjoy the soup so much, and I am sure I shall have a good night after it. Many, many thanks, Mrs Jones. I hope I shall be able to return your kindness some day, for this is a real good turn you have done me.'

'Well, pass it on!' said Mrs Jones, laughing. 'It's a good idea to pass kind turns on, isn't it, Mr Lacy!'

Now Mr Lacy lay in bed and thought about what Mrs Jones had said. He wasn't usually a very kind man. He was really rather mean. But now that he had plenty of time to think about things, he wished he had done more good turns in his life.

'Well, it's not too late to begin,' he said to himself. 'There's heaps of time to do plenty of good turns even though I am an old man. Now what shall I do? Who is there that I can do a good turn to?'

Mr Lacy had a toyshop: two people worked for him, a girl in the shop and a man who did odd jobs, delivered parcels, mended broken toys, cleaned the window, did the books, and many other things. Mr Lacy thought about him.

'Smith will have had twice as much work to do since I've been away with this cold,' he thought. 'He is a good workman. I think I will do him a good turn. I will ask him if he has any children and I will send a nice toy to each of them. That's how I shall pass on the good turn that Mrs Jones did me.'

He felt quite excited about it. He stayed in bed three days more and then went back to his shop. The man, Smith, had helped the young girl in the shop, and had done all his own work and Mr Lacy's work too. Mr Lacy was pleased.

'Have you any children?' he asked Smith.

'Yes, one boy,' said Smith, surprised. 'He is eight years old and his name is Billy.'

'Oh, I was hoping you had three or four children,' said Mr Lacy, quite disappointed. 'I wanted to send them each a toy. Well, as you've only one child, Smith, you must choose him a very, very nice toy. What do you think he would like?'

'Oh, Mr Lacy, how kind of you!' said Smith, surprised and pleased. 'Well, there's one thing my boy would be so pleased to have, and that's a good clockwork engine. He's just broken his, and he's so miserable about it. It would be a real good turn to him if you'd let him have another engine.'

'I want to do a good turn,' said Mr Lacy, delighted. 'See, here is the best clockwork engine in the shop, Smith, and take two carriages and a signal with it. Tell your boy I'm pleased to do him a good turn, and say to him: "Pass it on!"'

Smith was very anxious to get home that night. Whatever would Billy say when he saw what he had brought him! The little boy had been very sad over his broken engine, but now he would be happy. Smith did up the engine, the two carriages and the signal in a big parcel and ran home all the way that night!

'You're all hot and out of breath, Daddy!' said Billy in surprise. 'Why did you run?'

'Because I have a lovely surprise for you!' said his father, smiling. 'Undo the parcel and look inside.'

When Billy saw the new train and fine signal he was overjoyed. 'But did you *buy* it for me, Daddy?' he asked.

'No,' said his father. 'Mr Lacy said he wanted to do somebody a good turn, so he asked me to take this home for you. But he said I was to say to you: "Pass on the good turn!"'

Billy looked at his father in surprise and said: 'Oh, how funny! That's what I said to Wilfred the other day when I got his marble for him out of the cellar of that empty shop. Do you suppose it's my good turn come back to me, Daddy?'

'Well, that's a funny thing!' said his father. 'I wonder if your good turn *has* been passed on from one to another and has come round to you again. We'll find out! First of all you must ask Wilfred who it was that he did *his* good turn to.'

So the next day Billy asked Wilfred.

'Oh, I picked up all the things that fell out when a lady's bag fell open,' said Wilfred. 'I don't know who she is, but I see her every day. We could ask her if she passed on my good turn, if you like.'

So they waited for her that day, and when she came down the road as usual, Wilfred stepped up to her and asked her very politely.

'Oh, I remember!' she said, smiling. 'Yes, I did pass on the good turn! I helped an old woman across the busy road just there. It was just about this time of day, so maybe she is doing her shopping again. Look! I do believe that is the old lady over there! Yes, it is! We'll go and ask her if she passed on the good turn.'

When they asked the old woman, she nodded her head and smiled. 'Oh, yes,' she said, 'I did pass it on! Of course I did! I picked up all the washing when my next-door neighbour's line broke.'

'We'll go and ask her if *she* passed on the good turn!' said Billy, feeling very much excited. How wonderful that his good turn should have started so many others!

So they went with the old lady to Mrs Jones and asked her the great question – had she passed on the good turn?

'Of course!' she said. 'I took some hot soup to the old man across the road. If you want to ask *him* about it, you will have to go to the toyshop in the next street. He will be there.'

Off they all went, Billy, Wilfred, and the young lady, who was just as excited as they were. Mr Lacy was in the shop, and when he was asked the question he nodded his head and said, yes.

'I sent home an engine and two carriages and a signal to the little boy belonging to Smith, the man who works here,' he said. 'That's how I passed on my good turn.'

'And *I'm* the little boy!' cried Billy. 'So my good turn worked all the way round back to me! How marvellous! I must set it going again, because I've still got to pass it on! What fun!'

So the next day he set another good turn going, and said: 'Pass it on, please!' Isn't it a fine idea! I'm going to do it too, aren't you?

The Boy Who Heard Too Much

There was once a boy called Harold, who had very sharp ears. He heard a great many things he shouldn't have heard, and he listened hard whenever he thought anyone was telling a secret.

He listened behind doors, too, which was a horrid thing to do. And sometimes he hid in the hedge and listened to what passers-by were saying, hoping that he would pick up a good secret.

His mother used to get angry with him.

'Something will happen to you one day!' she said. 'And then you'll be sorry you were such a nasty little listener!'

Something *did* happen as you will see! Poor silly Harold!

It happened one day that he was going through Windy Wood when he saw a bent old woman trotting along in front of him. It was Old Mother Two-Shoes, who was supposed to be as wise as anyone in the village. Where was she going?

Harold made up his mind to creep after her and see what she was going to do in the wood. Perhaps she was going to pick some strange herbs to make magic from. Perhaps she was going to dig up some hidden gold she kept in the wood!

But she didn't do either of those things. No, she went trotting on, humming a little song without much tune, until she came to a small tumble-down cottage in the heart of the wood.

Harold was surprised to see it there for he didn't know anyone lived in the wood. Aha, he was going to learn something about Mother Two-Shoes!

The old woman knocked at the door. Someone opened it and she went in. Harold saw the door shut, and he was disappointed. He couldn't hear much with the door shut! But the window was open – if he crept underneath that he *might* be able to hear what Mother Two-Shoes was talking about to the person who lived quite alone in the heart of the wood.

So he crept up to the window and bent down underneath. He pricked up his ears and listened hard.

'And how are you keeping, Goody?' he heard Mother Two-Shoes say. 'See, I've brought you a fine medicine, and a pound of my best butter.'

'I'm better, thank you,' he heard a quavering old voice say. 'Make some tea, Mother Two-Shoes. The kettle's on the boil.'

Mother Two-Shoes took down a teapot and poured some boiling water inside to warm it. Then, taking it to the window she flung the hot water out, meaning to put in the tea-leaves and make the tea.

And, of course, the hot water fell straight on to Harold, bending down under the window. It gave him such a shock that he yelled out:

'Oooooh!'

'My goodness, whatever's that!' said Mother Two-Shoes, startled. She leaned out of the window and saw Harold there, wiping his face and neck with a handkerchief and wishing to goodness he hadn't shouted out like that!

'Oh, so it's *you*, is it!' said Mother Two-Shoes, who knew very well what Harold was like. 'Listening again, I suppose! I've just come to visit my poor old friend, Goody, and *I've* no secrets for you to hear, you nasty little boy. Come here!'

Before Harold could run away she stretched out a long, skinny arm and caught hold of him by one of his ears. She pulled it hard – and then

she pulled the other one. Harold squealed with
pain, tore himself free and ran off.

> 'The more you peep,
> The longer they'll keep!'

shouted Mother Two-Shoes after him.

Harold rubbed his smarting ears. How long
they seemed! That horrid old woman had pulled
them quite out of shape! He ran home and went
to his bedroom. He looked in the glass on the
wall – and then, oh dear me, what a terrible
shock he got!

His ears had been pulled out as long as a
hare's ears! They stood up above his head and
turned this way and that just like a hare's.
Harold looked most peculiar.

'Oh my goodness!' said Harold, staring at
himself in horror. 'Look at that! Whatever am
I to do?'

'Harold, Harold, tea-time!' called his mother
from downstairs. Harold didn't answer. How
could he go down to tea with ears like a hare?

'HAROLD!' shouted his mother. 'Do you
hear me? Come down at once!'

Still Harold didn't answer. Tears came into
his eyes, and he rubbed them away. His mother,

cross and impatient, came running up the stairs. She flung open the door – and then stopped in the greatest surprise.

'Harold!' she said. 'What have you done with yourself? Why are you wearing those silly ears? Take them off and come down to tea at once.'

'I c-c-can't, Mother,' said Harold.

'Well, if you can't, I will!' said his mother, and pulled hard at his ears, thinking that it was a sort of ear-toy he was wearing to make himself look funny.

'Ow-ooh-ah!' yelled poor Harold – for, of course, the ears were really growing!

'My goodness!' said his mother, in alarm. 'Harold! Those are not really your ears, are they?'

'Yes, Mother,' sobbed Harold, and he told her all about Mother Two-Shoes and how she had punished him for listening.

'Well, didn't I always say something dreadful would happen to you one day?' said his mother. 'It's a nasty horrid habit, listening and prying round after other people. Now see what's happened! Whatever are you going to do?'

'I can wear a hat always,' said Harold, wiping his eyes.

'But the teacher won't let you wear it at

school,' said his mother.

'Perhaps she would if you wrote her a note and said there was something wrong with my ears so please would she let me keep my hat on,' said Harold.

His mother agreed to do that. So the next morning, wearing his biggest hat, Harold went to school with a note from his mother. The teacher read it, looked surprised, but told Harold he could keep his hat on as his mother wished it.

So he did, though the other children laughed at him very much. When the time came for play he went out with the others – and then he noticed that two boys were standing by themselves in a corner, whispering to one another. A secret! What could it be?

Harold went as near as he could and listened carefully. He could just hear what they were saying – his ears listened hard – and then a strange thing happened!

Something pushed his hat right off his head and it fell on the ground! Harold put up his hand – and found, to his horror, that his ears had grown twice as long, very suddenly, and had pushed his hat off his head!

The other children ran up and pointed at him.

'Long ears, long ears!' they cried. 'Donkey's ears for listening! Look how they've grown! Aha, Harold, listen some more and your ears will grow even longer! Long ears, long ears!'

Harold burst into tears and ran home. His mother was horrified when she found that his ears were now twice as long. She at once put on her bonnet and shawl and ran round to Mother Two-Shoes.

'Oh, please, good mother, take away my boy's long ears!' she begged. 'They are twice as long as they were, and I'm afraid they will grow even longer!'

'That's quite likely,' said Mother Two-Shoes. 'I'm sorry, Mrs Brown, but I can't cure Harold. Nobody can – except perhaps my cousin who is half a witch, and lives on the top of Hoo-Hoo Hill.'

'Oh, I'll send him there then,' said poor Mrs Brown, and she hurried home and told Harold to take his things and go to Dame Clip-Clop who lived on Hoo-Hoo Hill.

Harold didn't want to go at all, but he had to. He felt that he really couldn't live at home and have all the children coming pointing and shouting at him. It was too dreadful. So he packed a few things, said goodbye to his mother and went off to Dame Clip-Clop's.

Dame Clip-Clop was expecting him. She was a tall old lady, with bright, piercing eyes. She wore a big bonnet with white lace inside, and a red cloak that swirled round her as she tap-tapped quickly here and there with her stick.

'Oh, here you are,' she said, giving Harold a sharp look, and feeling his long ears with her horny hands. 'Dear, dear – never did I see such long ears on anyone! Well, they will be *very* useful to me!'

'How?' asked Harold.

'Speak up, speak up!' said Dame Clip-Clop. 'I'm very deaf indeed. Can't hear a word!'

And she certainly *was* deaf! Harold had to shout his loudest to make her hear, and sometimes he had to write down what he wanted to say on Dame Clip-Clop's big black slate.

Dame Clip-Clop kept Harold very busy indeed. She used him as her ears. All that she couldn't hear and wanted to hear she made him hear for her.

'Now listen, Harold,' she would say one morning. 'I want to know what the thrush is saying today. He has come to me with a message from a friend of mine. Go out into the garden and listen carefully, please. Write down the message you hear the thrush sing and tell me afterwards.'

Out Harold went. First of all he had to find the thrush because, shameful to say, although he knew what a thrush looked like, he had never bothered before to listen to its beautiful song and so, unless he saw the thrush first, he didn't know which of all the many bird-songs to listen to.

The thrush was sitting at the top of an ash tree. Its throat swelled as it sang. At first Harold couldn't make out at all what it was saying. He sat down on the grass and looked up at the thrush, listening hard. The sky was very blue, the sun was very warm.

'Blue, blue, blue!' sang the thrush. 'Do you see it, do you see it? Pretty, pretty! Look at your ears, look at your ears! Why did you do it, why did you do it?'

Harold went red. To think that even the thrushes in the garden noticed his long ears and sang about it! He went on listening, and soon, because the thrush had a very lovely voice, he couldn't help feeling happy to hear its song. He wrote down its song and took it to Dame Clip-Clop.

'The thrush does sing beautifully,' he said.

'Didn't you know that before?' said the old lady. 'Dear me, wherever were your ears?'

Another day she sent him to the waterfall and told him to bring back the tune it sang. He took his lunch with him for the way was long. He sat down by the silvery waterfall, ate his lunch and listened.

The water gurgled and bubbled, it had deep, bell-like notes, it had silvery ripples of tunes. Harold listened in delight and surprise. Whoever would have thought that water sang like that? He took out a little flute that Dame Clip-Clop had given him, and tried a little tune on it. The notes came bubbling out like the water.

All the afternoon Harold worked hard, trying to get the gurgling tune that the water sang. At last he had it and proudly went back to Dame Clip-Clop. He played her the liquid, silvery tune as loudly as he could, and she smiled, pleased.

'Yes, you have listened well,' she said. 'That is the tune I used to love when I could hear.'

'I didn't know water sang so beautifully,' said Harold.

'You didn't know much,' said Dame Clip-Clop. 'You just knew the things you shouldn't know – everybody else's business!'

One windy day Dame Clip-Clop told Harold to put on his coat and hat and go to the woods. 'The trees will have a message for me today,' she said. 'Go to the woods and find out what it is.'

Harold went, warmly wrapped up, for the wind was strong and cold. When he got to the woods he found a thick bush which sheltered him from the wind and sat down. 'This is a horrid, boring job!' he said to himself. 'It's cold, and who cares what the wind says in the trees!'

His big ears began to listen. The wind rushed through the wood. The leaves whispered loudly, saying: 'Sh! Sh! Sh!' The branches tossed and shouted for joy. The trees bent over sideways and roared to the gale that swept through them. Harold was surprised. Who would have thought that the wood could whisper, shout and roar like that? He listened carefully and soon made out the mad, exciting song that the trees sang to the wind. He wrote it down, and then, leaning back, he shut his eyes and listened again. It was grand.

Dame Clip-Clop read the song and said he had got the message very well.

'Do you know, I'd no idea the wind in the trees sounded so grand,' said Harold. 'It was wonderful.'

'Yes, ears are wonderful things when they are used right,' said the old dame. 'Tonight, when it is dark, go out into my garden and sit on the old seat. I want to know what goes on there when day is gone.'

So, half-frightened, Harold went out into the darkness that night. He sat down on the old seat and listened, his great ears pointing this way and that like a rabbit's.

'This is a silly thing to do,' thought Harold. 'I shall only be frightened by something. Besides, there's nothing to hear!'

'Too-whoo, too-whoo!' suddenly hooted an owl. Then, far away in the distance came an answering cry, 'Ooooo! Ooo-oo-oo-oo!'

The moon came slowly out from behind a cloud. Three little bats flew into the moonlight and Harold could hear their shrill, high, excited squeaks as they caught beetles in the air. Then, not far off in the hedge he heard a few happy squeals as a tiny fieldmouse hunted for food, talking to his small companion all the time.

The wind creaked in a big ash tree, and some small sparrows, roosting in the hedge nearby, awoke and chirruped in whispers before they went to sleep again. A hedgehog came shuffling across the grass and brushed against Harold's

foot, giving a tiny grunt as it did so. Then a
nightingale began to sing.

Harold stayed out in the night so long that
Dame Clip-Clop had to fetch him in.

'Oh, why did you bring me in?' said the boy.
'It was lovely out there in the garden. You've no
idea what I heard!'

'Oh, yes, I have,' said the old dame, smiling.
'But you shall tell me.'

Harold told her everything he had heard.
'You wouldn't believe the little friendly sounds
that go on in the night,' he said, 'and oh, that
nightingale! It didn't sound like a bird. It
sounded like a fairy princess.'

'Well, now you'd better go to bed,' said Dame
Clip-Clop.

The next night, just as Harold was going to
sleep, he heard a sound a long way off. What
was it? It sounded like some little animal in
pain. It was a squeal. There! It came again!
Harold jumped up, flung on his coat and
trousers and ran downstairs.

'Where are you going?' called Dame Clip-
Clop.

'I heard an animal squealing for help,' said
Harold, and ran out into the night. He ran
stumbling down the garden and out into the

lane. He listened again. Yes, it came from the little wood down the hill. He ran on again, getting nearer and nearer.

The moon came out to help him. It shone down on a small rabbit, which had one of its feet caught in a trap. It was squealing pitifully. Harold forced open the trap and picked up the trembling creature. He put it under his coat and walked back to Dame Clip-Clop's.

He bathed the poor little paw and bound it up. The rabbit snuggled to him and looked at him gratefully out of big, soft eyes. Dame Clip-Clop watched.

'Have you ever heard a rabbit squealing in the night before?' she asked.

'I've never *noticed* it before,' said Harold, 'though I expect I've heard the noise many times.'

'I think you know now what things are right and good to listen to, don't you?' asked Dame Clip-Clop. 'Shall you ever waste your time prying and peeping and listening to other people's secrets again?'

'What, waste my hearing on things like that!' cried Harold. 'Why, there isn't enough time to go about hearing all the lovely things there are! No, I shall never make such a mistake again!'

'Then I think we will give your long ears to this little rabbit!' said Dame Clip-Clop, smiling. She stretched out her hands and pulled Harold's long ears gently from his head. They came away easily, leaving his own pink, rounded ears underneath. The old dame pressed the long ears on to the rabbit's furry head, and in a trice its smaller ears had vanished and it had fine, long ears instead.

'Now go, little beastie,' said Dame Clip-Clop, to the rabbit. 'You have long ears to hear enemies with. Use them well, and keep out of danger!'

The rabbit limped out of the door, turned to have a last look at the boy who had saved him and then disappeared. Harold went to a mirror and looked at himself in delight.

'Let your ears hear all the lovely songs and sounds of the world,' said the old dame, 'and let them hear, too, any calls for help, however faint. But close them to all secrets that are not yours, and to all things that are hateful or mean.'

'I will!' said Harold, and he meant it. He went home the next day and his mother was delighted to see he no longer had his long and pointed ears.

'Are your ears quite better now?' she asked, kissing him.

'Yes,' said Harold. 'They can only hear the right things now, Mother, and not the wrong things. I shall never grow long ears again.'

And you will be glad to hear that he never, never did.

The Skittle-policeman

Angela had a box of funny skittle-men. Each man was different. One was a clown with a pointed hat. One was a soldier in red. Another was a sailor in a sailor suit, and a fourth was a policeman in blue. There were nine altogether, and in the box were three balls, red, white, and blue.

Angela used to stand the skittles up in two rows and then she and Nanny used to throw the balls at them and see who could knock down the most. It was great fun.

One day the skittle that looked like a policeman was hit seven times in one morning, and the seventh time a dreadful thing happened. His wooden nose came off! Yes, it did, and it rolled over the floor into a corner. The policeman-skittle was shocked and sad. Fancy having no nose! How dreadful he would look!

When Angela picked him up she squealed in dismay. 'Oh, Nanny! He's lost his nose! I don't like him.'

'Don't be silly,' said Nanny. 'I'll find his nose and stick it on for you again. Then he'll be all right.'

But they couldn't find his nose, however hard they looked. Angela didn't like the policeman-skittle after that. She said he looked so horrid without a nose, and when Nanny had gone out of the room what do you think Angela did? She threw the skittle out of the window into the garden below! Wasn't it horrid of her?

Poor skittle! He fell into the wet grass and lay there, astonished and hurt. What was he going to do now!

All day long he lay there, and all day long it rained hard! When night came you wouldn't have known the skittle. All the paint had run off him, and he was just plain wood.

When the rain stopped and the moon shone out at night, the policeman-skittle sat up. He looked at himself. Goodness, what a sight he was! He felt his face. No nose! It was really dreadful. He wondered if he could find his nose if he went back to the nursery.

Somehow or other he climbed up the old apple tree by the wall and slipped in at the nursery window. The other toys were playing about on the floor very happily. When they saw the poor skittle-policeman with all his paint washed off him by the rain, they didn't know him.

'Who are you?' they shouted.

'I'm one of the skittle-men,' said the policeman, humbly. 'My nose was knocked off this morning and I've just come to see if I can find it.'

'How awful you look without a nose!' said the sailor doll, unkindly. 'And you've no paint at all.'

'I can't help it,' said the skittle, sadly. 'It isn't my fault. It's Angela's fault.'

'Well, we don't want you back here,' said the toys to the poor washed-out skittle. 'You look dreadful. Angela threw you away and you must stay away.'

'All right,' said the skittle, sighing. 'Just let me find my nose and I'll go. But I think you're very horrid and unkind.'

So they were, weren't they? Nobody helped the skittle to look for his nose, but he found it at last. He picked it up and went to the window.

'Goodbye,' he said. 'I'm sorry to leave you all.'

'Goodbye,' said the toys, and they turned their backs on him and began to play games again. The skittle slid down the apple tree and stood in the grass, wondering what to do.

He began to walk down the garden. He slipped under the hedge at the bottom and found himself in a field. He walked across it and came to a sloping hill-side.

The moon shone brightly. The skittle came to a little ring of toadstools, and then he heard a strange sound of grunting and panting. He looked to see what it was. To his great surprise he saw a small brownie tugging and pulling at the toadstools, trying his hardest to pull them up to carry away. But he couldn't drag the toadstools out of the ground, and at last he sat down on one, sighed heavily and said: 'I shall never do it. I shall NEVER do it!'

The skittle felt sorry for the little creature. He walked up to one of the toadstools and tugged. Plip! It came away from the ground at once. In fact it gave way so suddenly that the skittle sat down hard on the ground and said 'Oooh!' very loudly.

The brownie saw him and began to laugh. How he laughed! He laughed so much that the skittle began to laugh too.

'I say, I know I oughtn't to laugh at you when you were trying to help me,' said the brownie, stopping at last. 'But you looked so funny. Who are you?'

'I'm a skittle-policeman,' said the skittle. 'I've had my nose broken off, and Angela threw me out of the window because she didn't like me any more. Then the rain came and washed all my paint off me, so I haven't even a uniform on now. I'm afraid I look a dreadful creature.'

'You do look rather odd,' said the brownie, staring at him. 'But you can't help it. I say, aren't you strong? Could you help me to move these toadstools, do you think?'

'Of course,' said the skittle. 'But why do you want to move them? They look all right just here.'

'The silly things have grown in the wrong place,' said the brownie. 'They should have grown over there, where the magic bus stops – see, by that bush. They are seats for people waiting for the bus.'

'Oh,' said the skittle, looking in surprise at a bus that suddenly appeared round the bush. It wasn't much bigger than the toy bus in the nursery. It was full of mice, rabbits, and fairies. He stared and stared.

The bus drove off. The brownie began to tug hard at the toadstools again. 'Let me do it,' said the skittle, and he soon lifted two or three. The brownie carried them to the bus-stop and stood them there in a row. Presently little folk and three mice came along to wait for the bus. They were delighted to find the seats there and soon they were all full.

'It's very good of you to help me,' said the brownie, when they had taken up all the toadstools and moved them to their right places. 'I suppose I can't give you a cup of hot cocoa just to warm you up on this cold night?'

'Well, I'm quite warm,' said the skittle. 'But a cup of hot cocoa does sound very nice.'

'Come on, then,' said the brownie, and he took the skittle through a tiny door in the hill-side. Inside was a small and cosy room. A fire was burning at the end, and a kettle was singing on the hob. The brownie got out a cocoa tin and made some cocoa. Before long the skittle and the brownie were very friendly.

'It's a pity about your nose,' said the brownie. 'You would be nice-looking if you had a nose.'

'Well, I've got it here,' said the skittle. 'But what's the good of a nose in your pocket?'

'Oh, you've got it, have you!' said the brownie. 'Well, why not let me stick it on for you?'

'Oh, *could* you!' cried the skittle, delighted.

'Of course,' said the brownie. 'I can get some sticky glue from the buds of the chestnut tree, you know. The bees will go and collect enough for me. They are very clever at getting chestnut glue. Then I can stick your nose on for you.'

That night the skittle slept in the brownie's bed with the brownie. He was happy, warm, and comfortable. This was better than living in the nursery with unkind toys and a little girl who threw you out of the window because you had lost your nose.

In the morning the sun shone. The brownie went outside and made a strange humming sound. Soon twelve brown-and-gold bees came flying up to hear what the brownie had to say.

'Collect me some sticky glue from the chestnut buds,' he said. Off they flew. Soon they were back with the glue and they each put their sticky gift into a dish set ready for them. The brownie thanked them and went indoors. He heated the glue over the fire and then called the skittle to him. He took the little nose from him, smeared it with glue, and then stuck it firmly on the skittle's face. He stuck it on just a little bit crooked, but it didn't matter – it just made the skittle look comical and jolly.

'Ooh!' said the skittle, for the glue was hot. He stood still, quite brave, and in a few minutes there was his nose, firmly on his face again. How pleased he was!

'Many, many thanks,' he said, looking at himself in a looking-glass. 'That's fine! If only I could get myself a new coat of paint I should look just as grand as ever I did!'

'Well, perhaps we can manage that too,' said the brownie, at once. 'I know the elf who paints the bluebells in the spring, and if you don't mind rather a pale-blue for your uniform, I'm sure she would come and do it for you.

The skittle-policeman didn't know what to say, he was so pleased and grateful. Tears came into his eyes, and ran down his nose.

'I say, don't do that!' said the brownie, in alarm. 'Your nose is only just stuck, you know! If you cry tears, it might come unstuck.'

The skittle hurriedly dried his tears and smiled. 'You are very good and kind to me,' he said. 'I would simply *love* a bluebell-coloured uniform.'

So the next thing that happened was that they went to call on the elf who always painted the bluebells in May. She was pleased to see them and at once agreed to give the skittle a fine new

blue uniform. She set to work that same day and you should have seen the policeman-skittle when she had finished. He looked simply beautiful.

'You look grand enough to go to Toytown and be the policeman there!' said the elf, looking at the skittle, very pleased with her painting. 'The policeman there is old, and doesn't know how to deal with all the new traffic that's come in the last few years. You know, buses, trams, trains, motor-cars, and all that. Toytown used to be a peaceful sort of spot, but now it's all different.'

The skittle-policeman listened, his eyes shining. How he had longed to be a real policeman and stand in the road with his hand out! But he had never been anything but a skittle, made to be knocked down and set up again.

'Oh,' he said. 'Oh! If only they'd let me try to do some proper policeman's work in Toytown! How hard I would work! How careful I would be! I would see that no accident happened and that everything went at the right speed.'

The brownie and the elf stared at one another in excitement. 'Come along!' they suddenly cried to the surprised skittle. 'Come along!

We'll get you the job! Oh, how pleased Toytown will be to have a new policeman!'

Soon the skittle found himself being dragged along to the bus at the corner. They all got in and in ten minutes' time they arrived at Toytown. The skittle felt quite at home when he saw teddy bears, dolls, and toy dogs walking about the streets. Everyone stared at him in admiration, for he really did look smart in his beautiful pale-blue uniform.

Well, he got the job, of course. The old policeman was only too glad to give it up.

The skittle walked proudly into the middle of the town, where the traffic was thickest, and five roads met. He held up his arm. Everything stopped at once. That was a proud moment for the skittle. He waved his hand. The cars and buses chugged onwards again.

Everyone came to look at the new policeman.

'What a beautiful uniform he has!' they cried. 'What a lovely nose, just the weeniest bit crooked! Most unusual! How well he guides the traffic! He is a fine policeman, one to be proud of.'

What do you think happened one day? A big motor-car came up, driven by a sailor doll. At the back were crowded a pack of skittle-men, two dolls, and a teddy bear – and they were all from Angela's nursery, where the skittle-policeman had once lived!

'Honk, honk!' said the car, impatiently, for the sailor doll was in a hurry. The skittle-policeman knew that honk, and he looked round sharply. Ah, it was the toys he had once known! They were going too fast. He put up his hand to stop them. The sailor doll stopped, frowning. He was afraid of this policeman in his beautiful uniform.

Suddenly the teddy bear gave a squeal.

'It's the policeman-skittle from the nursery, the one whose nose came off! Just look at him! Oooooh!'

The policeman turned round and looked at the toys. He didn't smile. He didn't blink an eye. He just looked at them very sternly.

The toys in the car went pale. They felt uncomfortable. They remembered how unkind they had been. The little doll burst into tears. The policeman-skittle said nothing at all. He waited until the road was clear and then he waved on the motor-car. The sailor doll was so nervous that he put on the brake instead of starting the car and the toys nearly fell out with the jerk.

'Come along, now, come along, now,' said the skittle in his deepest voice. 'Don't hold up the traffic.'

The car at last went on. All the skittles stared back at the policeman in fear and admiration. What a grand fellow he was, to be sure! How sorry they were they had been unkind! Dear, dear, dear, what a mistake they had made! How they wished they were friends with him now!

But it was no use wishing. Once a chance of kindness is lost, it is gone for ever. The toys were very silent that day, and all of them were secretly making up their minds to be nicer in future.

As for the skittle-policeman, how he laughed when he told the brownie and the elf about the toys that night.

'You should have taken them all to prison,' said the brownie, indignantly, for he was very fond of his skittle friend now.

'Oh, no,' said the policeman. 'I just looked at them like this – and they felt dreadful, I know they did!'

'You are a kind and clever fellow,' said the elf, and she hugged the skittle. 'Let's get married and then I can paint you a new uniform every year when I do the bluebells.'

So they are married now, and very happy. And every day the skittle can be seen in Toytown, right in the middle of the street, stopping the traffic and waving it on just like any policeman in your own town. Wouldn't you like to see him? I would!

Tick Tock's Tea-party

Tick-Tock the brownie lived with the enchanter Wind-Whistle, and kept his house neat and tidy for him. He cooked his meals, washed his clothes, and sometimes he helped Wind-Whistle with his spells. He was hard at work all day long, but he was very happy.

One afternoon there came a knock at the door and Tick-Tock went to open it. Outside stood the Princess of the Blue Hills and two of her court, come to visit the enchanter and take his advice.

It was just tea-time and Tick-Tock knew they would all stay to tea – and oh, dear me – there were no cakes at all, hardly any jam, and just a pinch of tea!

'Pray come inside!' said Tick-Tock, bowing low, for he knew his manners very well. The Princess came in, smelling very sweet and looking very lovely. Tick-Tock gave her and the ladies-in-waiting some chairs in the drawing-room and went to tell Wind-Whistle of his royal visitor. All the time he was worrying about tea. What should he do for cakes and jam? You couldn't give royal princesses plain bread and butter – and goodness gracious, there was hardly any butter either! It was very worrying.

Wind-Whistle was pleased to hear of his royal visitor. He put on his best cloak at once and said to Tick-Tock: 'Get tea ready. Lay it nicely.'

'Oh, your highness, isn't it dreadful, there are no cakes, just a pinch of tea, hardly any jam, and not much butter!' said poor Tick-Tock.

'Well, go to the shops and get some,' said the enchanter snappily.

'But they're shut this afternoon,' said Tick-Tock. 'It's early closing day!'

'Dear, dear, so it is,' said the enchanter. 'Well, never mind. Now listen carefully, Tick-Tock. Lay the table as usual, but place the butter-dish, the jam-dish, and cake-dishes empty on the table – empty, do you hear? Put no tea in the teapot, but fill it with boiling water. I have a mind to do a little magic for the Princess, and at the same time provide a good tea for her.'

Tick-Tock listened open-mouthed. How exciting!

He hurried to do what he was told. He laid

the table, put out empty butter, jam, and cake-dishes, and filled the teapot with boiling water. Then he told the enchanter that everything was ready.

Wind-Whistle led the Princess and her ladies into the room where the tea was laid and bade them be seated. They were surprised to see nothing to eat.

'Madam, do you like Indian or China tea?' began the enchanter, holding up the tea-pot. Then he caught sight of the brownie Tick-Tock peeping in at the door to watch everything.

'Go to the kitchen!' he ordered. 'And shut this door, Tick-Tock.'

Poor Tick-Tock! He had so badly wanted to see everything. He shut the door and went to the kitchen – but in half a minute he was back again, peeping through the keyhole and listening to what the enchanter was saying!

'I'll have China tea,' said the Princess.

'China tea, pour forth!' commanded the enchanter, and the Princess gave a scream of delight, for pale China tea poured from the teapot into her cup.

'I'd like Indian tea,' said each of her ladies, and when Wind-Whistle said: 'Indian tea, pour forth!' at once dark Indian tea poured into their cups.

'What sort of jam do you like?' asked Wind-Whistle.

'Strawberry, please,' answered his three royal visitors.

'Strawberry jam, appear in the dish!' cried Wind-Whistle. Immediately a great heap of delicious jam appeared.

'And what cakes do you prefer?' asked the enchanter.

'Chocolate cakes for me!' cried the Princess in excitement.

'Cherry buns for me!' said the first lady.

'And ginger fingers for me!' begged the second lady.

'Chocolate cakes, appear!' commanded the enchanter, tapping a dish. 'Cherry buns, come forth, ginger fingers, appear!'

Three dishes were suddenly full of the most delicious-looking cakes, and the ladies cried out in delight. Then the enchanter struck the butter-dish.

'Now, butter, where are you?' he cried. Golden butter at once gleamed in the dish. It was marvellous. Outside the door Tick-Tock listened to all this, and tried to see through the keyhole what was happening. It was most exciting.

After tea Wind-Whistle called Tick-Tock to him.

'I'm going to the Blue Hills with the Princess and her ladies,' he said. 'She needs my help. Look after my house and see that nothing goes wrong. And don't meddle with any magic or you will be sorry!'

By six o'clock Wind-Whistle and the ladies were gone and Tick-Tock was left alone. He finished up the cakes that were left from tea and enjoyed them very much. They were much nicer than any that were sold in the shops.

It was whilst he was eating the cakes that the naughty idea came to him. He clapped his hands for joy and danced round the kitchen.

'Why shouldn't I give a tea-party and make all the cakes and things appear!' he shouted. 'I can wear the enchanter's magic cloak, and then all the things I say will come true too. Oh, how lovely! Won't I make everyone stare! My friends will think *I'm* an enchanter.'

He sat down at once and wrote six notes to his friends. One went to Big-Eyes, one to Little-Feet, another to Pippity, the fourth to Gobo, and the last two to Tubby and Roundy the two fat brownies.

'Please come to a Magic Tea-Party,' he wrote to each of them. Then he licked up the envelopes and posted the letters. How excited he felt!

He had asked his friends for the next day. So he was very busy in the morning making the house tidy and putting fresh flowers on the tea-table. Then after his dinner he washed himself, did his hair nicely, laid the tea-table with empty plates and dishes, and at last went to put on the enchanter's magic cloak. It was embroidered with suns and moons and shone very brightly.

Tick-Tock walked about in front of the looking-glass in Wind-Whistle's bedroom and thought he looked really very grand.

'Won't I surprise everyone this afternoon!' he chuckled to himself. 'Dear me! There's the clock striking half-past three! I must put the kettle on for tea.'

He ran downstairs, nearly tripping over the cloak he wore, for it was much too big for him. He put the kettle on, and waited for his friends.

They all came together, looking very smart in their best clothes. They were most excited and crowded round Tick-Tock, asking him what a Magic Tea-Party was.

'Wait and see, wait and see!' said Tick-Tock, laughing.

He led them into the dining-room, where tea was laid – but when they saw the empty dishes their faces grew long. Wasn't there going to be anything to eat?

'Wait and see, wait and see!' laughed Tick-Tock, again, running into the kitchen to fetch the kettle, which was now boiling.

His guests sat down round the table, and waited. Tick-Tock came back with the kettle. He was going to do better than the enchanter – he was going to make the cakes, jam, butter, and tea all appear at once!

'What sort of cakes and jam do you like?' he asked his guests. They all called out together.

'Gooseberry jam! Chocolate roll! Coconut buns! Cherry cake! Plum jam! Marmalade! Sponge fingers!'

'Right!' said Tick-Tock. He picked up the teapot, which he had filled with nothing but hot water, and then cried out loudly: 'Tea, pour forth! Butter, appear! Gooseberry jam, plum jam, marmalade, where are you? Chocolate roll, coconut buns, cherry cake, sponge fingers, come forth!'

Then, to the enormous surprise of all his

friends, the teapot poured tea into their cups, one after another, jam and marmalade began to come into the dishes, butter heaped itself up in another dish, and cakes fell into a pile on the rest of the dishes. It was perfectly marvellous!

'Wonderful!' cried Gobo.

'How do you do it!' shouted Tubby and Roundy.

'Goodness gracious!' cried the others.

'It's easy!' said Tick-Tock, pouring out his cup of tea last of all. 'I'm quite a good magician, you know. I'm sure I could teach Wind-Whistle a lot.'

A puzzled look came over the faces of the six guests as they watched the jam, butter, and cakes appearing in the dishes. They had been appearing for quite a while now, and the dishes were much too full. In fact the gooseberry jam was spilling on to the cloth.

'You ought to have put out bigger dishes,' said Tubby to Tick-Tock. 'Look, they aren't big enough for all the cakes and things.'

But Tick-Tock was also feeling puzzled about something and didn't hear what Tubby said. The teapot had filled his cup, but when he set it down on the teapot stand, it didn't stay there. No, it hopped up into the air all by itself and began to pour tea into the milk-jug! It was most peculiar. Tick-Tock took hold of it and put it back on the tray. But as soon as he let go, up hopped the teapot into the air again and poured a stream of tea into the sugar-basin. It was most annoying.

'I say, Tick-Tock, the dishes aren't *big* enough, I tell you!' said Tubby, as he and the others watched the cakes spilling all over the table. 'Shall we get some more?'

'No, just help yourselves and eat as much as you want to,' said Tick-Tock, still busy with the obstinate teapot. 'If you eat up the cakes there will soon be room for them on the dishes.'

So the guests began eating – but, dear me, they couldn't eat nearly as fast as those cakes, jams, and butter appeared! Soon the tablecloth was in a dreadful mess, for the jam slid over the edge of the pot and dripped on to the table, and the butter flopped down too, while the marmalade was in big blobs all round its dish. The cakes no longer fell on the dishes as they appeared out of the air, but bounced straight on to the table, scattering crumbs all over the place.

The guests were rather frightened, especially when they saw what trouble the teapot was giving poor Tick-Tock. But they said no more.

They ate steadily, though nothing really tasted very nice. Poor Tick-Tock could eat nothing for all the time he was trying to stop the teapot from pouring tea here, there, and everywhere.

At last it tore itself away from the frightened brownie and poured some tea down Gobo's neck!

'Ow!' squealed Gobo, jumping up in fright as the hot tea dripped down his collar. 'Ow! Ooh! It's burnt me!'

He wiped the tea away with his handkerchief and began to cry.

'Hoo, hoohoo! I'm going home! This isn't a nice tea-party.'

He ran out of the door and slammed it. The others looked at one another. The teapot moved towards Tubby, but he jumped out of the way.

'Good-bye, Tick-Tock,' he said. 'I must get home. I've some work to do.'

'I must go with him,' said Roundy, and the two brownies ran off in a hurry.

It wasn't long before the other guests went too. The magic was frightening them. It was all very well to have as many cakes as you wanted, but to see hundreds dropping on to the table was very queer. They felt sure something had gone wrong.

Tick-Tock was very unhappy and rather frightened. What had happened? Hadn't he done the magic just the same as Wind-Whistle? Why wouldn't everything stop appearing? Why didn't that horrid teapot stop pouring?

Tick-Tock looked round the table in despair. What a mess! Look at all the jam and marmalade! Look at those cakes, not even bothering to fall on the dishes any more! Look at the butter all over the place! And look at that perfect nuisance of a teapot pouring tea on the carpet now! Whatever was he to do?

Poor Tick-Tock! He couldn't do anything. He had started a magic that he couldn't stop. The teapot suddenly stopped pouring tea on the carpet and playfully poured some on Tick-Tock's beautiful cloak. He cried out in dismay.

'Oh! Look what you've done to the enchanter's best cloak! Oh, what a mess! Whatever will he say? Oh, my goodness me, I must go and sponge off the tea at once!'

Tick-Tock rushed upstairs to the bathroom. He took a sponge and began to sponge the tea-stain on the cloak. He was dreadfully afraid the enchanter would see it, and what would he say then? Oh, dear, dear, why ever had Tick-Tock meddled with magic when he had been told not to?

It took a long time to get the tea-stain out of the cloak, but at last it was done. Tick-Tock hung the cloak over a chair to dry and was just going downstairs when he heard someone shouting from outside the house. He stuck his head out of the window to see what the matter was.

Out of doors stood Gobo, and he was shouting at the top of his voice.

'Hi, Tick-Tock! Are you all right? There are a lot of funny things happening down here! Look!'

Tick-Tock looked – and out of the front door he saw a stream of tea flowing! Yes, really, it was running down the path! Mixed with it was butter, jam, marmalade, and cakes of all kinds, bobbing up and down in the stream.

'Oooooh!' screamed Tick-Tock, and ran downstairs in a hurry. Well! I couldn't tell you what the dining-room looked like. It was a foot deep in tea, to begin with, for the teapot was still pouring away merrily. And then the cakes! Well, there were hundreds and hundreds of them. The jam and marmalade and butter were all mixed up together, and still more and more things were dropping down into the room.

Tick-Tock waded in. The teapot at once

poured some tea on his nose and he gave a cry of pain, for it was hot. Whatever was he to do? This was dreadful.

'Can't you stop the things coming and coming and coming?' shouted Gobo, who was really very sorry for his friend. 'You made them start.'

'I know,' sobbed Tick-Tock. 'But I thought they would stop by themselves and they haven't. If only Wind-Whistle was here!'

Then Gobo gave a shout and pointed up the street. 'Here he comes!' he cried. 'He's come home sooner than you thought!'

So he had. Poor Tick-Tock! He didn't know whether to be glad or sorry. Wind-Whistle strode up the road and when he came to his house and saw the stream of tea pouring out, mixed with jam and cakes, he was most astonished. He stared at it in amazement, whilst poor Tick-Tock tried to stammer all about it.

'What! You dared to meddle with magic when I told you not to!' shouted the enchanter in anger. 'You wore my magic cloak! How dare you?'

'Oh, please, your highness, forgive me!' wept the brownie, as white as a sheet. 'I just thought I would give a tea-party like you did. It looked so easy. But nothing would stop. It just went on and on. The teapot is still pouring in the dining-room.'

The enchanter waded through the stream of tea and looked in at the dining-room door. What a dreadful sight! He frowned in anger. Then he clapped his hands sharply three times and said: 'Illa rimmytooma lippitty crim!' These words were so magic that Tick-Tock trembled to hear them. But at the sound of them the teapot at once stopped its pouring and put itself in the sink to be washed up. The cakes stopped falling from the air, and so did the jam, marmalade, and butter.

But the dreadful mess remained. Tick-Tock looked at it in despair.

'Aren't you going to make all this mess go too?' he asked his master.

'No, *you're* going to make that go!' said Wind-Whistle, sternly. 'Get brushes, cloths, soap and water, Tick-Tock, and clear it up. It will keep you busy.'

Tick-Tock went away howling. The mess would take him days to clear up. But it was his own fault, he shouldn't have meddled with magic. He never would again, never!

Wind-Whistle forgave Tick-Tock, when the house was clean and tidy again. But when he wants to tease the little brownie, he says: 'Would you like another tea-party, Tick-Tock, some day?'

But Tick-Tock shakes his head and cries: 'No, no, no. Never again!'

The Runaway Donkey

There was once a gnome who owned a fat grey donkey. The donkey was called Kick-up, because when he was angry he kicked up his hind legs. He had a good home with his master, the gnome Twiddle, and although Twiddle was very fond of the donkey, and did all he could to make him comfortable, Kick-up was always complaining.

Once Twiddle bought a dog, but the donkey made such a fuss that he had to sell it again.

'How can I sleep when that dog barks all night?' complained Kick-up. 'I won't work for you, Twiddle, if you keep him as well as me.'

Then Twiddle tried keeping hens, for he was very fond of boiled eggs. Kick-up kicked up his heels in a fury, and sent a basket of eggs, which Twiddle was carrying carefully, right up into the air – and, of course, all the eggs broke.

'Well, why do you keep those nasty, clucking creatures?' cried Kick-up in a rage. 'As soon as I lie down for a snooze in my field those hens lay eggs and start the most terrible cackling I ever heard. Is it such a grand thing to lay an egg? No, it is not. Even snails lay eggs.'

'Don't worry yourself,' said Twiddle, gently, for he was a good-tempered gnome. 'If the hens disturb you, Kick-up, they shall go. I will give them to my next-door neighbour. You know that I am very fond of you, and I want you to be happy.'

One day Twiddle dug up a great many potatoes and thought he would take them to market to sell. He had far more than he could eat, and he thought it would be nice to sell some, and with the money buy some paint to make Kick-up's stable smart.

So he spoke to Kick-up and told him that he must take him to market the next day, carrying a load of potatoes.

Now Kick-up had grown fat and lazy. He had planned to snooze in the hot sunshine all the next day, and he was cross to hear that he was to go all the way to market, carrying a heavy load.

'Master, you work me too hard,' he complained. 'It is too hot to carry loads to market. I shall get sunstroke and then you will be sorry.'

'Then I will get you a sun-hat today,' said Twiddle. 'I shouldn't like you to get sunstroke, Kick-up, because I am really very fond of you. But you MUST go to market with me tomorrow. I cannot possibly carry the potatoes myself.'

'I tell you it is too hot to go to market,' said the donkey, sulkily. 'If you treat me like this, I shall run away. As for a sun-hat, I don't want one. I should look silly wearing a hat.'

But Twiddle was so afraid that his precious donkey *would* get sunstroke, for it was certainly very hot, that he went off to buy a large straw sun-hat for him, with two holes for his ears, and a large pink rose in front, to make the hat pretty. When he got back he slipped it over Kick-up's head, and tied the ribbon firmly under his chin.

'You look very nice,' said Twiddle, admiringly. Kick-up jumped up in a temper and ran to the pond. He looked at himself and then flew into a dreadful rage.

'I look foolish, stupid, ridiculous, and a perfect silly!' he shouted in a rage. 'Take the hat off at once, Twiddle.'

'Who is master, you or I?' said Twiddle, quite firmly, for once.

'I shall run away if you don't take off this hat!'

cried the donkey. At that the gnome turned his back on him and walked away, hoping that Kick-up would be in a better temper by the next day.

But do you know, when Twiddle went to Kick-up's stable the next morning, the door was open and Kick-up was not there! He had gone, quite gone.

Twiddle stared in the greatest surprise. Then he looked all round the fields – no little fat donkey was anywhere to be seen. It was terrible. Kick-up had kept his word, and had run away!

Twiddle's eyes filled with tears. He had had the donkey for ten years, and had cared for him and loved him very much. He would miss him dreadfully, even though the little donkey had been so bad-tempered.

'I must see if I can find him,' thought the gnome, and he set off for his friends' houses.

'Have you seen a fat, grey donkey wearing a sun-hat?' he asked Gobbo, who was feeding his hens in the back garden. 'He's run away.'

'Good riddance too!' said Gobbo, at once. 'Let's hope he stays away.'

'But I'm lonely without him,' said Twiddle.

'Poor old Twiddle,' said Gobbo. 'It's a shame. Look, please will you accept three white hens from me for a present? They will lay you lovely eggs for breakfast, and now that Kick-up is gone there is no one to grumble about their cackling.'

'Oh, thank you!' cried Twiddle, pleased. 'I shall love to have eggs for breakfast tomorrow.'

So he took the hens home in delight and put them into the hen-run. Then off he went to his friend Tiralee, who lived at the other end of the village.

'Have you seen my fat, grey donkey?' he asked. 'He's run away, and he's wearing a sun-hat.'

'No, I haven't seen him, and I don't want to,' said Tiralee. 'Horrid thing, he was, with his bad temper and rude ways. You are well rid of him.'

'But I'm lonely without him,' said Twiddle.

'Poor old Twiddle,' said Tiralee, who was very fond of his gentle friend. 'Look here, old man, I've got three beautiful puppies here. I'd like to give you one of them to keep you company. He'll grow up into a lovely dog, and be very fond of you.'

'Oh, thank you,' said Twiddle, gratefully. He took the puppy home and called him Tinker, which the puppy thought was a lovely name.

Kick-up hadn't come back, so off went Twiddle to the next village, to call on his friends there. He knocked at Tiptoes' door, and she opened it.

'Have you seen a fat, grey donkey wearing a sun-hat?' asked Twiddle. 'He's run away from me.'

'Well, don't have him back,' said Tiptoes, at once. 'You're well off without him, the bad-tempered creature!'

'But I'm lonely without him,' said Twiddle, mournfully. Then Tiptoes was sorry for the little gnome.

'What you want is a cat sitting by your fireside!' she said. 'Look, here is a little black kitten for you; it will bring you luck!'

Twiddle was delighted with the cuddly black kitten. He put it under his coat and then went to call on Too-tall, next door.

'Have you seen a fat, grey donkey wearing a sun-hat?' he asked Too-tall. 'He's run away.'

'*That's* a blessing!' said Too-tall, at once. 'I never did like that horrid donkey of yours.'

'Yes, but I'm lonely without him,' said Twiddle.

'Poor old Twiddle!' cried Too-tall. 'I'm sorry for you. Wait a minute. I've two tame pigeons you would simply love. They say "Coo-rco" all day and are fine company. I'll give you them.

They will perch on your hat all the way home, so you won't have any trouble with them!'

Twiddle was delighted with the pretty white pigeons. They perched on his hat at once and were quite at home there, pecking Twiddle's big ears lovingly every now and again.

Last of all Twiddle called on his friend Very-Rich, and knocked at his door. Very-Rich was pleased to see him and shook hands in delight.

'Have you seen a fat, grey donkey wearing a sun-hat?' asked Twiddle. 'He's run away.'

'Well, you can thank your lucky stars that he's gone, the wretched thing!' said Very-Rich, who had once been kicked by Kick-up, and had never forgotten it.

'But I'm lonely without him,' said Twiddle, 'and also, it's very, very awkward, because I've a load of potatoes to take to market and I've no donkey to take them now.'

'Well, well, well!' said his friend, scratching his head and thinking hard. 'Let me see. How would you like me to give you my old pony? I don't need her any more, and she would love to come and live with you. She can carry heavy loads and doesn't mind working at all.'

'Dear me, no, I couldn't take a present like that!' said Twiddle.

'Dear me, yes, you could!' laughed Very-Rich, and he went to fetch the pony. It ran up to Twiddle and nuzzled its nose into his hand. He was so pleased.

'Well, I *would* love to have this pony!' he said. 'Thank you very much. I'll treat her very well.'

'I know you will,' said Very-Rich.

Twiddle climbed up on the pony's back and jogged happily home, with the kitten under his coat, and the two pigeons on his head. What a lot of good friends he had! He certainly wouldn't be lonely now that he had so many animals and birds of his own. Three white hens, a nice puppy-dog, a kitten, two pigeons, and a pony! How lucky he was!

He put the pony into the donkey's stable and told the pigeons they might live there too, and pick up any corn they wished. The puppy he put in a nice little kennel, and the kitten he said might live by the fireside. The hens were very happy in their run.

For a whole week Twiddle and his new friends lived happily together. The pony took him to market and never complained at all. The dog guarded him each night, and always went with him for walks. The kitten sat on his knee and purred lovely things to him. The hens laid him three eggs every day, and the pigeons called 'coo-roo' whenever they saw him, and flew down to his shoulders. He was very happy.

Then one night, when Twiddle was fast asleep in bed, the fat, grey donkey came back! He had tried first one master and then another, he had been disobedient and bad-tempered, and he had been beaten and half-starved. He was sorry he had ever left kind Twiddle.

'He'll be glad to see me back,' thought the donkey, as he trotted homewards. 'He'll have been very lonely without me. He'll treat me better than ever now!'

It was dark when the donkey reached home.

He trotted into the yard and immediately the puppy-dog in the kennel began to bark and flew at him. Snap! He was bitten in the leg and he brayed with pain!

He ran to his stable, but the door was shut. He kicked it open and went inside. But someone else was there – the little pony! He kicked out with his hind feet and the donkey was struck smartly on the nose – biff! Then the pigeons flew down from the rafters and cried 'coo-roo' angrily at him, and pecked the tips of his ears!

Poor Kick-up! How frightened he was! This was a dreadful home-coming! He left the stable and went to the house, but on the way he woke up the hens who all started to cackle at once: 'kuk-kuk-kuk-kuk-kuk-kuk, a robber, kuk-kuk-kuk-kuk-kuk, a robber!'

Kick-up pushed open the kitchen door, which was never locked. He ran into the kitchen, anxious to get away from all the frightening things in the yard – but the kitten, who was sitting by the fire, flew at him in a rage, dug all her twenty claws into his legs, and spat at him so fiercely that he backed into the kitchen table in fright and over it went!

That woke up Twiddle. Wondering whatever was the matter, he lit his candle and went downstairs. As soon as the donkey saw him, he cried: 'Twiddle, what are all these things you have, that bite, kick, and scratch? Order them away at once! I have come home to keep you company again, because I was sorry to think of you sitting here lonely and sad without me.'

'Dear me, but I'm not at all lonely or sad,' said Twiddle, sharply. 'I have plenty of good company and jolly friends. What have you come back for? I don't want you! You always were a bad-tempered, disobedient, selfish animal, and I don't know how I put up with you. Be off with you! There's no room for you here!'

Kick-up was so surprised that he stood staring at his master, and didn't say a word.

'Go away, I tell you!' said Twiddle, angrily. 'What do you mean by disturbing us at this time of night? If you want to see me in the morning, you may come humbly to me and ask my pardon. I don't want to see you any more tonight.'

The donkey ran out of the kitchen and went into the field. It was wet and cold, but he did not dare to go to his stable again. He lay in the field all night, grieving and sighing. In the morning he went to Twiddle again.

'Master,' he said, hanging his head, 'forgive me. Take me back. Send away these horrid creatures and let me work for you as before. I will be a good donkey to you.'

'Stuff and nonsense,' said Twiddle, patting the puppy and stroking the purring kitten. 'I don't want you any more. If you like to live in the field next door and earn your keep by fetching and carrying for me, you can do so. But I don't want you to. I've quite enough animals here already.'

Kick-up had to live in the field. He had to work hard. The puppy barked at him. The kitten spat at him. The hens cackled loudly whenever he passed. The pigeons pecked his nose when they could. The pony stood ready to kick; so he wasn't very happy.

But he is learning his lesson. He doesn't complain now. He works hard. He is humble and quiet. Twiddle watches him out of the corner of his eye, because, you know, he really is fond of that silly grey donkey. So I expect he will forgive him one day and take him back – but you may be sure he will still keep his other friends. Ah, it was a good day for him when Kick-up ran away, wasn't it!

The Surprise Party

There was once a brown teddy bear who was always miserable. You should have seen him! He went about with a long face, his whiskers drooping and his ears down. Nobody knew what was the matter with him, they just knew that he was miserable, and that it didn't seem to be any good to try to cheer him up.

As for the teddy bear himself, he was a foolish fellow. He thought that nobody liked him or wanted him. When he saw the other toys laughing and joking together, giving each other presents, and helping one another, he pulled a longer face than ever. He thought it was too bad that they left him out of everything.

And the toys thought that it was too bad that he wouldn't join in anything – so you see things got worse and worse, and soon the teddy bear went and moped in a corner all day and wouldn't even answer when he was spoken to.

The toys laughed about it at first – and then, because they were kind-hearted, they began to worry about the teddy bear. They sent to the pixie who lived in the pansy bed under the nursery window and asked him for his advice. He was old and very wise.

He peeped in at the window and saw the brown bear moping in a corner, looking very lonely and miserable. He shook his head and thought for a long while.

'I'll tell you the best medicine for him,' he said at last. 'Give him a great big surprise! That's the best cure for anyone who's moping.'

'What sort of surprise?' asked the French doll.

'Oh, any kind, so long as it's nice,' said the pixie. 'That ought to cure him. Don't let him guess what we're doing, though, or that will spoil it.'

Well, the toys sat in a corner together and talked about it. What kind of surprise could they give the teddy bear? They really couldn't think of anything!

Then the yellow duck suddenly thought of something. 'Why,' she said, flapping her plush wings in delight, 'I know! It's the teddy bear's birthday on Saturday. He came from the same shop as I did, and I quite well remember him telling me one day when his birthday was.

Couldn't we give him a birthday party? That would be a wonderful surprise!'

All the toys thought the duck's plan was a very good one. So they began to think what they should do.

'I will make the teddy bear a fine blue sash,' said the French doll, who was very clever with her fingers. 'He will like that to wear at his party.'

'And I will make some chocolate buns on the little stove in the doll's house,' said the sailor doll, who was really a very good cook.

'I'll make some toffee!' cried the clockwork mouse.

'Sh!' said everyone. 'The teddy bear will hear you! Remember, it must all be a great surprise!'

The teddy bear heard all the toys whispering together in the corner, and he felt more out of things than ever. What were they whispering about now?

'I expect they are saying horrid things about me!' said the bear sulkily. 'Oh, dear, how I wish I didn't live in this horrid nursery, with all these horrid toys always whispering horrid things about me. I've a good mind to run away!'

The toys went on with their plans for the party. They decided to build a big house of the pink and blue toy bricks, and to hold the party there. Besides the chocolate buns there should be ginger fingers and sugar biscuits. The pixie promised to bring them some honey lemonade to drink. There were plenty of cups, saucers and plates in the dolls' tea-set for the toys to use. What fun it would be!

They would have games afterwards, and the teddy bear should choose them. The clockwork train promised that if it were wound up it would give the bear six rides round the nursery, which was really a very great treat indeed, for usually the toy train was lazy and wouldn't give a ride to anyone at all!

Then there were presents for the bear. There was a fine walking-stick. It was really a pencil with a curved end like a handle, and it belonged to the children whose nursery the toys lived in. But they had thrown the pencil away because it wouldn't write properly. The toys found it and thought it would make a fine walking-stick. So they polished it up and made it shine beautifully.

Then there was a little red and yellow brooch that had come out of a Christmas cracker. It was very pretty and the toys felt sure the bear would like it. There was also a pair of small blue shoes,

too large for the smallest doll and too small for
the other dolls. They would fit the teddy bear
very well, the toys thought.

Nicest of all there was a wonderful little chair,
made by the pixie outside, out of bent hazel and
willow twigs woven together. That was really a
fine surprise.

All the toys were to be in their best clothes.
Those that hadn't best clothes, or no clothes at
all were to wash themselves well and brush their
fur or hair. The party was to begin at four
o'clock with a song made up by the sailor doll
especially for the teddy bear.

The toys were more excited that week than
they had ever been before. What whispering
there was! What planning! What laughing and
joking!

The teddy bear couldn't for the life of him
make out what was happening. He tried to listen
to the whispering but all he heard was 'the
party'. Then he was more unhappy than ever
because he felt sure the toys were going to have
a party without him.

'They don't want me,' said the poor foolish
bear. 'They're going to have a party and keep
me out of it. The horrid, nasty things!'

Now the toys didn't want the teddy bear to

see them building the brick house, or changing
into their best clothes on Saturday afternoon in
case he guessed their secret. So they decided to
ask him to go out for a little walk, and then,
while he was gone, they could get everything
ready for his party.

So the sailor doll went to him on Saturday at
two o'clock, and said kindly: 'Teddy, go for a
little walk until four o'clock. It is a sunny
afternoon and it will do you good.'

The teddy bear went red with rage. So they
were going to get him out of the way, were
they, while they were having their party! They were
going to eat everything up! They weren't
even going to let him *see* the party!

He rushed out of the door, with angry tears
in his boot-button eyes. It was too bad! He'd
run away! Yes, he would!

Off he went down the garden path. He
walked and walked and walked. All the time he
thought angrily about the toys.

'I *will* run away!' he said to himself. 'Yes, I
will! But first I'll go back and tell the toys just
what I think of them. I'll tell them how horrid
they are – how unkind – how selfish! I'll go
straight back now and tell them! Then I'll
smack that sailor doll on the head and walk out

with my nose in the air!'

Back he went to the nursery, quite determined to say some very horrid things. It was just four o'clock when he arrived; the toys had finished getting ready for the party, and were standing in a line ready to sing the song that the sailor doll had made up for them.

The bear stamped into the nursery and glared round at the toys.

'I've just come back to tell you what a lot of nast – ' he began – but he couldn't finish because at a sign from the sailor doll the toys opened their mouths and their beaks and began to sing very loudly:

'Here's a welcome hearty
To your birthday party.
Welcome, birthday-bear,
Hurry up and share
In our games and fun
Till your birthday's done!'

Then they stopped, took a long breath and shouted: 'Many happy returns of the day, bear! Many happy returns of the day!'

They crowded round him shaking him by the paw, and the little pink rabbit gave him a hug!

The teddy bear was so surprised that at first he couldn't think what to say.

'But – but – but – is it my birthday?' he asked.

'Yes!' shouted the toys. 'And we hadn't forgotten it! We've been having secrets about it all the week. We were so afraid you'd guess. *Did* you guess?'

'Oh, no,' said the bear, going quite red to think of all the horrid things he had thought. 'I didn't guess for a minute.'

'Here's a nice blue birthday sash!' said the French doll. She wound it round his fat little body and tied it in a big bow. He looked beautiful.

'And here's a brooch – and a pair of blue shoes – and a fine walking-stick!' cried everyone, giving the surprised bear the presents. The shoes fitted him beautifully, and the brooch looked lovely just under his chin. As for the walking-stick he was as proud of it as he could be. Dear me, could all this be a dream? How lovely! What a silly bear he had been!

They had tea in the splendid brick house. The biscuits, cakes and sweets were most delicious, and the honey lemonade was so nice that the bear had five glasses of it and felt rather like a balloon at the end. But he was so happy that he didn't mind anything.

Then they had games, and after that the bear rode in the clockwork train six times round the nursery. That was lovely. Then he was presented with the chair that the pixie had made for him, and he was so surprised that he could hardly sit down in it! But he did, at last, and it was exactly the right size for him. His very own chair! How proud and pleased he was. He wanted to thank the pixie, so the little creature was called and came in to eat a chocolate bun.

He looked at the bear with a twinkle in his eye.

'Do you know,' he said solemnly, 'I saw a horrid little bear this afternoon, going along muttering the nastiest things about dolls, and sailor dolls, and ducks, and every sort of toy.'

The teddy bear looked as red as a tomato. How dreadful! The pixie must have seen him going for that walk!

'But it couldn't have been you, could it?' said the pixie, his bright eyes twinkling more than ever, as he looked at the bear. 'It must have been a foolish, sulky, stupid little bear who didn't know what he was talking about.'

'Yes, it was,' said the teddy bear humbly.

'Well, pixie, that little bear will never be so foolish again. I know the toys are my friends, and I will be a friend to them. They have given me a lovely birthday, and I will never forget it. It was a wonderful surprise.'

'Ah!' said the pixie wisely, smiling round at the listening toys. 'A surprise is a fine thing – isn't it, toys? It's a splendid cure for the mopes – and don't you forget it!'

The teddy bear never forgot it. He is always planning lovely surprises for everyone, and he never *thinks* of sulking in a corner now!

The Enchanted Doll

Mollie had a pretty doll called Angela, whom she loved very much indeed. She played with Angela all day long, and the only thing she wished was that Angela could talk and walk, instead of just lying or sitting perfectly still, and staring at Mollie with wide-open blue eyes.

'I can pretend you talk to me, and I can pretend you run about and play,' said Mollie, 'but you don't really and truly – and it *would* be such fun, Angela dear, if just for once in a way you would really come alive!'

But Angela just sat and stared, and didn't move a finger or say a word! It was most disappointing, for she really was a nice doll, and Mollie felt quite certain that if only she *could* talk and walk, she would be a good companion to have. Mollie had no brothers or sisters, so she was often lonely. That was why she played so much with Angela.

One day a very strange thing happened to Mollie. She took her doll for a walk in Pixie

Wood, and it happened there. Mollie had never seen any pixies or anything at all exciting in Pixie Wood, although it had such a lovely name. It was just like an ordinary wood.

But today it seemed a little different. The trees seemed closer together, as if they were nodding to one another, and whispering about something. The sun couldn't get in between the branches, and the wood was dim and rather mysterious. Mollie took Angela by the hand and walked her over the grass, talking to her. Her doll's pram was broken and had gone to be mended, which was why Angela was not riding in it as usual.

Mollie walked on through the wood – and then she suddenly stopped short. She saw something most surprising in the wood! It was a tiny pram, a little smaller than a doll's pram, and it shone like pure gold. It had a little white hood with a silver fringe hanging down, and the pram cover was white too, with gold embroidery on it. It really was very beautiful.

'Whatever is a doll's pram doing here in the middle of the wood?' wondered Mollie. 'I haven't seen any other children about. I wonder if they've left their pram here and are playing hide-and-seek or something. I'll cuckoo to them and see where they are. Perhaps they would let me play with them.'

So she called loudly: 'Cuckoo! Cuckoo! Where are you? Can I play with you?'

But there was no answer. The trees seemed to lean closer to one another, and all the leaves whispered again. Mollie looked all round and ran here and there, but it was no use at all – she couldn't see any children.

She looked at the lovely little pram. It was the nicest she had ever seen. How pretty Angela would look if she were tucked up in it and taken for a ride! Mollie went over to the pram and turned back the cover. There was no doll inside – but would you believe it, there was a little bottle there full of milk!

'But this pram can't belong to a *real* baby! It can't!' cried Mollie, in astonishment. 'It's too small. Oh! I wonder – I just wonder if it belongs to a pixie! It would be just right for a pixie baby. Oh, how lovely! I wish, I wish, I wish I could see a real pixie baby riding in that dear little pram!'

Mollie waited for a little while to see if any one came, but nobody did. Then a thought slid into her mind – would it matter if she put Angela into the pram and just wheeled her about for five minutes? Angela must be tired with her long walk, and really, she would look perfectly sweet in that pram! It wouldn't spoil the pram.

So Mollie picked up Angela and put her into the pram. She sat her down firmly, strapped her in, and set the soft pillow up behind her so that she could sit up comfortably. Then she tucked the white cover round her and began to wheel her about. How pretty Angela looked in the pixie pram! It was most exciting to wheel her about in it.

Mollie gave Angela a ride for a few minutes and then she thought she saw a little pointed face peeping at her from behind a tree.

'Who's there?' she called. 'Come and see Angela in this dear little pram, pixie!'

There was no answer – so Mollie left the pram and ran to the tree to see if the pixie really was peeping there. But, wasn't it disappointing, there was no one there at all, except a scurrying rabbit with a white bobtail!

Mollie turned back to the pram, and oh dear me, what a shock she got! The pram was running away! Yes, it really was! It was wheeling off all by itself, between the trees, as fast as ever it could!

'Oh! Oh! Come back, come back!' shouted

Mollie. 'Angela, Angela! Oh, please, pram, do come back! Don't take Angela away!'

But the pram hurried on. Mollie wondered if an invisible fairy was wheeling it, or whether the pram was a magic one that could go by itself. Oh, why, why had she put Angela in it! She ran after the hurrying pram as fast as ever she could, shouting as she went. The pram went faster and faster. It was dreadful. Mollie caught sight of the doll's face. It was full of horror and fear, and the little girl was sorry for her doll. She must, she really *must*, catch that pram!

The pram turned a corner by some thick bushes, and disappeared from sight. Mollie panted after it, but alas, when she reached the bushes, she could no longer see the pram. It was quite gone!

Mollie ran wildly about, and began to cry when she could not see the pram anywhere.

'Where have you gone, Angela?' she shouted. 'Can't you call and tell me?'

But there was no answer. Angela had disappeared with the pram. Mollie sat down and cried bitterly. It was dreadful to lose her doll like that. She did love her so much.

Presently she felt a little hand on her shoulder and a high, twittering voice said: 'What's the matter? Would you mind getting up? You are sitting on my front door.'

Mollie looked up in surprise. She saw a tiny creature by her, with long, pointed wings, pointed ears, and pointed shoes. It was smaller even than Angela, her doll, and was looking at her with big green eyes.

'Are you a pixie?' asked Mollie, in astonishment. 'How small you are! Am I really on your front door? I'm so sorry.'

She got up, and saw that she was sitting on a small yellow trap-door, sunk deeply into the ground. The pixie opened it and then looked at Mollie.

'Why are you crying?' he said.

Mollie told him all about the little pram she had found, and how it had run off with her doll.

'Oh, that pram belongs to Mother Dimity, the old woman who lives in a shoe,' said the pixie at once. 'She is very forgetful, you know, and leaves it about everywhere! If she goes home without it, she whistles for it and it goes to her of its own accord.'

'Well, it's taken my doll too,' said Mollie, beginning to cry again. Her tears fell in at the pixie's trap-door and he frowned.

'Please don't do that,' he said. 'You are

making my home all damp. Why are you crying now? You can easily go and find your doll. Mother Dimity will give her back if you ask her.'

'Where does she live?' asked Mollie.

'In the Shoe,' said the pixie, getting into his trap-door home. 'Knock at the Big Oak-Tree six times, go down the steps, find a boat to take you on the Underground River, and then ask the Wizard Who Grows Toadstools where the Shoe is. He is sure to know, because the Old Woman is his sister.'

'Thank you,' said Mollie, getting up. The pixie said goodbye and shut his trap-door with a bang. Mollie looked round for the Big Oak-Tree. There were a great many oak-trees around, and they all seemed about the same size to the little girl. She chose one that looked a little bigger than the others and knocked six times. Nothing happened at all. She knocked again. Still nothing happened.

'It can't be the right tree,' said Mollie, disappointed. She looked round again – and then she saw the biggest oak she had ever seen in her life! It was a real monster, towering up into the sky, and as big round as a summer-house!

'That's the one!' thought Mollie, and she ran over to it. She knocked on the trunk sharply six times – rat-tat-tat-tat-tat-tat! Then there came a creaking noise, and to her great delight a small door swung open in the tree and she saw that a narrow flight of steps led downwards towards the roots.

Her heart beat fast. This was a wonderful adventure! She slipped through the door, which at once shut with a bang, and began to go down the steps. It was rather dark, but small lanterns which hung here and there gave a little light. Mollie went down for a long way. She thought she must have climbed down quite a hundred steps when she came to a wide passage, with doors on every side. She looked at them. They all had names on, or messages written on little cards.

One card said: 'Ring, don't knock.' Another said: 'Knock, don't ring.' The next door had a card that said: 'Don't knock or ring,' and the fourth one said: 'I am not at home yesterday or tomorrow.'

Mollie thought that was strange, and she giggled. The names were strange too. 'Mister Woozle' was on one card, and 'Dame High-go-quick' was on another. Mollie read a third one, 'Little Jiggy-jig', and she was just wondering whatever he could be like when his door flew open and someone rushed out and nearly knocked her down. It was Little Jiggy-jig himself!

He was a funny fellow, with small wings, rabbit's ears and a funny habit of jigging up and down. 'Sorry!' he said to Mollie. 'Didn't see you there!'

He was just about to rush away when Mollie caught hold of his arm. 'Wait a minute,' she said. 'Could you please tell me if I am on the right way to the Underground River.'

'Yes, yes,' said Little Jiggy-jig, jerking his arm away impatiently. 'First to the right and left and then straight on round the corner.'

'But how can I go to the right and left at once, and how can anyone go straight round a corner!' called Mollie, indignantly. The only answer she got was a chuckle, and Little Jiggy-jig disappeared into the darkness of the passage. Mollie felt cross. She went straight on, and at last heard a noise of lapping water. 'That must be the Underground River,' she thought, pleased. 'Now to find a boat!'

She soon came to the river. It was hung with fairy lights of all colours and looked very pretty. There were plenty of boats on the side of it, but none of them had oars in them. Mollie looked about for someone to row her down the river, but she could see no one.

'Isn't there anyone here?' she shouted. Then a little head came poking out of a funny little ticket-office Mollie had not noticed.

'Yes, I'm here, and you're here too,' said the person in the ticket-office. Mollie went up and saw that it was a grey rabbit with a collar round its neck, and a tie flowing down, very neatly knotted.

'Good morning,' said Mollie. 'I want a boat.'

'Here's your ticket, then,' said the rabbit, handing her a very chewed-looking piece of cardboard.

'Where's the boatman?' asked Mollie.

'Nowhere,' said the rabbit. 'There isn't one.'

'Then how can I go in a boat?' asked Mollie.

'Get in it yourself, silly,' said the rabbit.

'Don't be rude,' said Mollie. 'It's no use taking a boat if you haven't got oars, is it? Silly yourself!'

'Now who's being rude!' said the rabbit. 'You are being very simple, little girl. Why do you want to take a boat? Why not let the boat take *you*?'

Mollie glared at the rabbit, and then walked

up to one of the boats. She chose a blue one, dotted with gold stars and got into it. At once the boat glided off by itself.

'Good morning, good afternoon and good evening!' shouted the rabbit, but Mollie didn't answer. She thought he was rather silly.

The boat shot on down the river, and after a little while it left the underground darkness and came out into the open air. Mollie blinked in the bright sunshine, but she was very glad indeed to be in the light again. The boat sped on and on, and Mollie watched the strange folk walking in the flowery fields, and saw with surprise that the animals were dressed up like human beings.

The boat went on, rocking gently. Mollie suddenly saw a curious field, with a strange-looking old man waving a stick about in the middle of it. He was surrounded by toadstools of all sizes, colours, and shapes, and she knew that he must be the Wizard Who Grows Toadstools.

'Stop, stop!' she cried to the boat. It stopped at once and headed to the bank. Mollie patted it, said thank you and then jumped out. She went to the old wizard, who didn't see her at first and almost knocked her over with his waving stick, which the little girl now saw was a silver wand.

'Please,' she said. 'I've come to ask you where your sister, the old woman who lives in a shoe, is. I want to go and speak to her.'

'You'll find her on the other side of that hill,' said the wizard, waving his wand violently, and nearly catching Mollie in the eye with it. 'Look out! You are standing just where my next toadstool is growing!'

Mollie felt the earth pushing up under her feet and fell over. A big toadstool appeared through the ground and grew high and broad. It was covered with big red spots. Mollie sat on the ground and watched it in amazement. Then she felt the earth moving just under her again, and at once she was shot up high on another growing toadstool.

'Well, really,' said the wizard, in disgust, 'how you do get in the way, to be sure! Mind where you tread as you go through the field. There are toadstools growing everywhere today, for I have a very large order for them from the King himself, who wants three hundred for stools for his next party.'

Mollie ran out of the field as quickly as she could, and made her way to the hill in the distance. She climbed it, and as soon as she came to the top she saw the Shoe. It was an

enormous shoe, and it had windows and doors in it and a smoking chimney at the top. Mollie thought it looked lovely. She ran down to it, and at once she was surrounded by a crowd of small pixie children, not so big as she was, with pointed faces, pointed ears, and short wings.

'Who are you? Where do you come from?' they cried in excitement. 'Have you come to see our new child?'

'Look, our new little girl is in bed! You can see her through the window!' said a tiny pixie, taking Mollie's hand and leading her to a window that looked into the Shoe house. Mollie peeped in – and whatever *do* you think she saw? She saw a bedroom in the Shoe, with many little white beds in it, and in one of them, the bed nearest to the window, lay Angela, her own little doll!

'Do you see that new little girl?' said the pixie. 'Well, she came in today in Mother Dimity's pram, and do you know, she is very ill, poor thing! She can't talk, she can't eat, she can't drink, she can't even blink her eyes! Isn't it dreadful! I've never seen a little girl like that before, have you?'

'That isn't a little girl at all, that's my doll!' cried Mollie.

'A doll!' said the pixie children, crowding round Mollie. 'What's a doll? We don't know what a doll is.'

'Well, a doll is – a doll is – well, that's what a doll is!' said Mollie, pointing to where Angela lay on the little bed.

'But can't the poor thing move or talk at all?' asked the pixies in surprise.

'Of course not,' said Mollie. 'I'm going in to get Angela. Poor darling, she must feel so frightened!'

She ran in at the door of the big Shoe, and bumped into the Old Woman.

'Now then, gently, gently!' said Mother Dimity. 'You'll frighten the new little girl, rushing about like that. I've just given her some very strong magic medicine to make her come alive again.'

'She never has been alive!' cried Mollie. 'She's my doll!'

'Your doll!' said the Old Woman. 'Doll! Oh, I remember once seeing a doll in the world of boys and girls. Dear, dear me, so that's a doll, is it? Why, I thought it was a little girl that was ill, and so I've given her some stuff to make her walk and talk. I'm really very sorry indeed.'

'But, do you mean to say that Angela will soon walk and talk?' cried Mollie.

'Of course,' said Mother Dimity. 'Look – she is blinking her eyes now! Perhaps I had better make her go back into a doll again.'

'No, please don't,' said Mollie at once. She ran to Angela and looked at her. Wonder of wonders, the little doll was opening and shutting her eyes and she suddenly looked at Mollie and smiled a wide smile, showing all her pretty teeth.

'Hello, Mollie,' she said. 'I've often wanted to talk to you, and now I can!'

Mollie watched her in amazement. Angela threw back the covers and jumped out of bed. She danced round the room in joy and then ran up to Mollie. She hugged the little girl's legs, and Mollie lifted her up into her arms. She was so pleased to have Angela back, walking and talking, that the tears ran down her cheeks in joy.

'Oh, what fun we'll have together now!' she cried, hugging her doll to her. 'We can talk to one another, and play all kinds of games.'

'But you mustn't let anyone but yourself know,' said Mother Dimity at once. 'If you do, the magic will go, and Angela will be an ordinary doll again.'

'Oh, I won't tell anyone at all!' said Mollie, happily. 'Come on, Angela, we'll go home again now. It must be getting late.'

She put the little doll on the ground and Angela took her hand. Then, walking like a real person, she trotted beside Mollie, saying goodbye to all the pixie children.

Mother Dimity showed them a short way home, and they arrived there just in time for dinner. Mollie put Angela in her cot, and told her to be sure not to move if anyone came in, and she promised.

And now Mollie is as happy as the day is long, for she has a real, live doll to play with her, and they *do* have some fine games together.

'Really,' Mollie's mother often says, 'you might think that doll was alive, the way Mollie plays with her all day long!'

And then Mollie smiles a big smile – but she doesn't say a word! She has a wonderful secret to keep and she keeps it very well!

When the Toys Came Alive

Once upon a time there were two children called Peter and Gwen. They lived in a big house, and had a wonderful nursery full of marvellous toys. There was a rocking-horse far bigger than themselves, with a long tail and mane, and fine brown eyes that opened and shut as he rocked to and fro. There was a doll's house with electric light in every room, a bathroom with taps that really ran water, and fires that could really be lit. There were all sorts and kinds of dolls, animals and books.

They really were very lucky children, but you know, they had too many toys! They had so many that they didn't really love any of them, except two very old and ragged creatures that they had taken to bed with them ever since they were two years old.

These old creatures were so battered and worn that it was hard to tell that one had once been a monkey and the other had been a cat. When the children had had these toys their parents had not been rich, and the children had had few toys then – so they loved the two creatures, and always cuddled them at night.

But when they grew rich and went to live in a great big house, and had a nanny to look after them, they became spoilt and horrid. They had new toys every day and they didn't take care of any of them. I couldn't tell you how many they broke or how many they threw out of the window just for fun. It really was dreadful.

Once Peter wound up his clockwork engine with all its trucks behind it and set it going towards the pond in the garden. Splish-splash! The engine and all its trucks disappeared into the water at once, and when it was fished out a week later it was rusty and useless, and could never be wound up again.

Another time Gwen threw every one of her dolls out of the nursery window to the ground far below, and, of course, they were all broken to bits. Really, you would hardly believe the horrid, unkind things that those two children did to their toys.

But something happened one day – something very strange and peculiar. The children were playing in the nursery when they found a bag of little yellow sweets in the toy cupboard.

They were most surprised.

'How did they get there?' asked Peter.

'I don't mind where they came from but I know where they're going to!' said Gwen, and she popped four or five of the little sweets into her mouth. They tasted delicious and she took some more. Peter took some too.

And then they noticed a very alarming thing. The nursery seemed to be getting much bigger! The table looked enormous, and the chairs seemed far too big to sit on. The waste-paper basket looked big enough to hide in without being seen, and the flowers in the vase seemed like giant ones.

'What's happened?' said Peter, looking round in dismay. 'Why is everything so big?'

'I do believe it's us that have gone small!' said Gwen, staring round in astonishment. 'It must be those sweets, Peter. We shouldn't have eaten them. They were magic ones, I'm sure!'

Just at that moment their nanny came into the room and the children, now as small as tiny dolls, ran over to her, calling out. But their voices were squeaky now, and the nanny, who was short-sighted, thought they were mice. So she took up the hearth-brush and shooed them away, crying: 'You nasty horrid little mice! I'll set a trap for you, that I will!'

Peter was swept up by the brush and fell to the floor. He scrambled into a house of bricks that he and Gwen had built that morning. The little girl followed him and they hid there, trembling, until their nanny had gone out of the room.

'Whatever are we to do?' asked Gwen, at last. But, before she could answer, a furry face peeped in at the door of the little brick house, and gave her a dreadful fright.

'It's all right, it's only the teddy bear,' said Peter, taking a good look at him. 'He looks big because we're so small now.'

'*Only* the teddy bear!' said the furry face, crossly. 'I'll teach you to say I'm *only* the teddy bear!' and with that he pushed over the house of bricks so that it came toppling round the children's ears. Crack! Smack! The hard wooden bricks hit the children and made them squeal. The teddy bear danced for joy and called to the other toys to come and see.

'You horrid, unkind thing!' shouted Peter, crawling out from beneath the pile of bricks.

'Well, it's just what you did to me and the brown toy dog yesterday!' said the teddy bear, grinning. 'Tit for tat, you know! Wait till the rocking-horse catches sight of you. He's king of this nursery, and he has been in a very bad temper ever since you and your sister pulled all the hairs out of his tail.'

At the mention of his name the rocking-horse turned his head and looked straight down at the two children. He looked so big and fierce that they trembled in their shoes.

'Hrrrrumph!' he said, in a horsy voice. 'What's all this?'

'Do look, your majesty,' said the teddy bear, excited. 'Here are the two children gone small. They've eaten those magic sweets that the pixies left in the toy cupboard last night. They are smaller than we are!'

'Hrrrrrumph!' said the rocking-horse again. 'Call a meeting. This is important. We may be able to punish these children for all the unkind things they have done to their helpless toys. Hrrrrrumph!'

The teddy bear bowed to the big horse, and hurried off to the toy cupboard. Out came toy animals of all kinds, an old engine, a motorbus, four dolls, all with broken arms or legs or noses, twenty-four soldiers, marching in two straight lines, and all the wooden animals out of the Noah's ark.

They really were a sight to see. They all went to the rocking-horse and bowed to him.

'Hrrrrrumph!' he snorted at them. 'For a long time, Gwen and Peter, we toys have been in your power. Now, for a change, you are in ours. You have always been unkind to us. We shall now be unkind to you, then you will know what it feels like. Hrrrrrmph!'

'Oh please, don't hurt us!' begged Gwen, beginning to cry. 'We never really hurt *you*, you know.'

'Do you suppose I liked having all the hairs pulled out of my beautiful tail?' shouted the rocking-horse angrily. 'Teddy, pull a few hairs out of the girl's head. She can then see if it hurts.'

The teddy bear pulled a few hairs sharply out of Gwen's head and she squealed in pain. 'Don't! It hurts.'

'You pulled *all* the hairs out of my tail,' said the rocking-horse. 'I can't make up my mind whether to have all the hairs pulled out of your head or not.'

'Oh no, no!' cried Gwen, really very frightened. 'Do forgive me, please. I should look dreadful without any hair.'

'So do *I* look dreadful without any hairs in my

tail,' said the rocking-horse, gloomily. 'Well, toys, you had better take these children to Toytown, and we'll ask the toy judge there to say what had better be done to such unkind children.'

'Could we go on your back?' asked the teddy bear. 'We could get there so much more quickly if we could ride.'

'Jump up, then,' said the rocking-horse. Then with shouts of delight all the toys climbed up on to the wide back of the big rocking-horse. Gwen and Peter were pulled up too.

'HRRRRRRRRUMPH!' snorted the rocking-horse loudly, and he suddenly rocked himself right out of the nursery door, down the stairs, and out into the garden at top speed. Gwen couldn't help wondering what Nanny would say if she met them – but they didn't meet anybody.

The horse rocked down the garden and out of the gate at the bottom. It rocked down the lane and came to the wood. It rocked down a narrow path and went deeper and deeper into the wood. At last it came to a high gate. It knocked on this, with its head, and the gate swung open.

Gwen and Peter saw that they had come to Toytown. It was a queer place. The houses and shops were made of wood and cardboard and were exactly like toy ones. The trees were like the funny stiff ones in their toy farm at home, and the people walking about the streets were all toys. They stared hard when they saw the rocking-horse coming down the street.

At last the horse came to a tall building, and on the front was its name, Toytown Hall. All the toys got off the rocking-horse, pulled Gwen and Peter with them, and went into the hall. Gwen and Peter looked round. The hall was a big place with a platform at one end, and plenty of forms for people to sit on.

'The judge will be here in a minute,' whispered the teddy bear to the others. Sure enough in a short while there came the sound of heavy footsteps, and into the hall marched a toy judge, in a long, flowing gown and a thick white wig. He looked very fierce and grand. The toys all got up and bowed to him. Gwen and Peter thought they had better do so, too.

The judge sat on a throne-like chair on the platform and looked all round, frowning.

'Any complaints today?' he asked in a rumbling voice. At once all the toys jumped up and shouted, 'YES!'

'Quiet,' said the judge. 'One at a time, please. Rocking-horse, what is all this about?'

'Please, your worship,' said the rocking-horse, 'we have brought two bad children here to be judged by you. They have eaten magic sweets, become small, and so are in our power. How shall we punish them?'

'Well, what have they done to *you*?' asked the judge, biting the end of his pen.

'If you please, your worship, the boy wound up his engine, and sent it, with its trucks, right into a big pond of water,' said the teddy bear, jumping up like a jack-in-the-box.

'Truly shocking,' said the judge.

'And if you please, your worship, the girl threw all her dolls out of a high window to see if they would break,' said the rabbit, bobbing up excitedly.

'Then for punishment tie the boy in a railway train, wind it up and send it into a pond with him,' said the judge, writing busily. 'See how he likes it. And for the girl, take her up to the top of a high building and throw her out of the window to see if she breaks.'

'Ooooooh!' squealed the two children, in despair. 'Your worship, forgive us! We are not toys, we shall drown, we shall break out arms and legs.'

'Take them away,' said the judge sternly.

'No, no, have mercy on us!' shouted Peter. 'We will never be unkind again. We didn't know toys minded. Just give us a chance and we will be kind.'

'Have you *ever* been kind?' asked the judge, sternly.

'Of course,' said Peter.

'Then listen,' said the judge, 'if any toy will come forward to say you have been kind to him, then you shall go free. Now then, who will speak for these children?'

Peter and Gwen looked round at their toys – but not one of them moved! No, they just sat there on the forms, staring in front of them, not one with a kind word to say about the two children.

'Very well,' said the judge frowning. 'The two children must be punished as I said. Take them away.'

Gwen began to cry, and Peter bit his lip hard. What a dreadful fix to be in! It was no use trying to run away, and not a bit of good fighting the toys, for now they were bigger even than the children! Peter and Gwen were as much in the toys' power as once the toys had been in theirs. Things were certainly topsy turvy!

The toys dragged the children out of the town

hall and then stood outside talking about what to do next.

'There's an old train that lives near the big duck-pond not far off,' said the teddy bear. 'We'll take Peter to that.'

'Yes, and there's a tall tower not far from the old train!' said the rocking-horse, in his deep voice. 'We will take Gwen to the top of that.'

'Boo-hoo-hoo!' wept Gwen in fright. 'I don't want to be thrown out of the window.'

'Nor did your dolls,' said the brown dog, sternly. 'But it didn't make any difference. You threw them out!'

The toys took the children down a lane and out into a field. Nearby was a large pond on which toy ducks were bobbing up and down happily. An old engine with two trucks stood on a pair of rails a little way from the pond. Just behind rose a tall thin tower with a window at the top.

Gwen was hustled into the tower and made to climb a steep winding stair. When she looked out of the window at the top she saw that Peter was tightly tied to the engine, and the engine was being wound up so that it could go puffing into the pond.

'Ooooh, oooh!' wept Gwen.

'Now, are you all ready?' shouted the rocking-horse. The teddy bear caught hold of Gwen's arm, ready to push her out of the window, and the brown dog below finished winding up the big clockwork engine.

And, just at that very moment two strange creatures came into sight down the lane. They were hurrying as fast as they could, and as they ran they shouted something at the top of their voices.

The toys stared and listened. What was all this? They had no idea who the strange, shapeless creatures were.

But Peter knew! Gwen knew!

'Oh, it's dear old Monkey, that I used to take to bed with me!' cried Peter.

'And it's darling old Pussy that I used to cuddle each night!' shouted Gwen. 'Pussy, Pussy, come and save us!'

'Monkey, tell these toys to untie me!' shouted Peter, struggling hard to get free. But the toys held him tightly.

'Hi, toys, hi, toys, wait a bit, wait a bit!' yelled the two hurrying creatures. 'We've got something to say!'

The toys waited. When the two creatures came up the toys saw that they had once been toy animals, but were now very battered and worn.

'What do you want?' asked the rocking-horse with a snort.

'We've only just heard that Gwen and Peter are going to be punished unless a toy will speak for them and say that they have been kind,' panted the monkey. 'Well, we've come to speak for them.'

'To speak for Gwen and Peter!' cried all the toys, in astonishment. 'How surprising! Do you mean to say that these two unkind children were ever kind to you?'

'Kind! I should think so!' said the cat, mopping her hot forehead. 'Why, they loved us better than anything and took us to bed each night for years. It wasn't till last year that their nanny said we were too old and dirty to be in their clean beds any more, and she wanted to throw us into the dustbin. But Gwen and Peter wouldn't let her. They hid us away in the boot-cupboard, and do you know, they sometimes take us out, even now, and cuddle us at night when their nanny is away for her weekend!'

'It's true, quite true,' said the monkey, swinging what was left of his tail. 'I dare say the children have been unkind to *you*, toys – when people get rich they often change for the worse, you know – but both the cat and I must truthfully say that we have been loved and cared for by Gwen and Peter for a good many years. We don't want you to punish them. Please don't. We love them, you see, and we know that if children have been kind once they can be again. Give them a chance. I'm sure they will never, never be unkind to anything or anyone again.'

The toys talked together.

'Well, you know what the judge said,' said the rocking-horse, snorting loudly. 'If any toy would say a kind word for the children they should go free. So we can't punish them now. We must set them free.'

They untied Peter and took Gwen down the winding stair to the bottom of the tower. Both the children rushed gladly at their two old toys and hugged them until the monkey and the cat squealed for breath.

'Oh, you saved us just in time. I don't care what Nanny says, I'm going to have you in bed every single night, you dear old cuddlesome things!' cried Gwen.

'They look very battered and old,' said the rocking-horse, suddenly. 'How is it you didn't take better care of them? Look at the cat. She's a perfect sight, and hasn't even a whisker. And as for the monkey, he may call that a tail that he's got at the back, but *I* don't. It seems to me that you weren't very kind to these two toys, for all they say, children!'

'We're battered and old because we've been played with and loved such a lot,' said the monkey, at once, and he jerked his little bit of a tail up and down nimbly. 'Don't you know the difference between a broken toy and a well-used one? Look at this patch here on my back. I had a hole there and Gwen mended me. And look at the cat's ear. It came off, and Peter stuck it on again most beautifully. Oh, I can tell you, we're happy toys and have nothing to complain of except that we don't see our children often enough!'

'You shall see us every day and every night now!' cried Peter and Gwen. Then they linked arms with the two old toys and walked proudly off with them, all the toys following. The rocking-horse called to everyone to get on to his back again and up they all climbed, Peter and Gwen too. Then back they went to the nursery, rocking away hard.

When they were safely back again the

rocking-horse told Gwen and Peter to sit down on the floor with their eyes shut while he sang a magic song. They did so – and dear me, what an astonishing thing, when they opened their eyes again, they were the right size – just as big as ever! Their toys seemed very small to them.

'Oh, Peter!' cried Gwen. 'What a strange adventure! Let's be kind to everything now, shall we? It's much nicer than being horrid. Whatever should we have done without Monkey and Pussy?'

'Hrrrrrrrrrumph! said the rocking-horse loudly – but that was the last time he ever spoke!

The Brownie Who Pulled Faces

There was once a brownie called Twisty, who could pull the most dreadful faces you can imagine. It really was terrible to see him!

He could roll his eyes. He could screw up his nose till it looked like a withered apple. He could blow out his cheeks and he could pull down his mouth and make himself look most frightening.

Twisty thought it was funny to pull faces. He liked to meet a crowd of little pixies and stand in front of them, pulling the most dreadful faces he could think of. It frightened them very much indeed.

Nothing could stop him! Bron, the head brownie of the village of Puff, where Twisty lived, was always telling him to stop. His old aunt Chiffle-Chuffle shook her head at him and said he would make his face very ugly. And his next-door neighbour, Woof, said he would call in the policeman if he caught Twisty pulling faces at his baby in the garden.

Now one day old Witch Henny-penny came to stay for two days in Puff Village. She went out walking one morning and she met Twisty. She was a polite old dame, so she wished him good day.

Twisty thought it would be funny to give her a scare. So he turned up his nose, rolled his eyes round and put out his long, pointed tongue. The old witch watched him in silence.

Then she spoke in her deep, hoarse voice.

'Not very nice, not very pretty, and certainly most rude,' she said. 'One day the wind will change when you are pulling faces, brownie, and then you will be sorry.'

'Why shall I be sorry?' asked Twisty, surprised.

'Because whoever is making a face when the wind changes cannot pull his face right again,' said the witch solemnly. 'If your tongue should be out when the wind shifts from east to south, it will stay out! If your cheeks are blown out like a balloon, they will stay like that! You be careful, brownie! One day you'll be pulling a face when the wind changes and what a shock you will get!'

Twisty didn't believe her. He made an ugly face again.

'You're just making it up to frighten me!' he said. 'But I'm not frightened of the wind! Ho ho! You're a silly old witch, and I'm not afraid of you either!'

The witch looked strangely at Twisty. Her eyes seemed to go right through him – deeper, deeper, deeper, and the foolish brownie felt odd. He ran home quickly, looking behind him now and again to make sure the witch was not looking after him still!

He soon forgot what she had said. Two days later he was talking to a visitor at his front door. He thought it would be very funny to make a face at him, to give him a surprise. So he blew out his cheeks and sent his eyebrows right up to his hair. He waggled his pointed ears and made them stick straight out from his head instead of upwards. His visitor gaped in surprise and then looked offended.

'How dare you make a face at me!' he cried. 'I shall complain about you. Yes, I will!'

Twisty was just going to pull his face right again when something happened – the wind changed! The weathercock on the town hall swung round from east to west, just as Twisty made that face.

Twisty couldn't think why he couldn't stop

his cheeks from blowing themselves out. He couldn't make his ears stop waggling, nor could he make them point upwards. His eyebrows wouldn't come down again – they stuck up high on his head and gave him a most peculiar look.

Twisty began to feel frightened. He glanced up at the weathercock and saw that the wind had changed all at once. He remembered what the old witch had said and a cold shiver ran down his back. Ooh! Supposing she had spoken the truth! How dreadful!

He slammed his front door, much to his visitor's surprise, and ran to the kitchen. He took down a looking-glass, and looked at himself. Yes, it was quite true – he could not stop pulling that dreadful face! It was stuck like that.

'Oh dear! Oh my! Goodness, gracious, whatever shall I do?' groaned Twisty, in dismay.

His ears waggled and waggled. His cheeks stayed blown out. He really did look dreadful.

The worst of it was that Twisty was going to a party that very afternoon at Bron's. Could he go now? Would it matter if he went with his face like that?

'Perhaps it will go right again before this

afternoon,' said Twisty, wishing his ears would stop waggling.

But his face didn't go right. It stayed just like it was. Twisty changed into his green velvet party-tunic and stared at himself once more in the glass. He was more used to his strange-looking, blown-out face by this time, and he thought perhaps people wouldn't notice it very much. He could say he had toothache. That would be a naughty story, but Twisty wasn't always careful to tell the truth.

So off he went to the party, his ears waggling so hard that he couldn't keep his hat on for more than half a minute at a time. He shook hands with Bron, who stared at him very hard. Then Twisty went to join the others, who wanted to play a game of oranges and lemons.

Everyone stared at Twisty and he felt very hot and uncomfortable. At last a small elf came up to him and said: 'Why are you making such a dreadful face? Don't you feel well?'

'Not very,' said Twisty.

'Why are your cheeks blown out like that?' asked a gnome.

'I've got toothache,' said Twisty, going red.

'Why do your ears waggle?' asked a brownie. 'Have you got earache too?'

'I expect I have,' said Twisty.

'And what has happened to your eyebrows?' said a pixie, peering up at him. 'You don't seem to have any. You are a very strange-looking and ugly brownie. Are you sure you haven't been pulling faces? The wind changed very suddenly this morning, and perhaps it just caught you pulling a face!'

Everyone came round Twisty and began to laugh. They were all quite certain that that was what had happened. Twisty stood there feeling miserable.

'Well, well,' said Bron, shaking his head at Twisty. 'It's time you were taught a lesson, Twisty. I'm not sorry you've been caught like this! You won't pull ugly faces again in a hurry!'

'How can I get rid of this one and make my face nice again?' asked poor Twisty.

'Well, as the Wind made your face stick like that, I should think that only the Wind can make it come right again,' said Bron. 'I'd go and see if the Wind could help you, if I were you. You know where he lives, don't you? On the top of Breezy Hill, just outside Fairyland. You can't possibly go about looking as ugly as you are now. I wouldn't let you live in our village!'

Twisty ran out of the house, crying. He went

home and packed his bag. Then he set out on the long journey to Breezy Hill. At last he left Fairyland behind and came to the long, steep hill. Up he climbed and up and up. At the top was a long flight of slippery steps, and beyond these was the cloud-like castle of the Wind. It was forever changing its shape, and was marvellous to see.

Twisty knocked at the great gate. It swung open and he went inside. He stood in a big hall, and although he looked all round it, it seemed to be empty.

A small mouse was nibbling some crumbs on the floor. Twisty spoke to it.

'Where is the Wind? Is he here today?'

'Not yet,' said the mouse. 'He'll be here at any moment. He hasn't been in a very good temper lately, so if I were you I wouldn't make that dreadful face at him. He might be very angry with you.'

Twisty felt rather frightened. But it was no use, he simply could *not* stop his ears from waggling, his eyebrows from raising themselves high up on his forehead, and his cheeks from blowing themselves out. The little mouse stared at him for a few moments and then ran to its hole in fright. It really thought Twisty must be mad.

The brownie looked round the hall, wishing the Wind would come – and almost at once he did! There was suddenly a great draught, and all the curtains blew straight up in the air. The door banged loudly and the carpets flew across the floor. Then Twisty saw the Wind.

He was an enormous fellow, dressed in cloud-like clothes that swayed out round him all the time. His hair was long and curly and his eyes flashed like lightning. He saw Twisty as soon as he entered the hall and stood still in surprise.

'Who are you?' he bellowed.

'Twisty the brownie,' said the frightened brownie. 'I've c-c-c-come to ask you if you'll be k-k-k-kind enough t-t-t-to – '

'Stop waggling your ears at me!' roared the Wind angrily. 'How rude of you! Stop it, I say!'

'I c-c-c-c-can't,' stammered Twisty.

'Nonsense!' cried the Wind, jumping up and standing over the trembling brownie. 'If you don't stop your ears waggling at me, *I'll* soon stop them for you.'

Poor Twisty tried his hardest to put his ears straight up and stop them from waggling, but he couldn't. The Wind lost his temper and gave Twisty a big box on each of his ears – clip, clap! The brownie cried out in pain – but dear me, his ears had stopped waggling! Yes, they really had.

'And now stop blowing your cheeks out at me,' roared the Wind again. 'Stop it, I say!'

'I c-c-c-c-can't!' began Twisty, wishing he could run away.

'*I'll* soon stop you!' cried the rough Wind, and he slapped Twisty once on each cheek – slip, slap!

'Ooh!' cried Twisty, dancing about in pain. 'Ooh!'

But certainly his cheeks stopped blowing themselves out at once! They put themselves right again and stayed right.

'And now, where are your eyebrows?' asked the Wind. 'You are making faces at me, are you? First you waggle your ears, then you blow out your cheeks, and then you raise your eyebrows at me and look down your nose! Ho ho!'

'Please, please,' said Twisty, going down on his knees to the Wind. 'Don't be rough with me any more. I came to ask you for help.'

The Wind laughed, and then opened his big mouth.

'I don't help people who pull faces!' he said. 'Look out for your eyebrows, brownie! I'm going to blow them off!'

He began to blow. My, how he blew! The brownie felt himself rising in the air. He felt his nose being bent crooked. He felt his hair being blown straight up. He felt his eyebrows being blown right off! Then out of the door he flew, a great draught down the back of his neck!

The Wind blew and blew until a great gale came sweeping up and around the palace. Twisty was caught by it and rolled down the long flight of slippery steps. Bump! Bump! Bump!

All the way down the steps he went and rolled to the bottom of Breezy Hill.

'Ho ho ho!' roared the Wind. 'That will teach you to come pulling faces at me, brownie!'

Poor Twisty. He was bruised all over. He had lost his eyebrows and his hair was blown straight up on end. He limped home with his bag and went into his cottage.

There came a knock at his door. It was Bron, the chief brownie.

'Have you come back all right?' he asked. 'Is your face right again?'

'My ears are all right and so are my cheeks,' said Twisty. 'But my eyebrows are gone and I am all over bruises. I shall never, never, never pull faces again, Bron.'

'Dear, dear,' said Bron, looking at him. 'You certainly do look strange with your hair on end and your eyebrows gone – but never mind, you can brush your hair flat and your eyebrows will grow again. Cheer up! I expect you will be much nicer now!'

Twisty *is* much nicer, and he has never been seen to pull an ugly face again. Mind you don't either, just in *case* the wind might suddenly change when you do it; because that really would be dreadful, wouldn't it?

All the Way to Toytown

One morning Roger thought he would go for a ride in his little motor-car. It was a fine car, painted a bright green, and it had a hooter, two lamps, and a little extra seat at the back for one passenger. Roger was very proud of it. He had had the motor for his birthday, and he could work the pedals so quickly that the car shot along the road at a tremendous pace!

'I'm just going for a ride, Mummy!' he called to his mother, climbing into his car. 'I shan't be long.'

Off he went, pedalling fast down the lane. He thought he would go through the wood. The path was narrow, but just big enough for his little motor-car. There might perhaps be a few blackberries just beginning to get ripe.

Into the dim green wood he went. A rabbit ran across the path and Roger hooted at it, 'honk, honk!' He didn't want to run over a bunny! On and on he went and at last stopped in surprise.

He must have taken the wrong turning! He

didn't seem to know this part of the wood at all! He began to turn his car round so that he could go back – and it was just then that he heard the sound of someone crying nearby.

'What's that, I wonder?' said Roger to himself. 'Perhaps it is somebody lost.'

He jumped out of his car and went to see. Behind a tree he saw a small and very pretty little girl, her golden hair all over her face, as she bent her head and cried into a little pink handkerchief.

'I say!' called Roger. 'What's the matter? Are you lost?'

'No,' said the little girl, looking up in surprise. 'I know my way all right, but I can't walk any farther. So I'm crying because I am unhappy.'

'Why can't you walk?' asked Roger. 'Have you hurt your foot?'

'Well, you see, my leg has come right off,' said the little girl, much to Roger's astonishment. 'Don't look so surprised, boy. I'm not a little girl – I'm a doll, and dolls' legs easily come off, you know, if people are careless with them.'

'A doll!' said Roger, still more astonished. 'I didn't know dolls could walk and talk.'

'Well, they can't usually,' said the doll. 'Only when something important has happened. You see, Mary, the little girl I belong to, dropped me yesterday and my leg almost broke in half. So last night I made up my mind to go to Toytown and get it mended. They have a fine dolls' hospital there. But on my way my leg got worse and now, look, it's come right off!'

Roger looked – yes, it was true. The doll's leg *had* come off. No wonder she couldn't walk any more!

'Won't it push back into place?' he said, knowing that sometimes the arms and legs of dolls could be mended like that. But the doll shook her head.

'I'm afraid not,' she said. 'I'm not that sort of doll. But really, I don't know what in the world to do! I can't walk back home to Mary, and I can't get to Toytown. And if I stay here I shall be ill with cold and loneliness!'

'Where is Toytown?' asked Roger. 'If you know the way perhaps I could take you there in my motor-car.'

'Ooh! What a lovely plan!' cried the doll, delighted. 'I didn't know you had a motor-car. I thought you were just walking. Of course you can take me, if you don't mind!'

Roger helped the doll to her one foot. She carried her broken leg under her arm and didn't

really seem to mind much about it. She hopped
to the car and got into the little seat at the back.
Roger climbed into his seat and pedalled off
through the wood.

The doll knew her way very well indeed.
'Now round this beech tree,' she said. 'Now
keep straight on till you come to a little gorse
bush. Now to the left by that hazel. Now round
the corner by that tiny stream. You'll have to go
through it, but it is very shallow. That's right!
Now straight on till we come to a lane.'

At last they came to a winding lane. On one
side there was a farm, and Roger thought it
really looked exactly like his toy farm at home,
even to the funny stiff trees that seemed to grow
from the round piece of wood at the bottom and
not from the ground itself. White celluloid
ducks swam on a pond, and they quacked as
loudly as real ducks, but sounded rather hollow.

As they drew nearer to Toytown itself Roger
was surprised to see a large crowd on the road.
He hooted a great many times and the people
got out of the way. They were strange-looking
folk – all of them toys of various sizes. Some
were small and some were as large as Roger
himself. There were ducks dressed up, rabbits
in coats and trousers, dolls of all kinds, a clown

or two, a large pink cat whose ears wagged to and fro as he walked, and many other toys.

'Oh, dear! It's market-day in Toytown today,' said the doll, suddenly. 'I wondered why there were so many people. What a nuisance! I don't expect the hospital will be open. It shuts on Sundays and market-days.'

'But hospitals never shut!' said Roger, in surprise.

'Toy hospitals do,' said the doll. 'Now I shall have to wait till tomorrow to get my leg mended. What a nuisance!'

They drove into Toytown. It was a marvellous place! Roger could quite well see that every house, every shop, every farm was built of bricks or meccano. But they were all a good size, far bigger than toys. There was a wooden policeman in the market-square, and he stopped Roger as he pedalled along in his motor-car.

'You're going too fast!' he said, sternly. 'It's market-day today, so there's a low speed-limit.'

'Oh, policeman, is the hospital shut?' asked the doll, leaning out.

'Of course,' said the policeman.

'Is there anywhere I can stay for the night?' asked the doll. 'I want to get my leg mended tomorrow.'

'You might try at the big farm over there,' said the policeman, pointing to a fine toy-farm not far off. 'I know Mrs Straws has a few beds for visitors.'

'Would you drive me there, Roger, and go and ask the farmer's wife if she can let me stay the night?' asked the doll. Roger at once drove over to the farmhouse and got out at the little wooden gate. Toy cows and toy horses made of wood were everywhere. They ran up to him like dogs and seemed delighted to see him. He pushed them away and went up to the front door of the farmhouse. He knocked loudly.

Mrs Straws came to the door. She was just like the farmer's wife in Roger's farm at home. In fact, she was *so* like her that he really wondered for a moment if she had run away and come to Toytown.

'What is it you want?' she asked.

'Could you let a doll with a broken leg stay here for the night?' asked Roger. Mrs Straws shook her head.

'I'm sorry,' she said, 'but all my beds are quite full up tonight. It's market-day, you know, and Toytown is always crowded then. I'm afraid you won't find a bed anywhere at all.'

Roger went back to the car and told the doll.

Her big blue eyes filled with tears. 'What am I to do?' she said. 'I must sleep somewhere for the night.'

The farmer's wife came up to the car when she saw the doll crying. 'Don't upset yourself,' she said. 'You can easily get a box of bricks from the store-keeper in the middle of the town, and surely this boy can build you a nice little house for the night!'

That *did* sound a splendid idea! Roger climbed into his car again and drove the doll to the store-keeper's. He lived in a great barn-like building in the centre of the town. His house was stored with boxes of all shapes and sizes. When he heard what Roger wanted he took him inside at once. Roger stared at the great boxes everywhere. He saw that some contained railway-lines, some bricks, some farms ready to be put together.

The store-keeper pulled out a box and pushed it to Roger. 'This will build a nice little house for one night,' he said. 'Don't lose any parts because I may want it back.'

Roger managed to carry the box on his back. It was very big and heavy. He balanced it on his car, and then found that he couldn't possibly get in himself.

'Tell me where to go and I'll push the car along,' he said to the doll. So she told him, and Roger guided the car from outside and at last came to a small field.

'This will do nicely,' said the doll. So Roger put the box down on the ground and opened it. It had inside a great many small wooden bricks with little pegs to hold them together. Roger had had a building-set like that before, so he soon set to work. It was fun building a toy house that was nearly as big as a real shed!

Before he had done very much the doll said she was hungry. She gave Roger some cardboard money, and he set off to the little shops. He bought some strange-looking cakes and pies, which really felt like painted wood, but which tasted most delicious when he and the doll tried them.

Then he went on with his building and before tea-time had finished the toy house. It was very good indeed, and the doll was delighted with it.

'Now you can go and ask at that big doll's house over there if they can spare us two beds, a table, and chairs for the night,' she said to Roger. 'You *will* stay with me till my leg is mended, won't you? Then you can take me back in your car tomorrow.'

Roger promised that he would. He hoped his mother wouldn't worry about him, but he didn't feel he could leave the doll with the broken leg. He went off to the big doll's house and found that the doll who lived there was a cousin of the broken-legged doll – so she was very pleased to lend the furniture they wanted. She sent two friends over with it, and soon the little house that Roger had built began to look very real and cosy.

The two of them had tea together. Then Roger went out to have a look round Toytown. This really was an adventure, and he wanted to see everything! The market was crowded with people and toys of all kinds. Clockwork mice ran busily about, and little tin men on bicycles rode up and down the streets, sometimes stopping and asking passers-by to wind them up again. Roger wound up a duck on wheels and a clockwork clown who went along head-over-heels all the time.

The animals in the market were all like toy farm animals, and they made as much noise as real ones. After he had looked at them all Roger made his way to the railway station. This was a most exciting place! Clockwork trains rushed in and out, and toy signals went up and down all by themselves. Toys got in and out of the carriages, gave up their tickets, and behaved just like people. Roger wished he could have a ride in one of the trains, but he didn't like to in case it took him too far away.

He went back at last to the little house he had built. The doll was in bed and asleep. Roger got into bed too, wondering if his mother was missing him, and very soon he was fast asleep. He didn't wake up until he heard the doll hopping about on one leg, getting breakfast.

'Hurry up!' she cried. 'I'm getting so excited to think I'll have my leg mended soon. Eat your breakfast and we'll go.'

Soon they were in the little car once more, and Roger drove to the hospital. He helped the doll inside, and the nurse, who was another doll, dressed in an apron and cap like a nurse, told him to wait. He sat down and watched the one-legged doll go hopping out of the room, carrying her broken leg carefully in her arms.

A great many toys came to be mended while he was there. A doctor stood at one end of the room and looked at all the patients one by one. There was a teddy bear whose boot-button eyes had come loose. They were soon sewn on tightly. There was a poor little duck that had lost its clockwork key. The doctor fitted it with another and it ran off happily. There was a red dog without a tail and a blue rabbit with only one ear. The doctor sewed a new tail and a new ear on, and off they went, as happy as could be. Roger thought he could watch all day.

And then a monkey came running in – and now Roger stared! For it was his own toy monkey from home. The long-tailed creature pointed to a hole in his back, from which the sawdust was beginning to come out. Roger went red. He remembered quite well that he had caught Monkey on a nail by accident and had torn it. He had meant to ask his mother to mend him and had forgotten.

The doctor sewed up the hole quickly. The monkey was very grateful. Roger screwed himself up in his corner, to hide. He didn't want the monkey to see him there. He might tell the doctor that there was the boy who had caught him on a nail! The monkey skipped gaily out without seeing him.

Then the doctor came over to Roger, with a big needle and cotton. 'What's the matter with *you*?' he asked, kindly. 'Where do you want to be mended? Shall I sew you up somewhere? Or have you lost your key?'

'No, I'm quite well, thank you,' said Roger, half-afraid the doctor might really sew him up somewhere. 'I'm just waiting for a friend of mine.'

At that moment in came the doll. She danced in on two legs, singing a little song of happiness.

'See!' she cried, dancing a tiptoe dance. 'My leg is mended, Roger! Isn't it lovely! Oh, I do hope Mary never drops me again. I might not find a kind little boy like you again, to take me to Toytown. Come along. We'll go home now!'

They climbed into the car again and off went Roger, hooting through the busy streets of Toytown. They soon left them behind and came to the wood where Roger had found the little doll.

'You can leave me here, Roger,' said the doll. 'I can find my way home easily now. Thank you so much for all your kindness. I hope I see you again one day.'

She threw her arms round his neck, gave him a good hug, then jumped out of the car and ran into the wood, waving her hand merrily. Roger drove on and at last came to the lane that led to his home. He drove up to the door and got out.

'Hello, Roger!' said his mother, coming to the door. 'You haven't been long! It's just about dinner-time.'

'Haven't been long!' said Roger in surprise. 'But, Mummy, I've been away a day and a night. I've been to Toytown.'

'You've been gone just an hour,' said his mother, kissing him. 'Go and wash your hands. You must have been dreaming!'

Well, wasn't that odd? Roger really couldn't understand it at all. *Had* he been dreaming? Or was time quite different in Toytown? He couldn't make up his mind what to think.

But one day he went to see his cousin Mary, who lived at a farm about two miles away – and there he saw the doll again! He was quite sure it was the same doll he had taken to Toytown, though now she was smaller.

'Mary, did your doll ever break her leg?' he asked his cousin. Mary nodded her head in surprise.

'Yes, I dropped her once,' she said. 'How did you know? But, Roger, it was so strange, her leg got mended all by itself somehow. One day it was broken – and the next it was all right again. I can't think how!'

'Well, *I* can tell you!' said Roger, proudly. And he told Mary all about his adventures in Toytown with the doll. She *was* surprised. She picked up the doll and looked at her.

And Roger saw the doll smile at him, though Mary didn't. So he *knows* his adventure really did happen, after all!

Poor Old Scarecrow!

There was once an old scarecrow who stood in the middle of a farmer's field. The farmer had made the scarecrow, and really, he looked very life-like. He had a turnip for a head, with eyes and mouth scooped out, and a piece of stick for a nose. He had an old bowler hat on his turnip head. Round his neck was a red scarf full of holes.

He wore a dirty old coat of the farmer's and a pair of trousers so ragged that, really, it was a marvel they hung together. But they did. He had two sticks for legs and two sticks for arms, and that was all there was of him.

He stood in the field on the sloping hillside, and looked in front of him all day long. The birds were not a bit afraid of him except when the wind blew his coat and scarf about. Then they thought he was alive and flew off, frightened.

'Silly creatures!' thought the scarecrow, scornfully. 'Frightened by a bit of flapping in the breeze. Oh, dear me, what a life this is! Nothing ever happens. All I see are the foolish birds and a lolloping rabbit or two. I want somone to talk to. There are many things I think about as I stand here all day long. Surely I am not too ugly for other creatures to speak to me. What about the pixies in the hedge? Why don't they pass the time of day with me sometimes? Are they too high and mighty?'

The pixies were not too high and mighty, nor were the goblins who lived in the caves along the hillside. But they were afraid to visit the scarecrow. You see, he really was so ugly, so dirty, so ragged! So they kept away from him, and even when he beckoned to them with his stick-like hand they pretended not to see him.

Now one night something very exciting happened to the scarecrow. It was like this. He stood out there in the middle of the field, yawning and bored. It was cold and he was lonely. Only a rabbit had come near him that day, and he really was longing to talk to someone.

So when he saw two strange figures walking over his field, he was very much excited.

'They are coming to visit me!' he thought. 'At

last I shall have someone to talk to! How marvellous!'

But when the two people came nearer in the pale moonlight the scarecrow saw that they were almost as ugly as he was! They were witches, long and lean, bony and bent.

'Let us talk here,' said one witch to the other. 'No one will hear us, in the middle of this lonely field. We will sit down beside the scarecrow and whisper our secret plans.'

'What a scarecrow it is, too!' said the second witch, scornfully, looking the poor scarecrow up and down. 'Turnip head and turnip brains! Silly, gaping thing!'

The scarecrow was so hurt and surprised at these unkind words that he couldn't think of anything at all to say. He just stood and gaped all the more, and he felt as if his scarf was choking him.

The witches took no more notice of him. They sat down on the cold earth and began to whisper.

Now the scarecrow's ears were not much to look at, but they were very sharp, so he could hear every word that was said. And very strange was the thing that the witches talked about on that moonlit night.

'The Princess comes this way tomorrow night,' whispered the first witch. 'She will only be attended by two fairies, and she will be in her rabbit-carriage.'

'Then we will lie in wait for her under the blackberry hedge over there,' whispered the other witch. 'We will take her prisoner and throw the fairies with her into the nearest holly bush.'

Both the witches laughed at this. The scarecrow was so amazed at what he heard that his hat fell off. Both the witches jumped up in alarm, and when they saw it was only the scarecrow's hat that had made them jump, they stared at the scarecrow angrily. The first witch picked up his hat and jammed it down so hard on his turnip head that it went over one of his eyes so that he could hardly see. But he didn't say a word. No, he knew better than that!

'No one knows of our plan,' said the first witch. 'Meet me here tomorrow night, friend, before the moon rises, and we will go to the hedge to lie in wait for the Princess.'

They went silently down the hill together, their pointed hats showing up in the moonlight, two strange and ugly figures. The scarecrow blinked his turnip eyes and thought hard about what he had heard.

He wondered who the Princess was who was coming that way the next night. So when he saw a small rabbit venturing into the field to eat a few shoots, he called to him in his funny woodeny voice:

'Rabbit! There is something important I must say to you. Come nearer.'

The rabbit looked at the scarecrow in alarm. He lolloped just a little nearer and cocked his long ears up at the scarecrow.

'Don't flap your coat at me,' he said, 'or I shall run away.'

'Don't be silly,' said the scarecrow impatiently. '*I* don't flap it. It's only the wind. Listen, rabbit. Who is the Princess who is coming this way tomorrow night?'

'It's the Princess Peronel of Pixieland,' said the rabbit in surprise. 'However did you hear that news, scarecrow? Why, we thought only the rabbits knew, because two bunnies that pull the carriage told us. Don't you tell anyone, now!'

'There's no need to,' said the scarecrow. 'Lots of people seem to know! There were two witches here just now, and they said that . . .'

But the rabbit didn't wait to hear any more. At the mention of the word 'witches' he was off like a shot! Witches! Tails and whiskers, to think that he was out on a night that witches chose! Ooh!

The scarecrow looked at the running rabbit angrily. *Now*, what was he to do? Just as he was telling the rabbit, so that he might be able to lollop off and warn the Princess, the silly little creature must needs run away as if a hundred dogs were after him!

'Hi!' called the scarecrow, in despair. 'Hi! Come back! I've got something very important to say.'

But the rabbit had disappeared into a hole and had warned all the other rabbits that witches were about. So not a single rabbit showed itself again that night, and the scarecrow shouted himself hoarse.

He began to get alarmed. Just suppose he couldn't get help in time? Just suppose the little Princess Peronel should really be taken prisoner by those two horrid witches! Just suppose – but the scarecrow really couldn't suppose any more.

When the sun rose, the birds came flying into the field. 'Perhaps if I call and beckon to them they will listen to what I have to say,' thought the scarecrow.

So he began to call to the birds in his hoarse,

woodeny voice, and he flapped his arm-sleeves about to beckon them and waggled his trouser legs.

But, dear me, the birds came no nearer – no, they were frightened, and flew away at once, screeching: 'The scarecrow is alive today! Beware! Don't go near him! He'll be walking down the field next!'

The scarecrow listened to their calls, and then a sudden thought came to him. He never *had* tried to walk, but just supposing he could? If he managed to walk down to the rabbit-holes he could give the warning easily then. He could shout it down the burrows.

Now, you know, scarecrows are so stiff that they cannot usually put one leg in front of another. But our scarecrow began to try. He had all the day in front of him, so he had plenty of time.

First he tried to pull a leg out of the ground. How he tried! How he tugged, how he pulled!

It was no good at all. He couldn't seem to move his leg at all. The farmer had driven the stick-legs firmly into the ground, and it was more than the poor scarecrow could do to move them. He was really in despair.

He stood gazing in front of him, feeling hot

and out of breath, when he saw a peculiar thing. Not far from him he saw a little mound of earth rising. Then another. Then another. Whatever could that be?

He soon knew. A little velvet mole came peeping out of the ground, but when he spied the scarecrow nearby he gave a squeal of fright and made as if he would dive back into the earth again.

'Mole, mole, don't go,' begged the scarecrow. 'I won't hurt you. I really won't. Listen, two witches are planning to take the Princess Peronel prisoner tonight. Will you go and warn the rabbits?'

'What is a witch?' asked the mole. 'And what is a Princess? Are they things to eat? I should like to hear of some nice new beetles to hunt for.'

'No, they're not things to eat,' said the scarecrow, in despair. 'Oh, you silly little mole, never mind what they are. Just go and give my message to the rabbits. It's important.'

'Nothing's important but food,' said the mole. 'I'm sorry, scarecrow, but I can't go out of my way to tell a silly message I don't understand. You'd better be careful, because I may have to tunnel right under you, and if I loosen the earth around your legs, you may tumble over. Ho ho!'

The scarecrow listened – and a bright idea flashed into his turnip head. Of course! That was just what he wanted! If only he could get his wooden legs loosened from the earth, he would be free to walk!

'Mole, tunnel right under me!' he begged. 'Do. Do!'

'You'll fall on your nose!' chuckled the velvet mole. 'You will! How I shall laugh!'

'Yes, you do it and laugh!' begged the scarecrow. 'It is sure to be funny. Go on, mole.'

So the mole dived back again into the earth and began to tunnel at top speed towards the scarecrow, throwing up mounds of earth as he went. Very soon the scarecrow felt the mole at work round his wooden legs and he knew that the earth was becoming very loose there.

The sun sank down. Darkness came over the field. The birds went to roost in the trees and in the ivy. Still the mole worked around the scarecrow's legs, trying to make him fall down on his nose. And at last down he went, flop! His hat rolled off and a large piece of earth went into his right eye.

But did the scarecrow mind? Not a bit! He

was as glad as could be.

'Ho ho ho!' laughed the mole, and went on his way to tell all his friends what a joke he had played on the scarecrow.

The scarecrow tried to pick himself up, but it was very difficult. He tried and he tried. The night grew darker and the scarecrow felt frightened. Suppose he couldn't get down to the rabbit-holes before the moon rose? It would be too late to warn everyone then, for the Princess would be taken prisoner before the moon came!

At last he managed to pick himself up! How strange he felt with his legs out of the ground! He picked up his hat and put it on.

And then he got a shock – for he saw creeping along by the hedge at the bottom of the field, the two witches! Yes, there was no mistaking their tall pointed hats.

'Too late, too late!' groaned the scarecrow in dismay. 'Oh, dear, oh, dear! The rabbit-carriage will be by at any minute now!'

He tried to stagger along down the field and, dear me, once he got going, he couldn't stop! The field was steep and the slope took his legs along very fast indeed.

Suddenly he heard a scream, and he knew what had happened. The rabbit-carriage had

come along with the Princess and her
attendants, and the two witches had stopped it.
Down the field staggered the poor old
scarecrow, and as he went, he yelled at the top
of his voice:

'Beware, you bad witches! Here comes the
great wizard Boolamoolahippitty-twink with his
scratching nails, his pointed teeth, and his
terrible spells! Ooooooooooooh! Beware! I come,
I come, the terrible wizard Boolamoolahippitty-
twink!'

What made him call out all this he really
didn't know, but he felt that he must try to
frighten the two witches somehow.

And he certainly did!

When they heard this strange song coming
out of the darkness, and saw, with their green
witches' eyes, the queer, stumbling figure of the
scarecrow, with his bowler hat on all crooked,
and his scarf flying out behind him, they felt
quite sure it *was* a wizard. They had never heard
of the wizard called Boolamoolahippitty-twink,
and no wonder, for there was no such person –
but they quite thought it must be some fearfully
powerful magician, and they were frightened
almost out of their lives.

They screamed loudly, jumped on the two

broomsticks they had nearby, and sailed away into the sky at top speed. How glad the scarecrow was! He looked about for the Princess Peronel. There she was lying on the grass, looking as scared as could be.

'Princess,' said the scarecrow, in his hoarse, woodeny voice, 'Princess, I've come to . . .'

'Oooooh!' shrieked the poor Princess, in fright. 'Go away, you horrid wizard! I'd rather have the two witches than you! Go away!'

'But I'm not *really* a wizard,' said the scarecrow, humbly. 'I'm only a scarecrow, and I must beg your pardon, Princess, for daring to come near you, ugly old creature that I am. But you see, I *had* to rescue you from those horrid witches. I couldn't get anyone else to help.'

The Princess sat up and looked closely at the scarecrow. She saw his funny round turnip face, his stick of a nose, his wooden legs and arms, and his ragged old clothes – and she knew he wasn't a wizard, but only a poor old scarecrow. Very soon he had told her everything, and she listened in silence.

'You must forgive me for frightening you like this,' said the scarecrow. 'I know I am not fit to come near such a beautiful creature as yourself, Princess – but, you see, there was nothing else

I could do, was there?'

The Princess went up to the scarecrow. She put her warm little hand through his wooden arm and squeezed it hard.

'I think you're a darling!' she said. 'You are a dear, brave, clever old scarecrow, and I want you to come to Pixieland with me and be *my* scarecrow! I grow fine peas there all the year round and the birds do steal them so. But if you are there, the peas will be safe. Will you come?'

Would he come! The scarecrow couldn't believe his ears! He couldn't believe his eyes! To think that this should have happened to him, an ugly old scarecrow! Well, well, wonders never cease.

He found his voice at last.

'I'd love to come, Princess,' he said. 'But I can't. No, I can't, it's no use.'

'But why not?' asked the Princess in surprise.

'Because I'm too dirty,' said the scarecrow, mournfully. 'Much too dirty, and too ragged. I'd be ashamed to come to Pixieland like this.'

'Oh, is that all that is worrying you?' asked the Princess, with a laugh. 'How silly of you!'

She touched him lightly with her wand – and a strange thing happened. The scarecrow's bowler hat turned to gold. His scarf became red silk. His coat was made of thick brown satin with a thread of gold running through it, and his trousers turned to bright silver. My, he looked a real prince!

His turnip face was bright with joy as he saw all these wonderful things. The Princess touched him again.

'This is to make you able to walk and run like ordinary people,' she said. At once the scarecrow found himself able to walk to and fro without staggering and stumbling. He was full of delight.

'Oh, Princess!' he said, kneeling down before her, his wooden legs bending quite easily beneath him. 'You are too kind. Yes, I will come to be the scarecrow in your pea-patch. I shall be proud and honoured to scare away the birds for you. I shall walk all over your pea-patch and shout and wave my arms. Not a single pea of yours shall be eaten!'

'Well, that's settled, then,' said the Princess, pleased. 'Now, scarecrow, you shall come straight to Pixieland with me now. Look, there are my two fairy attendants with my rabbit-carriage. Go and bring them here, and you shall drive me home.'

Very proudly, full of joy, the scarecrow drove

the Princess and her two attendants home to the palace. Everyone thought that he must be at least a Prince, so magnificent did he look in his grand clothes. It was only when they saw his turnip head and wooden legs and arms that they saw he was really a scarecrow.

Now he lives in the garden of the Princess Peronel, King of the pea-patch. The birds are frightened of him and never eat a single pea, which pleases Peronel very much. You should see the scarecrow walking up and down, waving his arms and shouting at the birds! He is so proud and so happy – but he did deserve his good luck, didn't he?